I0831451

STARBORN

ALIYAH C. COULSON

Paperback – 979-8992088816

Starborn

Aliyah C. Coulson

ARCHERY PRESS

Contents

Calos
Arctic
Ocean
Rievo
The Void
Dragia
Kalhavar
The Dead Lands
Astro Academy
Astro
Celien
Hosheau
The Azaldir Temple
The Under City
Red
Sea
Iriea
Urish
Usnor
Wind Storm Valley
Owhana

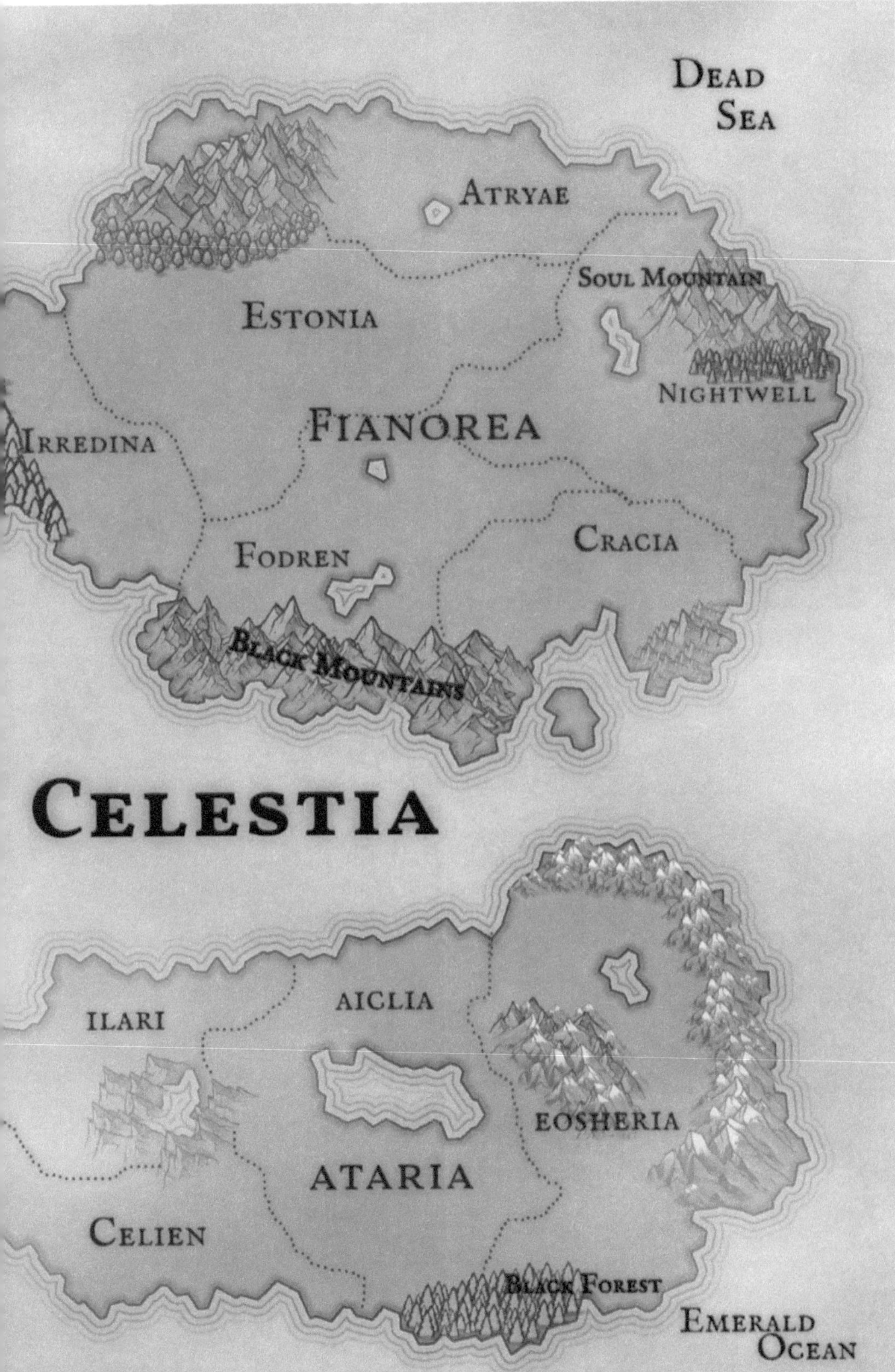
Dead Sea
Atryae
Soul Mountain
Estonia
Nightwell
Fianorea
Irredina
Fodren
Cracia
Black Mountains
Celestia
Aiclia
Ilari
Eosheria
Ataria
Celien
Black Forest
Emerald Ocean

Trigger Warning

This book contains
Gore, death, violence, blood, thoughts of self-harm, and violence against a child

Glossary

Keif - fabric made from the skin of northern Forian sheep; they were specially bred for the meet that came form them, but there skin was all most indestructible. They had blades made from Inconel, to cut through it.

Inconel – A metal stronger than steel and Iron, the only thing strong enough to cut through Keif, it is not easily forged.

Buony Berries - exploding berries the juice is used to make booms. They look like blueberries it will explode a person if they eat it, they are sweeter than blueberries but also deadlier.

Reight - Birthday in this world.

Ascension - The 18th birthday a mark of adulthood and the first time a Celerian gets to meet their Celestial parent.

Corviac - one week before winter comes the city of Asiza has a festival celebrating cultures on all four continents and people and performers come from all over.

Nives — A singing flower that blooms once a year, it has one of the most beautiful songs known to the world.

The Neovis - The General in the Forian language

Nioloes - soldiers in the Forian language

Ecuovea (Ec-cova) - when someone dies you little a candle and you grieve them Some of the candle burns out the grieving period ends.

Saels - the cart food and trinkets were sold on the road.

Veciesion dancing - a Ceremonial dance giving respect to the Celestials.

Gryphocart - a Carriage atop the back of a gryphon for traveling through the sky.

Greviger - Deathly plant created from the Blood of a Celestial Born.

Asphies- The Centinal Classifications

Centinal - The Celestial Borns and Celestial Blessed

Ecuovear - The three days of mourning while a Centinal's body is burned. It is done to watch over the body while the spirit can pass on and prevent demonic possession.

Riechea – A researcher, they are responsible for most modern technology, infrastructural, and medicinal advancement's

Sa'nchien – Sandworm, small in size. Enough of them together could eat an entire person bones and all.

Ryin – Training all Forian children are required to take, if they intend to hold any position of power.

Pronunciation Guide

Celerian (Ce-ler-ian)
Xiakary (e-ka-ry)
Nievar (Ni-va-r)
Keif (Ke-ef)
Buony berries (Buo-nny)
Reight (right)
Ascension (As-cen-sion)
Corviac (Co-va-c)
Nives (Ne-ves)
Neovis (No-ve-es)
Nioloes (Ni-ol-es)
Ecuovea (Ec-cova)
Sael (Sae-le)
Veciesion (Ve-ch-sion)
Gryphocart (Grypho-cart)
Greviger (Gra-vi-ger)

Asphies (As-phi-es)
Centinal (Cen-ti-nal)
Ecuovear (Eco-var)
Riechea (Re-sha)
Sa'nchien (Sa-ch-en)
Ryin (Ri-en)

Asphies

CELESTIALS

CELERIAN
(CHILDREN OF THE STARS)

XIAKARY
(CHILD OF THE BLOOD)

NEIVAR OR NIEVARIAN
(BLESSED BY THE STARS)

To my younger self, the world in your head is now out in the world.

Rules To Survive

In this world, death comes for everyone there are rules that we use to survive, to save ourselves.
Not just our lives but our souls.

1. *Do not get attached; death is more familiar than life here. —Noria C.*
2. *You will need to kill, or you will be killed. It is better to be the hunter and not the hunted. — Noria C.*
3. *Power has a price. If you want it, you must be willing to die for it, maybe even kill for it. — Noria C.*

Prologue One

Dahlia

Every mother was terrified of the day their child left home, and for Dahlia that day would come twice, for each of her three children. Once when they were sent away for Ryin and again when they were of age. Dahlia had already gone through it with her two oldest, and now she had to do it again with her youngest.

She thought she would have a few more years with her daughter for her to just be a child and not deal with the world ahead of her just yet, she was still at the age where in her mind the only evil in the world were the ones in the stories she loved.

But that was not the reality, because of how unique Veirella was she had to begin training two years earlier than most. She was devastated she had to leave home, she was only eight she did not understand why she had to go away it was not something she wanted to do, but it was what needed to be done.

She was not allowed to wield so she needed to learn control and discipline for the day when the power inside her did not wait to be called upon but came out on its own. As much as sending her off broke Dahlia's heart it needed to be done; the decision was not hers but her husband's.

He loved her as much as she did, but he thought coddling her would get her nowhere.

"Why must it happen now?" Dahlia had managed to hold herself together through the discussion she had with him when he suggested it; it was less of a suggestion and more him informing her of what he intended to do.

She almost yelled at him for asking for her support when it came to it, but after telling Veirella what would be happening and her crying begging for them not to send her away Dahlia could not hold the tears back any longer.

"My love, you have seen the signs of her magic this needs to happen, not only for her safety but everyone else's" he told her. He moved to hold her, but she stepped out of his reach.

"I do not care about the rest of the world; I care for my daughter." She hardened her voice as much as she could manage trying to keep it from breaking. As queen it was not something she should have said or even thought, but what mother would put others above her own, any who did was not to be considered a mother.

"And what about her, what happens if she hurts herself or Aspen or Iris, would you be able to live with that?"

"I love them all equally" she pushed back.

"That is not what I asked, and you know it." Dahlia turned away from him. She knew that was not the meaning behind his question, but she needed to fight, anything to delay what was inevitable.

"How am I to say goodbye?" Her voice cracked as she said the words.

She felt the hairs, on the back of her neck stand then felt his hands wrapped around her waist, his touch always brought her comfort no matter what the situation, but she did not know if it would in that moment.

He laid his head on her shoulder, even though she was not currently happy with him she could not resist looking at him.

"It will not be forever just a year or two." He moved his head and turned her in his arms. "It is the best thing for her, considering the restrictions she is under this is the next best thing." Dahlia had heard the words enough times to be able to repeat them in her sleep.

"I do hate it when you are right." He laughed pulled her closer and kissed her.

"If I did not make good decisions, I would not be a good king." The smile plastered on his lips was contagious and she returned one of her own not as bright but a smile all the same, he wiped away her fallen tears then kissed her again.

The day came when Veirella would be leaving, it had been several weeks since the decision was made, and it still had not set in for Dahlia that she would be leaving. She was not going alone, Iris would be travelling with her to Nightwell Castle where her Ryin training would take place, she had asked if she could accompany her.

Iris had trained with Elizabeth Nightwell and knew how hard she was on those under her command, royal or not everyone was treated the same.

"I was four years older when I trained under her and cried myself to sleep most nights, Ella is eight she will need the support." Iris told her father; this was not the type of responsibility they wanted to put on her but if it was what she wanted they would not stop her.

"Are you sure this is what you want?" Dahlia asked her, she could answer her own question, but she still needed to ask; Iris was not one to change her mind once it was set on something. It was a trait Dahlia both loved and hated about her, it would make her headstrong, but also stubborn.

"I am." She answered, Iris looked over at her father waiting for his answer to her request, she may have wanted this but if Dorian said no that would be final.

"Father, where do you stand on my choice?" she asked him.

"I think you are old enough to know what you want, so yes you may go." Dahlia could see Iris fighting her excitement and she was not winning the battle. She hugged her mother then her father then thanked them.

"Thank You, I promise you will not regret this."

"You should go pack your things; we leave in the morn—"

"Already packed" she interrupted her father. "Then get some sleep it will be a long journey and—" Iris did not wait to hear what he had to say she was already running from the room.

"She is just like you when we were that age." Dahlia told her husband.

"Really, I think Aspen is more me, patient and headstrong" she laughed, and he looked at her as if she had offended him.

"What?"

"You were nothing of the sort, I could hardly keep track of you, because of how unpredictable you were." He was always off doing something.

"But you loved me anyway" he stated.

"I did."

Their marriage was arranged but they found love within each other, and that was more than could be said for most political marriages. It seemed so long ago now, many things had changed since the beginning of their marriage and things were still changing, sometimes she wished she could make it stop and hold on to what she had for a little longer.

He placed his hands around her waist and turned her to face him. "I know this is a lot, they are growing up, we knew this day would come eventually the twins are three years away from Ascension and Veirella has a long road ahead of her. The best we can do is protect and prepare them for everything they will face." He was trying to comfort her, but it still did not change how much she hated what was happening.

Dahlia did not sleep much the night before, she could not stop thinking about Veirella's impending departure. She was so young she needed more time, but the reality was her powers had started to show themselves; they had been for some time now.

Dahlia had thought of getting someone to help her, but her blood mother did not want her learning how to wield, she did not give a reason, she always wondered why but she was never given an answer.

She watched as her daughter's things were packed into one of the two carriages, with every piece of luggage that was moved from the steps to the carriage she counted down the moments she had left with her.

But Veirella was ignoring her, she had tried speaking to her and she moved down the steps closer to the carriage as far away from Dahlia as she could get. Veirella had cried to her, begged for her not to let this happen but she had done nothing.

She had been through a silent faze with Iris, but she was much older, and she expected it from her, kids pushed their parents when they reached their teen years that was normal, but this however was not.

"Give her some time, she will come back to you." Dorian assured tried her she loved her, husband but that was not helping her at the moment.

"You made this choice, yet you are not the one she is ignoring." her words were more cross than she intended them to be, but it was how she felt why should she pretend it was not. "Because you are her mother, she expects you to make the things she does not want to do go away, and you did not do that."

Dahlia wished she could make it go away, but she did not tell him that. They had enough conversations about it which led to many fights and arguments, but he did not change his mind.

"Do not worry, in no time she will be back looking at you like you are the reason the sun rises." Dorian assured her. He kissed her then went to their daughter, he got down to her level and said something to her; to which she shook her head no.

He looked back at Dahlia then, picked Veirella up and placed her into the second carriage where Iris was already waiting, then he closed the door, and the carriage pulled away. Then he went back to her side, "were you not going with them?" she asked.

"I think they will be just fine on their own, and they have enough guards with them to form a small army. So, they are safe." he answered. Dahlia watched as the carriage moved further away until she could no longer see it.

"Only two years." Dorian told her.

"Yes, only two years."

Prologue Two

Iris

It had been two years since Iris had been home, she had only left Nightwell twice in that time she had been there and both were for her Reight which she shared with her twin brother Aspen.

She did not miss home as much as she thought she would have, it was not as if she would be doing anything different than she was now.

Iris intended to be her brother's hand when he became king, it required learning the history, customs, and traditions of every region not just the ones of Fianorea, but the other three Kingdoms as well.

Iris knew she wanted to work for the crown, so when her brother asked her if she wanted the role, she did not hesitate to accept it. And for three years she had been doing the work to prepare for when the day came. From meeting with the lords and ladies of the other houses, to joining her father's advisors.

She had helped with the new trade agreement with Dragia. It made trading easier between them, most of the world's food came from Fianorea as well as textiles, and Dragia was the only place Stardust can be found.

Her idea was to cut the cost of food, in exchange for more Stardust. The land there had not been suitable for anything to grow in years, so they had to rely on Fianorea more than they would have liked to.

And with higher demand came higher prices, so to offset the cost they would give them six units more Stardust for a quarter of what they pay for food. It took them some time to agree, they wanted to give two units for a quarter off; her father did not agree so they did a quarter of the price with four units.

That was the offer Iris wanted to give to begin with, but went higher knowing they would fight it. The queen took the offer because she was both saving money, making money, and ensuring her people did not starve to death. She had done many other things but that was the most memorable.

But she wanted more, and when she learned Veirella would be sent away for her Ryin Iris thought it was the perfect opportunity to show her parents she was ready for more.

Veirella was easy to be responsible for, she did as she was told she never skipped training or complained about how hard it was. Some days she would have bruises from how hard Elizabeth had pushed her, but she never complained or said anything about them.

Iris knew she wanted to go home, which might have been why she did not put up a fight. Iris had been trained by the same woman, and she was difficult as Elizabeth called her. She never paid attention or did what she was told, and because of it her time was extended three months. Veirella was ten years old and that was still two years younger than Iris was when she started, but she was by far a better student.

Veirella wanted to go home, she never said the words aloud, but her actions spoke for themselves. Their mother had written to them every week since they had been there. Veirella read them but never responded, she was still angry with their mother for not stopping their father from sending her away.

She wanted to visit for Veirella's ninth reight but she told Iris to tell her not to come. She respected her wishes and stayed away, Iris knew it was not what her mother wanted to do but she was still giving Veirella the space she wanted.

It had been a year since, and her tenth had come and gone some weeks ago. In the last letter Iris received from their mother she told Iris she would be coming for Veirella's Lovia Ceremony that would be happening in a week, but she did not inform Veirella of their mother's arrival and she would be there by the end of day.

She did feel guilty for not telling Veirella, so much so that she had been hiding in her room for the past week. But that changed when she heard a knock at her door, Iris opened it and Veirella was standing there dressed in blue Keives, she was either going to a training session or coming back from one. Iris could not always tell; her sister rarely sweat.

"What time are we leaving?" Iris had heard her sister's voice more times than she could count, but it was still the sweetest thing she had ever heard. "What do you mean, leaving for what?" she asked her. Iris could not think of anything where should they have been going.

"To see the Nives bloom, remember you said we could go see them this year"

The excitement in her voice made Iris feel so much worse not remembering that she promised to take her.

"I am so sorry; with all the studying I have to do I completely forgot." She forgot not because she was busy studying but because she was preparing for their mother's arrival.

"So, we are not going?" The disappointment in her voice was not what Iris needed in that moment; she was usually good at keeping up with everything she had to do but with the short notice she had gotten from her mother she had forgotten to finish preparations for the mountain climb they would need to make to go see the flowers bloom.

"I know how much you wanted to go before we left but we can always come back up here and do it next year."

The more she spoke the further Veirella's face fell until there was nothing, but disappointment written all over it.

"I know how much you wanted to go but it is not safe to do the climb without the proper preparations especially for someone as small as you are." Iris explained but the more she spoke the worse she felt. If they did not need a fire wielder to go with them maybe they could have gone and done it.

But Veirella was small, and she had not even crossed the five foot line yet. She would not make it up the mountain without one, and even if they could go getting a fire wielder to come with such short notice was not possible.

"How is my size a problem? I do great in training because of how small I am." She was not being defensive her question came from a place of curiosity. Iris knelt before her and took her hands into her own.

"You know how after a baby bird is born it still needs its mother to feed it because it cannot leave the nest?" Veirella nodded, "a Nestling." Iris smiled at her correction; she loved birds so it was the best way she could explain it to her.

"Well, you are like that bird—Nestling, you need someone to help you go up Soul Mountain because you are young and small. If I were to take you there without someone to regulate your body temperature you could get sick and then something bad could happen to you," she explained.

Veirella shook her head, taking in everything Iris said. "So, what you are saying is that without proper warmth. I could get hypothermia and then I would die?" Iris nodded at her in response, she should have just said that to her to begin with. Veirella was only ten, but she understood more than most children her age. Iris stood up because bending that way wearing a corset made it slightly hard to breathe.

"Yes."

"Okay well I guess it is better we be safe. I want to do a lot of things before I die."

"And you are also too pretty to die, so young" Iris told her then pinched her nose. Veirella slapped her hand away and stepped back. Iris laughed she hated when she did that, so she did it even more.

"Why do you always do that?"

"Because I know you hate it, and that makes it all the more fun." Iris reached for her again, but Veirella was quick and moved before she caught her. She got closer to the open door, putting some distance between them.

"Well, I am going to take a bath and do some reading, I am all sticky from training." She pointed at herself emphasizing her words. And Iris had her answer she did not have any wet marks on her clothes to indicate she had been sweating and she smelt like lavender, and something sweet Iris could not place.

"I will let you get back to your studies," she looked towards the open books on her desk behind her and the guilt Iris had felt before Veirella came returned. She had just lied to her sister. It was not a full lie but a lie non the less.

"Come here" Iris asked her sister, but Veirella stepped back now going through the door. "Why?" she said her tone was one filled with caution.

"I just want a hug from my baby sister is that such a crime." Iris moved her hands apart waiting for Veirella to come to her, she stood there thinking of what to do.

"You are not going to do that thing again are you?" Iris shook her head no in response.

"No, just a hug."

Veirella took a moment to think about it went to her sister and wrapped her arms around her waist, then Iris closed her arms around her small frame. The hug did not last long Veirella was not one for physical affection, but she did allow it in small increments; Iris wished it had lasted a little longer because after that night it may be their last for a while.

So, Iris took the opportunity to pinch her nose again and tickle her before she got away from her. Veirella looked annoyed but Iris could tell she wanted to laugh. "You lied." She said as harsh as she could manage. "What can I say." she raised her shoulders then dropped them. Veirella made her way out the door not saying another word.

"I will see you at dinner" Iris called after her. A dinner that might end with her sister hating her.

Not long after the sun set their mother arrived, but she did not come alone. Aspen, and their father was with her as well, her letter had said nothing of them traveling with her, but she was grateful for the surprise; it added to her mother's presence.

Aspen and Veirella had always been close having him there would soften the surprise of their mothers unwanted visit, or Iris hoped it would.

"Mother, this is quite the surprise your letter said nothing of Aspen and father joining you." Iris did not have a problem with the rest of her family coming, she was happy to see them, but she had only prepared for her mother's arrival. More guards were required for each member of her family, and she had only requested for her mother.

"They decided to come along last minute. Now come give your dear mother a hug."

She stepped into her mother's arms, preparing for how much she would squeeze. Her hugs were the tightest when she did not seen them for long periods of time, the first time they had been apart for more than a few weeks was when their father took them to Ataria for the winter festivities, and she did not attend. She had been too sick to travel, so they went without her.

They received plenty of hugs upon their return but mostly kisses which Iris loved and her siblings hated, which was the usual for them. The ones she was given when she came home from training where the most painful, mostly because of the bruises she still had.

The two she had received when she went home to celebrate her reight with Aspen, those had been air restricting, and this one was no different. She pulled away and looked over her.

"You have grown so much since I last saw you."

"Mother you saw me several months ago, I have not changed much in that time." She told her but she just brushed her answer off and looked her over again. She stepped away so Iris could greet her father.

"My sweet girl, your mother may be right you look taller. If you keep growing, you may pass your brother." Aspen rolled his eyes at their father's words. And he laughed at his reaction, she could feel his chest move when she hugged him.

"Maybe I will, just something else to be better at." They were all making fun, it was her shoes that made her appear taller and they all knew it. Her father kissed her head then stepped away so she could greet her brother, he hugged her and got close to her ear.

"The only times you have ever been better than me sister is in your dreams." he said in such a mocking tone she wanted to hit him, but she restrained herself in the presence of their parents.

She would not give him the satisfaction of making her look like the aggressor, it was his specialty, pushing people mentally so they would come after him physically. But no one would guess that the crown prince of Fianorea was such an instigator, if only they knew him as she did.

"I have beaten you...once." Iris knew she won their little game in the forest that day and he could not deny that.

"I am sure that is how you feel little sister, whatever helps you sleep at night." He squeezed her shoulders and stepped around her. "You are only older by five minutes." she argued.

"Five minutes is still five minutes, you know like how long it took for me to get across the pond and for you to fall in it." He gloated, she reached out to hit him, but he was too quick and moved out of her reach.

"Now." Aspen clapped his hands together it was so loud it echoed in the forest around them.

"Where is our guest of honor?"

He was the first to ask about Veirella, it was probably done intentionally, he would be the only one of the three she was not angry with, and he may be the only one she would be happy to see.

"It is time for dinner so she should be making her way to the dining hall" she answered. Aspen raised his arm to the entrance of the castle. "Lead the way." No one said anything as they followed Iris up the stairs, or down the hallways as they made their way to the dining room.

No one had said anything about washing up for dinner, which was a great show of how on edge they were for the reaction they would receive from Veirella.

When they finally got there the only ones present in the room were the servants getting dinner laid out for them. Veirella did not arrived yet. They waited for almost an hour, and she was still not there. "I should go see if she is okay." Iris told them as she stood from the table, and her brother did the same. "I'll come with you."

It would take them a bit of a walk to get from the dinner hall which was on the second floor to get to Veirella's room on the fourth. "So how has life been isolated all the way up here?" Iris could not tell if he truly cared or was just trying to fill the silence.

"It has been fine, I like the time I get for myself, Veirella hated it here when she first arrived. But then she made a friend." Her tone changed when she said the word 'friend' Aspen looked at her, he tilted his head to the side with a smile plastered on his lip, he had heard it as well.

"Is someone jealous?" He asked her mockingly almost laughing at her. "No!" Iris knew she answered to quickly and she was so loud it echoed in the empty hallway. She closed her eyes and waited for her voice to go quiet.

When she opened her eyes, she expected Aspen to be waiting to make fun of her for how she felt. But to her surprise he said nothing, he did not have a smug look on his face but one of sadness.

"It is okay to admit that you are. I can."

She stopped and looked at him, her face was pulled so tight together there was a chance it would leave her with permanent age lines. But she was just that confused she could not control the reaction.

"You have been jealous? of all things you could say to me that was not on the list." she said to him. He had not actually said the word, just something that implied it, and he did not correct her so there must have been some truth to it.

"Well surprise sister I have." He began going up the stairs, Iris did not notice they were standing before and she followed him, quickening her paise to catch him.

"When father said he was sending her away to begin her training I requested to go with her, she had never been anywhere without mother or father.

And I did not want her to feel alone. When we did it, we had each other, and she deserved the same. But he said you had asked first, and also that I had too many responsibilities as heir to leave even if he did not already given you permission to." his response was so unexpected Iris almost fell when she missed a step.

"You where jealous he sent me and not you?" She asked and she thought about it, Aspen and Veirella were together almost every day they were home, or he did not have some political engagement with their father. "Or were you jealous I would be spending more time with her?" He did not respond.

"Is that—" she was cut off by one of the guards "—Your Highness." he addressed Aspen, Iris was standing behind him, so he did not see her. She moved to see who it was. Sir William James, her sister's personal guard.

Iris had been paying more attention to her brother than to where she was going and did not notice they reached Veirella's chambers. When he saw her, he addressed her the same. "Sir James Veirella should have been at dinner over an hour ago why is she still in her room?" She asked.

He did not always accompany her to the dining hall but she had requested he have her there tonight. "The young princess has not returned to her bed chamber's since she left for training this morning, I had assumed she were with you Highness." he answered the panic in his voice evident.

"I saw her after her session with Elizabeth, but she was coming here after she left my chamber's." James was panicking he shifted from one side to the other, it was not much of a change, but Iris noticed it.

She did not fault him for not knowing where her sister was it was a death sentence for a guard when their charges were harmed, but his job was to guard her room not to follow her around. Veirella did not have a guard assigned to be with her at all times.

Nightwell was a fortress, it had an armory the size of Nelio Island, anyone stupid enough to try breaking in would not make it a fill step through the gates before the were killed. It was one of the reasons Veirella had been sent there for training instead of to one of the military bases like Aspen and Iris were.

"Well, she has to be somewhere around here, she probably heard mother was coming from a servant and hid somewhere. Gather some of the guards and look for her."

She ordered, Iris was unaware of where she could be, there were so many rooms in the castle that she could just about hide anywhere. Veirella did not have many places she frequented alone; she went three places. The training floor at the top level of the castle, the library and her room and occasionally the forest.

"We should go inform mother and father" Aspen suggested. Iris nodded to him, she did not say anything, there was nothing she could say if anything happened to Veirella it would be on her. So, she just followed him, it did not take them as much time to get back to the dining room. Maybe she was over thinking it but something did not feel right and with how fast they were moving Aspen felt it as well.

The guards greeted them, then opened the doors. Their father was standing by the window, and their mother was still seated but stood when they entered, the smile she had on fell when she did not see Veirella come through with them.

"She refused to see us?" she asked, her voice hoarse as if she was holding back tears. "She was not in her room they are currently looking for her." Aspen told her. Their Father went to them, "then we should do the same, it will go by much faster if we all look for her."

Two hours later every room had been checked but still no Veirella. "Anything?" Aspen asked they all responded no. "Maybe she is somewhere outside, she always liked going into the forest we should check there." Iris informed them.

Everyone made their way outside; all hundred and six guard's the castle and even some of the servants were with them. Iris was starting to worry, but no one said anything about something actually being wrong, but the tension around them was so thick one could see it.

But until they found her, she was just a ten-year-old throwing a tantrum because she did not get her way, and that is all she would be until they found her. When Iris stepped outside the cold air hit her so hard she almost lost her balance, it was colder than it had been in weeks but winter would be coming soon so it was to be expected.

If they were in the capital, it would not be this cold for another two months at least but, Nightwell was near to the water and surrounded by mountains the elevation plus the fact that they were next to Soul Mountain which was covered in snow all year round, was not helping.

"I hope she is not out here it is so cold if—" her mother said her voice broke Iris could hear how scared she was and she could also tell what she intended to say.

If Veirella was in the forest she was at risk of freezing to death, it was easy for her to go deep into the forest alone and get back no problem but if she had not gone back to her room she was still in her trainers and did not have the proper protection for this type of weather.

They broke off into teams, looking in sections. They called for her but there was no response, they called her name repeatedly.

"Veirella."

"Veirella."

"Princess Veirella."

But still there was nothing, they were moving deeper into the forest, then Iris stopped she thought she heard someone call her name. "What is it?" her father asked he did a better job at masking his true feelings better than her mother could, but she could still tell he was just as worried. "I thought I heard something."

Aspen told everyone to be quiet. It got so quiet that a leaf could fall, and it would be heard. *Iris* "There did you hear it?" she looked at the people around her, but no one reacted to anything but her.

Her mother stepped towards her, "darling I think you should go back inside" she told her. "B-But I heard something" she responded her family shared a look, they must have thought she was hearing things, feeling guilty that her sister had gone missing on her watch.

Then she heard it again. She felt something pulling at her telling her to move. And so, she did, she ran a parents called after her, but she did not stop. Her shoe got stuck, she kicked them of and kept moving. There was movement behind her, but she did not look back, all she cared about was getting to whatever she was being called to.

She felt close she knew she was almost there when she saw the clearing where moonlight was coming through, it was almost like a perfect circle had formed there was nothing there, then she got closer and saw Veirella, she was laying there on the ground with vines and roots moving around her and over her body.

She ran towards her, "Veirella ar—" before she could get to her sister one of the roots whipped at her cutting her arm open. She fell to the ground screaming in pain, the cut was so long it went from her upper arm all the way to her fingers.

Iris felt someone pulling her back away from her sister, she fought them trying to get free she needed to go forward not back. She looked back to see who was pulling her away, it was Aspen. "No! We need to get her something is wrong." she cried.

"We cannot, did you not see what just happened?" he pointed to her arm, Iris was in pain, but she was doing her best to ignore it. "We need to get her, or we need to at least try." She told him finally pushing him off.

Aspen looked at Veirella then back at Iris, he was going and whether he liked it or not Iris was going with him. He cursed then sighed, "Okay, but stay behind me, you do not have a weapon, and you are one hand down."

She nodded then they went, they moved slowly looking out for the roots moving over the ground they were getting higher and covering Veirella, they needed to move faster.

There was movement on their left, Iris turned so she would not get hit again but before the root could make contact, Aspen had it on the ground cut in half. She knew he had a great reflex but that was unreal. They did not stop the closer they got the faster they came at them and Aspen took them down just as fast.

When they made it into the center closer to their sister, the roots stopped coming. They stood in place waiting for more to come at them, but nothing did, Aspen held his sword up ready for anything that could happen.

Iris moved around her brother then ran towards their sister, but something pushed her away she fell on her injured arm it hurt but she managed to not make a sound, Aspen ran to help her up.

"I'm fine."

"What happened?"

"I have no idea, felt like I ran into something."

Aspen moved towards the still growing wall made of roots and vines. He tried putting his hand on it but it was stopped by an invisible wall, he pushed at it, but nothing happened. "What do you think it is?" She asked.

"It looks like a Cocoon—" he was looking at what Iris assumed was their sister his eyes wide with panic Aspen took his sword and began hitting at the invisible wall, the roots had gotten so high that Iris could no longer see her.

"What, what is it?" her words were quick almost illegible, but he understood her. "There is blood all over her." He answered his words rushed and panicked.

Blood, blood, blood.

That was all Iris could hear. Veirella was hurt, something was wrong with her sister, and it was her fault.

Her chest felt heavy, and it was increasingly becoming harder to breathe. They needed to get her out before it was too late. Aspen hit the wall again and a spark came from the collision.

Then she was moving through the air, Iris did not know what was happening everything was moving too fast, the last thing she felt was her head hitting something then it all went dark.

A Mother's Sorrow

Dahlia

There was no pain like a mother yearning for her lost child, for Dahlia it had been 1826 days since she had last laid eyes on her youngest daughter. She did not know if she was dead or alive, she hoped it was the latter, but it had been five years since the forest cocooned her.

And from what her son told her it was more likely the former and what she was standing before, was her child's grave and not a dome of protection.

One way or another she needed an answer if her child was dead, she needed to lay her to rest and give her a proper burial but if she was alive and trapped inside, they needed to get her out. But it was not for lack of trying that they could not.

They used the sharpest swords ever forged to try cutting into it, but they shattered upon contact with it, then they tried axes, hammers, maces, and finally archers, they shot arrows of fire at it, and they were sent right back at them. Nothing worked they cocoon looked perfect and unaffected.

Now, she was doing the last thing she could think of doing, using Wielders. The cocoon was made from magic and seemed to be protected by it.

The fact that it was impenetrable gave Dahlia hope that it was protecting her daughter inside.

Dorian sent letters to the other Kingdoms requesting the best Wielders they had to offer; he wrote of a challenge and if they completed it there would be a reward for the victor.

And now they were all in Nightwell, warriors from all over the world who fought and on countless battles they were mostly in arenas, but it still counted. They waited at the edge of the forest with Dahlia's husband and two other children.

She wanted a moment alone with Veirella before they began, it was her fifteenth reight and she wanted nothing more than to spend the day with her. The last one they were together she was eight.

Dahlia regretted the choice to send her away, she wished shed fought for her more then. Not only in that choice but the one to not let her learn how to wield the powers she had, but it was not what her blood mother wanted for her.

Dahlia never fully agreed with her decision not to have her learn how to control the powers she possessed. But one did not tell the Goddess of Creation she was wrong, even when she was.

Now, standing here looking at roots, vines, flowers, and not her daughter, the child she did not birth but considered her own in every way that mattered. Dahlia wished she had disagreed with that choice, because she now regretted not doing so, and she had to pay for not going against it with a broken heart.

She came to the forest every day to spend time with Veirella, hoping that would be the day the forest decided to open the ball of prison it had created around her, and she also did not want her to be alone.

There were guards around at all times protecting her but that was not the same, as having someone who loved her there to check in on her. Dahlia did not have much time left so she got to doing what she came to, she spoke to her as she did every day, she visited.

"Hi, darling it's mama, today is your fifteenth reight, or it should have been at least," her voice broke as she spoke. Doing it was never easy, and she did not think it would every get easier to do.

"I hope you are well; I really hope that whatever this, whatever is happening in there is not hurting you and as much as I want you to hear me, I hope to the Goddess you do not." Dahlia started to cry, and it became harder to get her words out. But she pushed through the best she could.

"I will be right here no matter what, I just want you to be home. I love you, bug."

Dahlia got closer, kissed her hand, and laid it on the cocoon. She stood there letting herself break, letting the tears she held in fall. She stayed that way until she heard footsteps approaching. Dahlia dried her tears, and pulled herself together, took deep breaths and remembered who she was to the people coming towards her.

She was queen, and not just any queen she was a ruler of the most powerful Kingdom, she was Queen Dahlia Graystone wife of King Dorian Graystone. And she could show nothing but strength, the kingdoms may no longer be at war but there were some who would love to explore a weakness within their nation, if they could find one so she could not and would not give them anything.

No one was aware of what happened to Veirella, after the incident the guards found the body of a male ripped apart not far from where Veirella was found, Dorian closed down the borders in case there were more than one assailant, and the others managed to get away.

One of Veirella's dogs had gotten free and killed him, the two large black creatures were put back in the cages, without Veirella to command them it was unlikely they would go back. Anyone who tried to get them away from her would probably be killed, the creatures were somewhere in the forest.

They were quite large, and they only got bigger every year but even if someone knew they were there they would be unable to find them. That was one of the many reason their guesses needed to be escorted into the forest they would kill anything that got too close to her.

Knowing how protective they are of her, Dahlia wished she did not insist on keeping them locked away all that time, maybe it would have changed the outcome of what happened that night.

“Here we are.” Dahlia turned at the sound of her husband’s voice. He was coming through the clearing in the trees, followed by Aspen, Iris and the Wielders from. Dragia (Fire), Ataria (Water), Iriea (Air), and two Forian’s as well (Earth). Each Kingdom’s sent two Wielders a boy and a girl.

“Now that you are here, this is your task” Dorian pointed at the cocoon. “Whoever opens this shall be given a great reward and glory of knowing you did the impossible, no weapon forged by man can cut through it, fire as not burnt it, and time as had no effect on it. The one who can get through this will be rewards generously." he continued. Dorian looked around at all of them smiling wider than what Dahlia thought was necessary, for the occasion.

"So, who would like to try their hand at the impossible?" Dahlia thought her husband's voice was filled a little too much excited considering this was their daughter.

The reaction they were having towards this made her want to scream at them. This was her child but to them it was nothing more than a game, something they were doing for fun, or for the gold they would get if they got the thing open.

But why would it be more than just a silly game for them after all that is what they were told it would be so why would they act any other way.

They broke off each set of Wielders to a different side of the forest, Dahlia moved around listening to them, most were laughing about how easy it would be, others were planning; the one that stopped her was hearing her daughter’s name.

“Where is princess Veirella?”

“No, one knows she has not been seen out in society since her eight year.”

“Well, she was sent off for Ryin when she was about that age, maybe she is still in training?

"Or maybe she did not survive."

Dahlia walked away from the Earth Wielders speculating about her daughters where abouts. Ryin did not take more than three, maybe four years. Veirella began her training when she was eight the latest, she should had been in for was age twelve, she would be in her fifteenth year now, and they had been telling the same lie for three years, that she needed more time.

After the borders were closed no one was allowed in or out unless they were of Forian blood or was married to a citizen. Many did not agree with the choice, but none questioned the decision once Dorian had told them it was the will of the Goddess.

They all knew he had a connection with her, considering he was raising her daughter. And Forian's were nothing if not devoted to their Creator.

If she had a problem with them using her name, she could come and see what her forbidding Veirella from learning has led to, or she knew and that was why she had not ended them for their lie.

"It is time to begin, who would like to go first?" Dorian asked. He looked around but no one was stepping forward, not being the one to show your skill was a great trait among warriors, on any other day Dahlia could respect that, but in that moment, she hated them for it. The Water Wielders were the first to step forward.

"We shall be the first." The girl was the one to speak she did not look very old, her warm brown skin lacked flaws, she was not old enough to wear the effects of the world.

Young, but power did not come with age if she was good that was that. She went to one side the boy went to the other, blue sparks moved around their hands as they pulled on their magic. Nothing seemed to be happening; then it got dark Dahlia looked up, there were storm clouds forming above them.

They crackled as they began to spin and got closer, it was not a normal storm, the Wielders were making it happen. It got closer and closer until it was above the cocoon.

The boy moved his hands, one was above the other, then the rain started pouring down but only onto the cocoon. They let it go for a few minutes then it stopped, and the cloud disappeared, then sun shined down on them once again.

The girl moved her hands stretching them out toward the cocoon, then the water stopped running down and began to freeze, she slowly closed her hands until it was solid ice.

She crossed her closed fists one over the other and spikes made of ice grew on every single side of it. She uncrossed her hands and moved them to either side of her head, and the ice shattered, for a moment there was nothing but a cloud of white falling around them, Dahlia's heart was beating so fast she thought it would pound out of her chest. She could not tell if it was fear or excitement of the possibility, she might have just gotten her daughter back.

But, when the ice shards and the snow cleared, her heart stopped. The cocoon was fine, not a single scratch on it, not one root cut or out of place. *Nothing,* she thought nothing happened to the cocoon it was still perfect. Shock blew across the Wielders faces, all that and nothing came of it.

It was midday when they started, and the sun was beginning to set, Wielder after Wielder but nothing. After the Water Wielder's then came fire, they set it ablaze. But one of the wielder's the boy tried again the second time the flames were so much hotter, to the point everyone had to move back, the lower hanging branches burnt, and they had not even been touched by the flames. But that was the one sign that they had done something, because the cocoon was still intact.

The boy who sent the second blast was breathing hard, he had a smirk on his face proud of what he had done, but it dropped when he saw it did not work. He cursed then walked off, back the way they came same as the Water Wielders did before them.

His partner followed after him, but she stopped to apologized for her partner's rudeness to Dahlia and Dorian. Then went to catch up with him. Air went next, the each through six blades formed from air (no effect), then the earth wielding boy tried using his power to pull the roots apart. Aspen and Iris moved back, followed them, unsure why they did so; then one of the roots came at the male hitting him across the forest into a tree, then it when back into place.

Why did that not happen with the others, was it because the elements were different, and this was formed from earth magic, Dahlia thought. The girl watched as her partner fell to the ground, for a moment she stood their looking at the spot where he fell unmoving, then closed her eyes and shook it off. She took a deep breath but did not release it. her brown skin turned a shade of grey, and her dark curls turned the same color.

She moved her hands, and green sparks began moving around her arms down to her fingers they wrapped around her hands continuously moving, they did not seem to have an end or beginning they just were. She moved her hands in the direction of the cocoon but instead of aiming at it she was going for the ground beneath it, then the ground began to shake.

Dorian pulled Dahlia to him and moved them beneath a tree, to keep her from falling or getting hit if anything were to start falling. The roots around the cocoon were hitting the girl but she did not look affected by it. She just kept going and she did not stop until she hit the ground.

The ground stopped moving and whatever she was trying to do did not work because the cocoon was still intact, unmoved by anything that had been done to it, impenetrable as it w the day it was formed.

Guilt of Thy Blood

Iris

It had been a few days since her parents tried to free Veirella from the cocoon. The thing was unaffected by everything they threw at it. Iris sometimes wondered if Veirella was stopping them from getting to her many be she feel save and this was her way of protecting herself.

Her parents really thought using Wielders would work, so did she. Iris saw all those Wielders and thought her broken family would finally come back together. But sadly, that was not the reality they lived in, hope was a dangerous thing for one to hold.

Those who had it either broke the world or themselves trying to make it a reality. For Iris and her family, it was breaking them, eating away at what little they had left. Every time there was a new solution they thought would get Veirella home, and every time they were left disappointed.

Iris saw the Wielders, and she thought things would finally change, and as they each went and failed one after the other. She lost a little bit more of herself. When she felt the earth move beneath her feet, Iris prayed to the Gods, not just the ones of her own home but any that would listen.

She would have her sister back; everything would go back to the way it was. Iris's heart moved as fast if not faster than the trees around her. But it stopped as they did when, the girl stopped wielding, she could not go anymore for fear of death taking her.

Iris did not pay her much attention; she could not take her eyes of the cocoon. It was still there unchanged, unmoved, unburnt, and unbroken.

She felt she was being mocked by it, telling her how much of a failure she was, that she was the cause of her family's pain yet again. Because using the Wielders her idea.

That was all she could think about, how she had yet again failed. Iris stood before the full-length mirror on the far side of her room looked at herself, she had on a dark green dress, with flowers matched in color the dress arrived plain, one would need to look at her for longer then was appropriate to take note of the designs stitched into the garment.

As a teen Iris loved wearing jewels and dresses that took weeks to make because of how extravagant they were. But she had lost her interest in such things over the years. She would still look presentable when it was called for, if she needed to attend a ball or a dinner to represent her family the best would be available to her.

Those things were mostly her mother's duties as the queen but since Veirella's attack she could not bring herself to leave Nightwell knowing her youngest daughter could not.

It was not always easy, women liked to gossip, and Iris would have rather done anything else instead of listening to them judge others for the dresses they wore, how much money they spend on weddings, or what betrothal gifts were given.

It was exhausting, but she needed to do it they were the wives, daughters, and mistresses of the lords who served the crown.

And they could be useful when it the time called for it. Women did not have much power, and they would do just about anything to get a taste of it, men did the same, so why should women hold themselves back.

Alliances were important to have, men had a tendance of killing their wives for not birthing sons, my no fault of their own, while this was not common it stilled happened. It was never a good idea to put your faith in the hands of a man.

Iris stood before the mirror looking at what she was wearing, she liked the color green it was what she favorite of their house colors. Blue did not match her as well as it did her siblings they had the perfect skin for it, but she was less focused on the color and took more interest in the design, it was all made from the same fabric.

They were rose vines; without the rose petals, they went all the way up to the shoulder and down to the end of the dress. Iris raised her hand to trace over the lines.

But stopped when she noticed the long scar that ran along her right arm. She removed the dress and threw it on her bed and then pulled another dress from her armoire, it was still green just much lighter than the first and the sleeves were long enough to cover the scar.

Only a small part of it was not covered but she wore gloves so it would not be seen.

The scar itself did not bring her any discomfort many women had scars, either from fighting or childbirth. And they wore both with pride, but Iris could not say the same, she did not get hers for being a warrior or becoming a mother, she failed to protect her sister, and it was her constant reminder and every time she looked at it all she felt was shame.

Iris was so focused on her arm that hid the scar, that she did not hear the knock at the door, of feel the tear that had fallen down her face.

"Yes?" Her voice was hoarse from the pressure building in her throat.

"Your mother has sent for you, Your Highness." The female voice on other said of the door informed her, Iris did not recognize it but considering her mother changed her staff so regularly that was to be expected. Iris cleared her throat before attempting a response "give be a moment." She did not get an answer back, Iris brushed her hand over her face wiping away the tear then pulled on her gloves.

She did not require assistance getting dressed she specifically choose to have her dresses made that way. She looked at herself once more, her hair was braided up, so she did not need to fuss about it, feeling satisfied with what she saw Iris grabbed a white pair flats pulled them on and went for the door.

When she opened it, a short dark-skinned girl was standing before her she was in a dark green and black knee length dress which was the uniform that was worn by those in her mother's court.

"You are still here?"

Iris was not expecting anyone other than her guard to be there. "Your mother told me to bring you to your father's study" she answered. Iris moved away from the door and Cole closed it behind her, she moves passed the girl who bows went she does so.

They walked in silence, Iris did not ask why she was needed because the girl was unlikely to know. Her family did not have anything scheduled for that day and she had intended go to the garden and read the day away; Iris did not think she would have the time after meeting with her mother and father.

They were almost to the study went another shock hit. It was bigger than the last few that had come in the past few days. One of the flowerpots was on the verge of falling, Iris moved to catch it, but the girl got to it before she could. The room stopped shacking, and they continued still not breaking the silence between them.

As they approached the doors to her father's study, Iris saw that the door was open, there were two guard's stations outside it. inside her family was sitting across the room away from the large dark red oak desk her father always used when he came visit.

They were sitting in the leather sofa's next to the windows, that have the perfect view in the direction of Veirella's cocoon. Iris thought that was the reason her father had his office moved there. Her parents were seated on one sofa and her twin the other, "Mother, Father" she sat next Aspen and looked at him wondering he knew what was happening, he shrugged at her in response.

Their mother was the one to speak first "Iris, Aspen, your father and I have been discussing this for some time now and we thought it best you hear it first." Iris was confused and worried, she looked from her parents to Aspen who did the same and shared the same look as she did.

What was going on why were they being so weird, did what they had to tell them had anything to do the Veirella. Iris hoped not because if it did and they were behaving this way it was nothing good or did they intend to marry them off.

Well, more Iris than Aspen he would get to live at home she would still be in court because of her role as his hand, but she would live with her husband.

Iris was hoping it was neither of those things, anything happening to their sister would be horrible but getting married at just twenty-one was also not ideal, she had only been of marriage age for a year, Aspen had been of age for three. Marriage law in Fianorea had been changed for fourteen years passed then it was sixteen for both groups.

It was eighteen for men because that was the age they could claim their father's titles if they were dead, and twenty for women because that was the age deemed safe for a woman to carry.

"We intend to reopen the boarders" their mother's voice broke off at the end, like the words were hard for her to say. Their father had them closed over five years before when Veirella attacked, Aspen told him he about the blood he saw on their younger sister that night, and in response he had them sealed.

He wanted to catch whoever attacked Veirella, they caught a man well he was more boy than man he did not look much older than Aspen at the time, and that was a weeks after.

When they got him, Veirella's blood was still on him and a knife with it as well. Artemis was the one to identify that it belonged to Veirella, he was one of her dogs. After their father questioned him, which did not get them anywhere because he kept repeating the same thing "I am a child of

Opherin and I will die for the cause." After a week of it him let Artemis ripped him apart, he died screaming.

It gave Iris some satisfaction, but it did not last long because that would not bring her sister back. Still, they did not find a partner, so the boarders were never reopened until know that is, four different sets of shoes sizes were found deeper in the forest so there were more than two of them.

“Why now? Why the sudden change?” Aspen asked. There was no change in his tone, no indication that the news affected him. Iris did not feel much different either, they caught and killed the man that attacked Veirella, and he may have lied about having a partner hoping that it would keep him alive, but he was caught tortured, then killed. Their father was never going to let him live long enough to hope.

“The people are becoming restless, they want the freedom to come and go as the once did, and if we do not do something we could end up with a problem on our hands” their father answered.

He was right, if people started feeling as if their rights were being impeded on, they could riot and considering not everyone cared for the crown; they could use this to gain supporters.

“What is the plan?” Both Iris and Aspen asked.

Their parents shared a look, they were expecting a different type of reaction from them, but they were old enough to understand how the world worked. It is better to be logical even in an emotional situation, emotions created problems it did not fix them, and when, not if when Veirella came home there needed to be a home for her to go to.

“We will be sending out letters to the different regions informing them of the changes, and we will also personally visit each of them together. The people need to see we are with them; they are losing faith in us and our rule we must get it back.” Their father explained, Iris did not completely agree with his plan, so she told him just as much.

“No.” she stood, and they all looked up at her.

“No, Iris we must do this I know tha—”

"I mean about your plan sending handwritten letters from the King himself is great and all, but it is still not personal enough, if says that you know what they hate this, but you do not truly care. You used the Goddess as your way into this, and that works for now, but what happens went they lose faith in her.

You should send us, as members of the royal family we represent you and her, more than a raven or messenger could." She told him, Iris was out breath from how fast she spoke.

Her father smiled at her, he stood and walked over to her giving her a kiss on her head, "and that right there is why you will be a great hand" he told her, then returned to their mother, who did not look pleased with any of it. Iris looked to her twin.

"What, I'm not going to kiss you" he told her a look of disgust written on his face. Iris wanted to hit her brother, but she would not touch him while her parents were still in the room.

She would wait until they were alone, and he least expected it. For him being praised by their father was a regular thing, and by most of the lords Iris was not given the same treatment because they did not see her in the same light, they did him.

Most of them did not agree with her father's choice to make her Aspen's hand. They thought one of their sons would be chosen for the role not a woman. Many of them made their distaste in the idea well known. But they could hate it.

All they wanted, it was his choice. He was the king, and their advice was just that advice so he did not need to take it so she would not let her brother ruin her mood.

Iris fell back onto the sofa when the room began to move, and things began falling vases of tables, paintings, somethings broke others shattered. There was no change it was an aftershock; no, it was a full-blown earthquake.

Their father pulled their mother to the opposite side of the room, far from anything that could fall and hit her. It felt like an eternity had passed before the quaking finally stopped.

But for some reason, Iris still heard movement, she pushed herself up off the couch and went to the window. A crackhead formed in the Earth, slitting all the way from the castle straight to where her sister laid, then trees all around her began falling one after the other.

Iris felt her heart stop; they fell right where the cocoon was. She tried to speak to tell her family what she saw, but she could not form the words. She turned to them and they were right there looking at the same thing she was.

"We need to go, and check that nothing has happened." Her father was the first to speak. In fact, he was the only one to speak, they did not have words, they did not know what to think, hey just watched as tree after tree fell to the ground.

They did not waste much time, the cocoon was a slight distance away from the castle, but not far enough that they needed horses, and it was better to leave the animals and go by foot in case another quake hit.

Aspen and their father moved faster than Iris and her mother did, it was the most convenient time to be wearing a dress, so long that you would trip if you did not pay attention to where you were going.

They had moved so far ahead of them that they could no longer see them. Iris pulled the hem of her dress into a ball, so there was no obstruction before her, and her mother did the same.

She did not realize how late in the day it was because by the time they made it to the clearing, the sun had begun to set. Iris saw her father ahead and pointed him out to her mother. As she got closer, Iris could see some of the fallen trees there were around the cocoon, but none were a top it. A crack ran beneath it.

Iris's heart was racing both from the running and how terrified she was because even though nothing could get into the cocoon, what about beneath it. She could not help but think the worst things maybe the Earth had opened up and swallowed her sister.

Or it would break open, and they would only see what remained of her little sister. She wished she could think more positive thoughts, but that was so far her imagination could bring her when reality was staring her right in the face.

Based on how long it had been since the cocoon had been formed and the scene before her, there was very little chance that her sister survived. Iris looked around seeing that Veirella's dogs had shown themselves they must have felt the quake and come to check on her.

"Look something is happening."

Aspen's voice was hard like he was trying to keep his true emotions a bay. Iris looked back at the cocoon at first, she did not see anything, but then she spotted the bits of gold peeking out of the roots.

It was as if there was light coming from inside the thing. The cracks of gold light became bigger and bigger until beams were coming from all directions of the cocoon.

The Earth beneath her feet shook she stumbled back, but her brother caught her arm before she could fall. She nodded at him thanking him and he did the same. Iris returned her focus back on the cocoon, the light become so bright. It was hard to see to keep looking without blinding herself. She did her best to see if something was happening.

It hurt, but she needed to know if Veirella was alive in there, and if she was the one doing this, she kept her eyes opened as long as she could manage but the pain became too much, when the light solidified It felt like she was looking at the sun.

Iris turned her head away, then felt a wave of air pass over her and a moment later the forest went dark. She looked back letting her eyes adjust to the darkness. Then she saw most of the cocoon was gone.

They moved closer, slowly hesitant to see what was inside. Iris closed her eyes as she moved forward praying to the gods that her sister was inside alive.

She heard a grasp, then opened her eyes and followed sound, it was her mother. She had tears running down her face and her hand covering her mouth, Iris quickened her pace to see inside what remained of the cocoon. Her sister was not dead. She was here.

Veirella was alive. She did not look hurt, she was definitely bigger she had grown, how that was possible Iris had no answer for it. Veirella did not look like the small 10-year-old girl Iris remembered but the 15-year-old girl she was ought to be.

She was curled up in a ball on moving. Iris could tell she was alive because she could see her chest rising and falling. Her clothes were gone, replaced by vines and roots all covering her most delicate areas.

"We need to get her out of here it is so cold she must be freezing."

Her mother told to them, Iris could hear both the pain and joy in her voice. Aspen pulled his sword from his sheath and begin cutting at the structure. Their father did the same, moments later they had cut out a clear path that they could get Veirella through.

Their father removed his coat and wrapped Veirella in it, then took her into his arms. None of them moved to say anything, they all followed behind him they could finally bring her home.

Blood Of Misery

Aspen

One Month Past

A month had passed since Veirella broken herself out of the cocoon, she was unconscious when the found her and she was still not awake. The Physician attending to her could not explain why Veirella was still sleeping; he was more fascinated by the fact that she had managed to sustain herself with food or water.

"Nothing seems to be wrong with her physically, other than the cut on her neck. But otherwise, the young princess seems well. I have never seen or heard of anything like this before." he told them.

"How is that even possible, she spent five years in there?" his mother asked, she was happy to have Veirella home, but Aspen could still see the sadness in her eyes, as much as she tried to hide it. Aspen could fault her they were all pretending to be okay.

They were close, more than most families were but talking about Veirella was hard for them, they never forgot her it was impossible to do so. But every year on her Reight they could light a candle and have dinner together serving only Veirella's favorite treats.

"It is not something I have an explanation for, but considering she is not a normal mortal child, I would not worry too much about it. The forest preserved her for five years I do not thing she will perish so easily now." The way the man spoke about his sister, Aspen knew what he would as next, it was the same with the three before him.

"Maybe I could take some of her blood and run some test on it" Aspen could excitement and hope in his voice.

"No!" he answered he may have been a man of medicine, but he was still a Riechea at heart, and if Aspen had lent anything from the Centinal's he knew, it was to never give your blood freely. He was startled by the base and tone in Aspen's voice, but he still tried. "I would not need much just enough to—"

"Like I said no, if you are done you may go" Aspen cut him off, the man whose name he did not bother to remember was starting to irritate him and every time he had to speak to him, his voice went a little deeper with the rage building within him. Aspen was trying his best not to hit him, Aspen watched him pack his things there was no chance he would be going anywhere close to Veirella again.

His sister was laying in a bed the most vulnerable she could ever be, and this man was trying to benefit from it. Celestial Blood was hard to come by Centinal's were very protective of their secrets and the few mortals who did not know anything about them, were of the blood if very distant.

Once he was finished putting his things together, Aspen walked him to the door. There were two guards stationed on the other side, Aspen had personally chosen them from his ranks to guard Veirella, he addressed the one on the left never taking his eyes off the Physician.

"Gregory"

"Yes. Your Highness"

"Could you show Doctor Lambert here, to the exit he has overstayed his welcome" Aspen ordered.

Gregory nodded then turned to the physician, for a moment he made no effort to move. He looked over at Aspen, then back at Gregory when he laid his hand on his sword, Aspen would never know what he intended to do or say, because he turned around and walked away.

Aspen returned to the room and seat by the window next to Veirella's bed. It was almost a natural reaction now considering how many times he had done it. Every day for the past three weeks he was there, doing nothing but watch her.

Her clothes were different each day, but she still laid in the same place in the exact same position, no movement of her own. If Aspen could not see her chest rise and fall, he would have thought she was dead. *Up down up down.* He counted every breath she took, making should there was no long pauses between.

When he felt satisfied with what he saw, Aspen turned his attention to their mother. She was sitting at the end of the bed, she had not said word regarding Doctor Lambert, in fact she did not say much of anything.

It was as if when Veirella was lost a part of her was too. Aspen did not see the light that had once shined brighter than the sun in her eyes, it was just darkness. She blames herself for what happened even though it was the farthest thing from the truth.

But guilt was one of the strongest emotions one could feel and once it too hold it had very little interest in letting you go, without a fight.

Aspen thought it was way Iris stayed away; she visited Veirella twice the first week she was home, but did not stay long. And two weeks prior when their father was leaving, she had chosen to go with him. It was Aspen's duty to travel with their father as the heir, but the last thing Aspen wanted to go do was place nice with the lords.

He also wanted to say with Veirella a little longer before he had to get back to his assignment in Irredin which had him leaving in a week. They were dealing with a string of deaths in the region, Nievar's were dying or being killed he did not know for sure which it was. Most people assumed they took too much Stardust and died from it. But Aspen was still not a hundred percent on board with that idea. Especially because there were so many bodies.

Two Month's Past

Aspen was going to be sick after seeing tree roots grow out of a girl's body. There was so much blood he did not know how she was still alive. She was screaming for help, as the vines came out her arms and legs wrapping themselves around her.

But there was nothing he could do but watch it happen; they were coming from inside her Aspen thought of cutting the off before they crushed her. But he did not know if that would cause her more pain. His choices were limited he could kill her and put an end to her suffering or stand there and watch it happen.

In the end he did not need to make a choice, her body did it for him. When the vines pushed her eyes from her head, she went silent hitting the ground with a loud thud, like an object falling not a person. And what remained of her blood rain into the ground beneath her. The girl was dead, but the roots and vines kept growing covering her body. Watching them consumer her, his mind wondered to him sister.

Aspen had been receiving weekly letters from his mother, updating him on Veirella's changes. A few days after he left, she woke it was wonderful news, and it was worth the looks he received from the Nioloes. They were surrounded by death, and he was walking around as if the world was not on the verge of burning.

But his joy was short lived; the week after she text another. Veirella did not speak or move, she tried speaking to her, but it was as if Veirella did not even see her, the weeks after every letter was the same.

Anastasia went to see her; they had been friends since they were children. The few times her family visited, Veirella and Anastasia became attached they were the best of friends, and their mother thought seeing her could help Veirella.

They hoped something would happen a quick glance in her direction, a smile, tears, even her screaming would have been something. But nothing changed not for another three weeks at least when she began eating on her own.

In that time three more people had died, two boys and a girl. Aspen stood outside the medical tent that had been built for a physician to come and examine the body. This was the first time there was a body felt behind. They collected blood from where they died but that did not do them any good.

All the vials that had blood in them had shattered when a flower formed from it. They tried going back to see if they could get more, but the same blood red flower had formed in those places as well. But now they had something physical to work with.

Aspen read his mother's most recent letter on his walk to the tent, hoping for some good news, but everything was the same. When he entered the tent, the smell that hit him was sickening.

"What is that putrid smell?"

His nose felt like it would fall off from how much it burnt.

"That would be the dead body you brought me." Link answered. "Well, it did not smell like that when we brought him here. What exactly around doing it?" Aspen's words were muffled from his hand covering his mouth and nose.

Link turn away from the boy's body to look at Aspen, his brow raised watching him cover his face. "He has been dead for a few hours now; decomposition has set in." Link told him.

"How is that even possible? It takes fifteen days for the human body to decompose." Link was the one with the license, but Aspen read enough books about anatomy to know that much.

"Yes. In humans, but this boy is not fully human his blood has been modified by the gifts he was given. Unlike Celerians and Xiakaries who have Celestial Blood, Nievars have Stardust in them, they age faster than either of the other two Centinal's and humans as well. Celerian's are half human half Celestial, and Xiakaries are somewhere between forty and eighteen percent Celestial, but Nievars have no blood connection to the Celestial's.

They have the ability to wield and use Stardust like the others but because Stardust speeds up the bodies functions it makes everything faster for them, including in death." Link explained.

Aspen was not planning on getting a lesson on how Centinal anatomy worked, but he had gotten something new to research in his free time. And it could have something to do with what was happening to them, and if this was just the beginning then whatever this thing was would eventually start going after the other two and considering Veirella was a Centinal, he needed to find out what it was and stop it before it got to her.

"So, because they do not have Celestial blood their bodies cannot neutralize the effects of Stardust the way the others can?" Aspen asked, from what Link told him it seemed like the right assumption to make.

"Precisely, now are you ready for what I have, or are you going to stand over there and ask, basic questions you have all people should have answers to?"

Aspen inhaled regretting it the moment he did it, he felt the bile building in his throat; he did his best to not let anything come up. Once he got it under control, he moved to where Link was on the other side of the tent. He had killed his fair share of people, but he did not like being around dead bodies it made his skin crawl.

They were alive one moment and dead the other, it creeped the hell out of him, and that was something he would never admit that to anyone. If Iris were to find out she would never let him live it down, he did not have a problem with killing people he was just not interested in being near the body after the fact.

"What have you found?" Aspen was close enough that it did not look strange that he was trying to keep some distance between him and the dead boy laying on the table, but far enough that he did not see him fully.

"Well for starters an overuse of Stardust is not what killed him, in fact he had very little present in his body, wielding should have been impossible for him." Link told him.

Aspen was going to have a headache; this was making no sense. "Let me see if I understand you, he did not have enough Stardust in his body to kill him, but he does not have enough to use the power that killed him?" Link nodded in response.

"Then how the hell did he die?"

"That I do not know, other than the fact that he has stones where his organs should be everything else is normal." Link declared as though that was not a strange thing for him to see. "Well, you have a lot of work cut out for you. I know how you Carters like to solve problems others fail to."

Link's his real name was Henry Carter. He was a doctor just like his father was and his father before him. His grandfather was the one to make stardust safe for Xiakaries and Nievar to consume, Celerian's were the only ones who could drink it before without it killing them. And his father and grandfather were response for a lot of modern medical treatments. The Carter family was blessed by a Celestial with knowledge and foresight. They knew what the world needed before they knew they needed it.

Link had yet to do anything to great he was only four years older than Aspen he still had plenty of time to save the world. And he had already started he was the youngest to ever earn a medical license and the youngest to be the head of a school, he was headmaster of Fianorea's Medical Academy Zolotia. It had only been several months, but he seemed to be managing well.

When he told Aspen the news, they went out drinking to celebrate. Link was like a brother to him; they grew up together, when he was not with his sister's or studying, they were together.

His father was the main Physician for his family when he was alive, they spend time together mostly preparing for Ryin. After he his father took ill, then died two weeks later, Link was sent away.

"It is not in my nature to do anything else." He responded. Aspen smiled at his friend then left, the sun would be setting soon, and he needed to prepare for his parole to start.

Three Month's Past

In the weeks past, there was not another death. Not just in Irredin but Atryae, and Fodren as well. Link still had not found anything else that they could use. And a change-out was coming, every six months they switched out the Nioloes, the had enough fighter's that they could rotate them regularly. Aspen would stay, if there were any new developments he wanted to hear it firsthand.

He could not stop thinking about how many more kids would have to die before they find a way to stop this. So far, the death count was at twelve and those are just the ones that were found. This was not just some overdose, especially now that one of the victims was an Xiakary. And they were not known to be as affected by Stardust as Nievar's were.

Something else was going on, but he did not know what and no one else had any ideas to give. Centinal's tend to keep to themselves human books did not have much on them. They usually dealt with things that concern them among each other, and Aspen hoped they were finding a way to stop, more kids from dying.

But the dead was not the only thing troubling him. In the last few letters he received from home, his sister only seemed to be getting worse. Aspen thought that after she started doing things for herself, Veirella would eventually start speaking again. But that was not the case, she still stayed in her room away from others, and most importantly away from their mother.

Veirella was close with her when she was a child. It was hard to get her to leave their mother to the point she slept in their parent's bed, up until the point she was sent off for Ryin.

Aspen had opted to do a shift the night before, it was his night off, but he chose to work instead of laying in the dark with his thoughts alone to keep him company, he could not remember the last time he had a proper night of sleep.

He could not recall when the voices started, he was always seeing the ones who had died, and it was not just when he was in bed, he saw them when he was around the base or in a meeting. They usually spoke to him asking why he did not save them, the rational part of him knew that it was not his fault, but that did not change how we felt.

Nothing out of the ordinary usually happened around the base most people were not stupid enough or suicidal enough to go and attempt to break into a Forian stronghold. He was sitting on the east end of one of the large walls that surrounded the base looking for a threat that would not come. He watched us the sun rose, counting down the minutes until he could go to bed. It was easier to sleep in the day than it was in the night. There was a lot going on around the camp, making it easier to block out the screams in his head.

It took a bit of walking to get to his tent, it was on the other end of the base right next to his father's. The base in Irredin was newer so only the wall had been built, buildings had not been added yet. Aspen did not care much were he slept just that he had a bed to do so. There was not much different about his tent than the others, other than the size. Four Nioloes shared and Aspen had enough space for ten.

When Aspen made it to his tent, he pulled off his sword, laid it on the table, kicked off his boots removed his shirt and got into bed, the moment his head hit the pillow he was out.

Aspen was woken up by the sound of trumpets, his father was there. He did not understand why even on a military base the king needed to be announced. He reluctantly got out of bed and put his Keives back on, strapped his sword to his waist then pulled his boots on. There was a cup of water on the table, he took it and pored it over his face to wake him up. Once he felt like a person again, he made his way out to greet his father. Whose dark blue carriage was coming towards him.

The base was quiet, which was strange for the time of day it was. Aspen had not slept for long; shifts were still changing, there were three hundred Nioloes on the base. And it was to be the second largest on the continent, even their smallest of the eight military outposts had more warriors than were present there.

The carriage pulled to a stop before him, and before one of the coachmen could get down to open the door, Iris did. She smiled at him waited for the steps on the carriage to extended for her to get out. Her eyes were red, and dark she was either tired from weeks on the road or she was crying. Aspen thought it was a bit of both.

"Hello, little sister." Iris rolled her eyes at him, then smiled her and hugged him.

"Are you well, how have you been?" She asked, Iris was always worried about everyone, her need to be needed was one of the many reasons she had asked for the position as his hand for when he took the throne.

"I should be the one asking you that, when was the last time you slept." They released each other. She shrugged at his question "it is quite hard to sleep when, every moment you are either hitting a hole or rock and shaking constantly, honesty I do not know how you and father bare it so regularly." she sighed the rubbed at her eyes.

"After years of traveling, you stop noticing it." Aspen answered.

"Well, I do not want to get used to it, being nauseated constantly and having my brain be thrown around no thank you." she added then rubbed her eyes again.

"You should go lay down get some sleep before your heart decides it has had enough of you." Iris shook her head, stubborn as always. "No, we are going back to Nightwell Castle I can sleep when we get there." Aspen did not think his father would be leaving again anytime soon there was too much happening for him to up and leave again, but he did not tell her that.

"Iris, the last time I check out of the two of us you are supposed to be the smarter one. So do you think you can survive an eight-day trip from here to there in this state?" he waved his hand over her. She opened her mouth intending to argue with him but the only thing to come out was a yawn.

"Go get some sleep, you can use my tent." He told, Iris she nodded in response knowing he was right.

"Where is your tent?" he turned and pointed at the dark green structure behind him. "Lucky for you not far." She walked around him and went inside closing it behind her, when he turned back his father was standing before him. "Father" he greeted him.

The carriage pulled away and they walked over to his tent where two guards were stationed, even when he was not there, they were. Aspen had reassigned his guards to helping with watch he did not see the point of having them around when they could be more useful elsewhere.

Royal Guards and Nioloes had similar training, both had to go the Ryin as all Forians did. It was mandatory if they wanted there Loiva mark, but they were then sent to different places to be trained for their assignments. Some were chosen for military service, others to protect the family.

Aspen had done both at once, Ryin and service training. He was the head of the military as all heirs were, but he was given more leniency than most, he could come and go as he pleased, and his father also did not give him control of the military. It was mostly a title given to the first-born child of the king. If Iris had been born first it would have gone to her, and he would have taken the same position she did.

Sex no longer played a part of the monarchy and who would rule it, the change was not only to their family but all the royal houses. Women and

Men could do the same jobs if they had the skills for it. But even so most men were still against the idea of such things, it had been more than thirty years and so many still did not accept it.

"So, what are the terms?"

Aspen did not intend to wait, the visit with the other regions was more than just about reopening the borders, he knew his father did not really need them to do that. He could command them as he did before, and it would be done.

"The same as always money, power, more control." his answered. The control they wanted was over their women.

"Nothing new there. You for people who are so willing to follow a Goddess, I would expect them to be more open to the idea of the equal treatment of women." His father removed his large coat made of a black wolf he killed two winters past and laid it on one of the chairs before his mahogany desk made from red wood. Then went around it and took a seat his chair made the same.

"Progress does not happen in a day."

"It does not seem to happen in a few decades either" he hissed. His father leaned back in the chair and sighed.

"It took time for people to accept your mother, it will take time for this too."

"Yes, but mother was chosen for you, and the Lords did not accept her lack of noble blood until they found out the Goddess who happens to be Veirella's mother, who is your daughter chose her for you." Aspen responded.

"This is not a problem the Goddess of Creation can come and solve for you. So, what is it that you intend to do?" he asked.

"The reason heads did not roll for the treatment of your mother, my wife." He said the word with more force than was need. "Is because I did not want your sister's birth to be overshadowed by bloodshed and death. That is not what it should have been remembered for." There was nothing that could have overshadowed the day Veirella was born, the color of the sky changed there is not much that could overshadow that.

"I have given my terms to both the lords then their more agreeable heirs. If they do not agree to the terms and conditions that I have set, then their son most definitely will." His father assured him.

That was another an advantage Aspen had, that may do not. His father did care for him and he for his father. If anyone tried to propose, he kill him to take power he would give them the death all Forian traitors deserved, Aspen sat in the second chair at the desk leaned forward and smiled.

"Then lucky for us most of them are shit fathers with greedy sons." His father smiled back "Yes, lucky us."

"So, what is our next move?"

"Our next move is finding out what is happening to all those kids that are dying, it will be a few months before they get back to me with their decisions. And that will be my job, you and your sister are going home to your mother." He answered then leaned over a document on his desk.

"Okay, I will bring Iris back to Nightwell then return to continue our search." Aspen was not expecting what his father said next. "No, you will not be coming back, this could become dangerous, and I want you and your sister's as far from it as possible." He told him. Aspen stood braised his hands on the desk and leaned over standing higher than where his father sat. "You cannot do that."

His father did not look up at him when he answered him. "Sure I can, last I checked I was still the king and your father, so I can tell you what to do." He countered.

"And what if I do not listen and return any way?" he asked. He could stop him from entering the base here but there were others he could go to.

"Then you will need to find yourself somewhere else to live." Aspen did not think that would be a hard task. "Not on this continent or with any of my money" he added.

"So, what is your choice, son?" He finally looked up at him and he was smiling like a mad man Aspen pushed back and sat down. "We will leave at daybreak tomorrow I shall not return unless called for."

"Good boy I knew you were smart." His father returned to the document he was reading, and Aspen sat there and watch not knowing if he was allowed to leave.

Misery's Blood

Veirella

FIVE MONTHS PAST

Age was a concept, something that grew with each year that passed. It was something people only noted in babes who were just learning the world, walking, talking, and rapid growth, and separating from their mothers, it was also noticed in the old their bodies grew weaker, their hair grayed, and their body pruned.

These things were seen because they were obvious. But for the ones not old enough to be gray or young enough to be explorers, society did not notice their changes until they became the object of one's eye.

Girls were noticed when men thought them desirable, and women grew green with jealousy of them. The same could be said for boys fewer people cared for their looks, for desire and jealousy, and more for their size, if they were big and strong enough to be warriors, protectors, and, most of all killers.

Iris was the first, and Aspen was the second. But Veirella did not know where she fell. She should be the same as her sister, but no man had ever looked at her with want, and no woman with envy. She was too young for either when she lived in the world.

Veirella would not be like her brother, either; she was tall but lacked strength she could barely wield a sword; she was no warrior, and Veirella did not think she could take a life. Some people could learn to be hard and ruthless, others were born with those things coded in their blood.

But Veirella was none of those things, she was a scared girl with a little mind in a bigger body. It was her Reight she was to be sixteen; she did not feel any different. To her it was any other day, not one filled with warmth and life, but darkness and death. Veirella should have been happy, she did not understand why she was not. She was home with her family, the people who loved her most. She honestly did not remember what it felt like to be happy.

Everything was hard, getting out of bed took more effort, she could not speak Veirella knew how to sign but she refused to, her voice was her own and if she relayed on another way of communicating, she feared she would never push herself hard enough to get it back.

Eating was also hard; Veirella had to force herself to eat her meals. She would fall sick every time she took a bite of something it was always something she liked as a girl, but took no interest in anymore.

She mostly stuck to fruits and would occasionally have bread, she ate enough to satisfy the servants, Veirella watched them as she ate waiting for the change that came to their faces when they though she had enough, it was a small change most would never see it. Veirella was always good at reading people, so she knew.

Everything was a reminder that she was different. Her hair was longer, curlier, and much fuller; her legs and arms were longer, and she had body parts that were not there before. As a child Veirella did not think she would ever grow, but now she was five and eight, similar to her mother, she was still taller by a few inches but it was not noticeable, Aspen still towered over her and she assumed her father did as well. Veirella had not seen him; he was not in the castle.

He wrote her letters, she received one every month, telling her how much he loved and missed her and that he would see her soon. He also asked how she was, but she never wrote back, so he never got an answer.

On the other hand, Iris was a floor down, and Veirella had not seen her at all; she did not know why her sister never came to visit. Veirella thought of going to her room herself but thought better of it when she remembered she could not speak. Veirella did not feel she could complain because she did not want to see her mother, the look of guilt and sadness she wore made it hard for Veirella to look at her.

Aspen came to see her daily. They never left her room sometimes they painted others he would read while she sat by the window watching the birds. It was about the time of day that he usually joined her.

Veirella heard a knock at her door, she did not move from her seat at the window or look to see who would enter. It would either be her mother, Aspen, or Rose, her lady-in-waiting no one else came to see her.

"There she is, the girl of the day," it was her brother. He was happier about her Reight than she was, which was not an impossible task to accomplish considering she felt nothing for the day.

When he got closer, she turned to he at him his smile so wide it should hurt. He was wearing a little blue shirt with black pants and black shoes. Blue was his primary color of choice; it went well with his brown skin, as it did hers.

"Not happy to see your dear brother? You break my heart." Aspen raised his hand over his heart for feigning pain. Veirella turned back to the window, he was like that every day; trying something new to get a reaction out of her. He was hoping she would eventually do something other than just stare at him, face as empty as she felt.

She heard him sigh, then his footsteps moving towards her. Veirella thought the seven feet between them was close enough, but apparently he did not. "Veirella I thought today of all days you would be happy, it is your Reight you are sixteen, that something to celebrate" he told her.

"Why?" The word was low and pained, as much as Aspen hated it, he was helping her speak. He tried to get her to say a few words a day, some long, others short. It helped, but it also hurt, the second she began coughing blood they stopped.

"Why not? These are special days, and they only happen once a year, and you have missed enough of them." Aspen explained.

Sure, he was right; it was a special day, but Veirella did not feel special, the way she felt she could not explain with words or even think of ones to describe it. She was a horrible daughter for ignoring her mother for weeks; she was a horrible sister for making her brother sad, and she was a horrible friend because she got Lily killed.

"Okay, what you want?"

"No, your day what do you want to do?"

"Paint?"

Veirella loved painting with him, when they were back home, it was one of the many ways they spent time together. It was the way they connected. She would draw him things and send him them in letters when he was away, and he did the same.

Aspen smiled at her. "Okay, we can do that is there anything else you want for, today or just painting?" Veirella shook her head, it was what they did most days nothing too different, but this time she was the one to suggest it.

"Alright, then can just do that if that makes you happy." Aspen moved to leave, Veirella stood, intending to follow him, but he stopped her.

"No, you stay. I will come get you once everything is ready," he told her. She did not know what he meant by that all her supplies were already in her room, but her was gone before she could ask.

Two hours later, Aspen returned. His clothes were different, white shirt with the same black pants. “Ready” Aspen rubbed his hands together. Whatever he did he was thrilled with himself for doing it.

“Do you need a moment to change?”

He looked her over and Veirella looked down at herself. Rose dressed her in a light blue dress; long sleeves and loosely fitted It was most of her current wardrobe. Veirella had no intention of going anywhere, so she had no need for corsets and layers. She looked back at Aspen and shook her head no.

“Okay, then we can go,” Aspen raised his arm toward the door, gesturing for her to go. But she did move, Veirella did not see the point of going before him when she did not know where they were going.

Veirella’s chambers were far from everything, including her family, her rooms, that was by designed just for her two rooms were converted to one so she would have as much space as she did back home in Estonia. Getting from there to the second floor took some time.

The halls were brightly lit from large windows she could barely see out because of how high they were. Castle windows were always high; they were built that way to protect from being shot by archers.

Veirella was not too disappointed by her lack of view the forest was the only thing there to be seen, and it was the last thing she wanted to look at. When they did make it to the second floor, Aspen turned down the right corridor, then it clicked for her where they were going.

The observatory it was the only thing down there. Veirella had been there only once since she had been at Nightwell, she wondered off exploring one night and discovered it.

She had seen the room in the dark of night, but it was different in the day, the sun filled the room with different colors that usually only appeared in the sky when it rained. The sofas were all covered with white cloth to protect them from dust, so were the paintings on the walls. And there were two large canvases in the center of the room and a stool before each.

Veirella looked outside, and she could see the mountains. There were snowing covering them year round, no matter how hot it was, it never melted.

"Thank You," her voice so low Veirella could not be sure he heard her.

"It was my pleaser." Aspen answered.

She sat at the canvas on the right, and he the one on the left. Veirella ran her hand over the blank space before it was prepped and ready to be used, she did not know what she was going to paint; the voices in her head were so loud it was hard to think.

She sat there with a brush in hand looking at it not knowing what to do; she looked over at Aspen, and he was in his own world. Veirella watched him for a moment longer, then stopped thinking and just do.

She opened a few colors randomly, not paying much attention to what they were. Then she began, Veirella dipped the brush in color after color filling her canvas until she could no longer find blank space, she moved her brush along it without thinking not knowing what would form from it but knowing something was happening she built up a motion of movement canvas, paint, canvas then paint once more, repeatedly until she felt satisfied with what she had.

Veirella looked up at what she created and lost her grip on the brush and palette in her hand, they hit the floor with a thud, the paint splashed halfway up her dress, but she did not notice her eyes were on one thing, and it alone had her attention. Her painting was the last thing she wanted to see, a place she never wished to return to the forest.

Not just any forest, but the one she had been prisoner to for five years, a place that had taken so much from her, and it was what she had painted. The sound startled Aspen; he stood from his stool so fast it fell over.

"Elly, what happened? Are you okay?" he frantically asked.

He looked over her eyes wide with panic. Veirella could see his heart slow when he saw nothing was wrong with her. His eyes found hers; Veirella's eyes were glass. She moved her hand to her throat, feeling the scar that went a crossed it, He looked from her hand to where she was looking. He sighed then moved the canvas from before her turning it so she could not see what was in it.

"Do you want to talk about it?" His voice was soft and calm he was being careful with what he asked her. She wanted to, she really did, but she did not know how to. Aspen looked from her face to where her hand still laid on her throat.

"Did that happen when you got hurt?" he was still calm, but she was not her crest rose faster just thinking about it. The knife, the cold sharp knife moving over her throat, going deep and spilling her blood. Breathe, she could not breathe she was bleeding out she was going to die.

"Hey, hey, hey breathe, Elly." Aspen told her, Veirella could hear his voice, but she could not see him; only darkness. Her head became both light and heavy in seconds. Aspen put his hand on her shoulder, trying to pull her back. The darkness faded, and she saw her brother's brown eyes, but she still could not breathe, and she could not hear him anymore.

Veirella could see his mouth moving, but she could not hear the words he was staying, Aspen raised his other hand lifting one finger after the other, and she counted them. Her chest felt lighter the further she counted. He dropped them, forming a fist then stared again.

One, she said to herself *two* she could hear his voice counting each finger as he raised them, *three* the heaviness in her head faded. *Four,* then the lightness followed, and finally *five* she could breathe again; her hand fell from her throat. Then, she fell into her brother's arms and cried silently.

Ten Years Before

Early morning the palace halls were mostly empty and dark, other than the occasional guard, there was no one around that early. Veirella followed behind brother, staying quiet just like he told her to. They were meeting Iris in the forest for one of their games.

Iris and Aspen were always challenging each other, wanting to see who was the best, from who was the better archer (Aspen), to which one was better with daggers (Aspen), who knew Fianorea history best (Iris). And now they were seeing who was better at wielding a sword better, it would more than likely be her brother.

Aspen spent more time with one in his hand than Iris did. Their father made sure they could both wield a weapon so they could protect themselves in case of an attack. It also helped them prepare for their Ryin. Aspen took more interest in it than Iris did, she liked being able to defend herself, but she hated to sweat. She stuck with the books, but that never stopped her from challenging Aspen to a match, if he thought she could not do something, it became her mission to prove him wrong.

Iris was wrong a lot, but for some reason she kept making the stakes higher. A few years before it got so dangerous that she got hurt in one of their games. Iris had challenged him to climb the whipping Willow at Nightwell Castle.

Her brother thought it was too dangerous, but she would not back done. She had beaten him at something and wanted to do it again; Iris did not care how dangerous it was. All she cared about was beating him, Iris did not make it far the tree hit her so hard it broke a part of her head. She was unconscious for days after and their father forbade them from playing their game any long; he let it go on for so long because he did not think a little competition between them could do any actual harm.

Their mother was furious that he knew about it and let it go on. Aspen told Veirella it was the first time he had ever seen them fight, and it was also the last. Now here they were, doing their best to not be spotted by any of the guards. They turned down a hallway and got halfway when Aspen saw light coming towards them and pulled Veirella behind a stone statue of one of their many great grandfathers.

He looked at her with a finger raised to his lips, motioning for her to stay quiet. Veirella nodded and copied his motion, telling him she understood. Veirella saw when the light passed, but nothing else with the way Aspen was shielding her.

"We are all most there. There is a corridor at the end of this hall, the exit is through there. When I say run you go straight for it." Veirella nodded at her brother again.

"Okay."

Aspen looked to make sure there was no one coming, then moved so Veirella could get out.

"Run."

She was gone the moment the word left his mouth. Veirella moved as fast as her legs could carry her; lucky for her, she was still two years away from wearing floor-length dresses.

Aspen took off the moment she made it down the hallway. It did not take him as much time to make it down as it took Veirella, and he was not breathing as hard as she was, it was nothing for him. "Why did. You wait?" Veirella struggled to get the words out.

Aspen smiled down at her, "because I bigger and faster" Veirella rolled her eyes at he, and he laughed. Aspen took her hand and led her to the doors.

They were on the southeast side of the palace, from there they had direct access to the wood. Aspen got down before her.

"Up"

"Why I can walk just fine?" He turned his head to look at her. "I now you can but if I carry you we get there faster and your feet will hurt less." he told her.

Veirella would not fight him on it she liked been carried, she hated went her mother told her she was old enough to use her own feet. It had being over a year and Veirella was still not over it.

She happy got on to Aspen's back, wrapped her arms around his neck, and her feet around his waist, Aspen made sure she was secures to him before standing up. "Ready?"

"Ready."

Aspen was right with him carrying her too less than half the time to get to the clearing in the forest, it got brighter the closer they got, and Veirella could see the sun rising. There was a small pond next to the clearing, Veirella looked around and saw her sister sitting on one of the many massive rock's around the clearing; most of them were hidden by the tree's. Aspen set Veirella done and Iris jumped off the rock and went to them.

She got done to Veirella "Hey Elly what are doing out here?" She asked her voice as soft and filled with sweetness. Veirella looked up at her brother "Aspen said I could come, he said you were going to play a game and I wanted to see." She answered excitement pouring from her.

"Is that so?" Iris said will looking at their brother. Her sister stood to facing Aspen. "Elly go and sit over there" Iris pointed to the rock she was sitting on. Veirella did as she was told, but she had trouble getting up. The shape of the stone changed before her and steps began denting which she used to get to the top, then they faded.

Veirella watched her siblings talk but she could not hear what they were saying, Iris did not look too happy. Aspen looking at her and she waved at him, he smiled at her and waved back. Iris sighed then moved to the other side of the clearing and Aspen went to the other closer to the water.

There were swords on either side stuck in the ground, waiting for them. "If her presence here is such a problem then, let's get this over with quickly so we can get back. Before anyone notices." Aspen told Iris then took up his sword and smiled at her, Iris did the same.

They circled each other so long Veirella grew bored with them and climbs of the rock, the steps reappearing was she did so. They were not looking in her direction so she moved around the stone, and walked into the forest. Veirella walked around looking at the birds flying above her, the squirrels running from tree to tree; the bees eating from flowers, and the dancing lady bugs.

Veirella heard pained noises above her, a bird bigger bird appeared out of nowhere and was attacking one of the smaller birds. It was biting at its neck, a part of Veirella felt the pain the poor animal was in. "Hey, stop it" she yelled at the larger creature.

But it did not stop, and she got anger, it was hurting the bird it would kill it. "I said stop!" Her eyes glowed gold and the larger animal was thrown back hitting a branch then flying off. The smaller animal fell to the ground, Veirella ran to the creature. It was bleeding and one of its wings was ripped through.

It was struggling to move, and she did not like the noises it was making. Veirella took the small white and blue creature into her hands as gently as she could manage. "Elly!" she heard Aspen yell for her, Veirella could hear the panic in his voice.

"Elly!"

"Over here," she answered, alerting him to her location. When she turned around, she saw him coming towards her, Iris right behind him. "You cannot wonder off on your own." Aspen told her his voice was heavy and short.

She did not acknowledge his words, she just showed them the injured bird in her hands. "Look" her voice was low and shaky.

Iris and Aspen shared a look, then looked at her. "We ... we need to get it some help," Veirella told them. They did not respond to her. "Elly, there is nothing that can be done, give it to be and go wait over there with Iris I—"

"NO!" Veirella stepped back, pulling the bird behind her. Aspen and Iris were taken aback by her reaction. Her voice had never gotten that high before.

"Elly,"

"No. No. No." She yelled again. "I am not giving it to you." Veirella's eyes started glowing again, "we are taking it home so see a healer, they can fix it." Her heart sped up.

Then the bird flew from her hands up into the trees. They all looked up as the animal, Veirella's eyes, stopped glowing, then she fainted.

Blood Or Water

Veirella

Aspen did not move he just stood there and let her cry into his chest. Veirella thought something was wrong with her, she could not have a simple conversation regarding the events that took place that night.

All she needed to do was tell them what happened, but she could not. Maybe she would never be able to do it no matter how much she wanted to or how hard she tried, and the fact she did not recall most if it made it even harder.

Veirella did not think she had the right to carry her families name, she was too weak to call herself a Graystone. She could not even say more than a few words without her throat burning in response, she considered herself an embarrassment to her family.

She failed to complete Ryin, and she was trapped in vines for half a decade of her life. She was the third child of the King and Queen of the most powerful Kingdom in the world and she was a pathetic excuse for a daughter and a Forian for that matter.

She needed to pull herself together, she needed to show strength, even if she did not have any. Veirella pulled away from Aspen and wiped away her tears.

"I... I am fi...ne. I a.. m going ba... back t... to my r...ro...room," she forced herself to say the words. She could feel the metallic taste of blood building in the back of her throat. It caused her so much pain to put such a simple sentence together. But she did not want to be weak; she refused to be her family's weakness. The thought of giving her family's enemies ammunition made her hate herself a little more.

Aspen intended to say something, but Veirella turned away from him and hurried to the door. Her guard following behind, she did not know where she was going, maybe her room? Or she could finally make the effort to try and go outside.

Veirella made her way to the doors on the first floor, but as she stood between them, she could not make herself go through. Her feet refused to move, making it impossible for her to take the final few steps necessary to complete this simple task.

There was nothing out there that could hurt her anymore as far as she knew. There were guards at every inch of the place, and her dogs were roaming the grounds. So, she was as safe as a person could be. But even knowing all that, she still could not do it.

Veirella stood there looking down at the line that stood before her, something that made her heart move faster than it should have. Finally, she gave up, turned, and headed back up the stairs, never looking up to see where she was going. Veirella heard voices; they got louder the farther down the hall she went. Veirella could make out the voices clearly the closer she got. They belonged to her parents; they were yelling, she was not even aware her father was there, she had not seen him in so long she did not remember what he looked like. Veirella intended to walk past; they were fighting, and it was not her place to listen.

But she stopped when she heard her name. "You cannot keep doing this, Veirella needs stability she needs her family, not to be shipped off to a place on the other side of the world!" her mother yelled. "This is happening whether you like it or not." Her father's voice was not as high as her mother's but still firm.

"This is what she needs."

"How would you know what she needs? You are never here!" She told him it was factual he was rarely ever home, but that was understandable; he was the king, he had the kingdom to take care of. He could not be there always.

"I know that I may not be the most present father to her, but this is the right thing to do. This will be good for her," he was trying to calm her with how sweetness he made tone.

"I am her mother; I know what she needs better than anyone else." She lowered her voice, but Virella could still hear how angry she was.

"Technically she is not yours, and it is time she claims her birthright. And it is time you accept that." Veirella did not hear anything else that was said; all she could focus on was her father's words *she is not yours. She is not yours,* her mother—well, could she even call her that? She was not her mother.

Veirella felt her chest tighten; she was moving to where, she could not tell, but she was going. She heard something hit the floor, but she could not focus enough to register what it was. Somehow, she made it to her chambers; somehow, she went up all those stairs without realizing where she was going. Veirella walked past the guard at the door, oblivious to his presence.

She is not yours, she is not yours, she is not yours; those were the only words going through her head. Veirella moved around her room, trying to get herself to breathe.

Nothing was working; finally, she sat on the floor at the foot of her bed, pulled her legs to her chest, and wrapped her hands around them, then began moving back and forth repeatedly until she felt the pressure in her chest lessen. Then she cried for the second time that day, within an hour of the last. Veirella cried herself to sleep right there on the floor.

Veirella did not have any nightmares; there was no blood, no screaming, or being paralyzed to the ground slowly suffocating to death. She was relieved she had a night for the first time since she had been home that she had a night of sleep free of fear, but it was replaced with the pain of her father's words.

But would that matter? She raised her, but was that a choice? Did she really love her, or had she pretended to for all those years? The thoughts consumed Veirella's mind.

Veirella could not help but question every moment they had spent together. Since she gained the ability to retain memories. Did she mean it all those times she told her she loved her?

Was that why Iris did not come to see her? She learned the truth of her birth and felt no interest in seeing her or hated her because their father had been unfaithful to their mother and was forced to take in the child created from his broken trust.

She was the topic of most of their fights when she was a child; was this the cause? she wondered. Veirella heard a knock at her door. "Elly, can you open the door?" It was Aspen her brother, not her brother.

Did he know the truth, or he did not yet, and that way he still came to visit. Would he stop caring about her the moment he did? Veirella did not think she could handle them both hating her for something that was not her doing. But if she were truly a product of one of her father's digressions, she would not hold it against them for rejecting her.

Veirella went to the door, listening to him try to coax her into opening it. "We do not need to talk; we could just sit at the window in silence if that is what you want." His tone was filled with desperation. He knocked again;

Aspen stayed for a moment longer, but when Veirella made no effort in opening the door he walked away.

Veirella looked down at herself, she was still in the paint covered dress from the day before. She did not wish to see anyone, but she wanted to take a bath, and she was clueless to those things. Veirella went up to her bed and pulled the rope attached to a bell that would summon her ladies.

There was a door next to her bathing chambers that was for staff only. It opened, and a dark-skinned girl, only a few years her senior, came through, followed by four others. Rose was her name; she was named the lady of the house; no servant served the same royal, so they each had their own household. "You called princess?" Her voice was laced with a hint of surprise, Veirella did not call for them; they just came in the morning to get her dressed for the day and again at night to get her ready for bed.

"A ba..th" she told her.

Two of the ladies, similar in shade to Rose bowed to Veirella and went into her bathing chamber to get her bath ready. The other two servants behind Rose lighter in color, only a few shades different from Veirella moved forward "Anything to eat or drink Your Highness?" one asked.

Veirella nodded at her woman, she looked older than Rose, closer to her mother's age but not by much, ten years below her at least. She bowed and left the room. "Come, let us get you out of those filthy clothes

"Sorr..y .. ruined" Veirella held up the dress, showing her the paint stains. "That is not a problem; there are ways to fix these things, and if painting will be a regular thing for you, I will have things prepared specifically for that," Rose told her, Veirella stood before the floor-length mirror as Rose unzipped her. She stepped out of the dress, then removed her undergarments and went to the bath.

They girl's were putting bath salts in the steaming water when she entered. Veirella stepped into the bath; one girl went for her hair, pulling it down from the braids it was in, and the other took a sponge to her skin. Her hair was washed and dried the best it could be considering how curly it was and how much of it she had.

The girl braided it and wrapped a towel around it to soak up what remained of the water, then it would be left to dry in the air the rest of the way. Veirella got out of the bath when her skin began to prune, she herself then went back into her room, where Rose had a yellow dress similar in style to the blue she had on before laid out on her bed with matching shoes and underthings.

By the time she finished getting dressed, the other ladies returned with breakfast. They brought plates filled with bread, cheese, dried meat, grapes, and tea. Rose set the table close to the window like she did every morning, and the ladies placed her breakfast atop it. Veirella sat, and tea was poured for her.

It was the first thing Veirella went for every morning; once she was finished with the first, a second was poured, and she slowly sipped it while she ate her meal. She did not know what type it was, but it gave her a tingling feeling she liked. When she finished, everything was removed and they all bowed then left.

A few hours later, Veirella was still at the window, looking out at the birds dancing in the sky. It was mating season given the way they were acting. She did not know what time of year it was; but based on how the wind blew, the warmer month's coming to an end. It was most common for them to start in the middle or end of those months. She watched as the smaller bird moved around the bigger one, they were Coileis.

Unlike most other species, they were the same in color, just different in size. The males were smaller and the females bigger. They were not the most appealing color; they were similar to that of soil.

Veirella watched as the male danced in circles around the female, doing his best to try and get her attention, but she showed no interest in him. She just kept flying as if he were not there, she was more than likely trying to get home to her nesting den before the sun went down. They lived deep in the forest and were the most likely to get eaten by a predator, even though there would be a few more hours of sunlight, but they were not the fastest flyers, so they needed to start early.

There was a knock at the door, but Veirella did not make any move to see who it was. She kept her eyes on the birds as they flew further into the distance. Another knock came, but still she did nothing. They knocked a third time then stopped. Veirella thought they had given up and left.

But then she heard a key turn, and her door was opened; the door could be opened and closed from both sides; there was only one key, and Veirella had used it to lock herself in the night before.

There was only one other key that could open the door, a Skilton key, which only one person had access to. Her father. As king, he had a master key that would grant him entry into every locked room within all his castles and the palace.

Veirella did not turn, she knew it would be him; he was the only one with access to the key. The last time she saw him, she was eight; when he sent her off to Nightwell.

"I have been told you rarely leave this room?" Veirella did not acknowledge him, she did not care for him being there knowing his intentions.

"I find that hard to believe considering the Veirella I know loved exploring and being anymore but inside," he laughed. Well, she had changed; that was not who she was anymore. In fact, she did not know who she was at all. But the last thing she wanted to do was leave her room, let alone the castle, she tried and could not build up the nerve to do it.

And as for exploring, she had learned everything she needed to about the world; It was a horrible place with evil people who liked to cut the throats of ten-year-old girls and leave them for dead. There was nothing else to know.

He sighed at her lack of response; he moved closer to her. The Coileis disappeared, Veirella was just looking at the empty sky; it was better than having to face her father. Veirella felt him sitting next to her.

"I will sit here and talk your ear off if you do not jump in and say something. I have been told I am quite the talker." It was intended as a joke, or he did not know she could not speak, it was bad either way.

Veirella looked at him after he spoke; she shock her head then moved away from the window. In his attempt to make a joke he showed how little he knew of her well-being because he would know she had trouble speaking. "I know what happened was har—"

"Stop!"

She cut him off, the word came louder than Veirella intended it to and regretted the moment she felt the burning in her throat. Veirella couldn't bear to listen to him attempt a conversation, not after what she overheard.

"It has been over a year since you came home, and you have made very little progress. So, I will be sending you away to a place where you will be able to get the help you need," he told her. Veirella could not speak, but she needed to get the words out of her head and into his. She turned away from him, looking around her room for something to write on.

She stopped at the drawing pad on the desk that Aspen left for her a few weeks before, that she had made no effort to touch until now. Veirella opened the pad took one of the pencils next to it and wrote every word she wished she had the ability to say.

It took her some time, but once she was finished, she ripped the page out, walked to her father, and gave it to him.

I cannot speak but that is not something you would know because you are never here. I know you have a job to do as king, but you have made little effort in looking in on me and sending letters in your absences to make yourself feel better about it is not enough. I needed my father, not just your words.

It may make me selfish to say these things, but that is the truth. And then the moment you do show up, you intend to send me away again.

He looked up at her, intending to speak, but she stopped him, pointing at the paper telling him to continue. *I heard what you said to mother yesterday; I could understand why you do not want me around so do not pretend what you are doing is out of love and care. You are getting rid of the problem you created.*

When he looked up at her, his eyes were so wide there was a chance they could stay that way permanently. "Veirella I... you do not know everything." He stood and walked towards her but Veirella moved back. She saw the hurt on his face before she looked away.

"There is more to this than you know, come sit and I will explain." His hand was stretched out to her, but she did not take it.

"Go. Please." Veirella did not look at him, she did not want him to see her cry. And she wanted to be alone when she broke. He did not move for a while, but when he did it was towards her. "I love you and so does your mother, so I will let you process this, and then we will talk about it." He kissed her on the head, then moved around her and left her room.

Veirella went to her bed, taking a nap seemed more productive than crying again. She would have gone to sleep after crying, but she would have a headache so she just went straight for the second half instead.

When she woke hours later it was dark, there were no candles or fae lights burning, so no one came to her room, after her father. But she felt strange, like she was being watched, Veirella looked around the dark room trying to see what direction the felting was coming from. She saw someone sitting at her desk, Veirella moved up onto the bed closer to where the rope was if she pulled it the servants would come in and alert the guards.

How had someone gotten into her room, to begin with there were always two guards at her door, and the staff entrance could only be accessed by those who had permission to enter.

Veirella grabbed onto the rope intending to pull it, she could not scream for the guards and this was her best bet. But before she could the person stopped her.

“Don’t” It was her brother's voice. Veirella felt herself relax. “I did not mean to scare you, and now that I think about it sitting in the dark watching you sleep was not the best way of going about this,” he told her. Aspen stood from the chair and walked into the moonlight, where she could clearly see him. Aspen walked over to her bed and sat at the end.

“Father said you knew the truth; Is that why you did not want to see me when I came to check on you?” he asked.

She could hear the amusement in his voice, as if learning the woman she had called her mother, as long as she'd known the meaning of the word, was not really that. Or the possibility that her father had been unfaithful to her.

“I can see you thinking and the answer that particular question is no.”

Veirella titled her head it was unlikely he knew what she was thinking. “Father has never stepped out on our mother; he may be a lot of things, but unfaithful he is not,” he told her. She did not expect him to actually know what she was thinking but considered it was obvious.

The question she would have first, considering she was the youngest. And mathematically, he would have needed for Veirella to exist, but then there was another option.

“He i..is not my fat..ther is he?”

If her parents were not her parents, then Aspen was not her brother, and somehow that felt worse.

“By blood no, but he is your father, and our mother is your mother.”

Aspen’s words made no sense to Veirella, she did not understand how her parents could be and also not be her parents. Either they were or they were not there was no in between.

Aspen went to speak but Veirella raised her hand, stopping him. She did not think she was ready to have that conversation. They sat in silence for a while, Aspen watched her, trying to gauge her reaction. But she gave him nothing, Veirella’s face was blank, it was a perfect reflection of how she felt inside empty.

Choices and Changes

Veirella

Nearly a week had since Veirella learned she was not the person she thought herself to be, her father was sending her off to a school, halfway around the world, and her family was not real.

Aspen told her the opposite, but Veirella had trouble understanding the concept of been someone's child without having any form of blood connection to them. She was struggling with it along with everything else, Aspen brought a variety of supplies to her room, and every day they did something different, one day it was sketching, another painting, or them attempting to make something with wool, it did not end well.

Aspen tried keeping brushes and pencil's out of her hand because without fail Veirella drew the same thing every time. The forest where she was attacked, it was the same thing every time, she did not do it with intent, once Veirella thought she was drawing a bird she saw by the window but when then her hand started drawing trees instead.

Her reaction was the same every time paralyzing fear and shock.

After the initial shock of her parentage dissipated, her nightmares returned, it was not the same one every night a new one presented itself. She was running through the forest, Veirella could not tell why she was running or where to, but she was terrified and needed to get away.

"Aspen?" He turned to her.

Do you know why she has not come?" Her question was not as clear as it should have been. There was more than one woman in her life was avoiding her.

"Our mother or Iris?"

"Mother." Veirella wanted to say both, but if her sister intended to keep her distance, she would ask her why herself, if they every spoke again.

"She has a lot going on, there are things happening back home that she is trying to control from here. She asks about you every morning, and she has your lady report to her." He told her.

Her mother, if she could still refer to her as such, was still the queen she had responsibility to attend to Veirella was with her at most social engagements, she was usually the only child in attendance. Most woman did not care for the children they birthed, for many children were a means to an end to help secure their place in society, .Veirella understood enough of the world to know woman who were unable to bare sons suffered for it.

"What. Happened. At. Home?" Veirella raised her hand to massage her throat, she was pushing past her limit, made it hurt swallow.

"No need to push yourself, I know it hurts. And it's all politics nothing for you to worry." Aspen answered.

His voice was low and comforting, Veirella wanted to know she was no longer a child she could hear the important things, her understanding of them was not the best but she would still like to know she could read books about the parts she did not grasp.

But she still nodded at him dropping the topic. There was something else they needed to talk about; the reason Aspen had being with her so consecutively. He was the heir she expected him to travel with their father but instead he was there with her.

Veirella could not pull together another word much less a whole sentence, so she flipped away from the tree she was drawing in her sketch pad and wrote her question. She waved her hand at Aspen to get his attention; he looked up from the girl he was painting. Someone Veirella had seen him create more than once now.

When he looked at her, she took the pad from her lap and turned it so he could read. *when do I leave?* Aspen shook his head attempting to deny what she already knew. Veirella raised her had stopping him, she turned the pad and wrote again. She moved faster this time, so her words were not as cleanly written.

I know it is happening, so how long? Aspen sighed and looked away.

"Four. Four days. I will be the one going with you, thought that was best after your talk with our father. I should have said something, but I wanted to pretend it was not happening a little longer," he told her.

Veirella put the sketchbook off to the side and moved over to where Aspen was sitting on the floor and hugged him. "Understand" she did not know if he heard her because the word came out so low, then she felt him nod against her shoulder.

The last four days had been absolute chaos. Veirella being measured from head to toe, the length of her hair was checked, her neck wrists, and fingers, for Jews, that she had little chance of wearing.

Dresses she did not thing would ever see more than her closet because all schools had mandatory uniforms, that was what the book's said any way. Veirella had tutors for everything she needed to learn, but in school's they were called teacher's and professors.

Veirella did not want to do any of it, the questions about what she wanted, what she did not, if she wanted a dress in more than one color, did she want a specific type of shoe, it wall all too much.

Veirella got overwhelmed by all of it and had Rose take charge. She knew what Veirella liked and could make the choices as best as she could, maybe even better. Rose would actually put effort and care in the decisions she made, Veirella would need to learn to function without the help of others.

It would be an adjustment, she did not like change but after thinking about it, going to this school was the most realistic thing to do. She had magic as far as she knew, Veirella did not attempted to use it, but she could tell something was different about her. It felt like something was moving under her skin, a feeling she did her best to ignore.

Veirella was terrified that feeling she could not control it, and lost five years of her life because of it and she had no interest in going for another take. And going away to learn control so she could not hurt herself or someone else. Veirella could life with causing herself pain but she did not like she could survive doing it to someone else.

"I think you've been in here long enough" she was pulled from her thoughts by the sound of Rose's voice. Veirella was in the bath she did not realize the ladies were gone until that moment.

Her hands were pruned, and the water had gone cold. Rose retrieved her robe and gave it to her when she stood. She walked back into her room and Veirella followed her.

Rose led her to the vanity, Veirella sat down, and the girl started combing through her hair end to root. Rose had woken her so early it was still dark outside. And her room was lit up by fae lights and candle sticks, she intended to braid her hair, and it would take a few hours to do so.

Head, neck, back, and every other part of Veirella was in pain, when Rose was finished. She'd been sitting in the same place for so long she could hardly feel her legs when she stood. In that moment she contemplated cutting off a few inches of her hair so she would never need to do that again, but once the pain and tension wore off, she would be back to her senses.

She looked in the mirror to see the end result, she wanted to see if it was worth the agony she would be in to the next day or two. And it most definitely was.

The braids were the small, so they would last for a few weeks, and the front was braided back to keep the hair out of her face, Rose added in small blue and gold gems all over, she said it would give it more life.

"Okay, it is almost time for you to get going, so which would you like to wear?" Rose asked, Veirella turned around to look at her, she was holding up leather suits, one black, the other blue.

"Dress?"

"It will be a bit of a journey, from here to Valria. Then you will portal from there to Asiza and from there it will be another four or five hours to get to the school. So Keives are better for this journey more comfortable." Rose explained.

Veirella had never been the biggest fan of pants, they felt too restrictive, unlike dresses where she had more room to move. But she would wear them, nevertheless. She pointed to the blue and Rose set the other down.

Rose helped her it to the leather like fabric, there were so many places she could conceal a weapon, daggers were her specialty, and she could carry at least eight without anyone spotting them.

The light blue shirt was a different material than the pants, but the jacket was the same, it close at the top but flowed free from mid waist down to her ankles. It imitated a dress which felt intentional.

"Almost there, you turn need boots." Rose ran to her closet and return a moment later with a pair of blue boots that matched. They had a short heel about two inches.

Veirella sat on the chair before her vanity and took the shoes from Rose.

"Socks. Please." Rose got her a black pair from the armoire Veirella never wore then most of her shoe did not call for any. She removed her bed slipper and replaced it with the sock then the boot and followed the same for the other.

She stood and moved around in them testing the feel and the fit. They were comfortable and fit perfectly, which was not a surprise they were custom, but leather needed to be stretched.

"Perfect" Rose almost squealed.

Veirella smiled at her. "We should get going. Your family will be waiting" Veirella looked at Rose through the mirror she was looking at the clock, Veirella did not ask what time they would be leaving, it was not required for her to know and no part of her much cared. Keeping track of things would now be her responsibility.

When they made it to the entry way, Veirella was surprised to see Iris there next to their mother. Both were wearing similar dark green dresses, with their hair pulled back into braids, and Aspen and their father were both in keives where Veirella's was blue theirs were black and both carried their swords on their left hip.

"Darling, you look wonderful" her mother told her as she approached. She raised her hands to Veirella's face squeezing her cheeks.

"This is my first time seeing you in a fighter's leather, you look adorable." Veirella pulled but out of her reach, she heard a sound coming from behind her, she looked over and saw Aspen trying his best not to laugh.

Veirella did not like that word in regard to what she had on most people wore keives when they intended to fight and her mother looked at her and called her

'Adorable.'

How would others react to her if that was what her mother thought. Granted she was not going to fight anyone, but it did not matter, it was not how she wanted to be preserved.

"How are you?" She could see the concern in her mother's eyes and Veirella could feel the discomfort building inside herself. She did not know what to do her voice made her question sound genuine and caring but, how she felt asking it was the complete opposite, there was guilty mixed in.

The clock bell rung, which was perfect timing in Veirella's eyes. "We should be going, if we intend to get there my nightfall" Aspen told them.

He went towards the doors and Veirella followed, but she stopped at the threshold looking down at it. The fear was mostly in her head she knew that but that did not stop it from existing.

Aspen got halfway down the stairs before he noticed she was not behind him, he walked back up to her.

"What is it?"

"I can't"

"Can't what Elly?"

"Go. Out."

Aspen looked over at their parents then back at her. "There is nothing out there that can hurt you. And even if there was, I would not let anything happen to you." His voice was low and soothing.

Veirella did not look away from the ground at her feet the small space that separated in and out. Aspen's hand came into her line of sight, open and waiting for her.

"Do you trust me?" she nodded.

"Then take my hand and we can do this together." She looked up at him, he smiled at her, for a moment all Veirella did was look at it, then she took it, Aspen squeezed her hand.

"Ready?" Veirella nodded at him, took a deep breath closer her eyes and stepped out. She let Aspen lead her down the stairs towards the a waiting carriage. "If you do not want to fall, I do suggest opening your eyes" he told her. Veirella did not realize she was had them closed until he said something, but Aspen would never let her fall. She breathed in deep, swallowed so hard it hurt, then did as he asked.

She kept her eyes down looking at the gray steps beneath her feet letting him lead her. Veirella counted all fifty-two steps as she walked down. Until she was finally standing before the dark grey carriage been pulled by two large black war horses.

Veirella looked back at her family, one last time then got into, Aspen followed and sat across from her. He hit against the glass behind him, and they were moving, in that moment Veirella felt she was reliving the beginning of the start of the worse day of her life once again.

A New Beginning

Veirella

They had been moving for hours. The only sound between them was the carriage hitting the rocks and holes in the road, and the galloping horses. Neither Veirella nor Aspen spoke hours together in silence, one of the many things they shared as children they could be in a room together and never say a word. It was not awkward or uncomfortable; it was just how they were. But Veirella now did not have the option to speak and because of it, Aspen would never attempt to speak to get to her. Aspen had his eyes close, and she was playing with her hands.

There was a commotion outside. Veirella was so out of it she did even notice they were nearing people. That last time she looked out the window, all she saw were trees and thought could have been hours ago.

The noise woke Aspen; he followed her so see what was happening. There were people gathering, looking at something. Veirella did not see much, before her Aspen closed the curtains, he did it so quickly her brows cruised at the action.

"It's a little bright and I am trying to sleep," he told her. She closed the ones on the other side for him, then he laid his head back as it was before and went back to sleep.

From what Veirella saw before he closed the curtains, there looked to be a tree forming on the side of the road before the buildings. It was what everyone was looking at, but she could not be curtain she did not see much of it, but a part of her thought it was a person based on the shape.

It got darker, and they should be at their first stop at any moment. According to Aspen anyway. Veirella felt the carriage stop, then she tapped on Aspen's arm to wake him.

He jumped from his sleep, hand instinctively reaching for his sword. "What's wrong?" He looked around, but looked at very when he realized he could not see outside.

"Stop" Veirella pointed to the top of the carriage. She saw the tension in his body dissolve the moment he looked out the window, seeing where they were. He released the curtain.

"Stay here. I will be right back." Aspen looked at her, waiting for a response before he would open the door. Veirella nodded. Then he opened the door and closed it behind him. Veirella saw a caravan a head of them off to the side before he closed it.

She heard voices, one belonging to a woman, the other she assumed her brother's. They were too far for her to know for certain. Veirella took no interest in the conversation, she was more interested in the carriage's interior she than what was taking place outside of it.

Gray carriages were common transport, for the public blue was privately owned by those who could afford them. Some families had one, others more. Her family had one for each member. They were not allowed to travel together. They all had black interior, but the roofs were different; blue carriages were designed with gold and gray silver.

The outline of the windows was coated in metal, all of which were moving in vine patterns similar to the Lovia Marks Forian's earned after successfully completing Ryin. Veirella never finished her training, but somehow she had them. At first they were just on her back, so she did not need to see them, but then they grew and now ran up her chest.

She avoided looking at them when she took her baths or when she was getting ready before a mirror. ***"You are not worthy. Those were stolen not earned. You are a fraud and a fake."*** Veirella did not know if it was her own voice or there was someone else in her head. Most days she did her best to ignore it, or them, because sometimes there were so many. There was always more when she was alone and they were also louder.

"Everything is ready for us to go" hearing Aspen, she realized he was back in the carriage. Veirella did not hear the door open or felt anything when it did.

His brow rose as he watched her. "Are you okay?"

"Yes." she answered softly.

"Ookayy, well we are about to go through the portal. And considering this is your first time, it might be uncomfortable." He warned her, Veirella nodded, then the carriage began moving again.

Then something happened. One moment she heard the horse's hooves, then nothing. She felt a wave pass over her, making her feel strange. Veirella saw green sparks hitting the window; she pushed the curtains to the other side to see. There was a vortex of green around them, mixed with different shades.

Then a moment later everything was normal again and she could hear the horse's again, it was bright out. The sun was still out because of the change. They would get a few more hours of light.

Veirella moved to sit back, then looked at Aspen who was smiling at her. "I am sick," she told him. The words were so low she was not sure he heard her. But his smile fade and his body tensed. Aspen did not say anything and Veirella was not sure there was anything to say. In the silence, the voice made its way back in. ***Poor little Veirella, broken, useless girl do you think anyone would care if you just disappeared.***

It was dark when they finally stopped. Veirella's head felt as like her brain had been shaken to bits. She pulled back the curtains to see the school, but there was nothing but trees before her.

"Where are we?" she asked him.

"Outside the gates of the Academy, come." Veirella turned to see Aspen leaving the carriage, then turned and offer his hand to help her down. She took it and followed him out; she looked around. There was not much she could see. The trees were dense and filled with darkness. The only reason she could see the ground before her was a combination of both the moon and the carriage lights.

They moved before the horses where there was a closed gate; it was solid gold and so tall she could not see where it stopped.

"State your business" Veirella looked around to see where the voice came from, but saw nothing. It stated her, she was not expecting anyone to be out there in the dark and, also never heard a voice with so much base in it.

"My sister, she is here to attend" Aspen's voice was firm, unwavering at what was in the dark. "Approach." Veirella swore she felt the ground shack beneath her.

Dark and creepy voice, that was a no Veirella thought. She tried pulling her hand from Aspen's, but his hold on her only tightened; they did as the voice order. There was nothing but blackness before her. Then torches came to life on either of the gate. Veirella looked up, she could see the gate more clearly now and at the top she saw symbols. It was still too dark to make them out, but she saw a woman in the center with a sword pointed down in her hands. Halfway down in the middle of the gate, there was another symbol going across, but it was more of a crest. Two swords crossing with symbols, each representing the four elements.

At the top was earth flowers, rocks and vines going towards the center of the crossing where the swords crossed, air was on the right and water on the left doing the same, and finally fire on the bottom going up to meet the other three. They all came together in the middle, mixing into each other but never blending.

"Place your hand on the gate" Veirella ripped her eyes away from what was on the gate to what was behind it. She saw legs, then she looked up until she spotted a face. The creature before her had four eyes, two like hers and one on its forehead, the other where its nose should have been. A troll Veirella read about them but never thought she would ever come face to face with one.

That is far from face to face. That thing is at least sixty feet tall. It could flick me with its finger and I would probably fly away. Veirella tried her best not to show it fear. She did not know how well she was doing, but considering she was still standing there; it was working.

Remembering its words, she looked down to find where she was to put her hand, but there was nothing; a moment passed, and the gate started melting. The gold was not dripping on to the ground but coming together to form something. When it solidified again, then words began carving themselves into the smooth metal. ***"Ites laco entaor"*** *for one to enter the truth must be revealed.*

Veirella did not know how it intended to reveal that truth or how she even understood the words that were written there. So she slowly moved her hand down on it. At first, nothing happened. She looked at Aspen, who was looking back at hand.

Before she could ask what was supposed to happen, she felt her hand burning Veirella tried pulling away but her hand would not move. She wanted to scream from the pain, but no sound would come. She gritted her teeth together, doing her best to push through without crumbling to the ground.

She kept pulling her hand until it finally came off the pad. Veirella looked down at her hand, it was covered in her blood, she looked away from it not wanting to trigger a reaction. Veirella forced her attention at the pad that burned her, her blood was absorbed into the gold, Veirella looked back at her hand where the pain had faded as well and the blood was absorbed back into her skin, as if it did not happen at all.

"There is truth withing her blood." The troll said then walked away going towards the forest. Once it was no longer in sight, the gated opened. They returned to the carriage. Once they were open wide enough, they went through.

The ride up did not take long. Veirella hoped it would take more time. She was counting down the minutes she had left before Aspen left her in this strange place she did not know.

"You will like it here" Aspen stated his enthusiasm was not needed.

I would like to be home. I like that much more.

Veirella thought the words she so wished to speak.

Aspen was looking out at what part of the castle he could see.

Veirella looked out long enough to see them going around a water fountain with a statue of a woman holding a spear. Then she saw the castle. There was light two to three floors up, but everything else other than the bottom was dark. The student were either all in bed or on that floor.

When the carriage stopped, a guard in blue opened the door.

"Your Majesties" he moved to the side and bowed to Aspen when he exited, he turned and raised his hand to her, Veirella looked from his face down to his hand, she did not what to do it, she wanted to stay and hoped her brother would just take her home. If she did not comply, but she had no interest in having people talk of her family's lacking control. Guards talked as much as servants did, and she also did not know who else was out there so she took his hand.

When she stepped down, Veirella was standing before steps. At the sound of heels coming down them she looked up.

A woman a very tall woman was walking towards her. Her hair was pin straight and onyx black, her eyes were a monolid shape, they were the same color as her hair, and her skin was olive. And she was wearing all black shirt, pants, her long coat, and shoes.

"Veirella I presume, I have heard a lot about you" she was smiling at her. It was warm, welcoming, comforting for most, but it made Veirella run cold.

Having strangers smile at her did not bring up fond memories. The last person to do that asked her mother for her hand. He had a son so her mother had considered, but then he looked at her and smile when he said it was not for his son but himself.

Veirella was only seven, and he was two years her father's age. When her father heard of his request, he had him hung for treason.

The woman was still looking at her, Veirella moved closer to Aspen, almost standing be hide him.

"She does not speak much, her vocal cords were damaged" he explained. Veirella could feel the woman looking at her, but she moved her eyes in every direction but hers. Veirella had seen how people reacted to hearing that she could not speak. The pity was uncomfortable and unbearable.

Her servants were changed three times because they all looked at her the same; she understood why they did it. She was a walking tragedy, but that did not mean she had to like or endure it.

Her eyes landed to her right where she saw two guards, one of the school, the other one of the men that had accompanied them to Astro, unpacking her bags.

"Not a problem. Wielding does not come with such limitations." she told her.

"Come, let me show you around, and my name is Genevieve Conley. I and the headmistress of Astro Academy." she turned, and went back up the stairs. Aspen looked at Veirella then followed Genevieve him.

Veirella did not pay much attention to what Genevieve said, after talking about the different levels of the school she stopped listening. There were seven levels. The first was not the one they started on but the one above, the first was considered the ground floor, consisting of the Greenhouse, supply storage, the weapons room or were they cleaned the weapons.

Veirella was busy trying to see into the greenhouse to catch which it was. But considering the ground floor was where the entrance was, it would not be strategic to have weapons there. In case the school was ever attacked.

The actually first floor was where Genevieve's offices was along with the other teachers. The second was teachers' quarters, which were the only floor students did not have access to, third and four were class, training center, library, dining hall, and test rooms. Each element had their own. The other three were the student dormitories. As Genevieve led them up the stairs, Veirella blocked her out more, focused on the paintings on the walls. They were quite beautiful, not just the paintings, but the women in them. They all looked different.

"Those are my predecessors. This school has only ever been lead by women. The High Priestesses makes the choice, once one Headmistress dies or retires. Another is chosen by one of the other three High Priestesses."

Genevieve explained. She was standing above her on the stairs. Genevieve smiled at her, then turned and started going up again, she must be the Iriean choice. She did not look as old as the woman in the paintings; she looked closer to Iris in age.

Two more flights later and they were finally on the first floor, they went all the way to the end of the hallway, moving past fourteen doors spread four and a half feet apart. Then up four steps were there was another door, the same dark oak as the others just twice the size. Genevieve's office.

When she opened the door, the torches came to life, lighting up the room. It was massive; the desk was so far into the room it took a decent walk to get to it and a few more to the floor to ceiling windows behind it. The left side of the room was lined with shelves filled with books, both old, older and new-ish. Before them were two sofas dark in color to match with the rest of the room, they faces each other with a table in between.

On the right there were also shelves, but they did not have books they had weapons, three long swords on the top, and an axe in the middle of the one beneath that with daggers short and long no either side of it, the last two shelves had trinkets, there was a golden crown that took her attention. It stood out even in the dark; it had a ruby red gemstone it the center, but that was the only gem on it. Every other part of it was solid gold.

She also mainly focused on it because she did not recognize any of the other things there, and ignoring them was better than admitting that she did not have that knowledge, even if it was just to herself.

There was a knock at the door. “Right on time” Genevieve said mostly to herself. “Enter” she called to the person on the other side. When the door opened, a girl with similar looks to Genevieve walked in. She was a wearing black and teal uniform: black skirt, jacket and vest, with a teal undershirt. She moved farther into the room and Veirella saw the same crest on the upper left of her uniform.

“You called for me Headmistress?” There was something familiar about her voice to Veirella but she did not know the girl’s face.

“Yes, your new roommate is here.” At Genevieve’s words, the girl looked in Veirella’s direction and smiling. She made her way over to her and hugged her, Veirella pulled made. she did not know much about Iriean culture, but it was not common in any part of the world to hug random strangers you just met.

Veirella looked at her brother for help, but he was just standing there looking at the girl touching her without reason.

“It has been so long since I last saw you.” Veirella raised her brow at the girl. She did not know who she was. Veirella pulled her hands away from her and moved closer to her brother. Her smile slipped for a moment before returning. She looked past Veirella at Aspen as he raised his shoulders, then dropped them.

“Veirella this is Anastasia, from what I have been told you two spent sometime together as children. You will be sharing the dorms with her,” Genevieve explained, but the name was not one Veirella remembered she spent most of her time with tutors and trainers. And occasionally she would see a friend.

"Sorry, you many not remember me by that name, but what about Gemma? Like Gemi" That was Veirella's favorite necklace. It was a reight gift she got when she turned seven. It was made of blue sapphires. That she named Gemi. Gemma did not like her name, so Veirella called her after it.

"A name given to my favorite person after my favorite gemstone" Veirella knew those words they were hers. She had said that to Gemma the second time she came to visit.

Veirella looked at her again. She had some of Gemma's features. She mostly grew out of most of them, so Veirella did not take note of who she was at first, but she still did not move to hug her. That was not her thing.

"Anastasia, would you show Veirella to her room?" Genevieve asked. Gemma nodded in response, then moved for the door. Veirella did not follow, she turned to Aspen instead.

"I do not want to stay here" her voice was so low the others could not have heard her. "I know you do not, but this is for the best. We can write to each other." Veirella did not move or say anything in response. Aspen sighed.

"Look, give it eight weeks. If in eight weeks you are not happy and you want to go home, I will come and get you myself. Regardless of what father wants, if you want to go, we will go. That is my promise to you, but you need to at least try. Can you promise me you will?" He asked. Veirella thought about it for a second. She wanted to get better, she wanted to fix what was wrong with her.

So she was willing to try. She nodded "Yes. I can try" She turned away from Aspen and went towards Gemma, who was standing at the midpoint of being in the room and outside of it. She moved through fully when Veirella got closer, before she followed her Veirella turned back to look at her brother one more time. Then went after her. The door closed behind her on its own. She looked around it to see if something was there, but she found nothing.

"The Headmistress is an Air Weidler. She did it." Gemma explained. She turned and continued down the hall, when they reached the end to go up the stairs, Gemma stopped and went to one of the paintings on the wall, it was slightly lower than the others.

"I do not know about you but, I have zero interest in walking up four hundred steps to get to the top flour" Gemma told her, she put her hand over the painting and light blue and white sparks appeared moving around her hand rotating with no end or beginning. The painting, of what looked to be a storm or fire, disappeared and in its place, a vortex similar in color to the sparks on her hands appeared.

"This is called a pocket space or a port key. They are all over the school, they help us get around. By for easier than taking the stairs. Once someone uses it until it is closed and a new cannot be opened it will take you to the same place, lets go," Gemma explained, then stepped through the port key and disappeared.

Veirella closed her eyes, took three deep breath's in and out and with her eyes still closed she stuck her hand through. She did not feel anything happen, so she kept moving. She opened her eyes again when she heard Gemma's voice, "thought I was going to need to come back and get you." Gemma went around Veirella and closed the vortex again.

She looked around and, on her right, there were stairs at the end of the hall leading to a massive set of doors. There were eight doors on each side of the hall. With two sets of windows on this level, one behind the staircase and the other at the end of the hall.

"Only Celerian's live on this level. We live in the royal court because our parents are upper four the originals." Veirella did not know who her parent was or who any of the other Celestial were, she assumed that would be something she would learn in one of her classes, which she was not looking forward to.

They got to the end of the hallway and Gemma pushed the doors open, where they were met with another sent of doors. She opened them and was met with a massive room.

"Welcome to the royal court," her voice rose slightly when you said that. Veirella looked around. They were standing at the top of a staircase, there were large windows, one on each side of a fireplace in the middle. There were two sofas facing each other, with a table in the center. Veirella walked down into the room, where she got a better view of the room; there were four identical doors, two on each side of the room.

"Our rooms are on the right, and the boys are on the left." Gemma went left. "Now, this hall is our very other private training area; I rarely go. Not a fan of getting sweaty, and a kitchenette we mostly only use for breakfast." Veirella followed Gemma down the hall. "All other meals we take in the school dining hall, but if you would like to get all your meals here, that can also be arranged." Gemma continued, Veirella liked that option, she was not ready for large group settings yet.

It would take some time for her to adjust to the three people she was now living with. Veirella was not entirely against the idea of being around others.

She eventually wanted to be comfortable doing so, but she could not go from barely being around people to being around a lot of them every day. She would try getting comfortable with the other three and, based on that, she would slowly try to be around others. But that was thinking too far ahead.

Veirella heard a sound coming from the room on her right, which Gemma had pointed out as the training area. She slid the door open, and there she saw two boys fighting or training. She could not tell which it was. They did not seem to be holding back at all. The boy on the right got hit in the face, but he did not seem affected. He just kept going after the other one.

He went in to hit back, but he dodged his punch, but he got another attempted he got down and swept his feet from beneath him. He hit the mat with a light thud. "As hot as it is watching you two go at one another, we have company." Gemma said, getting their attention. They looked at her in unison. The boy who knocked the other one down helped him up.

They were laughing with each other as they walked over to them, so their fighting was not serious. "This is Veirella, a friend and the princess of Fianorea," Gemma introduced her. Both boys look at her. "Lovely to meet you, Veirella. I am Lorenzo, but most call me Luka." Luka had dark hair and light green eyes. His skin was tan, like he bathed in the sun; he had on a long sleeve shirt, which was strange considering he was sweating.

Veirella did not say anything she just nodded, it was slow and easy to miss. She looked at the boy next to him, who she somewhat recognized as prince Sebastian. He was just as tall as Luka. He had dark brown hair, his eyes were also brown with a bit of gold within them and he his skin was bronze.

"Hi, Veirella. Away from home, every just calls me Pax." he told her.

"She lost her voice, in an accident, so she cannot speak." Gemma told them. They both nodded, Veirella waited for the look of pity that they would give her but it never came.

"Let me show you to your room," Gemma told her, Veirella followed her out. She took her to the second room on the right, which was closest to the window. Veirella opened the door; and her things were inside; there was not much to the room. It was a large space. There was a bed, a small sofa at the foot of the bed, a vanity, and a large mirror on the wall for the most part it was plain.

"They do not decorate much, so you can do whatever you like with it," Gemma exclaimed gleefully. Veirella walked around the room. It had big windows on either side of the bed, which was good. She liked her space bright.

There were two doors on the right side of the room; she opened both; one was her changing room; it was not as big as the one she had at home, but it was still great in size. The other door led to her bathing chambers; a large golden bath was in the center of the room. It had a contraption on it she had never seen before.

She moved it, and water came rushing out. She pushed it down, and it stopped. "That is called a called a fau, it was developed a few years ago. And it is the most amazing contraption the Atarian's has ever come up with." Gemma explained.

"Where does the water come from, and where does it go?" Veirella signed. "The whole thing is made with Cai, so my guess is pocket space," Gemma answered. Veirella was tired she just wanted to have a bath and get to bed.

"I am going to go. I am next door if you need me." Gemma left and Veirella went and took her bath. It took little time for the bath to fill and it was the perfect temperature. She thought it would be cold, but it was very much not.

Veirella did not know what to expect for the next day, but she hoped it was nothing magic-related. considering she was here to learn control, it was unlikely that would be the case, so she was hoping for the best but preparing for the worst.

Ten Years Before

Veirella spent most of her days in the library; that was where she took all her lessons. Only for four days each week, but she had to spend all day there even when she finished early.

However, this day was different. They were hosting the royal families of Iriea and Ataria. Treaty negotiations were starting and Fianorea had the honor host the first.

That morning, as her mother braided her hair, Veirella asked if her day would be different. She loved learning, but any breaks she could get, she would gladly take.

"Are my lessons off for today, mama?" Veirella looked up at her through the mirror. Her mother always focused completely on her hair when she did it, like it was something important that needed to be absolutely perfect. They had braiders who could do it, but her mother insisted on doing the task herself. The servants could take do styles and wash Veirella's hair, but they were never allowed to do it. Those were her mother's orders, as far back as Veirella could remember, no one but her mother had ever done her hair.

She did not understand why; Veirella was old enough to know how her mother was and what it met. So the time she took everyday morning to come and do her hair felt wasteful.

She did eventually answer her once the braid was completed. "It is a learning day. You can either do study history or you can live it. But you will be learning something, your choice." Her mother looked down at her through the mirror, smiled, then started another braid.

So she ended up in the library, learning how treaties worked and why they were made, Veirella went to one of her father's council meets once and she fell asleep because of how boring it was. Her mother knew which choice she would take. Most children her age, royal or not, would not want to sit there listening to adults talk about trades, alliances, port access, and entry fees.

It would have been exhausting. Iris was the only person going that did so by choice, Aspen, as the heir was required to go. So were the other heirs as well, and her lessons would also end hours before the meeting would. And considering her mother was busy, Veirella could do whatever she wanted once her lessons were finished.

It was the third day of the week and unlike the other days were she had math, science and language analysis, she only had history. On history day, she only did that and language analysis, it was mostly just reading.

"Now let's go over what you learned. Once I know you understand what I have taught you, then you may go." Isabelle told her. She was one of her two tutors; Isabelle was the one she liked better. She always made learning fun.

That day, Isabelle made up a board game. Every spot had a word or phrase that they would go over. Every time Veirella landed on one, Isabelle would tell her a fact or meaning that went alone with it. It gave Veirella some control over what she was being taught, even with going over the board until she got every single one.

"No two treaties are ever the same, and modern ones are very different to earlier versions, today they can get up to hundreds of pages when once it was only a verbal contract. They would then write down a summary of what they agreed to and then sign it.

But that would sometimes cause more conflict, so they became more detailed and everything that was agreed upon was written down, so they could refer back to it if they needed to."

Isabelle smiled at her, then started with her questions. "What are some things they can stand for?"

"Resolving conflict, trading, and security,"

"And what is the primary reason for creating a treaty?"

"To protect the people of each nation, considering they are the ones who fight and die in war, not the ones who started the conflict." Veirella answered.

"Very good and last thing what did you get from the story you read last week?" She was given a new story every week. The story Isabelle had given her was called 'A Stolen Heart'. She said it was a love story, but it did not read like one.

"It was tragic, she loved him and all he wanted to do was use her and when she did not want to use her magic to do bad thinks he took it and made her do them anyway, for a story about love it does not have a very happy ending."

"It does not, but it was her love story. He may never have loved her, but she did him. And unfortunately, not all romances had a happy ending." Isabelle told her.

"It however it did have a nice rhyme. A place she knows but came not reach her heart lays and weep, banished away never to return so she could never be set free." Veirella resited.

Isabelle stood from the table and began collecting the things they used. Veirella go up and started putting the books back on the shelves, only the ones she was not allowed to claim the ladder, as much as she wanted to.

"That is all for today. I will see you in a week for our next lesson. Lucky for you, we finished up a few hours early, so you have much more free time." Once Veirella finished, she left.

"Outside, go outside,"

Veirella did not know where the voice came from. She never did, but she did listen.

Outside the library there were three guards, only two needed to be stationed at any post, so one of them was there for her. Most days she saw George, he was her mother's guard, he always brought Veirella to her after her lesson's, but of all days that was one she did not expect to see him.

Veirella went back into the library to look at the clock. Noon was an hour away. She had time before she needed to go to the dining hall for lunch. She could see what was outside and be back before she was missed.

Every moment in her day was scheduled where she needed to be for every hour of the day was written and her mother, her guard and everyone who attended to her knew where she was at all times.

Veirella did not say anything to the guards, she just walked past them. George would tell her mother what she did, but he could not say anything to her.

"Right, Right, Right."

"Now left,"

"Down, Down"

"Two more lefts and you will be there"

"Out those doors and you'll see."

One of the guards before the door opened it for her. On the other side there were two more guard's neither dressed in Forian colors. Veirella stood there, looking at them for a moment before going through the doors. If they were a threat to her, the guard behind her would have done something. As she went down the steps, she heard voices coming from the forest. The wind got a heavier the further she moved and the water in the fountain moved unnaturally.

"Go around and you will see."

Veirella did as the voice told her. Behind the fountain was a boy and a girl. The girl was an inch or two taller than Veirella and the boy was at least five. The girl had pale skin with dark eyes and dark hair that was pinned up, completely opposed to Veirella's curls, and she had on a red dress similar in style to Veirella's blue.

And the boy had brown skin, light eyes and dark hair, but not as dark as the girl's and he had on a dark blue tunic. They each matched in color to the guards standing at the door.

There were little sparks of color going around their fingers, but it stopped when they noticed Veirella watching them.

"Who are you?" the girl asked, walking towards her.

"I should be the one asking. You are in my home." Veirella countered. The girl smiled at her. She stuck her hand out for Veirella to shake when she was close enough to do so.

"I'm Princess Anastasia of Iriea, pleased to meet you and that over there—" she pointed to the boy behind her who also got closer. "—Is Prince Sebastian of Ataria." Anastasia turned back to Veirella. "Now that you know who we are, who are you?" she asked again.

"I am Veirella, second daughter of King Dorian Greystone." She told them that was how she always introduced herself. Her mother told her it was unnecessary, but it was not a habit Veirella cared to break.

"What were you doing over there?" she asked. Anastasia seemed to stand taller if that was possible, "We are Celestial Blooded. We were just showing each other our abilities. I can control air and he can control water." The boy said nothing he just looked at her.

"What does that mean, exactly?" Veirella knew who the Celestial's were history could not be learned without knowing the creators.

"Well, we have their blood. We are half Celestial and half mortal—"

"—Celerian that is what we are." Sebastian added.

"And because of that, we have gifts."

"You have gifts. Tell them."

"I have gifts." They both looked at her. Anastasia's smile grew wider she tilled her head to the side. Sebastian was unchanged. "Really, what kind?" Anastasia asked. Veirella did not know what to say. She heard voices in her heard was that her gift.

"Dance, you can make the birds dancing."

"Do it show them."

"I can make the birds dance. Would you like to see?" she asked, hoping they would not because she did not know how to do that.

But Anastasia nodded. Veirella turned away from them and looked up at the sky. There were little blue birds flying above her. She had spoken to birds once before months ago, but it never happened again. Veirella did not know how it happened or how to make it happen again. But she reached out to them with her mind, hoping they would answer.

"~~Hi there~~," no, that was wrong, she thought. "Can you help me?" A moment [passed of silence then it happen. **"What would you like help with, princess?"** they all answered at once. "Could you dance for my friends and I please?" they got closer, dropping from the sky.

"What kind of dance would you like?" they asked. "Any kind will be fine thank you." Than got closer, the closer they got, the more in line they became. When they were close enough, they flew around the statue in the fountain, then circled around each of them.

Then they flew back up into the skin and used their bodies to form the first letter of each of their names.

"Thank you."

They broke apart and flew away. "Anytime daughter or daughters."

"That was amazing. What are you? Blood or Blessed?" Veirella did not know what she was asking or how to answer the question. Anastasia stood there waiting for an answer than would not come. But she did not need to say anything. Sebastian saved her.

"She is right that was amazing, now I think it is our turn to show you some or our gifts" he turned to the fountain reached his hand out, blue sparks started moving around it, Veirella wanted to get closer to get a better look but she did not know what he was doing so she stayed back.

The water in the fountain began to rise and move towards his hand. He formed a fist, then it turned into a ball. Veirella stepped forward, but before she could get any closer, something cut through it.

"Ana warning next time you come seriously hurt someone." Sebastian told her, "sorry, I was just so excited, I could not wait anymore—" one of the guards calling for them, cutting off Anastasia.

"Our time's up. We need to get back," Sebastian told her. They walked around her. "It was nice meeting. I hope we can see each other again," Anastasia hugged her. "See you around Ella." Then she followed Sebastian inside.

First Of Many

Veirella

"I need to get away. *Run, Run, Run." Veirella felt something moving behind her. She would not look back, she needed to get away. The ground, one second she was running, the next she was laying on the ground. Then something pulled her up. Then she was on the ground again, but it was hard to breathe, and her hands were covered in blood. Screams. Lily, she was died her limbs bent wrong.*

Veirella jumped out of her sleep, breathing hard, heavy. She was covered in sweat and she was cold all over. It was the same dream; it was always the same. Her running from someone, then her bleeding out, then the screams.

She thought it was Lily, Veirella saw her that night. It was in her head, but she was in the forest with Veirella from what she saw.

The nightmare did not come every night. Most days she had them. Some nights she had peace. Two, three days would pass and nothing, then they would come back. Veirella wished it would always come or very at all. It was tiring living like that.

"Who knows, maybe next time you just won't wake up."

"*Stop*", Veirella hated voice, but getting it to go away and stay away was hard.

"How about this? I stop when your heart does."

"Good Morning" Veirella turned so fast her vision blurred it too a moment to adjust before she saw who was there. It was a girl and was green from top to bottom, she was similar to that of a leaf, her hair was thick with dark green curls touching her shoulders, her eyes were different in color the left was as dark as the hair and the other was a light brown.

Her dress matched her skin perfectly, her arms and both sides of her face were covered in vines detailed into her skin.

"I did not mean to scare you, but I arrived three hours ago and you were still sleeping. I got your things unpacked while I waited for you to a wake."

The girl told her. She walked over to the bed and pulled the sheets off Veirella. "Come, it is time for you to get up. You have two hours before you need to get going." Veirella stood from the bed. It was an automatic reaction for her.

The girl started making her bed the second Veirella was out of it, but she did it with a turn of her hand. "I set a bath for you, go wash up while I get your things ready."

Veirella went into her bathing chambers, undressed and stepped into the bath. The heat was perfect to the touch. There was already soap in the bath. It took little time to wash herself considering she did the before bed. Veirella go out dried herself and returned to the room. A uniform similar to the one Gemma wore was laid out on her bed.

Veirella guessing wear her undergarments were but most kept them in the same place, so she looked in the armoire she got a black set, she went back to the bed and get the uniform, there were three pieces a shirt, a vest, and a skirt. The only it she remembered bring in something that was not a dress was during training, the skirt was shorter than she was used to. A Ladies legs were always covered. Veirella held up each piece, there was an order to things but she did not know what order she was to dress.

"Shirt first, then vest, and skirt last so the shirt can be tucked without wrinkling." The unnaturally colored girl told her emerging from the closet. When she was finished getting dressed, the skirt went above her knees, which was not common for women's clothing or any clothing for that matter.

"Here." Veirella looked at the girl, she was holding a pair of long socks that matched the uniform. Mostly solid black with two teal bands at the top, in her other hand she held black shoes with a short heel, nothing too noticeable.

Veirella took both from her and put them on, then went to the vanity to fix her har. She removed the covering, and the girl came over and put half of it up and left the other down with two pieces felt out in the front.

Veirella looked at herself in the mirror, it would take some time for her to get used to what she looked like, so many things about her were different. Veirella turned to the girl who's name she still did not know, hoping for an introduction. "Who are you?" her words were low and slow, so she did not struggle getting them out.

"I am Willow, your Nyx it my pleaser to survive you. We do not have time for a better introduction than that but I will tell you more later, it is time for you to go." Willow walked her door and led her over to the hall Gemma showed her the night before. Veirella took a few steps forward then stopped and turned to ask her something but Willow was gone.

There was voice's coming from down the hall, when she got closer, Veirella the other's seated at a circular table covered in food. There were four seats, three of which were occupied by Gemma, Pax, and Luka. Gemma was in the same uniform as Veirella but both boys were dressed in black leather's.

"Hey, come sit" Gemma called to her, Veirella took the last empty seat between Gemma and Pax.

"How did you see? I know being in a new play can be hard, it was for me but it will get easier after a few weeks. I still can't believe you are here. When we finish here, I need to take you to the headmistress's offices. And after class—" Luka raised a hand her shoulder.

"Breathe, your are going to overwhelm her if you do not calm down." Gemma took a deep breath then laughed.

"Sorry, I am just really happy that you are here. I have not seen you in so long." Gemma told her; her face fell a little, Veirella could understand why she felt that way. Unfortunately she did not share that feeling more much of any feeling.

"Okay." Gemma looked up at her when she heard her speak, Veirella smiled at her and her smile brightened again.

Veirella wanted to now, why Luka and Pax were in different clothes. She touched Gemma's arm, pointed from herself to Gemma's uniform them at the boys.

"What is?" Pax asked, looking from her to Veirella. "Different?" Veirella asked her. She down herself then back at Veirella understanding what she meant. "She wants to know why you are dressed differently." Veirella nodded at Pax when he looked at her.

"We are second years, so we have more options, then first years like you. First years are not allowed to leave school grounds, second years like us get to chose if we what to say and study for what we will do when school ends or we can get in field assignments, supervised by an underclassman third or fourth year. So instead of a school uniform we wear keives, to protect us." Sebastian explained.

Veirella nodded in response, she knew enough about the fabric to know it was stronger than leather, harder to make and was more expensive. Most invested in it because it was harder to cut through it with a blade or strick with arrows.

Gemma started talking about how hard one of her classes was and Luka was giving her advice on things that could help her but she was just getting more frustrated because everything he told her, Gemma had already done. Veirella did not pay much attention to the conversation, she was trying to decide what to eat considering she did not recognize most of it.

There were a few types of bread, but all bread did not taste the same, some were bitter, and she hated that. So Veirella did not touch any of it. She looked at Gemma's plate, she was almost finished and she did not want to have her wait, so Veirella settled on fruit, that was good no matter where you were in the world. Then she poured herself some tea, the taste was similar to the one she drank at home, and she still did not know the name.

"Ready?" Gemma asked, Veirella nodded then they stood together. "See you guys when you get back, please don't die." Gemma told them, Luka looked up at her "You say that every time we leave, feels like you are hoping for it to happen." He answered, Gemma rolled her eyes at him.

"Well I say it every time, and you come back every time so lets not start breaking tradition." she responded then walked away, Veirella following behind. "Do you need to get anything before we go?" Veirella shook her head no. "Okay" Veirella followed her out of the court.

Gemma went down the hall and opened the port key they went through the night before. This one was a painting of waves hitting rocks. They went though and walked to the end of the hall before Gemma could knock the door opened.

"Come in, Anastasia you many go." Genevieve told her, Gemma turned to Veirella smiled then left closing the door behind her. Veirella stood there looking at the door for a moment, she did not understand why she sent her away, Veirella did not know where she needed to go for her classes.

As mush as she did not want to be around others, she was there to learn control, it was going to inevitable.

"I will be, heading your studies from what your brother has told me that is for the best." Genevieve walked around her desk so she could get closer to Veirella. "But if you do well with me and living with the others, if you decide you would like to be with the other students, then that can be arranged."

Genevieve informed her Veirella was not expecting special accommodations for her. She knew something was wrong with her, but having it so open and out there was not what she wanted.

Veirella hated it but it was the logical thing to do considering, she could hurt someone with how uncontrolled her magic was she and it had more to do with her mind than anything else, it was better to be safe.

"Speaking is hard for you but your vocal limitations will not be a problem. If there is something you need to say, write it down."

"I can speak, just not much" her voice was low, Veirella did not think Genevieve heard her. Veirella closed her eyes and sighed.

She did not what to waste what little she could say on repeating herself.

Veirella opened her mouth to say it again, but Genevieve raised a hand stopping her. "I heard you, Air wielders have better hearing than most. If that is as high as you can speak, we can work with that, or like I said, you can write." Veirella nodded.

"Come sit." Genevieve led her to the sofa's, on the table between them was a book 'History and Knowledge of the Centinal's'. "before we start on accrual wielding you should know what you are first, and how it all works this book contains basic things all Centinal's learn the moment they learn what they are."

Everyone but me apparently Veirella thought.

Her parents felt no need to tell her anything. "First thing to know you fall into the first Asphies, which is Celerian, meaning you have a Celestial parent and a mortal parent, your blood mother is the Celestial in your case. Now get reading, the faster you finish, the sooner we can start on the fun stuff," Genevieve smiled at her, then returned to her desk to read through files

.

Veirella did not think anything about this would be fun. That was also the first time someone had referred to her mother and was not speaking of the woman that raised her. It was strange, and it made her chest tight, thinking about it. She tried pushing it away to somewhere in her mind she did not want to go, the dark side where she pushed the bad voices.

Giving me some company, tell me what does it feel like to be a kings bastard? Do you think the people would have you killed if they learned the truth of your birth? We should tell them and see what happens.

Veirella did not want to listen to it. They were right, they always were. No matter what, the moment something bad happened, they were always there to make it worse. Her reaction to the voices must have shown on her face because Genevieve was looking at her, concern written all over her face.

Veirella closed her eyes, took a deep breath trying to calm herself, *in and out* she repeated that to herself three times, until she could no longer heard them, she wished they would go away for good.

Instead of dwelling on something she could not control, she would focus on something she could, knowledge learning what she was and the things she could do were things she could control no matter how terrifying it was she needed to do it.

Veirella tried picking up the book off the table, but it was so heavy it did not move. She tried again but still nothing, so she took a pillow off the sofa, laid it on the floor and sat down. The table was not that high, so she still had enough space where she could open the book and read it comfortably.

On the first page was a chart, 'Asphies Classifications.' At the top was Celerian (Children of Stars), then Xiakary (Children of Blood), and last Nievar or Nievarian (Blessed by Stars). On the next page, there was another chart: Source and Wielding Levels, Base Magic (Elemental), Specific Magic (Signent), and Incora (rarest and least known).

The Source for wielding was called Celicai. It is a gene, passed from the Celestial parent, another name for it was Cai. If one did not pose the gene, they cannot naturally wield. There are three ways to have the gene one from having a Celestial parent, two being a descendant of one a Celestial, and three being blessed by a Celestial. Those are the Nievarian they were given power in exchange for their loyalty to the Celestial houses they were born into.

A child born of a blessed bloodline could not wield naturally, but they could do so temporarily by taking stardust. It bonded with the Celicai in the blood and enhances wielding. For those who are born to a Celestial or are descendants of one, it enhanced whatever abilities they already posed, and it also works as an amplifier for them.

For those who are blessed Stardust is not recommended for long-term use or it can become addictive, and slowly kill them. For those who have the blood of a Celestial, there is no limitation with the substance.

With there being more than one type of wielder, they were split into different classifications. The first were the children of the Celestial's they were called Celerian's named after the first world before the break, second were the Xiakary, who were descendants of the Celestial's children and of their children, it was not uncommon for the gifts to skip some children but most had then, and last were the blessed they were known as the Nievar they were chosen by the Celestials to survive their houses; before the break they were protectors, advisors and the link between the children and their parents, but after they became teachers, guardians, and now held positions of the priestesses, mostly only women were ever put in these positions.

There were also male Nievars but their positions stayed the same, protectors, and advisors to the kings and lords of each house.

As for Cai, Wielding levels all had an elemental power based on one of the four elements: Earth, Fire, Water, and Air. There were three Celestials per element making up the twelve.

Then there were Signent's. They were unique for every Celerian that had then, mostly only Celerian's and Xiakaries rarely ever Neivarians. Their power was given and rarely every grew past what was given to them, but it was not impossible.

A few examples of Signent's are Fire wielders ability to bond with dragons, Earth wielders ability to weave plants and trees into fabric Water wielders ability to breathe underwater, and Air wielders enhanced senses.

Those are all common Signent's that most wielders have, and it allowed for then to possibly develop more, up to three. Most of these common Signent's are given to Nievar's by the Celestial's those gifts are common amount the three that share a domain.

And last, the rarest of the three Incora, not much is known of it, but there have only ever been three of them recorded in history and there has not been one since the Great War a thousand years ago that led to the first world breaking and becoming the four continents.

It took Veirella almost three weeks of reading to learn most of that, there were signs in the book she studied that were common for opening portals and getting things to move for her some of them did not apply to her because she could not control air, water, or fire. It may have been a waste of time, but she wanted to know everything and the moment she was finished the real work would begin, and she was not looking forward to it so stalling by consuming information was her way out.

In that time she had received a letter from her mother and one from Aspen, none of wish she could bring herself to open and read. A part of her wanted to know what they wanted to say, but another would not let her.

What scared your dear mother will tell you how much she hates you.

Veirella tried focusing on anything but the voice, it was hard but she was getting better at it.

Every day after Genevieve was finished with her, she opened a port key inside her office and send Veirella through, and in the morning, Gemma would open one for her. Veirella could tell something was off about her, as the days went by her smile looked at little more forced and little in her eyes a little darker, Veirella did not ask her about it she was sure if she wanted to talk she would say something.

Maybe not to her but she was sure she had other friends in the school she could talk to, and Veirella did not ask mostly because she was not ready to talk about the accident, it did not seem fair to push someone else to talk about their problems when she could not talk about her own.

A few days earlier, she returned from Genevieve's and heard noises coming from Gemma's room. She was crying, Veirella thought of knocking, but when she raised her hand to the door, she could not bring herself to do it. No matter how hard she tried, she could not lay her hand on the door.

"How are you going to comfort someone else when you cannot even do it for yourself? Leave the girl alone. I am sure the last thing she wants to see is your pathetic and miserable face."

Veirella tried making the voices go away but she could not. She went to her room; closed the door. She was moving slowly so not make a sound.

"If you really want to help, go to the window."

"Come on, I know you can do it."

"If you go out, you can help a whole lot a people."

"Do it. Do it. Do it."

They said over and over. Veirella laid on the other side of the room as far from the windows as possible, covered her ears and begged them to stop, but they did not. At some point, she cried herself to sleep on laying on the floor.

Power and Pain

Anastasia

The few weeks Anastasia spent at Astro had not been easy. Nothing was working the way it should.

Every skill she had mastered as a child slipped away from her. Nothing she was doing worked. Shielding, echo waves, Levitation; nothing worked considering how shit her luck was at the moment Anastasia opted not to try using the cut. She could kill someone if she lost control of that particular move.

Anastasia was in class watching everyone else get progressively better, but somehow she was managing to get worse.

Liam was doing the best out of all of them. A boy who she out performed most of her life was doing better than her. He never missed a chance to gloat about it to her face. It was infuriating, she never did that Anastasia's talent's spoke for themselves.

That was one of the only new things about him and his height and the muscles he grew over the break. His onyx black hair was the same cut, straight and swept back lower on the side, and his skin had more color.

They were working on Levitation while Anastasia struggled to keep the blue glass vase two inches from the table. He had it floating above him; it did not even look like he was trying. It was effortless for him. Anastasia was once able to do that, make everything look easy and effortless, even though it was not, wielding required focus something her mind did not seem to remember.

But that was the past. Something had gone wrong with her magic, and Anastasia needed to figure out what it was. At the moment, she was completely useless. Anastasia looked around at the others, they were all air wielders. It was an Elemental training course; they kept the Elements separated where wielding was concerned. For physical defence, and hand to hand, everyone trained together because of the lack of magic. And it began in two days.

Anastasia almost dropped the vase, she pushed all the energy she could find into it so it would stay up. She looked around at the others again most of them were getting better. Some were struggling at first when they started, so her struggles did not stick out as much, but now most of them got the basics down and knew what to do.

Anastasia knew they were talking behind her back, but that was not new she was the heir to Iriea. She was the first and only woman to ever be named heir and kept the title after a boy was born; she had two younger siblings, Andrew and Olivia. Andrew was three years younger and Olivia was five.

They only shared half their features, their father's. Unlike her brother and sister, she did not have any of her mother's.

Maybe the fact she looked nothing like her made her care about her less. Her mother told her she loved her but, those were just words she could say then but not mean. If she really loved her, why would not have said those things about her.

"Andrew should be first in line, he is your son, your only son Richard. Why pass him over for a girl?" Her mother asked her father. Her words angered him.

"That girl is our daughter, and she was born first. It is her birthright, and I will not take it from her because you are too stuck in the past to look at her as an option." Anastasia could hear the anger and frustration in his voice. "Well, she is more your daughter than mine."

Anastasia was pulled from the memory when she heard something hit the floor. She looked around to see where it came from, then realized the vase she was floating was gone, and everyone was looking at her.

"What the fuck, Anastasia." She looked over at Liam, and there was blood running down his neck.

"Oh god, I am so sorry. I did not mean for that to happen."

She apologized. Anastasia felt worse the further down the blood went.

"It's okay accidents happen. We just need to be more careful." Professor Zelma told her, she was a short woman whose eyes always made it seem like she wanted to sleep.

"Lola, do you mind helping Liam to the med center?" A girl sitting four rows down stood up and went to Liam he who was holding his head. The blood was still coming. Anastasia could not see it move, but she heard it.

"No problem, Professor" Lola answered in the sweets voice she liked to force, you would never know how much of a snake she was, but now was not the time to think about the she devil who liked pretending to be an angel. Anastasia seriously hurt someone. It was someone she despised, but he still counted as a person.

Lola led him down the levels, passing the rows of desks filled with student's then out the double doors at the front of the room. Anastasia could hear them talking.

"If little miss unstable over there is going to be our queen, we are some done for."

"I hope they change the law back and make her brother King, when the time comes."

"She may be one of us, but she's more likely to get us killed than anything else."

Anastasia wanted to do nothing more than run out, but all that would do was give them or to talk about and she would be proving them right.

So she sat there in silence for two hours listening to them bad mouth her.

The second the bell came, Anastasia was the first out the door. The class had two exists, one at the top and the down at the bottom, that Liam and Lola went through.

She choose to use the one at the top; the room was between two levels, and she had no interest in sitting at lunch and listening to them talk about her more, so she made her way to the court.

Death Or Glory

Lorenzo

There was nothing better than killing someone first thing in the morning. Breakfast was a close second. The first thing you ate could make or break your own day.

Lorenzo, for having someone bleed out on his blade screaming in agony as he ran them through, was more adrenaline inducing than anything else.

Weeks away from the Academy and three demon dens and he was yearning for another kill. More demons were appearing on the Astro plane recently, and no one could figure out why where the coming for something or running from something.

They were not new to the demons. Incubus and succubus have always preferred the mortal lands to their own mortal's were easy prey for them.

There were laws they had to follow. Some followed them, others strayed and were killed for it. Lorenzo had the pleaser of handing out some of the punishment. Sometimes an Alp would appear, every few years are so.

They were sealed in their dimensional plane after the damage they caused during the war, familiars were the most common and least harmful to mortals, well mortals without small children. Because of how normal it was not to find one, people painted sheep's blood over their doors to keep them out and made jewels filled with the mother's hair to hide their smell. As long as they stayed away from babies, they were left alone.

Those were not the demons they were sent to kill. Those were mid-level demons, they could understood what they were doing. Lower-level demons known as abominations could not even speak. All they knew was killing. Over the past three-four years, more and more have been appearing all over the continents.

They did not like the daylight, so they did not go far from their den or underground caves in the mountains. They found places with heat to hide that had people around them; they were not the smartest creatures, but they did know how to hunt. Small villages were wiped out overnight. They stayed for a few weeks until they got hungry again, then found somewhere else.

Abominations were dangerous to the average person, but someone with basic training could kill them. So instead of calling in the guard to deal with them, the student of Astro Academy were given assignments to track and kill them.

They tracked another den to a small village called Usnor. A boy said he saw a monster with bright green eyes and dark gray skin the night before. There was a chance it was not true, but Cyrus thought they needed to check it out just to be sure. The last town they were in was now a ghost time.

They stayed the night, then left before the sun began rising. They climbed up the side of the mountain outside the village, which was the only place they could be hiding there was nothing for miles around Usnor and abominations did not stay too far way from their prey.

With little to no visibility, the sun would rise above them, making it hard to look up Lorenzo hoped there was something at the top that made it worth all the work. "Tell me again why we are doing this instead of waiting for it to get dark?" Pax asked.

Cyrus and Griffin were a little far a head of them so he was asking Lorenzo that question "Because this is unauthorized, and we need to be back to school, in a few hours." He answered.

"Right, because asking permission to help people was so hard." He grunted out. Asking permission was a little hard in this case. Nothing had happened yet, and rulers were a pain to deal with when things did not affect them. The last attack was in Ataria, and it was unlikely King Richard would have given them permission to enter his lands on the word of a small child.

So they used Owhana Island to get to Usnor. The island was close to Iriea, but they did not have control of it. No one did, so that made it open territory, and wielders of any element could portal in and out without restriction or permission.

When they finally made it to the top, Griffin went in to check if the demons were inside. The cave was deep. It would take him some time to get in and back. Cyrus went to the left side of the opening and sat down on one of the massive rocks formed there. Pax and Lorenzo did the same on the right.

Lorenzo could tell something was off with Pax. They had been friends for half their lives; they knew each other better than anyone else. "You have been quieter than usual. Are you okay?" The anniversary of his sister's death was approaching, and that was always a hard time for him, Pax did not take about her much or every Lorenzo never met her or even knew her name it was the one thing about his friend he had no knowledge of and Lorenzo never pushed for him to tell.

If he ever wanted to take about it Lorenzo would be there to listen, there were thing about his own life he did not like talking about with anyone, including Pax.

"Just thinking about all the people that have died in the past few months, I know everyone is saying they pushed themselves too far with Cai, but something just feels off about it." Pax answered.

Lorenzo did not think about it much, he was not close with any of them, so he never concerned himself with it. Outside of Pax and Anastasia, and maybe Veirella she was close with Ana so he might grow to care for her. He did not care what happened to anyone else.

"That happens every year. Kids get cocky with their powers and do something study that gets them killed." Lorenzo told him. Pax sighed and dropped his head. "Yeah, I know that but that, usually on a few nine or ten, maybe not thirty."

Lorenzo shrugged, he did really care. The number did not change that. Knowing Pax, he went out of his way to find out. He would just about do anything to try and help anyone he could. Lorenzo thought he was projecting the fact he could not save his sister on anyone and everyone he could.

He could not save her, so he wants to and save everyone else. Pax told him about her two years ago. It was the only time they talked about her, it was also when Lorenzo found out he even had a sister.

"So I guess we have more idiots than average this year, I am sure everything will be fine."

Lorenzo told him. He reached over and squeezed his shoulder, then stood and went to look inside the cave. There was nothing there to see, but he needed something to do and Griffin was taking too long.

The sky got brighter by the time it took Griffin to reemerge from the cave. They all went to him the moment they saw him coming out. "So, what are we dealing with?" Cyrus asked. The air was getting hot, his dark curls were sticking to the sweat on his forehead.

"There are a few in there, but from what I saw, it was not a whole nest. Half a dozen the most," he answered. Lorenzo was disappointed, but it was something.

Anything less than a full nest did not require all of them, when less than twelve were together, they were always weak, even if they were only off by one. The same amount of strength was not present.

"So, how are we doing this?" Pax asked. Lorenzo was placed with Cyrus and Pax Griffin when it came to picking who would supervise their in-field training and, luckily for them, they got to stick together because Cyrus and Griffin were also a team of their own.

But they never worked together. One reason Lorenzo was happy they got to stay together was that they could work together. It was one thing to train together, understanding each other's every move in training but entirely different in a real-life situation.

This seemed like the perfect opportunity for them to test their ability to work together. "How about Pax and I take them out?" Lorenzo asked. Cyrus and Griffin looked at each other, then at them.

"This is our what fourth time in field, and or eight mission. Do you not think it is time to see if we sink or swim when there is no one to save our asses but us?" Lorenzo asked, it was trying to convince Cyrus more that Griffin, he was the more responsible of the time, and they were already breaking one rule why not break another.

It would happen at some point, they would be tested to see how well they did on their own, but Lorenzo had no interest in waiting months, to show everyone exactly what he could do. "Well, considering neither of you have done anything stupid or reckless on our last few assignments, why not?" Griffin answered.

Pax glanced in Lorenzo's direction for a moment before turning and retrieving his bow. It was a regular school issued; it was made of oak wood harder to break, and easier to learn, his arrows were the same. The only differences with them were the metal melted onto the on the heads, a gift from Lorenzo.

"Okay, you know the drill by now. Make as little noise as possible if you can take them out without waking up great, but remember to expect it if they do. They may not be as strong, but they are still twice your size, so be careful." Cyrus told them.

He was the one always reminding them of what to do and do not before every mission, Griffin on the other hand. Just did it and expected them to get it by watching him.

Because according to him "they were not babies and this was the real world not everything will be explained to them before going in." He was right they could assess the threat and do as much reconnaissance as they wanted but that would not change the fact that there were still unknowns they could not prepare for.

"You have half and hour, if you are not back by then, we come in to make sure your not died." Cyrus told them, "so little faith, I am a little hurt actually" Lorenzo told to him, he raised his hand over his heart faking pain. Cyrus rolled his eyes.

Lorenzo laughed, then followed Pax to the opening, that was nothing but darkness. "Ready to do this?" Pax asked, "as long as you are." They looked at each other, nodded at went in.

Griffin did not say how far in they were, which was intentional. He wanted them to find it, just as he had. Lorenzo formed a ball of fire in his hand, so they could see where they were going. There were rocks everywhere, which made more sense why Griffin took so long.

And Lorenzo did not sense and magic in the air, so he did not use his powers to get around. That was probably his Signent, Lorenzo did not know much about him, other than them having the same element. Maybe he could see in the dark. It would explain why he rarely ever used his abilities like Lorenzo needed to.

"We should move a little faster, considering the time we have." Pax told him. They upped their pace. They were not as quiet, but they needed to compromise on something. If they wanted to going fast, they would be louder, if they wanted to be quiet they would need to move slower, and with a time restraint the former it would be.

The further they went, the wider the cave got, the rocks also got bigger, and the stalactites were getting longer. Lorenzo pulled on pax's arm to stop him from taking another step, he almost stepped on the tail of of an abomination. It was so similar in color to the rocks around them.

"What?"

Pax asked. Lorenzo pushed the flames towards the sleeping body on the ground for Pax to see.

If this one is here, then the other's most be close by

He thought. He was eager to get his blade wet. Pax pulled his dagger from its holster at his side, bent and stabbed it through the heart. The beast grunted that was all the sound it made before turning to ash.

Pax wiped it black blood from his dagger on his pants, then returned it to its holster. "If they are all spread out like that, it will be good for us less chance of them waking up." Pax stated, keeping his voice low.

That was something they could do, but there was not fun it that. "I have a better idea." Lorenzo pulled his sword from its sheath. Pax dropped his head and sighed. Lorenzo hit his sword against the stalactites above them until a few broke, hitting the ground with a loud thud that echoed into the cave. Once the sound faded, he hurt the growls come one after the other.

"Perfect."

Guardian

Sebastian

His best friend was an idiot. Not only that, he had a death wish. Sebastian readied his bow as Luka, pushed flames to four corners of the cave. He saw their dark green eyes before their bodies.

They both moved back, giving themselves enough room if they started running at them.

Sebastian placed a silver coated arrow in the nocking, ready to shoot the second he got a clear view of the creature. He moved left, and Luka right. Sebastian did not know why they were waiting to attack. Then he heard something behind him, Sebastian looked over his shoulder.

There was another abomination a few feet away from him. It swiped at him. Sebastian divide towards Luka out of its reach and released the arrow, hitting one of them in the head.

Then all six came at them at once. Sebastian quickly fixed the bow over his head and grabbed his daggers. Times like this made him wish he carried a blade instead of a bow, a dark cave, where he could hardly see with something twice his size coming towards him was not the time to test how fast he could nock arrows.

He was good, great even, but that was when he had proper visuals. Sebastian trained for years to be one of the best. But the predicament he was in currently in proved he still needed work. The creature scratch at him with its long, dark inky claws. It was bigger than the others. He ducked before it could grab his neck.

He needed to be careful if it caught him. He would die. Once they had you, they never let go, and they had poison in their claws, so even if he managed to get away, one scratch would kill him and there was no cure for i t.

Just like him, it having trouble seeing in the dark, for a species that was nocturnal. It was surprising that they had such poor sight when they had no light to see, but that gave Sebastian an advantage or left them both a disadvantage. At the moment, either way, it made it harder likely for it to get him.

It swiped at him again, but this time Sebastian swung the daggers cutting its hand off. It stream in pain, shaking the cave around them, while it was distracted Sebastian ducked under its arm and stuck a dagger into his heart.

It vanished before it realized what happened, Sebastian out of breath turn to see Luka had taken do four out of the five, while he was busy pushing his sword into the last one's chest, another one ran for him. Sebastian grabbed his bow, and an arrow placed it.

With the why it was turned even if he shot it, he would not get to its heart. It would get to Luka before Pax could shoot.

"Hey!" Sebastian yelled. The massive creature turned its attention away from Luka and placed it on him. He waited until it turned its body enough getting ready to run at him, then he fired.

Abominations moved fast, so it met the arrow halfway. Seconds passed then it turned to ash.

"I think Griffin needed to relearn how to count," Luka stated.

Sebastian looked at him. He was annoyed he should have expected Luka to do something like that he would not be him if he did not do something reckless and stupid that could get them killed.

A pattern he followed consistently since they were children. Luka walked over to him and Sebastian pushed him back against the wall.

"What the hell?" He asked, a look of confusion crossed his face.

"I should be the one asking you that. You could not do things the easy way for once. Everything just needs to be hard and complicated, doesn't?" Luka said nothing.

"It was an easy job. I know you have issues with that thing growing up your arm." They both looked to the spot Pax was refusing to. "But that does not mean you need to cut your life any shorter than it already is."

Sebastian signed. He wanted to be mad; he wished he could stay angry with him, but he understood why Luka did the things when he did. He waited for Luka to say something, but all he did was push past him.

"No point in protecting something that will end soon enough."

Nine Years Before

Like every night before, Maria got Veirella ready for bed, and as always she took down her hair and left it undone, then left her waiting for her mother. It was the routine Veirella followed since she could remember.

Maria could take done her hair, wash, and oil it but she was not allowed to do it. That task was reserved for her mother only.

Veirella did not understand why her mother did it. She did not have the time to come and do her hair every day, but yet she did. Some days she would come earlier than others depending on what she intended to do to it, but she was never late; Veirella had a lot of hair, so it always took a lot more time to do some styles, took hours and required her to sit for a long time.

She hated having to sit for long, so some styles were reserved for traveling and important celebrations, like balls, dinners, and reights. That was the compromise Veirella made with her.

She sat at her vanity waiting for her mother to come and prep her hair from bed, which anyone could have done. Veirella read the latest letter she received from Anastasia, they did not spend much time together, they only met in person a few times but their friendship made it seem much different.

A week after their first meeting in the garden, Veirella received the first letter where she told Veirella she would be her best friend. Veirella did not seem to have a choice in the decision, but she did not mind. Veirella did not know any children her own age, so she did not know if that was normal.

The only other children Veirella knew were her brother and sister and they were a little older and had less time to play with her, plus they were gone and Veirella had no idea when they were coming back. Aspen told her they were going to a special place to get stronger, Veirella did not want him to leave her behind she asked if she could go with them, but he told her she was too young, but she would get to go when she was their age.

Since she had no one to play with, Veirella spent most of her non-study time, which is what her mother called it, because princesses did not have such a thing as free time. When she was not with her, Veirella was in the lab her father built for her.

So Anastaisa was her only friend. They wrote just about anything in their letters, Anastasia told Veirella about all the boring things she had to do with her father because she would rule their kingdom someday. Veirella did not think it should still be a kingdom if it did not have a king. Veirella told Ana she should change it and call it a queendom instead. Anastasia thought it was funny and considered the possibility of a name change.

The things Anastasia found boring, such as council meetings, law studies, and mapping. They were problems Veirella wished she had, it would mean spending more time with her father and siblings.

"Ready for me as always," her mother's voice pulled Veirella from her thoughts. She had on a light blue silk robe with her night dress beneath it.

Veirella looked up at her through the mirror. Her mother smiled at her, then reached down and kiss her on the side of her face. Then took the comb and fixed Veirella's hair into four sections.

"Mama?"

"Mm"

"Do you think father, love me the same as he does Aspen and Iris?"

Veirella asked. Her mother stopped and looked at her through the mirror, Veirella did not see her. She was too busy drawing flowers in her letter to Anastasia to notice.

"What type of question is that? Of course he does, he loves you all the same." She told her.

"Are you sure? Because he is with them right now, and he is always with Aspen, and he does not see me as much." Veirella responded. It made her sad sometimes he was rarely ever home and when he was, he was always working.

Her mother got down next to her, so she could look her in the eyes. Veirella did not turn her to look at her so she place her hand on the side of her face and turned Veirella's head.

"Aspen and Iris are much older than you are darling, so things for them are different than, they are for you. And they have responsibilities that you are way too young to understand." She explained.

"I understand plenty, and if I do not, I can always read about it." her mother laughed. It was low and light, something that barely existed. It made her feel warm inside. "Wrong chose of words, but what I am saying is your father loves you just the same as he does them, and when he comes home, I will ensure he spend all his time with you, that sound good?" Veirella nodded it response.

She touched her nose, then stood. Veirella scrunched her face and pulled away, her mother laughed then returned to her hair. "The birds tell me the same thing, so maybe it is true." Her mother stopped again. "The birds? That do you mean?" she asked, confused and concerned evident in her voice.

"The one's in the sky, Mama. what other birds are there for me to talk to?" Veirella laugh looked up at her mother, whose eyes were open wider than was natural.

"Are you okay? Your eyes look weird," she asked.

"I am fine darling, d-do these birds in the sky speak to you often?"

"Yes, almost every day. They wake me up sometimes."

"And how long has this been happening?" the tone in her voice changing.

Veirella shrugged at her question. "A while." Veirella yawned, she was tired, for most others the night was still young but Veirella needed the sleep. Less than twelve hours and she would be horrible to deal with.

"Are you almost done? I want to go to bed." The mother looked away from her and shook her head.

"Yes, we are almost finished" her mother quickly finished the last two braids and helped her into bed. Once she was comfortably under the covers, she sat next to her.

"Darling, do you mind telling me when the birds talk to you again?" Veirella was already half asleep but nodded.

"Okay, I love you" she bent and kissed her on the head.

"Goodnight." That was the last thing Veirella heard her say before she fell asleep.

World A New

Veirella

It was dark out when Veirella woke. She was still on the floor; in the corner she passed out in. She heard the main door open, then close, it was followed by two male voices. The boys were back from their assignment. She originally thought they would only be gone for a few days. But it had been weeks since they left. Veirella only knew that because of all the times she went to Genevieve's office, time did not much register for her, so she understood what day it was based on when she had to go and see her. Classes were four days out of the week. Veirella knew day and night and she went to Genevieve four days in a row, then nothing for three, then repeat.

Veirella did not understand why time was so hard for her to understand. There are things she remembered happening but could not recall when. If it was not for Willow coming to see her every morning, it was unlikely she would get up in time.

Veirella could hear some of what they were saying, something about being reckless, but she did not pay any attention to them. Whatever they were talking about was not her concern, and she would not make it so. Veirella went to her closet, changes covered her hair, got into bed.

Veirella woke up wet and cold as she did most days. There was one new addition, Willow the green girl was standing at the foot of her bed every morning Veirella woke. Well, not everyday just the ones she needed to see Genevieve.

"Good Morning, your bath is set. By now we should have a routine down come." Willow pulled the covers away and Veirella got up, and went to her bathing chamber, stripped and got in the bath set exactly how she liked it.

Veirella did not stay in for long, she never did. When she got back in her room, her uniform was laid out for her like it was every morning. She got dressed. Fixed her hair, just as she was about to leave her room, she stopped and turned to look at Willow. Something Veirella had not noticed before was her color. Willow saw her looking at her and raised her brow, waiting.

"What is it?"

Veirella was in surprised. She did not know what to say. She watched the girl move around her room, tiding it and her eyes followed her. It took her a moment, but she found her words.

"You are green?"

Willow stopped, and turned to Veirella her brows creased, then she tilted her head. "I was also green, yesterday, and the day before that, and well every day since birth I think" her sarcasm was well deserved. It was not something Veirella had noticed before that should have worried her, but she did not have the time to think about it.

"What are you?"

Veirella asked. She read about many creatures in her studies, but she did not recall anything about green people.

"I am a Nyx, a guardian for magical beings like yourself," Willow answered.

"Guard for what?" was someone else coming after her that Veirella needed to know about, she did not want to speculate, if she did that, Veirella would send herself into a panic, so she waited for Willow to answer her.

"I am a protector and a guide to help you with anything you need from learning about your magic to help you in any way I can. It is whatever you need," Willow explained.

That was interest an all, but who sent her here? Veirella thought.

"Your mother." Willow answered. A question Veirella knew she did not speak. "If you think about me while say something to yourself, I can hear it." She explained.

"*How is that possible?*" Veirella thought, hoping she heard what she was thinking.

"I was made with your blood. I am bonded to you. Nyx's are Celestial creatures. We were created by the Celestial's to guide and protect their children." She explained.

In that moment Veirella realized she was not talking about her mother, the one that raised her but the one whose blood ran within her veins. Veirella did not want to talk about her. She would need to do it some day but that day would not be this one.

"*I need to go. I do not want to be late.*" She projected to Willow. "Okay, we can continue this conversation at another time." Veirella nodded at her, then left the room and went to the kitchenet to have breakfast. Everyone was there Gemma, Luka, and Pax. Gemma was dressed in her uniform, the same as Veirella but the boys were where in regular clothes or tunics were a part of their uniform, Veirella had yet to meet another person let alone another boy to know if their uniforms were different, but they did not match like she did with Gemma.

They just got back, and they were a year above them. Maybe their classes were different, or they did not have any. Veirella could ask, but that required caring.

"Good Morning" all three said to her. Veirella nodded in response and sat at the table. They went back to their conversation she blocked them out Veirella took more interest in what was in the table than what they were talking about. And considering she lacked an appetite, nothing looking appealing.

She took a slice of bread with cheese and some eggs, some grapes, and a cup, which she still did not know the name of. Once she was finished, she waited for Gemma to be done so she could open the port key for her. Veirella hoped it would be the first thing Genevieve would show her how to do. She felt like she rushed Gemma in the morning to do it for her and wanted to stop.

When Gemma finished, they when into the hall. Gemma waved her hand over the same painting she did every morning, then she turned concern or worry etched into her features. "Was everything okay with you last night you didn't come to dinner?" She asked. Veirella nodded "fell asleep." She answered. Her voice was too low many would never hear her, but with Gemma being an air wielder, she could.

Gemma nodded, moved so Veirella could go through. Veirella looked down at Gemma's hands they were shaking.

"You okay?" Veirella asked, looking up at her. "Yes, I am fine. You should go the headmistress is not big on tardiness." Gemma hid her hand being her and smiled at her. Veirella waited for a moment, then stepped through.

Veirella raised her hand to knock at the door but dropped it when it opened and two boys came out. One with dark curls, dark brown eyes and warm brown skin, the other had little hair, similar colored skin and little hazel eyes. She moved to the side, allowing them to pass, as they did the one with little eyes looked her over. He went to say something to her, but the other boy hit him on the back of his head.

He winced in pain, then looked over at him. The curly-haired one gave him a hand signal, telling him they were leaving. Before the boy could turn his attention back to her, Veirella went into Genevieve's office and closed the door behind her.

"You are a little earlier than expected." Genevieve told her she was looking down at something on her desk. She was busy with something, but Veirella did not know what time she should be there. She hated her magic, but she hated being late more.

Veirella moved to the sofa and waited for Genevieve to final reading her file. Once she was done she closed to added it to the massive stack forming on her desk then joined Veirella.

"Now that we are finally finished with the basic's, we can get started on your wielding. Have you done it before?" Veirella shook her head. It was not something she had ever tried or intended to do. She was too scared of what would happen if she did.

"Okay, come with me" Veirella stood and followed her behind her desk, where she had a table with two green pots filed with soil a top it.

"Earth is a complex element, it as may variations, but something that is consistent is growth. It is the trigger for almost all earth wielders because it requires a connection to nature, but with oneself. Close your eyes," Veirella did as she asked.

"Now, count your breaths, level it out." Veirella counted every time she breathed in and out until it was even. "Then your heartbeat. Feel every pulse moving through your body, in your head, hand, chest, and feet." Veirella felt something pull her, and she pulled back without meaning to, "Do you feel it?" she nodded. "Now pull them together, make them go where you want them to." Veirella did as Genevieve told her. She could feel every beat of her heart not only in her chest but all over and how it all s ynced.

Then she pushed it all into one. Veirella could only feel and hear one beat, then the pulse when towards her hands. There, she felt something electric moving over them. It was intense and hungry, Veirella opened her eyes and looked down at her hands. There were green sparks with spots of blue going up her arms and around her fingers. They had no end or beginning, they just were. She woke something inside herself, and it was happy with her. It called for her, wanted her to take more.

Veirella felt the pull get stronger and more intense. It became too much, everything was happening too fast. Veirella wanted to let go, but it would not let her. She tried to let go, but it pulled her back in, it wanted her to keep going. *No.*

"What happened? You were doing so well?" Genevieve asked. Veirella could hear the disappointment in her voice. "Too much," she answered. It was terrifying that she had so little control, but so much power.

Trials

Veirella

Over the next few days, that was all she did, worked on pulling on her magic and controlling the energy. It was tiring and most of her sessions with Genevieve ended with Veirella laying on the sofa drinking tea, while she worked on other things.

"Do you think you're ready to try growing something?"

Veirella looked up from where she was seated with a steaming cup of tea in her hand. She did not look at Genevieve but at the table behind her desk.

"If you need some more time to get comfortable with your abilities, we can work on your summoning a little more." Genevieve assured her, the tone and voice she used when speaking to Veirella was always light and sweet, one a mother would use, not your teacher.

Veirella knew it was something she did specifically with her. A few times she came to her office for her lessons when Genevieve was with someone and she spoke with more authority.

Veirella wished she did not do it but, what could she do about. People tended to act differently around her and treat her a certain way, after the learned what happened to her, pity was a common reaction, so was the change in how they spoke to her, Veirella was used to people being different around her because of her status, but this was something different.

It was a feeling she would need to get used to, because the world would never look at her as anything but broken, and as for getting more comfortable with her magic, that was unlikely to happen.

Her powers were the reason she was in that cocoon for so long. No matter how hard she tried, there was no part of her that would never not hate them.

I may never find comfort in what I can do or what I am, but I need to learn how to control it. If not for myself, then for everyone else.

Veirella told herself. She was still looking at the pots when she nodded at Genevieve's question.

"Ready."

Something had changed in her voice. It was slight, but her words came out with more clarity that they had before did before and she could speak a little louder. Genevieve stood from her desk and moved to the table and Veirella did the same.

"Nothing will happen."

"You are weak, pathetic to make it grow."

"And *you are wrong." She pushed back.*

"Really? You think so?"

"Then prove IT!"

The voices got so loud Veirella did not hear what Genevieve said to her. She touched her arm, pulling Veirella bad to reality. "You do not need to do this if you are not ready, no pressure. This will take as much time as you need," Genevieve assured her.

"I can do it," Veirella answered, not only to the woman standing next to her, but to the voices in her head that wanted to see her fail. So they could make her feel worse that she already did. They duplicated, she did not know how but they did. And they were more present now than when there was only one.

Veirella moved to stand before the pot closest to her. Then raised her hands over the soil and closed her eyes, remembering what Genevieve told her to do, she ran through the steps in her head.

First closed eyes. Done

Second, count my breathing until it evens out.

She slowed her breathing until she inhaled and exhaled at the same count and speed.

Done.

Three, feel my heart heartbeat and all the pulses all over my body.

Veirella counted them off in her head.

Heart.

Head.

Neck.

Hands.

Feet.

Done.

And Last pull them together until they became one.

She felt every part of her body coming together, the invisible connection that they shared, she could feel it all. When they no long felt individual but as one single part, Veirella pulled on it until she until she felt the electric pulse moving through her.

Done.

Once she finished checking all the boxes in her head, Veirella opened her eyes and pulled the energy towards her hands. It was her first time doing with her eyes open, she was always too scared she would fail, so she kept them closed. But she had something to prove, not only to herself but to the voice and Genevieve. She was not weak.

Veirella saw as the green sparks mixed with a hit of blue it was so faint someone would need to know it was there to find it. The sparks move from halfway up her arms, moving around them and down to her wrists, then over her fingers.

She turned her hands back to the pot and pulled. Veirella did not how if she was doing the right thing but based on the fact that Genevieve was not staying anything just watching it was something she had to figure out on her own.

Flowers grow towards the sun, so pull should get it to grow.

Veirella knew she was correct when she felt something moving, how she felt that was strange. Her hand were not even touching the soil or the pot. It was moving down digging; the roots were growing out. They hit the bottom of the pot, then another part of the seed split open and moved up towards her hands. Veirella moved them when she felt something touch her, it was the stem.

I did it. It's working, she thought to herself. Her eyes began glowing, and the sparks from her hands faded.

Genevieve did not say anything because the flower did not stop. Bud formed, then cracked open, the white petals coming out, then the yellow center. Once it was finished growing, the gold in Veirella's eyes faded. She smiled at what she did.

"A sunflower."

It was the last thing she said, then she fell to the ground, unconscious.

When Veirella woke up, her head was pounding. She winced when she went to sit up.

"I think you should stay laying down."

She did not recognize the voice. It belonged to a woman; it did not sound much older than Gemma's. Her eyes were still adjusting, so it took her a moment to see the face. When her vision cleared, the first thing Veirella saw was red, red hair to be exact. It was dark, not close to black, but not too far from it either. Her eyes were a light green, and she had pale skin.

"I'm Scarlet."

She introduced, scarlet was sitting on the sofa opposite her. Veirella looked done confused as to the why she was laying down, and where this girl had come from and where Genevieve had gone.

Then it all came back to her. She was growing the flower, which turned out to be her third favorite the sunflower, then everything after that was blank. She looked over at the table behind Genevieve's desk to make sure she was remembering correctly, and there it was. The white plant was exactly where it should be.

"If you are wondering where the Headmistress is she, had to step out for a moment, she will be back in a moment" Scarlet informed her. Veirella did not attempt to say anything to her. She was not one to be rude, but it was better to not say anything than embarrass herself by saying something and it barely coming out.

They sat there together in silence, looking at anything but each other. Then the door opened and in came Genevieve entered. She was holding a tray with two cups and a pot of what Veirella assumed was tea.

Scarlet stood and went to greet her. When she reached to take the tray, Genevieve pulled it back and stepped around her, setting it down on the table.

"How is she?"

Genevieve asked, not looking at the girl. As she waited for her to answer Genevieve turned one of the cups over and ported the hot dark liquid into it. Then pulled a veil of white sparkly power from her pocket and poured it. It dissolved the moment it came into contact with the liquid, like nothing.

Scarlet looked at Veirella, her brows creasing as she did so. When Genevieve stood straight, the girl's face returned to normal, with a smile plastered on her lips, when Genevieve looked at her.

"She does not have a concussion, but she has been drained of most of her Cai. A good night's sleep and some stardust, and she will be fine." Scarlet informed her.

"Thank you. Scarlet you may go." Genevieve dismissed her. The moment the door closed behind, Genevieve took the cup and have it to her, "here drink this. It will make you feel better." Her tone change from authoritative to soft and welcoming, Veirella took the cup from her hands, blow on the hot liquid then took at it sip. It was the same tea Veirella drank at breakfast. She still did not know what was in it, but it made her feel better.

"What is it?"

Veirella asked it was a question that she should have maybe asked before she drank it, but she had done it so many times that if something was wrong, it was already too late to turn back, but she still wanted to know.

"Peppermint leaf tea with a little stardust added in," she answered.

"Stardust?"

Veirella had heard of it, but was not too sure what it was. "Stardust is something that helps people like you and me. It speeds up our body's natural progress's, gives you a temporary boost of energy. It is the remnants of a dying star that has been harvested and cured." She explained.

"Now" Genevieve moved away from her and towards her desk. "For your homework, I will be away from the Academy for a few days and in that time, I want you to work on your wielding.

You are pushing out too much energy, and it is making you burn out faster." Genevieve explained as she reached for the other pot on the table. She brought it to Veirella, who stood and took it from her.

"I will arrange for one of these to be sent to your dorms every day until I return. That with add up to six, on the day you do not receive one you will come back to see be the day after. And when you do; you should be able to make this little flower grow with ease, and in seconds," she instructed her.

She was truly an educator I get hurt and she still gives me homework to do

"Okay."

There was nothing else Veirella could say. It may have sounded like she had a chose but she did not. Her mother had done the same thing to her enough times for her to know it was not optional.

"You may go."

Genevieve waved her hand and the painting next to the door turned into a port key. Veirella went to it. She had been seeing her long enough that Veirella knew when Genevieve dismissed someone that was the end of the conversation.

Veirella ended up right outside the entrance of the court, she pushed the doors open and when straight to her room. Not only did she have an assignment to do, she also had to undo her hair. The roots had begun to grow out, and there were was red dust in it. Veirella did not know how she ended up with red dust in her hair, and she did not care. Veirella just knew it needed to be washed.

Halfway through undoing her braids, she got tired. Veirella remembered the connection she shared with Willow and decided to use it.

"*Willow, if you can hear me, I need you help.*"

A moment later, she appeared out of thin air. "What do you need help with?" Veirella pointed at her hair. Willow walked over to where she was sitting at the vanity and waved her hand over her hair. Then it all puffed up, all the braids were out.

"*Where have you been all my life.*"

Veirella directed at her, Willow laughed. "You think that's impressive? There is so much I can do. Would you like some help washing it?" she asked. Veirella nodded. She had too much hair to turn down the help.

Willow went into her bathing chambers to set the water and Veirella undress and put a robe on. When she went in, the bath was ready and waiting, Veirella got in and Willow started porting water on her head.

An hour and three washes later, she was dressed and seated back at the vanity with a towel wrapped around her head. Willow took it done and dried her hair with magic. Veirella liked this side of magic. If she did not need to wait long hours, drying, undone or doing her hair, she would love every second of it.

"*Now this is a part of magic I could be comfortable with.*"

Errors

Anastasia

Anastasia hit the ground so many times she was sure her ass left a permanent indentation in it. Combat training had only just begun it was only the first day, and by the end of it she would have a week's worth of bruises. It was times like this she was grateful for Stardust, which made healing faster.

"You think its fare that they have us going up against upperclassmen?"

Isa asked, she was thrown off the platform landing right next to Anastasia. It was twenty feet up in the air, why it was that high she had no idea, but whoever designed it that why really wanted it to hurt when you lost.

"I have no idea, and I am in way too much pain to care" she responded, wheezing from how tired she was. Every time she inhaled, Anastasia felt like there was a dagger repeatedly stabbing her in her side.

A moment later, the other girl she was paired with Amaya came falling. She latest the longest and also fell the hardest. "If she did not break something the other three times, that one definitely did it."

Isa stated, tensing up when she hit the floor. Isa was a water wielder, she was a Nievar one of the many in the school, of the three Asphies they were the most. Her skin was a warm-yellow brown and her dark brown hair was up in a braid. She had on dark red trainers, similar to Anastasia and Amaya, each team was given a different color, she liked that they got red, helped hide the blood more than anything.

Anastasia walked out to Amaya, who was still laying on the floor, not moving. *Is she dead? If she was, then they would need to cancel the class out of respect."*

She knew it was a horrible thing to think or wish for, but this class was three hours long and Anastasia did not think she would survive another hour of getting knocked on her ass. The floor was made of stone; it hurt badly.

When she got closer, she looked over at her. "Are you still alive down there?" she got a mumble in response.

How unfortunate.

Hell had a nice hot place just for her, and if it did not, then one just formed. Anastasia reached a hand out to help her up.

"Come on"

She told her, pulling her up when Amaya raised her hand to her.

"Do you think they are trying to kill us? Because it really feels like they are." Amaya was grouting, she was lending over. She was probably in too much pain to stand up straight.

Her wavy brown hair had come loose from that last fall and was covering half her face. It was the side Anastasia was on, so she saw the pain on her face.

"I do not have an answer for you there" Anastasia looked up as two the kids were knocked of their platforms, "but I think you need to get to the med center" Amaya shook her head. "No, the pain will pass. I just need a moment to heal," Amaya told her. Leaning over to rest her weight on her knees.

Amaya was a Xiakary, her element was fire. All Centinals healed fast, fire and water wielders could recover from an injury in minutes, Anastasia felt envious for a moment then remembered how creepy their powers could be.

Water Wielders were natural healer's it was one of their Signent's so their healing speed was understandable, but for Fire Wielders their healing it was burning. If it was an open wound, you could smell the burning flesh as if closed itself, it was disturbing and looked painful.

"Okay, I'm ready to go again," Amaya stated a moment later. *You know now I do not feel as bad for hoping she was dead.* Anastasia thought.

She looked at Isa, who threw her head back and sighed before walking over. "Are we quitting or going again?" she asked. Amaya walked under the platform and disappeared.

She rolled her eyes, "what do you think" Anastasia walked under the platform and appeared at the top. There was an invisible port key beneath all the platforms. It was smaller and took less magic than others. Even though port keys themselves did not require much magic to begin with, it was the one thing she could do without fail.

"Ready for another beating so soon? You first years are really something." The boy, whose name Anastasia was told when they started, but she had been hit so many times she did not remember it. And in all honesty, she did not care to.

A second later, Isa appeared next to her. They were placed with third years and the girl was sitting on the side of the platform with her legs hanging over her hair was so white it rivaled snow.

She looked back at them, then pulled herself up. Anastasia did not remember her name either, but she knew she was an Air Wielder. *Fourth times the charm.*

It was not. Fourth was definitely not the charm. Anastasia latest a little longer than the three times before but not by much a couple seconds at most. That last time, she managed to pull enough power together to make the landing hurt a little less.

Why she had not thought if doing that before was beyond her. Then again, her magic had not been doing her any favors of late, so it was probably for the best she did not try.

Anastasia got up off the floor and instead of heading back to the platform she went for the door, "giving up already" she turned and instructor Rowen was looking at her. Large arms crossed over his chest, dark hair brushed back, with a smug smile on his face.

Anastasia had no problem admitting when she failed. Her father told her it would make her a good queen because she did not allow her ego or pride to get the better of her, like most men did.

Fire Wielders did not understand that concept, they would rather die than admit defeat. "My ass and pride have taken enough of a beating for one day. Thank you very much."

She responded. Then continued to the door, "Anastasia always give up so easily" Anastasia looked over up at the stands where Lola was sitting with her friends. It was not her turn to go yet, and Anastasia really wanted to stay to see how she did. But her pain overrode her need to see her get hurt.

"Lola, did you happen to forget that I can make blades from air, that I could use to cut your tongue out" Anastasia shot back. Terror crossed her face but disappeared a moment later, replayed with a conniving smile.

"Well, considering you barely have control over your magic, that is unlikely." She responded.

"Well then, I might just miss and cut your head off instead" Anastasia stepped forward, and Lola moved, make the fear return to her eyes. "What to see what will happen" she moved closer and closer, but someone stopped her, pulling on her arm. Anastasia turned to see Pax standing behind her.

"I know how much you hate her but now is not the time to start drawing blood," he told her. Anastasia looked back at Lola, her smug demonic smile had was back in place. "Fine" she pulled her arm out of his and felt the room.

"She got luck. Next time I will get her alone first."

Bonded

Veirella

Day after day passed, Veirella had been working on her wielding she barely left her room most days. She managed to grow the last five sunflowers that Genevieve sent to her.

Veirella needed to work on how much magic she pulled on when she did it. The first two days, she managed to get up to the stem before stopping.

She thought she could do it again without pushing it too much, and on days three and four, she did just that. Instead of not pushing enough, she pushed too much and killed the plants. The only thing she had going was that she did not pass out again, just a headache here and there.

Something else was happening, every morning she woke up there was red dust on her pillows and in her hair, Veirella did not figure out where it was coming from, and she hated having to wash her hair so often to the point it felt dry and brittle.

Willow changed her bedding every day so far that week. Veirella woke a little earlier than she usually did, and thankfully it was a nightmare free night. Veirella had been having more of those in resent days. The sun had not come up yet when she woke, so she got dressed in a simple little blue dress.

Veirella opted to wear comfortable clothing on her off days. She watched the sun come up as she waited for her final pot to show up. Or what was to be her final pot, she would not know for sure until the next day.

A little will later someone knocked on her door. She made her way over, opened it to find Luka standing there, with a little blue pot of soil in his right hand and a box in the other.

"Hi" he said smiling down at her.

"Hi" she smiled back, she had not spoken to him much, in all honesty Veirella could not remember if in the few weeks she had been there if they had spoken directly to each other at all. "This came for you" he raised his hand out to her with the pot and she took it from him.

"Thank you," she told him. Veirella looked down at the brown package in his other hand, "is that for me too?" she point at it. "Well, unless my name is Veirella Doviena Greystone, I think so" Veirella dropped her head at hearing him say her second name out loud. It was missing one, but she did not know it, only her parents did and based on her second name she did not what to know what it was.

Luka laughed at her reaction. "Not a big fan of the name I see," he asked.

"No, not really." She answered, of all the names her parents could have chosen, that was the choice they made.

"Well, whoever sent this for you either really loves you or knows how much you hate it," he gave the package to her. "A little of both. My bother is the only one whoever calls me that.

He knows how much I hate been called it so he always uses it," she explained. Luka nodded at her, holding back a laugh. She could tell it was not the name he was laughing at, but her reaction to it. It was not a terrible name, but she was already named after one plant. Why did the need to make it two.

"Well, I should get to working on this. I still have a lot to do." Luka nodded at her turn to leave "Bye" Veirella told him, "see you are around Dove." Veirella closed her eyes and groaned. He smiled at her, then walked off. Veirella really hoped he would forget it by the next time they speak to each other.

"This is so hard,"

Veirella groaned. She laid her head on the table, she needed to find a balance, but Veirella did not know how to get there. "What is it?" Willow asked.

"I need balance. *But I have no idea how to find it."* She looked up at Willow, she was getting better at communication with the link they shared, and switched naturally when she did not feel like speaking.

"*Your thinking about it too much. Your ability to wield is a part of you. Its like breathing."* Willow told her, "*so what should I do?"* Veirella needed all the help she could get, so she was willing to try just about everything and anything.

"*Like everything in nature, things naturally pull to you. The same can be said for your magic. Instead of pulling at it, let it come to you, flow naturally."* Veirella nodded.

Okay, think about it and then make it happen. She thought to herself, so Willow would not hear. She closed her eyes and went through her steps, but unlike the other times, she did not pull at the ball of electric pulses she formed in her body.

She let it wash over her; it went through her entire body. Then Veirella opened her eyes, and they were glowing bright and golden. Willow moved to the other side of the table. Her eyes grew wide when she saw Veirella's.

"Wow"

It was so light Veirella barely caught it. Veirella focused on the soil before her. Something she remembered from when she was young. Birds did what she asked of them, so maybe she could get plants to do the same.

"*Grow.*" She commanded.

Veirella did not know if it would work on plants there were living, but seeds lived more in the space of being both living and dead, so there was a higher chance that it would fail.

But then she felt something move, and the stem broke through the soil growing up, but it did not stop, it grow the bud, then it popped open and bloomed into the sunflower. Veirella smiled at what she did, and the glow in her eyes faded, and she did not feel faint.

"I did it."

"That you did" she looked up at Willow and her eyes were still wide open.

"What?"

Veirella asked, the smile falling from her lips. "Nothing, just surprised you did that without your hands." Veirella had realized she thought she did. "Things most work differently for Earth Wielder's I guess," she shrugged.

"Yes, or it has something to do with who your mother is" Willow stated, Veirella looked away from her. That was one topic Veirella did not like Willow bring up, and she did it often.

"I will go get you something to eat. You have been in here all day. I am sure you are famished," Willow told her, then felt the room.

Veirella was not to be honest. Food was not something she ever felt for. She ate breakfast every morning, and sometimes dinner, but she did not get very hungry so she only ate sometimes.

Veirella stood from the desk. She was going to put the sunflower by the window, so it had as much sunlight as possible. It was the only plant she had in her room, something she would eventually need to change.

But one was a good start. While she was looking for the best place to put it. She felt something run down the side of her face, Veirella raised her and to feel it when she pulled her fingers away, they had blood on them. At the sight her chest tightened.

Breath she could not breathe no matter how hard she tried, Veirella could not get air to go through her body.

Veirella pulled herself back and remembered where she was. She hurried to her bathing chambers to clean the blood from her fingers and her face. It was the only thing she could not to distract herself from the sight before her.

get clean, get clean, get clean.

She repeated in her head, as she took a wet cloth and whipped her hands with it, then her face. She rubbed and rubbed faster and harder to the point it hurt.

Get clean need to get clean she kept going.

"Anastasia put something together for you considering you missed breakfast" at the sound of Willow's voice her hand stopped moving, then Veirella noticed how fast her heart was going. She dropped the cloth into the bowl of water.

Veirella did not remember pouring. She dried her hands and the side of her face, Veirella hissed at how much it burned. She felt the spot. There was no visible damage, it would just be sensitive for a day or two. Then it would be fine.

She took a deep breath in and another one out. Then returned to her room where Willow was setting up her meal. It was a plate with bread, cheese and with fruit. It would be something she would choose for herself. Veirella did not notice Gemma paying attention to what she ate. But then again, Veirella did not notice much on anything.

Veirella sat at the table just as she poured her a cup of tea. "Thank you" Willow smiled and returned the pot to the tray. "I am going to go. Call if you need me." Veirella knew how things worked by now, she did not need to keep reminding her. But all the same Veirella nodded, then Willow disappeared.

"Did you really think doing one good thing could change everything? Still pathetic, as always. Remember, dead girls can't disappoint anyone."

Veirella knew they would come. They always did every time she lost herself, and pushing them away did not always work. So she just sat there and listened to them at point they would eventually give up or she would.

Changing Tides

Veirella

The following day, Veirella did not receive a flower. Meaning Genevieve had returned. Veirella had nothing to do, so she thought it was time to see what was in the package.

Veirella did not know for sure it was from Aspen. But he was the only one who ever used the name. She retrieved the brown package from the table and brought it to her bed.

She got the wrapping off revealing a black box with an envelope an top. Before Veirella could start opening, she heard a loud crash coming from the other side of the wall. Gemma's room. Veirella hoped she dropped something and did not hurt herself, Veirella jumped off her bed, grabbed the box and went to check on her. Veirella heard her curse, her voice was coarse like she was crying or was about to. Veirella knocked and waited for an answer.

"Come in."

Veirella opened the door and Gemma was turned away from her, picking up pieces of a broken glass of the floor. It was hard to tell what she broke, but from the shape of the fragments, it was a vase.

"Hey, Ella"

"How do you do that? Know who's there without seeing them?" She asked Veirella to put the box down on the white vanity similar to her own and went to help Gemma collect the shards.

"You move through the world quieter than most, for most you could go unnoticed. Plus, you hesitated when you knocked. And more importantly, you, me, Pax, and Luka are the only ones who can get into the court without an invitation simple deduction."

Gemma explained; that was new information to Veirella, and it also gave her some relief knowing the place was protected.

"Are you okay?"

Veirella asked. Gemma's skin was a light shade of red, either from anger or her trying not to cry. She stood with the pieces she collected and took them to the trash next to the door, Veirella did the same.

They moved to her bed, which had a red and white cover with a mix of red and white pillows. Everything in her room was mixed between those two colors with some black splashed in.

"Yes, I am just having a little trouble with my wielding." *So she was not okay.* Gemma always loved her abilities. It was one of the many things she talked about the most in their letters. She took it up on herself to learn one of the most difficult and dangerous wielding forms for air wielders. 'The cut' she called it.

It took almost cutting her arm off to get it, but she eventually did. Veirella did not remember every bit of her childhood years, but she recalled almost every part of their distanced friendship.

"You must hate that?"

"I do not know what is wrong with me. A few months again, I could do this stuff like it was nothing. And now levitation, something a baby could do is impossible."

Her frustration was evident, and her annoyance radiated off her to the point Veirella felt it. "I am sorry. I know saying that does not help you much, but I am. I have not done much, I just learned how to grow a flower so I am not exactly an expert in much of any of this" Veirella was trying to comfort her friend but it was not something she had every down before so she did not know how well she was doing.

"I can get there, will get there. I know that I just have no idea how long it will take me to get back, is all. To return the favor for where you are I think you have made a lot of growth in more ways than one," Veirella's brows drew together, she did very little in the six weeks she had been at the school so she did not know what Gemma meant.

"So, what do you want to do? Would you like some help to work on your wielding?" Veirella asked, pushing the conversation back to her. Gemma picked up her hand.

"Ella, this thing friendship" She pointed between them "works both ways. Just because I am dealing with something does not mean you cannot talk about what you are dealing with, okay?" Veirella nodded in response.

Gemma looked around her. Whatever she saw made her tilt her head to the side.

"What is that?" she asked. Veirella turned to see what she was looking at. It was the box she had brought in with her. Gemma let go of her hand and got off the bed to get it. "I think it is a gift from my brother. I have not looked at it yet, so I have no idea what it is." She told her Gemma picked up the box and returned to the bed.

"Then we can see what it is together" Gemma took up the envelope and started opening it, while she did that Veirella started undoing the ribbons around the box. "See you soon" Gemma read aloud. Veirella looked up at her and she turned the white card so she could see it. '*See you soon*' written in dripping red ink.

Now she knew for certain it was from Aspen, it a strange way to leave a message but it got her attention considering Veirella had answered any of his letters. He would be coming to see her in a little over two weeks to see if she still wanted to go home.

Veirella had still not decided if she wanted to stay at Astro Academy just yet. That could still change. She had the time, Gemma was there so that was one reason to stay. And a more important one would be she needed to learn control, so she did not hurt someone.

While Gemma put the card back in the envelope, Veirella pulled the lid off. Inside was a flower, she thought it looked a hydrangea, but that could not be. It was not the color right color; it was red, not purple or blue. It was an unnatural shard of red, closest thing she could compare it to was the blood coursing through her veins, "is this a Hydrangea?" Gemma looked down at what she was holding.

"*Hi there.*" The voice was sweet but made Veirella's skin run cold. Before Veirella could answer it, Gemma slammed the lid back on to the box. She jumped off the bed and ran for the door. "What is it? Where are going?" Veirella asked, getting off the bed and following her. Confused at what she was doing.

"Luka, Pax, come here hurry!" Gemma yelled, her voice filled with panic. She stood in the middle of the room, and a moment later, both boys ran into the room, coming from the training room. "What? What is?" Luka asked her, his confusion was just as evident as Veirella's. Gemma put the box on the table and opened so they could see the flower, then move back.

"Fuck," Luka cursed. Veirella looked at all three of them. They were all wearing similar expressions, worry. She looked back at the box and four red vines similar to the petals started coming out, moving towards each of them.

"Gemma," Luka called, he was pulling at his power. Red and orange sparks started moving around his arms, same with Gemma with her light blue ones. "Please work," she said beneath her breath. Gemma turned to the flower and in started going up into the air. It was shaky but it moved.

Gemma was struggling to keep it up. She got it halfway above the table, then nodded at Luka, then he blasted flames at it. Veirella heard it screaming, not in her heard Veirella could also hear it. A few minutes passed before it finally stopped. So did Luka's flames, the blackened flower fell back to the table, breaking as it did.

"Why did you do that? That was a gift from my brother." Veirella went towards the pieces, but before she could touch them, Gemma stopped her. "Ella, Aspen would never send you a Greviger" Veirella looked at her face pulled together.

"What?" she asked.

"That may look like a hydrangea but it is called a Greviger. Dangerous to our kind, the only why to kill them is with fire." Gemma explained. Luka said something to Pax, and he left the court.

"Why would my brother send me that?" Veirella was not asking them for an answer, because only Aspen could answer that question.

"He did not and also he would not." Luka told her, "but the note" Veirella stopped herself from continuing. "What note?" Luka asked, looking between them.

Gemma said something to Luka, but Veirella did not hear what was said. All she heard was her heart pounding in her ear's, it got faster and it was becoming harder for her to breathe. Her eyes were focused on the burned plant before her.

"*They were coming, they were coming for me again*" whoever attacked her in the forest that night was coming back for her. They knew where she was and could get to her. Those were the thought running through her head making her feel even worse.

"Let's hope they finish the job this time."

"Then everyone can finally move on with their life's not constantly, wasting time worrying about you."

"Or you could do it yourself, make it easy for everyone, and end it."

The voices grew in size and volume. Veirella was shaking, and not breathing. She felt a hand on her knee. Veirella pulled her eyes away from the flower to see who it was. Genevieve was next to her. She was speaking but Veirella could not hear the words.

Genevieve raised her hand, then raised her fingers. Veirella counted as she dropped them. She got to five and Genevieve opened her hand again and Veirella counted. When Veirella got to five, the second time her heart slowed and she could hear again.

"There you go, better?" Genevieve asked. Veirella nodded, Genevieve stood and helped her up. "Anastasia, can you take Veirella to her room?" Gemma nodded, then took Veirella's hand and let her to her room.

"Their coming back." Veirella told Gemma, her voice broking as she said the words. "Who? Who is coming?" Gemma asked. Veirella shook her head, "I don't know who they are, but they did this." She showed Gemma her neck, where the scar on her throat was.

Gemma gasped, her eyes grew wide looking at it. She steered at it for a moment, then back up at Veirella's face, her eyes returning to normal. "Hey, no one is going to get to you. It does not matter who they are, if they come for you again. We will deal with them as a team. I will not let anything happen to you and neither will the others." Gemma assured her.

Veirella did not want to burden anyone with this, but she also did not want to spend the rest of her life looked over her shoulder waiting for someone to kill her.

Veirella woke up from the same nightmare she was used to having, it never got easy to go through the same motion over and over again. She wished she could go back further into the nightmare so she could see who was chasing her. If she had a face, to look for things would be easier, but there was none, and everyone was a threat until she knew the truth.

Veirella laid in bed looking up at the dark ceiling hoping she would go back to sleep, but after an hour of nothing, she got up. Veirella moved slowly because Gemma was sleeping next to her.

She moved around when Veirella stood, but did not wake. She quietly made her way out of the room, then closed the door behind her. Veirella intended to go out to the balcony but wanted some water. She went to the kitchenet and poured herself a glass. She finished then went to leave, but a sound coming from the other hall stopped her.

It was Luka or Pax, at less she was not the only one that could not sleep. Veirella went down the hall and the door was open. Veirella looked inside, and Luka was in the center of the room, back to her. He was hitting a training dummy.

He was not wearing a shirt, so she could see how toned he was. The muscles in his back flexed every time he threw a punch at the dummy. Veirella saw a part of his right arm, there was a tattoo going up it. He usually had a long shirt on, so it was her first time seeing it.

"Like what you see Dove?"

His voice was low and deep. Veirella's skin ran warm hearing it. She got caught watching him without his knowledge, or with it considering everyone there could tell when she was in the room. Luka stopped hitting the dummy, then turned and went over to her. He stopped inches from her, looking down at her sweat running down his face and body.

Luka raised his hand up next to her head and took a small towel from the hook that was next to the door.

They did not stop looking at each other, as he stepped back and used the towel to wipe the sweat off his face. Then he turned and went to the window where he retrieved his grey shirt and a canteen.

"Sorry, I should have said something," she apologized. Luka laughed in response. "No need to apologize, I like you watching," he turning and looked at her. Veirella stepped into the room, it was her first time in the training room. The first days she arrived, she did not go past the entrance.

Veirella looked around the room. There was not much she could see there were no fae lights on or fires burning. The only light in the room was coming from the moon outside the window. "You interested in fighting

Dove?" Veirella could tell he was calling her that because he knew it would get a reaction out of her. "Can you just call me by my name?"

She asked, Luka smirked at her. "But that is your name," he stated. He was not wrong entirely. Dovi was a part of her name, but she knew he was staying it as Dove with an e. So Veirella could argue for that, but that would just encourage him to continue. She was going to try and brush it off. Maybe if she did not give him a reaction or acknowledge it, he was eventually stop.

"Why are you up this late?" Veirella asked. She went and sat next to him on the window seat. The windows were big so there was a decent about of space between them.

"Working off soon of the energy I have, and you? Why are you up this late?" He turned to the side the same way she was, so he was facing her. Veirella had both feet crossed beneath her, facing him.

"Woke up and could not fall back a sleep, the flower thing was a lot." She answered. Her voice got lower than it already was when she spoke of the Greviger.

"Hey, whoever sent it cannot get to you here, and I am sure Pax and Gemma are currently plotting murder. So no need to worry, they won't let anything happen to you and neither will I." It was nice to know she had friends willing to put themselves at risk to help her, but Veirella did not want that.

She did not know what the threat was or how much danger it could put the people around her in. "That's nice to know, considering I could barely protect myself. All that training and I could use none of it." Veirella felt like a disappointment for not stopping what happened, and it reflected badly on Elizabeth, who trained her.

"What do you mean?" Veirella could see the lines on his face. Luka did not know she assumed he did because he knew Pax and Gemma. She thought one of them would have told him. "Do you not know what happened to me?" he shook his head no.

Veirella liked that he did not know about her tragic past. At least she now knew his interest in being around her did not come from a place of pity. She thought about not telling him but, considering everyone else around her knew why shouldn't he.

"Someone tried to kill me when I was ten. Left me with this." she showed him the scar on her neck. His face hardened when he saw it. "What happened?" he asked. His voice somehow got deeper, if that was possible. "I cannot remember much. All I know is that I was running from someone, then I was on the ground bleeding out." She told him, "so you think that was your fault?"

"I did Ryin for two years and I could not manage to get myself out of danger, and I am pretty sure I left my friend for died." He did not hear the second half of what she said.

"No one is going to expect a ten-year-old to be able to protect themselves from an adult, someone who was probably twice your size. Dove, you should not put that on yourself." He was trying to comfort her, but after so long of telling herself the opposite, Veirella's mind would not change so easily.

But she nodded none the less, "Well, I am going to bed. I can be sure that Miss Genevieve will have something for me to do tomorrow." She told him Luka nodded, then Veirella stood and went for the door. "Goodnight" Veirella turned her head to look at him.

"Goodnight" she returned, then left. Veirella was sure there was very little chance of her getting any sleep, but she was going to try. The sun would not be up for another few hours, so she had plenty of time to try.

Veirella followed the same routine she did every morning. Willow set her bath, helped her get dressed, then breakfast with Gemma, Pax, and Luka and last Gemma open a port key for her.

But Veirella stopped her before she could do it. "Can you show me how to open it?" she asked. Based of the fact that Gemma said she was having trouble with her powers, it must not have required a lot of wielding to get one opened.

"Sure, it only needs a small amount of power to get it opened, then think about where you want it to send you." Gemma explain, Veirella nodded then moved before the painting of the water she had seen so many times. Then raised her hand and pulled on her magic. When the green sparks appeared around her hand Veirella waved her hand over it and a green vortex opened before her, Veirella thought about Genevieve's office.

She looked back at Gemma who nodded at her, "what if it sends me to the wrong place?" Veirella asked a little panicked. "No problem, these are limited to inside the school. Just come back through and we can try again." She explained.

Veirella hesitated for a moment, then closed her eyes and steps through. "*Please be the right floor.*"

She took a deep breath then opened her eyes to see the familiar hallway, that led to Genevieve's office. Veirella looked back at the port key, she forgot to ask Gemma how to close it. But it faded on its own when the sparks around her fingers did. Veirella turned at the sound of a door being opened and saw a tall, white-haired man coming out of Genevieve's office.

She was behind him, Genevieve said something to the man. He nodded then walked off, passing Veirella like she was not there to begin with. Genevieve did not wait for Veirella she just turned and went back into the room. When Veirella got into the room, she saw way more files on her desk than there were the last time she was there. Genevieve was quite busy, but somehow, she made time to help Veirella.

"I saw you what you did with the sunflowers. For a beginner, you have done well, far better than I thought you would." She told her, had she expected her to fail? "The flower was the same, but the soil was different, both in density and what was used to make it." She explained.

"Did you expect me to fail?" Veirella asked, "Gods no, if I expected my students to fail, I would not be very good at my job. That was your first test, and you passed above average. The ones you did not get to grew into full flowers. I am guessing you thought you were not wielding enough?" Veirella nodded.

"Well, they were never going in grow, the soil that they were placed in was not compatible with the flower, most students figure that out in the test but considering they have weeks to learn all of this, you did what you could with the time you were given. Your brother said you were a fast learner I guess that applies to magic as well. So I think you can move to the next level." Genevieve told her, "and what would be?" Veirella asked.

"The greenhouse."

Then Genevieve opened a portal and sent her through. The hall Veirella ended up in was mostly dark. There was light coming from one direction, so she went towards it. She followed the light to a dark green door, Veirella opened it and went inside.

There were rows of tables starting from where she stood going back to where the glass walls ended. Each had flowers on them varying in size, color, and type.

There were other tables closer to the walls, all filled with plants as well. A few were so tall they would eventually touch the roof. The sun was shining brightly above, but Veirella could not feel it on her skin. She walked around, looking at all the plants.

"Hello there" Veirella turned at the sound of the soft feminine voice, she was met with a brown woman wearing a guarders cover, she holding blue lilacs and her black hair was in two braids, and her dark eyes were filled with peace.

"You must be Veirella" she put the lilacs done on the closest table to her, took her gloves off and laid them next to the plant, then walked over to her.

She raised a hand to Veirella, and she took it. "I am Thora Heart, I am the keeper here," she introduced.

"Nice to meet you. Miss Genevieve said you would be overseeing most of my lessons from now on." She released her hand and clasped hers together. "Yes, I will. She informed me that you can wield without using your hands, which is quite interesting. Most of your work will me research based, so you will more than likely spend more time in the library than you will here with me. This is not a regular class.

Only upperclassmen and rarely a few lower classmen who excel come here. You grew up in nature. You just need to take the rules and tweak them a bit for magic." She explained. Thora went to the back of the greenhouse to retrieve something and brought it to Veirella. It was a green flower bud. It had seven levels, meaning the flower inside was a type of rose.

"What is it?" Veirella asked, Thora handed it to her. "That is where the research comes in. You need to figure out. And just so you know, this cannot be opened with brute force. If you try, it will not end well," she warned.

"Okay."

"You can head to the library and then return here if you would like or you can go to your dorms, whichever works for you." Thora told her then walked off. Veirella assumed this would be more teaching but considering she was not taking regular classes with the other earth wielders. Things were expected to be different.

Veirella used the same port key that Genevieve sent her through to get to the library. *What was the point of the tour if I could just move around the school like this?* She thought to herself. Veirella opened the large wooden doors to the library, it was a massive room.

There were fourteen shelves that she could see each labeled with a different letter of the alphabet. There were students sitting all over the place, some with friends, others alone.

Considering she was dealing with nature, Veirella figured her best bet would be to start looking in the 'N' section. She did not know how long she was there for looking at book's but nothing stuck out.

Veirella was going to give up. Then she thought of something else. If the flower required magic to open it, then a book on magic and nature would be the best bet, but she did not want to spend the rest of the day looking for something that may very well not be there.

Veirella found a girl taking books from a cart and putting them back on the shelves. "Hi, could you help me find something?" she asked. The girl stopped what she was doing and went over to Veirella, "What can I help you with?" she asked. She did not look much longer than Veirella, she maybe had one or two years on her.

"Is there by chance any books in here on how magic affects nature?" The girl thought about it for a moment. "I think so stay here, I will be right back" she told her then moved around her and disappeared behind one of the bookshelves.

It took her a while to get back to Veirella, but it was not something Veirella noticed. When she returned, she was holding a large dark green book.

"Here, I think this is what you're looking for?" Veirella took the book from her. It was a lot heavier than she expected. Veirella turned the book so she could read the title. 'Cai's Presences in the Natural World."

"Thank you. Can I take it with me?" Veirella asked. The girl nodded. "You're welcome, and yes, just remember to return it once you are finished." She told her. Veirella nodded, thanked her again, then left, opening a port key and went back to the court.

Gemma was in class and Veirella had no idea were the boys were. She liked being alone and now she had some reading to do so that made it even better.

And for the next few days all she did was read, Willow came and made her bed every morning as she usually did, but Veirella did not require her help so she did not stay for long after. So far she had learned about other plants with magical influence like the Keives which were made from a mafic collision between earth wielders and water wielders. That was why they only bloomed when it was cold, specifically the coldest night of the year.

But nothing on the mystery plant miss Heart gave to her. Veirella's head started pounding, so she stopped reading and laid her head down on the book, waiting for it to pass. She had been getting headaches for the past two days, eating some things helped, but she did not feel like moving. When the pounding finally stopped, she decided to go get something from the kitchenet.

Veirella did not get to do that because when she opened her door, Gemma was standing there her hand raised, prepared to knock. "Gemma, is everything okay?" she asked "No, everything is not okay. You have been hiding it here for days; it is time you have some healthy dose of human interaction." Her frustration was palpable.

"You saw me, the other night at dinner and in the morning for breakfast" Gemma pushed passed her and went to her closet. "What are you doing?" Gemma was going through her clothes "finding you something wear, tonight."

Gemma was taking things down, and Veirella went and stopped her "Okay, before you make a mess of my room, would you tell me what this is about?" Veirella asked. "The upperclassmen are having a bonfire in the woods tonight and we are going to it, so would you rather pants or a dress?" Gemma was showing her the different things she picked out.

"You are, but I am not, I will be doing some reading for my assignment," Gemma looked at her with shock and disgust "you want to do schoolwork on a none school night, when there are hot older boys as an option?" Gemma looked at her as if she had grown a second head.

"If the options are books or boys, I chose books." Veirella tells her. Gemma sighed "well if not for a boy, then for me" Veirella wanted to say no, but she did not know how to "I am not much of a party person, Gemma," she told her "Look I can understand that but you have been here for weeks and you have kept to yourself, I want you to make friends outside of myself who you live with, so you really have no choice but to be friends with me."

Gemma told her "if that is your reasoning, then the answer is no" Veirella did not want more people to deal with. "Well, you are going and as long as we are friends isolation is not an option for you" Gemma pushed back "Well go luck with that" Veirella responded she was not going.

Veirella was following Gemma into the forest. She was wearing a purple dress with dark flowers designed on the front, and her hair was braided up. Gemma had gotten Willow to help her get Veirella dressed for this party she had no interest in going to.

Gemma was wearing red pants with a black shirt and black boots. "It is not much further, I think," Gemma told. Veirella wondered if they were lost, but then she saw the fire, and heard the students.

There were people all over the place. Some of them did not look to be in their right minds; they must have been drinking. Veirella stayed close to Gemma. She did not like crowded spaces; they made her nervous. And she was now surrounded by drunken teenagers who could do magic. Those two things did not seem like a good combination. Someone could lose control and hurt someone or, worse, kill them.

"You will be fine. It is okay to let yourself have fun," Gemma told her. Veirella did not think they had the same use of the word. Music and people were what Gemma liked. It was to be expected; she was Iriean, and they loved nothing more than people looking at them. And a party was the perfect place for that. So, Gemma was where she was comfortable, but Veirella was not.

She would have rather sit by herself reading somewhere quiet. "Did not expect to see you here," Veirella was frightened by whoever spoke, she stepped away, before she noticed who it was "Sorry did not mean to spook you" Pax apologized "no worries just was not expecting it, is all" she told him. "What are you doing here? Social gatherings are not really your thing."

He asked, “Gemma did not give me much of a choice” Pax laughed “why am I not surprised by that, she can be very persuasive.”

“That is not the word I would use, but it works.” She told him.

Veirella did not noticed Gemma was gone, but she returned with two cups moments later “here, I got you cider very little on the alcohol you should not even taste is” Gemma told her. Veirella took the drink from her; she was hesitant to drink it, but when she finally took a sip, it was not as bad as she expected.

“How is it?”

“Not the worst thing I have ever tasted.” A girl Veirella had never seen before came over to them. She was swaying a little, but seemed fine otherwise. “Hey, we are going to play a game, want in?” she asked them “What kind of game?” Veirella asked “a drinking one”

“Andras won last year, and he never shuts up about it”

The girl told her Gemma, she looked back at her. “You two have fun. I am going to stay here.” Veirella told her, “you sure?” Gemma asked. Veirella nodded. She lingered for a moment before walking off with her friend.

And when she could no longer see them, Veirella turned to Pax “I know I have not been here very long—“she started “—But you are leaving,” Pax finished for her. Veirella gave him her unfinished drink, then walked back the way they came.

Veirella was not very far from the party. She could still see the fire, just not hear the music. It was not very dark out; the moon was out, and the sky was clear. She tried her best not to lose it. The last time she was in the forest, it did not end well.

But the school was safe, and the only thing around that could hurt her were than animals and there was very little chance that would happen.

Veirella heard something behind her. She turned to see what it was, but there was nothing there. Veirella did not say a word. When alone in an unfamiliar place, it was always best to stay quiet. A moment passed of nothing, so Veirella turned to continue, but there was someone in front of her.

She jumped back and gasped before she saw it was Luka. "Sorry, Dove did not mean to scare you," he apologized. "Well, when you see someone in the woods, it is best to announce your presence so as not to scare them to death," she told him.

"I will remember that if it ever happens again." He looked around them then back at her. "Are you lost? I can help you get to the bonfire" he asked her, she could not be lost in her own element. Veirella could always navigate her way around a forest no matter where she was or how far in she went. It was not possible for her to get lost.

"No, I am actually leaving; crowds are not really something I enjoy." Luka nodded at her response. "I am going back to the dorms. Enjoy your fire party." She moved around him and walked away, but he walked with her. "I do not need an escort back. I can find my way back, just fine," she told him. "I would just like to ensure you get back safely," he told her.

"So how have you been? Gemma said you have been doing well with Cai usage" he asked. "Yeah, I grew a whole sunflower, it was pretty badass" she said, her voice laced with sarcasm "I am sure it was, but once you get the basics down, then you get to do all the fun stuff." Luka informed her.

Veirella had no interest in fun she just wanted enough control to live her life, but she did not say that to Luka. They all seemed proud of what they were and of the things they could do, so telling him she hated it did not seem like the right thing to do.

"Looking forward to it, I know you leave so assignments regularly but would you be able to help me train if I manage to do well here I know once I get home my parents will have me back on a routine, and I would like to be somewhat ready for it," Veirella asked. "It would be my honor to train with you. Maybe I can learn the secret of what makes Forian's such great fighters," he told her.

Veirella did not think there was a secret; they started training at a young age, so it made them more advanced, and that was something anyone could do. "No secret, just skill and dedication." She told him "Okay, we could work on your sword work first, that is my—"

"—Nothing sharp," she said cutting him off.

"Okay, bow staff is fine too" she nodded at his response Veirella and sharp objects did not mix much anymore.

They did not speak for the remainder of their walk. The silence was not awkward, but comforting. Luka went with her all the way to the entrance of the court. "Well, thank you for walking me here; it was nice of you."

She thanked him. "I would not be much of a gentleman if I left a lady to walk through the forest alone at night now, would I?" he asked smiling down as her "No you would not" she answered, Luka opened the door for her "Goodnight" she told him "same to you" she entered, and he waited for her to get to her room before closing the door.

It was not late; she could still do some more reading to see if she could find what she needed. However, Veirella could not gauge how long that would take, so she changed and went into bed, leaving that task for the next day.

Wild Cuts

Lorenzo

The last assignment, Lorenzo had was ended two weeks prior. It usually took time to get a next because of how many students were and he was restless waiting. But they had a high success rate, so that gave them more power in the choosing process. He needed to kill something and fighting Pax was not helping anymore; it was not the same as fighting a demon. He had no intention of hurting or killing his best friend. Lorenzo could not say the same for the demonic bastards from the dark realm.

At the before he went to the bonfire the night before, Cyrus told him they had an assignment, and they would be leaving in the morning. Lorenzo was too excited to drink. He could if he wanted, he blood burnt so hot it would barely have any affect on him, but he held himself back none the less. Pax and Lorenzo did not stay there long.

He grabbed his black pack along with his sword and met Pax in the court; it was important to travel light no matter how long they would be gone, they needed to be prepared for anything and a bag take up your energy was not ideal.

"Why is it that they tell us when we are leaving, but never where we are going?" Pax asked. Lorenzo thought it was a power play keeping the information to themself until they absolutely needed to tell them, he thought it was a shit way of maintaining control they did not have did not have. All it did was make it harder for them to prepare for where they were going and what they would be dealing with, then they got there. “Look on the bright side. Next year you get to know everything firsthand, then we get to choose how we run our team.” Lorenzo told him.

They went into the hall, and Pax opened a port key to the map room. When traveling through a portal, it was best to have either being to the place you were going to or knew the exact location. Going through a portal without knowing where you were going led to one of two things, one you made it but dead because half your body gets left in limbo, a place beyond time and space. And considering they did not know, most of the places they were assigned to using the world map was necessary.

It was also the only full map in Celestia. Each continent had its own map with all their regions detailed in them, but their knowledge on the other three was limited. They spent most of their time fighting each other, so it was not strategic to share such information. Astro was allowed to exist because it was common ground for all four continents. A small part of the island touched each on each of the continents. They all tried to claim it, but none wanted the other to have access to their waters without permission, which control of the island would give. So Astro was left as free territory and three centuries later, they built the school there.

Not everyone was allowed in the map room, mostly third and four years. Second years could entire but with permission of a teacher, the headmistress, or the map reader on their team. Pax and Lorenzo, on the other hand had royal blood so they could go in without asking. But they still needed Griffin and Cyrus because they did not know how to read it.

Cyrus was their map reader. And he would teach Pax to be the same. The map readers were the only students given positions in the military the moment they graduated because of the knowledge they held. They had to get a rune carved into their necks, preventing them from using what they knew against the other continents. The map was made up of five stone slabs lit by flames, touching the place on the map you intended to go absorbed its location into your skin, the rune also preventing the process from killing the reader. It was all in a dead Celestial language, one Lorenzo did not bother to remember because he had no interest in learning how to read the map.

He did not know what Cyrus was teaching Pax about the map, because in order to understand it, he would need to go to one of the temples.

"They tell us to be on time, but they are late." Lorenzo was done with waiting; he was ready for some action. Only one team was allowed in there at a time, but there was never anyone waiting to use the map.

The assignments were not only to give them in field training; they were graded on their performance and their efficiency in dealing with a threat without putting civilians in danger. The teams with the highest marked benefited the most.

For second years it gave them first pick of the first years they wanted on their team, for third years it was an opportunity to be seen by the royals for either positions at court or in the military, and it also gave them a nomination for the War Games that happened every four years. That was the only way students could take part in it.

The trials would begin soon to determine who would get to go, considering it was almost time for the next one Lorenzo had a lot of work to do. Fourth years were the only level to take part in the games. Third years never made it in, so the school rarely ever nominated them anymore, but Lorenzo intended to be a player and would do whatever he needed to get a spot. Second years have been nominated in the past, but none made it pass the trials to actually be in the games.

Even if Lorenzo had the time to wait until after graduation, he would not. It was more impressive winning the War Games, when you were younger than everyone else in to. And he did not have four more years to wait around for the next one. The black marks on his arm were growing faster now that he was getting older, and he got closer to D-day.

One of the many paintings that lined the walls opened and Griffin and Cyrus came through. They told them to be there before the sun came up, but there was light in the windows above them and they were just getting there. "How long have you two being waiting?" Griffin asked. His eyes were half closed, and his hand covered half his face, shielding his eyes from the brightness of the fire. He was hungover. It was to me expected when Pax, Lorenzo, and Anastasia left the bonfire. He was still drinking.

"We got here the time you told us to." Pax told him his tone was harsh. He hated having people waste his time as much as Lorenzo did.

"I still have trouble comprehending how those two were the best of that last year's second class," Pax told him low enough for the others not to hear. Pax was the top of his classes, in everything the same for Lorenzo. Like it was, every year, the top ten best students were chosen for the best teams. Lorenzo was beginning to question it that was indeed Cyrus and Griffin.

"Where are we going?" Pax asked. If one of them did not push for them to get going, they would spend another half an hour listen to Griffin tell them the most uninteresting story about his night. Cyrus moved through the slabs, passing Dragia and Fianorea, then going around Astro and stopping before Iriea.

Lorenzo and Pax sighed and went over to it. They did not need him to tell them why they were going there. There was only one answer to that question. *Sex Demons.*

Winter was coming, meaning everything was ten times worse than it usually was on a normal day. The people were more riled up, the thieves were bolder, and the worse of all it was mating session.

The only people that were happy this time of year were the rich and the drunk, the rich never went hungry or cold, and the drunks had too much rum in them to care what was going on around them.

That was normal for most of the world, but it was always somehow much worse in the under city. Where those who could not afford to live in the Hosheau took up residence, they did not have many other options. Most of Iriea was either covered in deadly windstorms or were demon feeding grounds.

Because the city was so densely population, incubi and succubi loved it. There between 50 and 60 babies born in the warmer months and almost half of them were fathered or mothered by the demons.

They did not come out during the day so the boys spent the day doing whatever they could to pass the time. Lorenzo was trying to learn a new sword maneuver, Pax was making more arrows, and Cyrus and Griffin had gone out to do god knows what. Cyrus was more than likely looking for some new plant life to study and Griffin was probably in a brothel somewhere. Lorenzo did not care what they did on their own time as long as they got the job done, was all that mattered.

And the second the sunset, they were both back at the inn; it was high up. The further up the room, the better it was. Which was perfect, considering they would need to move fast to catch as many as possible.

They climbed to the roof and began hunting. Not push time passed before Cyrus stopped, one of the benefits of having an Earth Wielder on your side, one of their Signent's came in handy went tracking. They had the ability to sense changes in the dimensional plain.

"Two houses over," he told them. Pax opened a portal and Griffin went through. Pax was skilled enough at opening portals in enclosed spaces without leaving much of a signature behind or causing too much damage.

A few minutes passed and Griffin came back through he nodded and they keep moving. Their weapons were coated in water from a ceremonial pit in Astro. No one knew what it was exactly, but a demon had fallen in and was burnt up by it, and ever since they used the water to clean their weapons and whatever is in it stuck to them.

House after house they took turns going in and taking killing them. Lorenzo killed fifteen by the time they made it to the edge of the city. An hour passed and Cyrus had not found another was strange. The city is a lot bigger than the amount they killed. But Lorenzo knew they were not finished because Cyrus was tracking something.

He stopped and pointed across from where they were standing, they all looked at what he found. There was a single white house across from them. The building was so damaged, anything could finish it off, whoever lived there was long dead and no one had bothered to keep it and up time or the weather took it for themselves and the house next to it did not look any better.

"There are at least three of them inside," Cyrus informed them.

"What the hell happened here?" Griffin asked, something they were all thinking, it was not common for homes to be left unoccupied in the under city given how many people lived in the streets, no one said anything because they did not have an answer to give. Pax opened a portal, and they went through one after the other.

They were on the main floor of the three-story house. "We split up and we can each take one out. There are three, so one of us is getting lucky tonight" Cyrus told them. His voice was low whispering, so whatever was in the house did not hear him. Cyrus could track any demon but he could not tell what they were, and there were things more dangerous that a succubus.

They broke off, Griffin moving around the ground floor, and the others going up the stairs. Cyrus took the second floor and Pax and Lorenzo the third. The house was bigger on the inside than it was in the out. Pax went down one hallway and Lorenzo the other. He looked in all the rooms as he went. Slowing his movements so not to disturb the wooden floor beneath him. Lorenzo came out of one room and was about to go in another when he heard a sound coming from the last room at the end of the hall.

He slowly made his way towards it, careful not to make a sound. The door was not locked just pushed up. Lorenzo used the tip of his sword to push it open from where he stood all he could see was a part of the window and the small bed in the corner.

He moved further into the room, looked around as he went, but he saw nothing. Lorenzo moved around the bed and saw a girl in the corner curled up in a ball. He called on his magic and sent a ball of fire into the air.

When the room light up, he saw she was covering in blood; Lorenzo did not see her face, but he could tell she was scared.

"Are you okay?"

He looked away from her, looking in the bathing chamber attached to the room, making sure there was nothing in there with them. The space was small, so he cleared it with one look around, then he sheathed his sword.

"It hur-hurts." Lorenzo turned back to the girl whose voice he recognized. He pushed the flame closer to her so he could see her. The face belonged to someone Lorenzo had since many times before. He called her name, and she pushed herself up, looking at him. "Luka?" he went to say something, but she screamed. Her clothes soaked with blood, *her blood* then she dropped to the floor, and so did Lorenzo, the last thing he felt the pain, then it went dark.

Preparation

Veirella

Veirella knew she would have bruises with how many times Gemma hit her with the ball. It was not intentional, she could not control where it went, but somehow it almost always ended upcoming at her. It was soft, something a child would play with. But the speed at which the ball hit her made it hurt a lot more.

Over an hour of working on her levitation and she did not seem to improve at all, with every failure, the more frustrated she became. It was Veirella's second time in the training room. The first was too dark for her to see anything, but now she could see the back wall that was lined with weapons, both steel and wooden.

Ranging from bow staffs, swords, dangers, and bows; on the wall above the door and next to it there were stacks of small towels, and on the other side there was a storage container, with training dummies and rocks for some reason.

Veirella did not understand why they needed their own private training area when the school had one for all the students to use. Then Gemma told her it was a new addition after Luka almost burned it down. Veirella they were powerful, but being able to destroy something designed to handle their power was something entirely different.

In fact, the court just appeared out of nowhere when the boys started attending the academy, and it was designed just for them. Their magic was stronger than the others and the court acted like a shield to keep their power contained within it and adapted to accommodate them as it grew.

"I will never get this" Gemma kicked the ball away after dropping it again. Veirella lost count of how many times she had thrown it to her in the time she began helping her. And her arms were beginning to hurt, unfortunately it was not because of the amount of throwing she had done, but the eight times she had been hit, three on her right arm and five on her left.

"You will. I think you think about it took much." Veirella told her. "Why is this so hard?" Gemma sat down and threw herself back on the mat.

"Well, I am pretty sure defying how gravity works and stopping objects in midair is not met to be easy. You are trying to control something that is not meant to be controlled," Veirella told her. Air was a wild element, so was fire. Both could do massive amounts of damage in seconds. The difference lied within their needs.

Fire needed oxygen to grow which air provided, take the air away and it would die. But Air did not have such restraints, it could move as fast or slow as it wanted to and never stop. In most situations, it was run or die.

"I would like your element right about now; earth seems easier to learn," Veirella sat next to her. "Things always look easier when you are the one looking and doing, just because something is hard for you does not make it easy for someone else," she told her. Gemma sat up and sighed.

"I know. I just hate not getting this. I have been able to wield Cai since I was five; it should not be that hard to get this."

"Come" Veirella stood and pulled Gemma up onto her feet. "I do not think my ego can take another fail," she protested. "How about you stop thinking about it and just do? When we were kids, you could summon your power without thinking about it. Mostly because you wanted to prove that you were the best, you care what others think and how they perceive you, so focus on the opinion that matters the most." Veirella's idea may not work, but it was worth a try.

Gemma was the first girl to be named heir and kept the title after a son had arrived. Most expected her brother to be given the title. That was what every time a daughter came before a son, everyone thought that would happen. But her father did not take the title from her.

His council did not agree with his choice, and because they all had opinions, that for some reason they felt the need to express in her presence, Gemma felt she needed to prove something to them and everyone else who had something to say.

Veirella retrieved the ball. "I can do that." Gemma nodded at her, shaking her head a few times, then closed her eyes. Gemma stood there leveling her breathing for a few minutes, then she opened her eyes and nodded to Veirella signaling her to throw the ball.

Veirella threw it. Instead of moving out of the way preparing for the ball to come back, she stayed. Gemma needed to believe in herself, and so did Veirella. She wanted Gemma to see how much she believed in her and her abilities.

Light blue sparks began moving around her hands, then Gemma raised them to stop the ball, holding it up. The longest she managed to hold it was forty seconds Veirella counted.

But Gemma did not drop it, and Veirella kept counting. Then Gemma passed a minute, and then two; the ball moved around a little, she was losing her grip on it, but Gemma crossed three minutes before that happened.

Gemma dropped the ball and bent over, resting her weight on her knees. She was breathing hard and heavy, and there were beads of sweat forming on her forehead. Doing that would have drained what she had left.

Veirella grabbed her canteen and handed it to her. Gemma thanked her for it and moved to rest herself on by the wall. Veirella went with her. "That was your best attempt yet," she informed her, but Gemma did not respond. She was too busy downing her water to care. There was stardust in it and it would help her heal faster and give her some artificial strength while she recovered.

It tricked the body into thinking it had more Cai to use while her body created more. Gemma's breathing slowed as she finished her water. "I think it was, but I do not think I am in a position to go again," she answered after calming herself.

"You'll get there, I know you will." Gemma was too headstrong to let anything stop her from getting back to the top. " I believe in you." Veirella continued. "I believe in you too," she responded.

"And I wish you had a better mother. You may not want to admit that just yet, but I know what she thinks matters to you. She is different with your brother and sister and that is not fair to you." Gemma stiffened at Veirella's words, then sighed and dropped her shoulders.

"I cannot blame her. They are her children," Gemma answered. As much as she tried to brush it off, Veirella heard the pain in her voice. "But so are" Gemma shook her head, "she gave birth to me, but she is not my mother." Veirella's brows drew together. "What? How does that work?" she asked.

"They do not refer to the Celestial women as our blood mother's for nothing. They come and conceive us with mortal men and once they find women to marry the child is placed inside them. It is similar for Celestial men, but they find the man that will raise their child as their own. In some cases anyway. Most times the men are married and their wives do not know the child they carry is not theirs until after birth, same for men they are unaware that the child they are raising is not theirs until they learn they can wield." Gemma explained.

Of all the things Veirella thought Gemma would say, that was not one of them. She did not have a long list of choices to go off of, but that would have never made it.

"And I thought we could not get any weirder. But aside from your issues with your mother, you also have a temper, and frustration will only make things worse."

"What do you suggest?" she asked.

"Find balance with yourself, anger make people irrational, but optimism can make you naive. Your positive emotions will not always come out on top, but you can't let the negative ones be all you feel make them to coexist."

Veirella had been trying to do that herself, mediating her emotions if she thought too much about the bad things that have happened in her life she found it hard to get out of bed, but she could not just forget them and focus on the positives no matter how much she wanted to, so she off balanced it out by remembering all the happy memories she had, it was the only way she could function.

Based on how alike they were, it may work for Gemma. "That is not a bad idea, I will work on that but not today I am spent and I do not have to energy to push myself any further" Gemma threw her head back against the wall and sighed. Veirella stood, then took Gemma's outstretched hands to pull her up.

They went to leave the room when a portal opened before them. They moved back, not knowing what was on the other side. A moment passed, then Pax, Luka and the two boys Veirella saw leaving Genevieve's office came through. The portal closed behind them. "Get a medic," Pax told them, Veirella heard fear in his voice. He looked back at Luka, who was being held up by the other two boys.

Luka was barely a wake, Veirella looked him over then saw the one color she could never *escape. Red.* He was bleeding from his abdomen, his jacket was open with cuts on both sides and the light colored shirt he had on was soaked with his blood.

Gemma ran from the run, doing as he had asked. But Veirella she did not move, she watched as the two boys laid him down on the mat.

Her hands were covered in her blood, and she could not breathe. Lily was bleeding out. She was already dead, but the blood did not stop coming.

"Useless, if you were stronger, you could help him. But you are weak."

Stop, Veirella did not want to hear the voices, not now or not ever for that matter. She needed to do something, find a way to help him. She would not let him die too, not like that. Veirella looked around the room, looking for something to stop the bleeding. Her eyes landed on the towels. *You can do this,* she told herself, then ran to get a few and brought them to Luka.

Pax and the others were just standing there looking at him. Veirella dropped two of the four towels she grabbed and started pressing them into his wound.

"Stop!" Pax yelled. She jumped from how much how loud he got. Veirella looked over at him. Pax's eyes grew when he looked down at her hands, which she could feel Luka's blood on. "What?" she asked. Pax looked from her to where hands were again but said nothing.

The other two boys had similar expressions, "How are you doing that?" it was not Pax that asked her the question but the boy that had tried speaking to her that day.

Veirella did not know what they were referring to, and she did not get to ask. Luka started groaning. "What happened to him?" her question was directed at Pax. "We were scouting out this abandoned building, when—"

"—It was rigged with shatter booms and one of them went off and the shrapnel hit him." the curly haired boy cut Pax off and finished. Pax looked at him, brows raised.

Veirella was confused by his answer. She did not think something like that could do that type of damage. "A shatter boom did this?" she asked, voice slightly raised. Pax nodded at her, still looking at the boy. *That was a lie* they were lying. Because that was impossible.

Veirella felt her magic rising. It was strange because she was not calling on it. She could feel it moving through her body, going through her hands and in Luka. Veirella could feel the blood slowing down, but it did not stop. Luckily Gemma was fast. She returned moments later, and she was not alone. Following behind her was the girl that was there when Veirella fainted. If she remembered correctly, Scarlet was her name. She did not stop to ask questions about his injury.

She put her medical bag on the floor, opened it and pulled out a pair of gloves. They were green, not white like most physicians used. Veirella, Pax, and the others moved to give her space to work.

When Veirella stood, her vision got blurred. She tried shaking it off, but it did not work. The last thing she remembered was falling.

When Veirella opened her eyes, she was lying in her bed. She tried looking around, but it was too dark in the room to see anything. Veirella sat up but her head did not agree with her chioce to do so.

Veirella felt the left side of the bed move. She looked over to find Gemma sitting there, looking at her. Gemma snapped her fingers and the fae light's next to her bed came to life. The change burned Veirella's eyes; it took a moment before they adjusted. "I guess blood is not really your thing." Veirella scrunched her face up. "Not really, the sight of blood has never made be pass out before."

Made her forget how her lungs though. "Is Luka, okay?" she asked. It was the worse possible time to lose conscious. But there was not much Veirella could do about that. "He will be. His body already started healing itself, he will be out for a few days but he should be fine after that. A few stardust covered wraps, and it will be like it never happened," Gemma answered.

"I think something really bad is going on." Gemma looked at Veirella her face pulled together, "meaning?"

"Pax and that boy lied about how Luka got hurt." Gemma sighed, her shoulders dropping for a moment. "You think so too?" Veirella nodded. "I thought I was crazy for thinking that, but what he said does not match up with how Luka looks." Gemma continued.

"Yes, one of the other boys said Luka was hit with shrapnel from a shatter boom, that just does not seem physically possible, shatter booms shatter it is quite literally in the name, something like that cannot cause that type of damage." Veirella explained.

"Someone did that to him. From the way he is injured someone can to have cut him. But why are they covering it up?"

"It may have something to do with the assignment they were on," Gemma told her. "It could. The headmistress came here to check on Luka, which is normal, but then she took Pax, Cyrus and Griffin into his room and put up a sound barrier so I could not hear what they were talking about."

"I want to know what it is. I do not like being lied to," Veirella told her. Gemma looked at her, and a smile broke across the face. "Then let's go find out what it is" Veirella looked at her friend, her confusion shown on her face. "Asking them is not going to get us anywhere." They would just tell them another lie, to cover for the first.

"Then we don't ask, lets break into the headmistress's office and find out for ourselves." Veirella raised her hand to Gemma's forehead. "What are you doing?" Gemma asked as she removed her hand. "Checking to see if you are well, because if you have not fallen ill, then you have lost your mind," Veirella answered.

"We want answers they will not give them to us, so we need to go it ourselves, besides we will take anything, just read whatever we find. She will never know we were there." Gemma seemed to have her mind already made up and would do it ever if Veirella did not agree.

She was right, but that did not change the fact that breaking and entering was a crime and if they were caught, they could be expelled. "Okay, let's do it. You said Genevieve is talking to Pax and his friends, so her offices is empty at the moment, and I just so happen to have a have a copy crystal." Gemma raised a hand to her chess, and she looked like she was going to cry

.

"I can't believe I am getting you to do something bad" she whipping away a nonexistent tear. "I am so proud" Veirella rolled her eyes. She was being ridiculous. Veirella went to retrieve the crystal. It was on her desk in a black box. The base was a dark shade of blue, mixed with purple, and the terminations got lighter as it went up, till it got to the tips, which were clear.

"That is beautiful. How did you get it? They are so rare, especially the blues," Gemma asked. Veirella gave it to her and grabbed one of her sketchbooks from the bottom drawer. They were all still empty.

"It was a gift. I do not know who from. There was no name attached to it," she answered. "I have seen a few white ones, but never one this dark," Gemma told her. "We should do this quickly. We do not know how much time we have before she goes back to her office."

The chances of them getting caught were high, and as much as she wanted the truth, she did not like breaking rules; they were there for a reason they made order. Veirella always did what she was told, no matter what. She was obedient to a default, so this was not the most ideal situation for her to be in.

"*This is a bad idea, a very bad idea. But they lied, so this was justified. Right.*" She was doing her best to make what she was doing okay with her conscience. Getting to Genevieve's office would not be hard. Veirella knew she had a port key inside. "We can go directly into her office with one of the port keys in the hall" she told Gemma. Veirella went to leave her room, but Gemma stopped her.

"We do not need one of those paintings specifically to open a port key, any painting in the school will work" she informed her, then looked at the portrait of Veirella, it was the most recent painting of her and she was eight when it was done. It was a lot higher than the others they used to get around the school, but it could still work.

Veirella pulled the chair from her desk and pushed it over to the painting so they could stand on it. She was not short, and neither was Gemma. They both stood around five and eight, but the painting was at least six feet high.

The paintings they traveled through regularly were all eight inches from the ground.

Veirella opened the port key and pushed herself up the wall, then through. It was not the most comfortable position to be in, but she made it to the other side in one piece. The room was dark, the only light shining in was coming from the portal and the moonlight behind the desk. But it would be enough, it had to be.

Veirella moved towards the desk and moment's later Gemma came through the port key. With the crystal and the sketchbook in hand. "Now I understand why all the painting are so low, that was painful."

Gemma went over to Veirella and gave her the crystal, "What are your command words?" she asked. Copy crystals were unique to their owner once it absorbed her blood. It was hers. The only way someone else could use it was if they knew the command words.

"Give me Glory," Veirella said into the crystal, then placed it on top of the large stacks of files and watched as the blue at the base spread up to the tips, then done on to the folder.

"What can you tell me about that plant? The one I was sent," Gemma's smile faded, Veirella seemed to have that effect on others. "Greviger, it means greed or consumption. Back home they grind them into a power and use it to torcher prisoners. It is quite painful to be honesty, it comes from blood and it requires blood to survive, specifically our blood Celestial or anyone with stardust in them. If one of us bleeds somewhere, then die not long after, Greviger's grow from it." Gemma explained.

"You mean death? It comes from death," Gemma nodded. "Yes it does, one drop of blood from anyone with Celestial blood and it kills. When they kill, they can create more of themselves." She continued.

"But they are not only dangerous to people like us. If not dealt with, they can destroy entire environments, so they must be killed. Whoever sent that thing to you was sending a message," she tells her.

Veirella could not think of anyone that would want to hurt her other than the people who tried to kill her. But she did not know who they were, and that was terrifying.

"*The Headmistress is coming, out the door she goes*" Veirella heard the voice in her head, it was different to the others, it was rare that she heard it at all. It did not come from her, that much she could tell, Genevieve was still on the top floor they needed to leave before she tried opening the port key to her office and considering they were inside it and the key Veirella made was open Genevieve could not get one open.

"We need to go. She is coming back." Gemma looked at Veirella brows raised. "How do you know that?" Veirella reached for the crystal. The blue light made it halfway down the stack and was still going, but they did not have time to wait for it to be done.

"Glory has been found" she told it and the glow faded. "That is even worse than the last one."

"We need to go. You can make fun of my coding later," Veirella told her, then they ran back to the glowing green vortex.

"*All most there*" an image of Genevieve wielding flashed through her mind. She was getting ready to open the key. Veirella jumped through, falling on the floor of her bedroom. She forgot that it was different on the other side. Veirella rolled her body to the side so Gemma would not land on her. She came through falling on her back protecting the crystal from break.

It was hard to move, but Veirella pushed herself to close the portal. Then another image of Genevieve flashed in her mind. She opened the key seconds after Veirella closed hers.

Then she fell back and signed in relief. Gemma stood and helped Veirella up, "I hope us breaking into the headmistress's office was worth it." Gemma smiled at her, then gave her the crystal. They went to her bed, Gemma put down the sketchbook and Veirella placed the crystal atop it.

Then she repeated the words to activate it. "Do you think there is something there, and we did not just steal private student information?"

Veirella asked her friend she was trying to be okay with what they did. It was a violation, and she hoped there was something there.

"Well, most of this probably has something to do with the assignments that they are given, so either way, this is private student information," Gemma stated. Veirella moved to sit on her bed next to her and watched the blue glow from the crystal going down the pages.

"What do you think we will find?" Gemma asked, breaking the silence that had fallen over them. Veirella shrugged "I do not know." She just hoped it was nothing too bad. Pax and his friend lied, but people lied for many reasons. It did not always need to be something bad for them to do so. Veirella did not know how their assignments worked, maybe they could not share the information.

"I think it's finished" Veirella looked over at Gemma then at the fading light. Gemma picked it up and gave it to her. Veirella said the second command, then got off the bed and brought it back to the box it lived in.

"Would you like to do the honors?" Gemma asked her, waiting to open the book that was newly filled with information they should not have.

"You can do it. I still need to figure out what this is." Veirella answered, then showed Gemma the flower bud behind her. Gemma nodded, then opened it and began reading. Veirella sat and did the same.

A few hours had passed and Veirella still did not find what she was looking for. The book was not small by any means. She was nowhere close to being halfway through. Her eyes got heavier the more she read. The words were small, so it was harder to read.

"What the hell" Veirella turned to Gemma, hearing her speak for the first time in hours. "What? Did you find something?" she asked, standing up and going to her.

"Yes" she answered. Veirella could hear the fear in her shaken voice. "People are dying. Wielders like us," Veirella dropped onto the bed, not knowing what to say or how to feel. "How? Is someone killing them?" Veirella managed to get the words out, without her voice breaking. "No, not—not quite. Their magic killed them."

Nine Years Before

"What colors should I use?"

"Blue, green, and white. Those colors look the best. Blue is your color of choice, green us, and white for what you have on the inside."

"Insides are not white, they are red; Aspen's insides are always coming out; he calls it blood. It happens when he fights. It looks like it hurts. I do not think I want to fight. I do not want to be in pain."

"Then you do not need to fight. We can protect you, keep you safe, daughter of daughter. It is what your mother would want us to do."

"My mother has big men called guards to protect me."

"Not that mother the other one the one in the sky"

Veirella laughed at what the plants said she always did when they said something funny. Like her having another mother, that was not true. She heard the story of how beautiful and painful her birth was from her mother many times.

Veirella was born on a rare day, known as the Aurora Phase. A day that only comes around every three millennia or so. The sky was purple, blue and white, and the stars were the brightest they had ever been. And the moon shined down on her the moment she entered the world. Everything went silence listen to her beautiful cries.

"The Goddess is not just my mother. She is the mother of everything. She created all of it," *she told them.*

Veirella was in the throne room which was in the middle of the palace, far from the world outside she did not always know where the plants, trees or flowers were when they spoke to her, sometimes they were by her window or freshly cut from the garden, placed in the vases all over the place.

But the throne room did not have any flowers. All the old ones had been removed earlier that day and would not be replaced, until late evening.

And the room did not have windows to prevent people from hurting her family. The only form of light in the room came from the big glass above where she could see the sky and sometimes the sun, when it passed over. So the origins of the voices were unknown.

"What color should I start with?" *she asked them, when she was alone Veirella spoke to the aloud, the told her she was never allowed to do it when others were around, for other's would think her sick if she was talking to something no one else could hear.*

"White." *They answered.*

Veirella took the biggest brush she had, which was still small in comparison to the ones they used to paint the walls, and her white jar of paint, then climbed up to the head of her father's throne. And began covering the wall in white paint, forming the flower she intended to paint.

Veirella enjoyed painting flowers. It did not matter what type they were; she did them all. Her favor to do were Anemone's. There were so many different species in so many different colors she rarely ever had to paint with the same colors twice. In some paintings, she could use up to seven colors to finish one, but this time she wanted to see what she could do with only three.

Veirella did not come up with the idea on her own. She saw Aspen paint a portrait of their mother using only red, three different shades of the color. Veirella thought it was a wonderful idea after seeing the how amazing it turned out. Their mother thought so too. She called it magnificent.

And Veirella wanted to do something similar, but she wanted to make it her own, she did not like painting people or sketching them, nature on the other hand she was quite good at, it became her medium of choice after seeing how very little color was added to the drawing in books of the natural world around her.

Because the world was constantly changing, she wanted to capture what it looked like in the present because it would look different in the future, for better or worse.

It was her way of making up for not being able to see what the world looked like before her, and she wanted those who would come after she was gone to see how beautiful her world was. The doors behind her were pushed open. It was probably her mother coming to look for her.

"We will set sail for Dragia in four days' make the arrangements. It is imperative that this treaty signed" That voice belonged to her father.

Veirella turned to see him. She smiled, looking down at him. He was finally home. But it faded when she remembered the words he spoke moments ago. He would not be staying; he opened his mouth to say something else.

But stopped when he saw her. His eyes grow in size seeing where she was, then they returned to normal in a matter of seconds.

"Veirella darling, what are you doing up there?" he asked there was panic and surprise present in his voice but Veirella did not notice either, she just thought he was mad at her for messing on the walls when he had an entire room built for her to do whatever she liked.

"I was painting you flowers, so you would have something pretty to look at when you came home," she explained.

One of the men got close to his ear and said something Veirella was too far away to hear. "Out all of you." He ordered.

"I am going to have a word with my daughter. We will meet in my study at nightfall." He told. As all seven men left the room one after the other, they bowed, but her father's eyes never looked away from her. Veirella did not speak until the door was closed after the last one was gone.

"Would you like me to come down?" she asked moving, but he raised his hands, stopping her. "No, I will get you down. Just stay where you are." He instructed. From where he was standing, Veirella was far above him, but then he walked up the stairs of the dais and he was as tall as the throne itself. He lifted her up and off the head of the throne, then seated himself in it and sat her atop his leg.

"Veirella why would you do something like this?" he asked. Veirella dropped her head. She was in trouble and would rather not look at him while he scolded her for her wrong doings.

"I am sorry, I should have asked before making a mess of the wall" she answered, her voice as small as she felt. She heard him make a sound, then he took the brush that was now covered in white paint and the jar from her and place them on her mother's throne next to his.

He then placed his finger beneath her face and raised it, so Veirella was looking at him. "This is not about the wall. Paint where every you like, just please do not climb anything to do some. My heart almost gave out seeing you up there," she nodded to him in response.

"What even gave you the idea to do something like this?"

Veirella smiled again at his question, "it was the plants idea, they said you would think of me every time you entered this room" she answered her voice filled with glee, but her father did not smile or laugh at her words, his face grew tight well tighter than it already was that is.

"Right, and do these plants tell you to do dangerous things regularly?" he asked.

"No, mostly they give me ideas of things to paint, considering I do not go outside much and when I do, I mostly play with the birds." She informed him.

He nodded, taking in every word she said.

"Okay, but remember not to let anyone or anything. People, plants and animals, all groups included, tell you what to do or make you do something you do not want to. And if they try, you tell me or your mother understood?"

"Yes, understood," Veirella answered, shocking her head for emphasis.

"Now I will be home for the next few days, so what does my little girl what to do?" her father asked.

Veirella's smile grew in size and so did her eyes, she waited for him to have some time for them to spend together, and she made a list for when the day came.

"There is some much and so little time." He laughed

"Well then, we shall do and many as we can then,"

"Yes, we shall."

Rising Sun

Veirella

Veirella was trying her best to keep herself together. Her magic already scared her and, as much as she tried to deny that, it was still the truth. And that same magic could now kill her. Veirella needed to figure out if this was some form of sicken that only affected those with Celestial ties or someone was doing it.

From what she was reading, it was mostly affecting the Wielders of the second generation, the Xiakaries they have been dying on all the continents, their power suddenly imploding on them.

From what Genevieve's as documented said they were not overusing their Cai, and in some cases, they only used it once before dying, and others not at all. "How is that even possible, I understand dying from overuse but been kill for just using it" Veirella said to Gemma "there as to be more to it, a sickness or something there has to be an explanation," she continued. "And why is it only effecting Xiakaries and Nievarians?" that was the strangest part of all of it.

They needed answers, but considering they stole the files from the Headmistress it was unlikely she would be of any help. There was a higher chance they got expelled. Veirella was willing to risk that it would mean she got to go home, but she would not put Gemma in that position. Veirella wanted answers, just not bad enough to get her friend in trouble.

They had two working theories, one someone was doing it. If there was an illness designed specifically to kill those with Celicai in their blood, more people would die before a cure could be created. Veirella was more convinced that there was a person behind it. Because from what she read, no Celerian's had been killed yet, and they had the most amount of Celicai out of all three groups. It would make them the most affected. If it was a person, they would want to go after those with weaker magic and built their way up.

Xiakaries had Celestial blood, but it was for less potent than what Celerian's had. They were more mortal, which made them more valuable to an attack on their bodies. But that theory could be questioned because of the Nievarian factor. They did not have Celicai. They were blessed, so they had stardust into their blood.

Veirella spent most of her morning in the library. She did not know what to look for exactly, so she started with the details. Veirella focused on Luka, if she could find something on what hurt him, it could lead her somewhere. Veirella closed her eyes and tried thinking about what she could remember from that night.

Luka was bleeding. He was on the floor in pain, his clothes were cut through same as his wound. He had on his Keives. That was it, Veirella opened her eyes and smiled to herself. Someone cut through his clothes, and there was only one type of metal that could cut through the fabric.

Most swords were made from Iron or steel, and neither were strong enough to cut through Keif, one of the few metal's that could was Inconel, and very few ever chose to forge weapons with it not only was it hard to melt it was expensive, because of how difficult it was to work with and mine for. And unlike other metals, in could only be found in one place Fianorea.

Veirella needed to look for a sword made from it. Based on the size of Luka's wound it could not be anything smaller. Which should be easy because there were very few willing to work with it.

First, she search through the blacksmiths who worked with the metal; there were only three. One lost his hand, making a short blade. Then he died of an infection. The second only made daggers and arrowheads. So it had to be the third Sir Killian Tarrenbrook. He was one of the most renowned blacksmiths of his time, a weapon forged by his hands was coveted by all, but he turned away most who requested something crafted by him. He used Inconel to make a blade for his son; named death singer.

His son killed many in the war of Cecaila before falling himself, the sword had changed owners of the centuries but then it went missing two hundred years ago. Then Veirella looked through the blacksmith logs to track the history of the sword, but there was nothing. But it could have been recorded elsewhere. Astro Academy was the neutral ground for the continents. The school's library would have the most up to date information about everything.

And if there was something not in the book's and there was a chance there was another weapon out there that could do the same thing Veirella could ask Aspen about it, as heir he had control over trades and needed to sign off on everything before it left or entered Fianorea, she would write him a letter when she got back to her room. Veirella wanted to do more research, but she was interrupted by Gemma. "Have you found anything?" They both agreed Gemma should go to class and Veirella would go to the library to see what she could find.

Well, it was more Veirella told her what to do. Gemma was looking for an excuse not to go to her combat class. They had assessments coming it two weeks and were given a break from their other classes to prepare for them. From what Gemma told her, she was doing better, just not by much.

Veirella showed her what she found. They had a lead of sorts, it had less to do with the dead wielders and more to do with Luka, but Veirella thought they were connected some.

"I just need to see if there are any mention of the sword, but fifteen hundred years is a long time." Veirella informed her, Gemma looked down at the book and nodded.

"Well, you can do that later. It is time for lunch," Veirella tried protesting against going with her. She ate breakfast, so she was not mood for food. "I will not take no for an answer. I would like to know what is happening as much as you do, but I will not let this consume you." Gemma tells her.

"Where I would usually fight you on this, I do not have the energy to do so today." Gemma smiled at her response, then her browse knitted together "Are you okay?"

"Well, since I woke up it has felt like something has been stabbing me in the stomach and my headache is back," Veirella answered. "Well, I am sorry you feel that way, but I guess you feeling like shit is beneficial to me" Veirella tilted her head to the side not knowing how to respond to that.

"Believe me, I came in here prepared to drag you there myself, but thank you for not feeling well so that I did not need to do that." Veirella tried hiding the smile that was forming on her face, tried and failed, "you would not."

"Oh, I would, and if you are ever interested in testing me, I am willing to drag you down the halls with everyone watching. Remember no isolation, and after what you did on bonfire night the only way I am leaving you out of my sight is if we are so far away from school you need me to get back." Gemma told her, seemed like she was both making a promise and threating he r.

"Well, I will be sure to remember that. One extreme sibling is enough for me." Veirella told her. "Well, best friend by fate, and your sister is my choice, but either way, you are stuck with me for life." Gemma answered as she made her way to the door. "Then it shall be a wonderful life."

It did not take them long to make their way to the study hall, which was not where Veirella thought they were going, but she did not question it, the less people around the better. "I thought this was better than throwing you into a crowded room of students." Gemma explained as they made their way into the massive room.

Everything was made of a grayish red wood Veirella could not place. The overhead lights were low and the few students who were in the room were sitting with books before them. They did not need them, the massive glass above them provided enough light. That every corner of the room was brightly lit.

Gemma went to one of the tables by the lower windows, which had three plates covered with cloches on it. Veirella looked over at Gemma as they moved into the chairs sitting opposite each other.

"I wanted to tell you before she came, I invited someone to have lunch with us. I hope that is okay," Gemma told her. Gemma watched Veirella waiting to see how she would react. Veirella did not mind having someone else around but she would have liked the chance to prepare for it, knowing a few weeks in advance would have been very helpful, but knowing herself she would have found something to do at that exact time so she would not need to be there. Gemma ambushing her may be the only why Veirella would mean anyone else.

"I have no problem with it; I would love to meet some of your other friends." Gemma sighed, then smiled at her. "Okay, she really wants to meet you as well." Veirella smile widened. She was unaware Gemma talked about her with her other friends. Veirella did not even know any of their names. Veirella was sure that was not a good thing.

It took a while for Gemma's friend arrived. She wore the same uniform as Veirella and Gemma. She had warm brown skin and loose curls that brushed against her shoulders when she walked. And she had a stack of books in her hands that she placed on the table next to the bowl that was for hers. Veirella saw it was soup when Gemma removed the cover. After she got sick of waiting.

"Sorry to keep you waiting, Madam Thora took so long to finish up; I thought we could never get to leave," she explained. "No need to worry, we have not been here long," Veirella assured her. She did not know how long they had waited, but it was long enough for Gemma to finish her soup.

"Time for introductions, Veirella this is Ivy, Ivy considering you are Forian, you already know who Veirella is." Gemma stated. "It is an honor, my lady," she said to her, then she lowered her head. "Same and you can call be Veirella." she told her. They were not at home, so formalities felt unnecessary. "What year are you?" Veirella asked, she looked a little older than them.

"Second year, I am a late bloomer. My abilities did not come to me until I was thirteen; I was lucky they did one more year, and I would have been too old to attend the Academy." Veirella found that to strange because she was three years past that age so Gemma. "What do you mean? We started this year and we are most definitely not thirteen." She asked.

"For a Xiakaries and Nievar's to be accepted here they must be tested on their Celicai level and how compatible you are with stardust if you fail the test, you do not get in, they take some of your blood mix it with stardust and cael root to see were you land. There are three colors: red, green and white. Red is an automatic rejection, green you get in, but it is probationary, and white is your acceptance," Ivy explained.

"Why is it like that? Why is it different for you?" It did not seem fair that one group could go to the school without question while the others were tested. "The second and third Asphies, are not like the first, Celerian's can take Stardust whether or not their abilities have presented.

But the others cannot, if someone without enough Celicai or stardust present within them to take, they will lose themselves. So they do the test to ensure that we can handle it without consequence. It can fade within us on like you, if we start consuming it regularly it stops the deterioration or slows it down," she continued.

"And after fourteen, it starts fading." Ivy nodded in response. "Okay, we can talk about the workings of our magic system some other time; we do not have much time left, so let's get to why we are actually," Gemma exclaimed; Veirella looked at her, brows raised. "What do you mean" she turned to Gemma. "Ivy here knows what's going on" of course she was a second year, meaning she left the Academy on assignment just like Pax and Luka did.

"Not exactly, my assignment has nothing to do with death—" Ivy stops herself before continuing "well it does, I am researching a dying forest on Dragia. Which is not the point, the second year's talk, and one of the boys assigned on Ataria said something about a Xiakary girl exploding, only thing left of her were bones," Ivy told them.

That was something not much, but she would work with whatever she could get. "Is that all?" Gemma asked. Ivy looked at her and nodded. The clock on the wall chimed. The lunch hour was over. "Sorry I could not help more, but if I learn anything else, I will let you know. See you around Gemma. Princess." Ivy told them, then stood and grabbed her books and left.

"Can what she said help us?" Gemma asked once she was out the door, "it could, there is also a chance she ate some buony berries." Veirella answered. "What are buony berries?" Gemma asked, "it is what they use to make booms and anything you want to explode, they look identical to blueberries just a little darker. If you have never seen both, you would not notice they were different and they are also sweater." Veirella explained, it was not uncommon for someone who did not live on the continent to know what it was and ate it by mistake.

"So, we have nothing" Gemma sighed and sat back in her seat. "It is not nothing, things are not definite. If we do not consider all possibilities, we are likely to make mistakes." Veirella told her.

"You should probably go, you don't want to be late for your next training session" Veirella told her, "yes because going to combat training is more interesting than finding out why people like us are dying and looking for the person who tried to kill our friend, yes that is by far a better option."

Veirella could hear the sarcasm in her voice. "Think of it this way if you learn how to shield you can protect us, and what happened to Luka won't happen to us. And by the time you are finished with this class, you will be able to kick ass."

Gemma thought about it for a moment before responding. "You're not wrong"

"And in order for you to do that you need to go to training" Gemma sighed in response, then stood. "Sometimes I do really hate how logical you are," she told her.

"I am happy to be your voice of reason" Veirella proclaimed, laying a hand on her shoulder, "and I both love and hate you for it"

They both left the room and opened port keys, Gemma to the training room and Veirella back to the court. The pain in her lower abdomen became more intense and constant as the hours passed, she needed to finish going through the book to find out what the flower bud was but she could not see through the pain to focus, so she took a bath and got into bed.

Blooming Flower

Veirella

Veirella was pulled awake by the pain in her body. Somehow it manage to get worse through the night, and she could no longer bear it. Veirella tried sitting up by the pain was too much. She could not move, so she called for Willow. Moments later the Nyx appeared in her room wide-eyed.

"What is it? Are you hurt?" she asked frantically, looking over her for injuries. But she would find nothing, because what Veirella felt was inside. Willow snapped her fingers, and the fae light came to life. The room brightened, and she saw Veirella. Laying in her bed, curled into a ball.

"It hurt, why...why does it hurt so much?" She never felt pain like that before, like she swallowed a knife, and it was trying to cut its way out of her. The panic in Willow's eyes disappeared, then she walked over and sat next to Veirella, on the bed.

"Have you never bled before?" She asked, Veirella contorted in both pain and confusion. "What are talking about?" She asked. "Did your mother not have this conversation with?" Willow asked as she made her why into the bathing room. "What conversation? What is happening to me? Is this death because it feels like I am being ripped apart from the inside." Veirella asked.

Willow returned a moment later and helped her out of bed, into the bath, helped her out of her nightdress, which she hid before Veirella saw it. Then helped her into the bath. "The warmth should help with the pain."

A knock came at the door, and Willow when to see who it was. A second later, Gemma entered. She smiled at her, then got down and hugged her.

"You blossomed. I am so happy for you." Veirella did not understand what was happening. She was in pain and Gemma thought it was a good thing. "Why is this a good thing? It hurts so much." Veirella had tears in her eyes. Then Gemma pulled away and looked at her.

"Your first bled is a major part of womanhood, did your mother not tell you any of this?" Gemma's brows rose. *Womanhood I don't remember how to be a person much less a woman,* Veirella thought to her to herself. "The last time I had a conversation with my mother, I was eight and she was sending me away. So whatever this is, no she did not explain it to me," Veirella told her.

Gemma went to say something, but Veirella stopped her. "You know what, if it is so important that I have this conversation with my mother, then she needs to be here. I want my mother. Someone go get my mother and bring her here so she can tell me what is wrong with me." She told Gemma.

"Ella—" Veirella. "I want my mother; someone just please get me my mama" then the tears finally fell. Gemma got up and left the room. Veirella hoped she would do as she asked, but a moment later, she was back at her side.

Veirella did not look in her direction. She focused on the night sky. She watched as the clouds moved and the moon began shining through. Veirella did not know how late or early it was. Her inability to understand time was just another thing that was wrong with her mind.

"Veirella" she knew that voice. She heard it so many times it she could pick it out in the dark, she would still find her mother. "Mama," she looked over at the entrance of her bathing room just in time to see her mother walk through it. She looked right at her and smiled; her mother was still wearing her nightdress covered with a robe to match.

Her mother looked at Gemma, smiled then went to Veirella. Gemma stood squeezed her arm, then left. "Mama, something is wrong with me. There is blood in the water." Veirella's voice broke as she spoke.

"My sweet girl, there is nothing wrong with you." She laid her hand on her cheek and caressed it. "This is a very normal part of growing up. I am sorry I never got to explain any of this to you."

"What is happening to me?" Veirella asked. Her mother moved away from the bath and retrieved her robe. "Come, let us get you into bed." Veirella stood and got out of the bath, then she pulled the robe around her. She walked Veirella into the room, her bedding was different.

Her mother helped her get dressed, then her mother gave her a cloth. "This goes in your undergarments, so you do not make a miss of your clothes," she explained. Veirella laid the cloth in place then, her mother helped her get into bed.

There was a tray next to her bed with a white pot and a matching cup next to it. Her mother poured her a cup, then added four drops of an amber liquid in, then handed it to her. "This will help with the pain, and if you take it regularly, it will stop this from happening, if that is what you want."

She explained. Veirella looked at her sideways. Why would she want this to happen again? The pain was not as intense, but it was still there.

"What is it?" Veirella asked as she sipped on the tea. "It is tonic, designed to stop the menstrual process, and pregnancy which at your current age that second part does not really apply to you." Her mother explained, "why did you not tell me this would happen?"

Her mother raised her hand to her face, then slid it down to her chin. "Because you were eight." Her mother's face fell, remembering the last conversation they had before Veirella left home. "I thought I had years until it was time for this particular conversation. I did not have it with Iris until she was twelve. That was when I planned on doing it with you," she answered.

Veirella regretted how she acted in the weeks before she left for Ryin. She thought about it for months after and still thinking about it even now. “I am sorry. I should have said that to you a long time ago,” Veirella told her. Her mother looked confused. “What on the Goddess are sorry for?” She asked. Veirella looked away, unable to look at her, “for the way I was in those years away. I should have been more understanding, and I never should have ignored your letters.” Veirella answered. She could feel the tears building inside.

“Hey” her mother’s voice was soft and warm. Veirella wished she could wrap herself in it. She looked at her, her mother’s eyes mirrored her own. “You have nothing to apologize for. If anything, I should be the one apologizing. For more things than I can list at the moment, but most of all, for sending you away when you did not to go. My little miracle.” She continued, a tear rolling down her left cheek.

“I love you. Now get some sleep. When you come home, we can have this conversation fully, I promise.” Veirella nodded, then gave her the cup. She put back on the tray. “Can you say until I fall asleep?” Veirella asked as she went to stand. “Of course I can.”

Veirella stayed in bed for the next week. She wondered when the pain and the blood would stop; she hated every second of it. Willow and Gemma answered all the questions she asked, from how long it would last, which was between three and seven days. For her, it was four. Time was lost to her, but Veirella counted those days. The other days, she was too exhausted to get out of bed.

Which, according to Gemma was normal. Veirella wanted her mother to be the one answering her questions, but from the letter she left by her bed, she was busy with something at home.

When Veirella finally found the energy to get out of bed, she got dressed in her uniform; she was growing comfortable in. Veirella did not know if she was required to wear it, considering she did not attend classes, but she wanted so she would. Willow appeared before her bed as Veirella was pulling her shoe on. She looking down at Veirella's empty bed, then spun around to look for her.

"I guess you were not expecting me to be up yet?" she asked. "No not really. You do not usually get out of bed before nine on the days I do not come and it is—" she looked over at the wooden clock on the wall next the door "—seven thirty in the morning." Willow answered.

Veirella turned in to look at the mirror and began taking down the three braids Willow did for her after washing it the night before. "Well, I have being in bed for several days. I think I am all full-on sleep. Plus, I have things to do" Willow walked up behind her and Veirella dropped her hands, letting her finish. "Like what? It is not as if they can give you anything to do here." She stated as she pulled all of Veirella's hair into one, then tied it in place with a black band, then braiding it and tying it off with a smaller ban d.

"I know, but I still need to do some research for my assignment." Veirella also needed to do research on Celicai. It was a part of her, and she still knew very little about it. Everything had strength's and weakness's, if she could figure out what they were, maybe it would lead to what how the wielder's were dying.

"You and your books. I think you spend more time with them than you do, your friend or friends, if we count the two that are never here." Willow said to her. As she went over to make her bed. "I spend a lot of time with Gemma, and if she wins her fighting thing tomorrow, we can spend the whole week doing nothing. And as for Luka and Pax, I do not know what I would do with either. I know very little about boys." Veirella answered.

Willow looked over at her as she removed the pillows to fluff them. Veirella's eyes met hers. She shook her head and left the room. She could deal with Willow's judgement of how Veirella spent her time later. But now she needed food. Veirella did not remember the last time she felt hunger, but she had not eaten anything in almost a week, and tea and soup provided little sustenance.

When she reached the kitchenet, there was fruit on the table. Veirella ate some grapes and the reddish pink thing called a strawberry. It was quite sweet and was quickly becoming her favorite. Once she was finished, Veirella started making her way out, but stopped next to the hall that led to the training room. Pax or Luka was in there, and by the sounds it was Luka.

Veirella went down the hall, then slid the door open. Luka in the center of the room, throwing punches as a bag. With each hit ge groaned, the bag dented moving back with ever hit he took. The last one burnt a hole in it and the white grains started falling out, "I am sorry for who every has gotten you this riled out." There was so much anger and frustration behind his punches they had to be directed.

He looked back at her and some of the tension in the body faded. "Hard to direct my anger when I have no one to give it to." There was pain in his voice. Veirella went into the room and stopped at the edge of the mat. "So the bag gets it?" he nodded. "So the bag gets it."

She kicked her shoes off and stepped on to the mat. Luka's left brow rose as he watched her. "What are you doing?" he asked, his eyes following her to the other side of the mat, that was free of grain. "It is better to have someone to spare with." She told him. "I will not spare with you, not when I am like this." The last time Veirella was on a training mat with someone else since she was ten. Helping Gemma with her magic did not count, that was a one-sided encounter.

"You think you can hurt me? I was trained my one of the most amazing fighters of this era." She informed him. There were not many that could hold their own with Elizabeth Nightwell. She was not in the military but she over saw most of their Ryin's.

It had been six years since Veirella worked with her and just as long since she used any of what she learned. "You really want to do this?" Luka asked, moving towards her. Veirella shrugged. "Why not? You did promise to help me. So help me, and maybe I can also help you." She told him.

"Okay." the side of his mouth move an inch, before he hardened his face but Veirella could tell he was fighting a smile. Luka took up an offensive stans and Veirella a defensive one, she was good at both. She could attack if she needed to, but she was not the attack first type. Luka nodded at her and Veirella returned it.

Then he threw in her direction. It was not a punch, his hand was open. He was not really trying to fight her. Veirella grabbed his arm, pulled it over her head, twisted her body into his and kicked his foot out from beneath him, and he fell to the floor, but before that happened, he wrapped his other arm around her pulling her down with him.

Veirella landed on him. She saw his face scrunch up and pulled herself up. "Sorry, are you okay?" she asked, looking done at his covered abdomen. "Yeah, all healing up, but the pain still lingers." He sat up and she sat back, folding her legs beneath her.

"How did you get hurt?" he was unconscious most of the time he was on the ground, so there was a chance he did not hear what the boy told her. "We were hunting. I found this girl, I think she was hurt it was hard to tell. Then she screamed, next thing I was on the floor in pain. That is all I remember." Veirella nodded. No shatter boom, so there was more going on. "What happened to the girl?"

"She died. Whatever was wrong with her, it killed her." Luka answered Veirella though she was probably sick. Not every region on the continents had access to proper medicine. "How?" Veirella asked. It would tell her where he was. Some sickness developed in some regions and were specific to them.

Luka looked down, his shoulders dropping along with his head. "I have no idea. On second she was their telling me she was in pain, the next she was dead, cuts all over." Veirella's eyes widened, but she pulled herself together before he could see. *Air Wielder* she thought, it had to be. Whatever happened to her affected Luka in the process. *So not a sword.*

Luka shook his head as if trying to not see it. That was a feeling she understood well. "I am so—" Veirella did not get to finish was she was saying because a bird came crashing through the window. Veirella jumped to her feet, running for the creature. She was careful not to step on any glass. She picked up the little blackbird. It had a piece of glass in its neck. Veirella gently pulled it.

"Here" she looked over and Luka, who holding out a towel to her, "Thank you" she took it and wrapped it around the bird, stopping the blood from running. "It's okay little one, you're going to be okay" it felt like a lie, there was very little chance there was someone in the school who could help it and even if there was by the time they got help the bird would be died.

Veirella held it in her arms as it struggled to keep its eyes open. Luka started cleaning up the broken glass, but she paid no attention to him. "Is it going to be, okay?" he asked. Veirella shock her head, but he was turned away from her. A tear ran down her face, then her eyes glowed. A few seconds later the bird flew from her hands. It went up, and she went down.

"Veirella, Veirella" the voice calling out to her was panic ridden. She slowly opened her eyes, and Luka was standing about her. Wide eyed and his chest moving faster than was normal. "Mm" was all the sound she could get out as she pushed herself into a sitting position with Luka's help.

Her head was throbbing, and she could feel every pulse in her eyes. "Gods, are you okay? I was just about to call for someone," he asked. Luka was still holding onto her. "What happened?" Veirella raised her hand to her temple and rubbed it, hoping it would help the throbbing pass.

"I was just about to ask you the saw question. One second you were talking, the next I heard you hit the ground, and that bird flew out the window." Veirella looked over at the window where the creature had broken through. It was strange she could have sworn he was going to die but flew away no problem. Veirella thought she was imagining things. But there was blood on the floor.

"How long have I been out?" Veirella moved to stand, and Luka helped her up. "About five minutes or so" he answered. She looked up at him and his eyes were still roaming over her. "I guess my aversion to blood is getting worse. First you and now a bird," she told him, Veirella attempted to laugh, but the movement did not help with her head.

"Is this a regular occurrence, passing out at the sight of blood?" Veirella shock her head. Yet another bad idea. "No, happened when I was helping stop your bleeding. It also happened when I wielded that time in Genevieve's office, and now with that bird." She informed him.

Luka looked away from her to the broken glass on the floor then back down at her. Veirella could tell he was thinking about something, and it somehow involved her. "Were you wielding all three times or just when you were with the headmistress?" He asked.

"Just when I was with the headmistress" Luka intended to say something, but she stopped him. "Okay, thank for caring, but I need to get to the greenhouse. I may not have a normal class schedule, but I still need to be there on time." A lie, she was a liar now.

She stepped around him and retrieved her shoes; Veirella pulled them on, then made her way out the door. Before she disappeared, Luka called after her. Veirella stopped and looked back at him.

"Drink water just to rule out dehydration"

"I will."

Dying Will

Anastasia

Where the hell is Amaya? Anastasia thought. There were two teams left before them, and if she did not show up by the time they needed to get on the mat, they would need to forfeit their place.

"Where is she?" Anastasia whispered to Isa. She shrugged. "Last time I saw her was at dinner." Half the school was in attendance, and she let Pax kick her ass for three days to be able to hold her own in assessment, or long enough to earn some points.

Considering she was barely getting anywhere with wielding. Anastasia needed this to happen. The last time she was off school grounds was the day she came. And that was months ago. First years were not allowed to leave.

But there were special occasions like assessment's. There was one every three months to evaluate the student's progress, so she would get another chance to go out, but that would be after Corviac. Anastasia had never been to one, only heard about it from Julia from her time at the Academy. It was once a year where people from all four continents came together in celebration of the winter solstice.

Anastasia looked over at the platform just in time to see Neal get thrown off. He was not moving, there was a fifty fifty chance he was dead. His team still had a chance if they could get two of the others off before they got one more, but then Kol was thrown off, and they were out. The third member of their team piper, a tall blond fire wielder, appeared under the platform. She walked off towards the bench, not even stopping to see if the others were okay.

The next team went up Anastasia only knew one of them, Lola. She wanted to knock the grin off her face. Anastasia wanted her to stay on just for that reason only. They went beneath the platform and disappeared; Anastasia looked around the room, seeing if Amaya finally showed up, but no such luck. Then she looked over at the stands where she spotted Veirella. She was sitting between Luka and Pax.

Veirella saw her looking, then smiled and waved, Anastasia tilted her head, smiled and waved back. If her teammate did not show then she would find another one. She was a part of the school and was allowed to participate. She turned to Isa. "I'll be right back" She walked off before she could responded. Anastasia moved past the other two teams and made her way to the stands. "Hey just remember, go on defense. All you need to do is stay on, get some point on the board." Pax reminded her. She nodded at him, then turned to Veirella.

"I needed a favor" Veirella at both boys on either side of her, but they were looking at her. "Me?" She asked, her face scrunching up. Anastasia nodded. "You." She answered, "the other member of my team is not here and if we do not have three people, we are going to need to forfeit."

"Are you sure I can help? I am not exactly in this class." Anastasia nodded. "This is a mandatory class for first years. So, even though you are not taking it, you are allowed to partake," Anastasia informed her. "Okay."

"Are you sure about this, Ella?" Pax asked.

"Yeah, I think so" she nodded, then stood up. Anastasia went back to Isa and Veirella followed. "Isa, Veirella, Isa" they looked at each other. Isa smiled and Veirella nodded. It was a good then Veirella was already wearing keives, because they were up next and they did not have time for her to change. "What exactly are we doing?" Veirella asked. "The team that stays up on the platform the longest gets the most points. Each person you knock off is five points. The team with the most points at the end wins," Anastasia explained.

"Win what?"

"A day pass to leave the school. Go into the town." Veirella nodded "okay." The team before them did not last. All three of them were knocked off within seconds. The girls went under the platform, then they were pulled to the top. Rowen appeared on the mat between them. "Quick reminder of how this works," he looked to Veirella. "Two out of three, whichever team gets two of the others off first, wins and faces the next team. If you are the last team standing you win, but if you do not have the highest points, then you go up against the team that does. Got it" They all nod. Then he was gone.

The others attacked first; Anastasia was depending on Amaya being there. Both her and Isa could wield well, but that was no longer an option, so they had to work with what they had. Lola tried blowing them back with air, but Isa blocked her with ice. It shattered, and she threw the pieces back at them. Anastasia wanted to go for Lola, but there was a fire wielder on her team, so taking him out was first priority.

While Isa's ice storm distracted them, Anastasia ran towards her and shoved her off. She jumped back before their earth wielder Ivy could hit her with a blast. Anastasia switched places with Veirella so she was standing before Lola.

Ivy moved towards Veirella. Anastasia moved to stop her but, Veirella stopped her from doing so. Ivy threw rocks at her and Veirella dodged them effortlessly. Anastasia looked around the platform to find where rocks were coming from, but she found nothing. While she did that Veirella got close then grabbed her arms, spun behind her and threw herself down and threw Ivy over and off the platform. Anastasia, Lola, and Isa looked at her, eyes wide

.

Anastasia knew it was wrong, but she could not help herself. She pulled on her power and sent a small burst of air towards Lola, then threw her off.

Lola screamed as she flew back."Bye, bye" Anastasia whispered and smiled to herself. "Was that really necessary?" Isa asked, her head tilted to the side, looking at Anastasia. "Yes, yes it was."

The next two rows passed in a blur. Mostly because Isa was knocking them off with ice. On the last round, they each took one of them out. That last team opted to not wield, which ended badly for them. Once Veirella kicked the last person off, Rowen appeared again. "Congratulations, not only did you stay on the longest, you have the most points," he told them. Anastasia turned to Veirella and hugged her. "We did. We can go to Corviac" she jumped with excitement.

"What?"

Dancing Flames

Veirella

Veirella did not intend to go with Gemma, but she was so excited about it, she would do it. The third years that were to accompanying them were Cyrus a Xiakary earth wielder, and Griffin a Xiakary fire wielder, they were the boys with Luka and Pax that day in the training room.

All the boys wore black Keives; Veirella and Gemma chose to wear dresses. Well, Gemma chose Veirella just went with it, so she let her friend do all the work. "What dress would you like, the green or the blue?" Veirella shrugged. Gemma dropped her head and signed.

"I chose the blue dress because you look great in that color." She threw the green one on the bed and held the other out to Veirella. "Now you can either put this on willingly, or I can put it on you myself." They stared each other down, waiting to see who would break first.

Veirella rolled her eyes, took the dress, and went into her closet. She did not doubt Gemma would follow through with her threat. On another day, she would have pushed back more, but they won. It did not take much to undress and then redress herself. All the dresses that were sent with her were designed for her to not need help getting them on or off. when Veirella came out, Gemma was standing before the door.

Veirella did not think she was in there that long but Gemma was dressed she had on a red dress with white patterns in the shape of the wind, she had on a ruby necklace and matching, bracelets one each hand over the sleeves of her dress. "You look wonderful. I love the detailing a call to what you are" Veirella told her.

"Thank you." Gemma spun around so she could see all of it. "You should look at yourself; I love the blue and gold." Veirella went to the mirror to see the dress. It was dark blue with gold all over, forming connecting vines with small Jews in the shape of flowers petal's all along the top half.

"And these to complete the look" she turned to Willow, who was holding a gold platted necklace with small rubies within and a larger one on at the center with matching bangles. Veirella put the bangles on and turned to let Willow put the necklace on her. "Perfect."

Veirella pulled on her boots, similar in shade to her dress. Veirella was sure she had a pair of shoes that matched every dress she had in her closet. "We should be going; we have kept the others waiting long enough," Veirella stated, "they are boys. They should be waiting on us." Gemma told her.

Luka and Pax were sitting across from each other in the commons when the girls came out. Pax was the first to notice them. "Finally, with how long it took you to get ready, I thought you were making the dress yourself" Gemma rolled her eyes at Pax, they met by the stairs. "If you think that was long, you have not spent much time around women," she told him. Veirella did not pay much attention to their squabbling. She had all her attention on Luka, who had his on her.

"Hi."

"Hi."

He looked her over, then his eyes returned to hers. "You look lovely" She looked down at herself as if she did not already memorize every detail of her dress in the mirror. "Thank you. You look nice as well."

"Thank you, shall we?" Luka raised his hand toward the stairs. Veirella nodded, then went to the top him following behind. He opened the door for her. "Thank You" he nodded, and they walked out together and he opened a port key that led them to the ground floor of the school then they went out to the courtyard, with Gemma and Pax still arguing about what time and what was an acceptable amount to make someone wait.

When they got to the courtyard, the boys were leaning against the wall, with Isa standing in the center of the stairs between them. Her hair was pulled back, and she was wearing a black dress that ended beneath her knee. Cyrus and Griffin straightened when they saw them, they were dressed similar to Pax and Luka.

"You all took your sweet time?" Cyrus asked. He was the one that lied to her. "It takes time to look this good," Pax answered. For a moment Veirella thought he would tell them, her and Gemma were the reason for their tardiness.

"I don't see much difference between what you look like now and what you looked like yesterday." Griffin pointed out. Veirella did not know what the relationship between them was like. They were paired up, but that did not mean they were friends. Veirella thought she missed something because they were laughing. "And who is this beauty?" Griffin asked her. Luka moved closer to her, almost shielding her from his view. Griffin stepped back with his hands raised. "No need to go all breast, I was just asking." A flash of fear crossed his eyes, then was quickly replaced with a smile.

"Veirella, we have met" she did not move away from Luka. Veirella did not think the boy would try anything, not with him there or otherwise. After all Genevieve did trust them to keep them safe, but Veirella did not know him. "A beautiful name for a beautiful girl," she smiled at him. "Griffin, stop trying to flirt with her." Isa told him as she pulled him down the steps away from Luka. "I guy can try." he raised his hands and winked at her. "We should get going. We need to get to the gate in order to portal," Pax informed them, breaking the tension that had formed around them. It stopped the death glare Luka was sending Griffin's way.

They took a carriage to the gates. Pax opened a portal for them a bright blue spinning vortex opened before them, Griffin went, first then Gemma,

Isa and last Pax, leaving behind Luka and Veirella. He walked to the portal floating two inches off the ground, then turned to her, taking notice of her lack of movement. "Is something wrong?" he asked.

"I have only gone through one of those things and it was in a carriage. I do not know what will happen if I go through with something between." She told him, Luka held his hand out to her "then we go through together, it will be fine," he assured her. Veirella looked down at his hand, hesitating for a second before taking it. "It will not be noticeable. It only lasts a few seconds and then we will be on the other side."

"Ready?" Luka squeezed her hand. Veirella nodded. As they entered, she squeezed his hand. Luka stroked his thumb over the back of her hand. She closed her eyes as she stepped through. Then she heard Gemma and Pax arguing about what they should do first.

Luka was right it was hardly noticeable. The first time was so much different. Pax closed the portal and the blue light faded. Griffin turned to them, "you know, for a second there I thought you two were trapped in limbo." He said to them. Veirella looked up at Luka, who was looking everywhere but at her. "We could have been trapped?"

Her voice was filled with both panic and fear. "Yes, but we were not, so no need to worry," he answered, smiling down at her. Veirella attempted to walk away from him, but he pulled her back. "Now let us see what this year's Corviac has to offer."

There were people everywhere, which made it hard to move around. Because of how crowd it was they split into two groups, Gemma, Pax, Griffin, and Isa went to the saels and Veirella, Luka, and Cyrus went to watch the performers. They walked in a line, led by Luka, and he was still holding her hand.

Veirella's hold on his hand tightened as they moved through the densely packed streets. But Luka did not react, he either he did not care, or he did not feel it. Her options were limited it was either used him to help ground herself or panic, and considering there was nowhere for her to go. The former was her really her only choice.

They turned down a dark alleyway. There were far fewer people moving through them than on the street. Most of the people around them were laughing and dancing with dark bottles in hand. "We can get there faster if we cut across Celien to get to the center of the city." Cyrus informed them, this was not ideal to Veirella anything could happen in the dark. But she also did not want to go back in the crown.

It was not so dark they could not navigate their way; the moon gave enough light for them to see where they were going, and every so often there was a torch lighting the way. One left and two rights later they emerged from the shadows, onto a street that had fewer people. It was still crowded but there was more room to move around. The city was booming with life, some many colors from all over the world. Not all the people were native to the island, by their difference in clothing, most of the men were dressed in tunics along with some of the women others dresses.

The differences were in the color and dark reds and small touches of dragon scales, which was common amount Dragians. It was harder to get than gold, so it was expensive and a show of status. Atarians were more colorful than most, rich blues, yellow, orange, purple, and some red here and there.

Irieans also took to the color red, but they mixed it with white and grey. But there were no Forians attending solstice. From what Veirella recalled, there was a celebration of the eve of solstice and then there would be a week of worship of the three Celestials that ruled over them.

When they got onto the street, everyone seemed to be heading in the same direction, so they followed hoping it would lead them to one of the many performances that were going on. As they got closer, Veirella heard people cheering and the sound of drums.

"Come, it is about to start," Luka said, the excitement noticeable in his voice. Whatever it was, he knew. The beats were not something she was familiar with, Veirella could not place which continent it originated from, but them again music was not one of her interests that was Iris.

If she were here, she could place it in seconds. But based on Luka's reaction, it had to be Dragian; three short beats, then two long, and two fast. As they got closer, the drums became louder, telling her they were in the right place. Though Veirella could not see what all the excitement was about, there were so many people around it blocked her view.

They pushed through the onlookers that gathered to get to the front for a better view. Then Veirella saw why everyone was cheering. There were three women in the center wearing bralettes and short skirts covered in dragon scales. They were each holding a small dragon; blue, green, and black. Veirella did not know how small the creatures were as babies. She had only ever seen pictures of them in books, and they were always massive. The women released them into the sky together, flew up turned, and shot flames towards their holders.

The fire formed a ring that went over the women, then burnt out when it hit the ground; the drummers began playing a faster tune, and the ladies began to dancing, the dragons came back towards them and moved themselves around their bodies, following along with their movements perfectly in sync, when they flipped the Dragons went in between their arms then around their bodies and up their legs. They flipped back to their feet, and the creatures repeated the movements.

Then they moved away from the women, preparing to blast flames once again. They released the flames, and it formed lines of fire moving around them like they controlled them. The drums stopped, and the dragons flew down to their out-stretched arms, then the drums stopped, and everyone around them including Veirella, gave them applause.

"What was amazing, I have seen others do veciesion dances before but not like that," she said to the boy standing next to her. "Well, what can I say Dragians like to do things to the extreme" everything was competing for them, even something like a ceremonial dance they found a way to make it a competition.

"What would you like to do next?" Luka asked. "Whatever is as amazing as that just was," Veirella answered, "well we could go see the animal—" Luka did not finish what he was saying. Because someone walked into Veirella. The smile faded from his face, replaced with anger. It was almost surprising how fast Luka went from sweet and relaxed to looking like he wanted to murder the person who bumped into her.

"Hey, watch where you're going," the bass and his voice made the hairs on the back of her neck stand. Veirella was not scared of him. She was just not expecting it. She turned to tell the person that Luka was giving death glares to not to worry about it, but she was stunned to silence when she saw who it was.

"Aspen, what are doing here?" Veirella asked, looking up at her older brother, then she hugged him. He had a delayed reaction to seeing her but then he reciprocated, "I was coming to see you, this is the last place I expected you would be." That was the last place she expected herself to b e.

"Veirella, you know this man?" Luka was still looking at her brother as if he were a threat to her. "Yes, this is my brother Aspen" she could see him visibly relaxed at her answer. "Sorry about that," he said to Aspen with a light laugh. "No problem. It is nice to know that there are others as protective of my sister as I am," Aspen said, looking from Luka to Cyrus, who Veirella just noticed had gotten come closer due to the commotion.

"It is quite loud here. We should go somewhere else to catch up," Veirella nodded in agreement. "I spotted a tavern a few buildings down. We can go there," Luka informed them. "Lead the way."

"What is a tavern?" Veirella asked, looking from Aspen to Luka. They both looked down at her, then at each other. But neither answered her question. Aspen moved to her left with Luka still on her right, leading the way, with Cyrus behind them. They passed six buildings Veirella did not remember seeing, then Luka moved to enter the seventh 'The Stormy Bell' the sign read. It was larger on the inside than it looked on the outside. Everything was made of wood and there was a fire lit just about everywhere.

There was a bar in the middle with patrons scattered around it eating and drinking, there were booths and tables around it the bar that was in the center of the room, and cut the two sides, some tables were exploding with life, while others were empty or only hosting one or two people.

They moved for the stair that led to the second floor, which was even more lifeless than the first. The few people that were up there were all on the left side of the room. There was a group of men drinking and laughing about the bore they killed, and what parts of it they would sell and how they would use the money from it.

They made their way to the far right of the room, which hosted no one else, and was dark and quiet. "I am going to get us some drinks, any particular requests?" Luka asked, "whatever tastes the least shit will do" Aspen answered. Luka turned to her to wait for her answer. "Cider would be fine, thank you" When he walked off, Veirella noticed Cyrus was not the re.

"If you are looking for your other friend, he went to the bar when we came up here." Aspen informed her. "Now that we have a moment of alone, would you like to tell me way it is that you are late for our visit?" Veirella asked, the last time someone mentioned how long she was there it was six weeks, her nightmares were almost not excitant now and she had slept eighteen full nights since. "I am not that late—"

"You should have come four days ago, I would consider that late." she cut him off. Veirella was no longer smiling. She was annoyed with him, and Aspen could tell. "Something happened that needed my immediate attention. I was busy I did not notice that much time had gone by," he explained, but what could have been so dire that he could not find a moment to spare to send her a letter.

"What, was so urgently in need of your attention that you lost time for so long?" she asked. As[pen smiled at her in the way he always did when he was not telling her something. "Nothing to worry your pretty little head about, little sister" he reached for her hand, but she pulled away before he could take it. "Do not patronize me." There was hurt and anger in her voice. He sighed, then threw his head back against his seat. "I am not."

"You are, you are treating me like a child" Aspen raised his head and looked at her "you are a child, and you will be a child until you ascend" he told her, something that did not much matter considering he treated her the same way long when they were children. "You have been this way our whole lives, and it does not seem like that will ever change, no matter the situation." She pushed back.

But as much as Veirella wanted to push him until he answered her, she did not what to draw too much attention to them by arguing with him. "Has anything new happened at home since I left?" Veirella did not expect much to be different.

Their mother would busy herself with planning social events, talking to the ladies of the other noble houses, both Celestial Blooded and mortal, while her father dealt with their husbands and affairs of state, and Iris would do what Iris did best, analyze. It did not matter what people, books, paintings; she did it all.

Their mother always told her the role of a lady is as important as her husbands, if not equal to it. Balls and dinners were a way of nurturing those connections. A lady needed to have alliances not just for her house, but for herself. Because no matter how much money one had, or the title bestowed upon them, a man still held more power than a woman ever would.

Aspen confirmed her thoughts, "Father and Iris went back to the palace in the capital, and Mother remained in Nightwell; she said she had things to do before she followed them." Veirella learned she had not been to Estonia since her accident. Maybe she was not ready to go back to the world that awaited their queen for six years.

Or she liked the lack of chaos the Nightwell offered. Veirella had not been to Estonia since her eighth reight. so much could have changed in the time. She did not know much about how they hid her absence. Her parents did everything possible to keep suspicions away, Veirella knew that much, but she wondered what it cost them to do so.

"Now the big question, will I be returning home alone or with a travel companion?" Aspen's body went rigid, waiting for an answer. Veirella had not thought about leaving. If she was being honest with herself, she was with her closest friend, and she was making others she wanted to stay. "No, I will be staying here for the remainder of the school term, then I shall return home. I am already four months in. It would be absolutely ridiculous to just up and leave." She answered.

Aspen looked both relieved and happy with her answer. "That is good. I am happy you have decided to stay. You have changed so much in the short time you have been here, it seems to make you happy." Veirella went to speak, but he cut her off. "For logical reasons or otherwise," Aspen knew her better than most, so he could predict what she was thinking and what she would say.

Veirella would never admit to him that she actually liked it there because that would mean admitting he was right, and his head was already the size of a door. It did not need to get any larger with a stroke of his ego. "Now tell me, what have you done since you have arrived here? Have you learned any cool spells?" his excitement and intrigue radiated off him like a glowing ball of fire.

"No, not particularly I have mostly being learning how to control my wielding, making it last and I mostly spend my time reading Genevieve says it is important that I do this slowly so not to burn myself out," she told him, Aspen did not seem disappointed at her lack of extraordinary achievements. He picked her hand up. "I am sure you will get there in due time,"

"I know that as badly as I would like to have control over this fully, I know it will take time" Aspen nodded, their conversation was cut short when Luka returned with their drinks. "I went save and got Ale. There are so few ways to mess it up" he handed the deep amber drink to Aspen, and he gave him a nod of thanks.

"And for you Dove one cider, don't know how well it tastes though so sorry in advance" Veirella took the drink from his outstretched hand, "thank you" Luka smiled at her then slid into the booth next to her.

Veirella looked up at her brother. His face had hardened, and his eyes were moving over them. "What is it?" she asked, her brows creasing. Aspen looked at her, then focus entirely on Luka. "Lorenzo, what are your intentions with my sister? You two seem to be very familiar with one another" Luka sat straighter than he was before. "Aspen, do not be rude. He is my friend."

Luka touched her with his arm in a way her brother could not see. "It is all right," he told to her low enough for Aspen not to hear. "What she said is correct. We are friends, there is nothing more to it" he asked.

"And if your friendship ever went beyond that, I would hope you honor her properly." Aspen's tone was stern, emphasizing the word 'properly'. And was telling, not asking. "I would not think of doing anything less," Luka answered. Veirella looked between them, not understanding what they were talking about. What did Aspen mean by honoring her? Most of all, he called Luka by his given name. Veirella should not have been surprised as she was; they were both heirs. Surely they would have met before.

But if they knew each other, why did Luka react the way he did before? "If you are going to sit here and talk about me, I might as well know what it is you are discussing." They both look at her and then back at the other. "No need to worry, Ella, just ensuring he keeps you out of harm." Aspen told to her while still focused on Luka. "I do not see how I would be in any harm if I never leave the school. My been here is a onetime exemption," she told to him. Aspen released her hand and sat back, nodding his head.

"Well, you will be there four years and the other three you are given infield assignments," he knew how Astro worked, she should have expected that, you never went into a fight without knowing your opponent, why would Veirella be sent to a school her parents did not know every detail about. "Nothing too life threatening, and she can choose not to do it," Luka informed him. "I have allied myself with a few of the attendees over the years, and I would not call what we did non-threatening." Veirella did not like the way Aspen was looking or speaking to Luka.

She did not know how they knew each other, but she did not think it warranted the looks Aspen was giving him. Luka, on the other hand, did not seem fazed by it. His face was void of emotion, like the way her brother was acting towards him did not affect him at all. It may have not bothered him, but it bothered her. He was her friend, and Aspen was being so hostile. "Why are you being so rude?" Aspen looked at her for the first time since Luka sat with them and his eye softened.

"Your safety is important to me, and I want to make sure he takes it seriously." Aspen told her, but the words were not for her. "I can understand that, but that does not make the way you are speaking to him okay, he is my friend, and I would respect it if you treated him the same as you would treat Gemma."

"My apologies," he told to Luka. "One is not needed; I can understand wanting to protect her." Aspen did not get a chance to say anything back. Someone approached their table. It was Cyrus, "it's getting late, we must head back" he told them. Luka and Aspen drunk half their drinks, and Veirella had not even touched hers; she was more focused on the two boys before her than anything else.

"We are going to need to find the others," Luka told him as he exited the booth. He gave Veirella his hand to help her out. "No need, they are at the bar downstairs," Cyrus answered.

When Luka and Cyrus went down the stairs, Veirella stopped her brother, "Aspen, I love you and I know you mean well, but treating my friend as if he was an enemy was very much uncalled for and out of character for you" he looked at her then dropped his head and sighed Aspen said something under his breath that she barely caught *"maybe if I was more like this back then you would not have gotten hurt"* Veirella was surprised by what she hard, did he blame himself for what happened.

"What?"

He looked at her and smiled. "Nothing, I love you too and I do not want to see anything happen to you for putting your trust in the wrong person." Trusting the wrong person is not the way she got hurt. They went down the stairs together, then separated at the end. Veirella saw Gemma at the bar, alone, and the boys standing by the door. "Hey, how did you like your very first Corviac?" she asked, her excitement evident. "It was nice. I got to see fire dancers."

"I wanted to see them, but by the time we got there they were finishing their last performance, but I have no regrets all the amazing foods I got to try was worth missing baby dragons for," Veirella gave her a look knowing she did not mean that "okay, maybe I felt a small amount of regret, they are baby dragons after all and when their small is the only time they do not scare the hell out of me," Gemma confessed.

"Well, maybe you can see them at next year's Corviac," Veirella assured her. "I love the idea of us doing this next year, no permission needed and two designated chaperones that would not dream of saying no to us," she stated, looking at the boys deep in conversation. Aspen had joined them, he looked more civil than he did upstairs. Which Veirella was grateful for, she did not need him scaring anyone off.

"I am not sure about you, but I am ready to go."

"Ella, you were ready to go before we stepped into the city." Gemma pointed out. Gemma jumped off her chair and walked over to where the boys were standing, Veirella following behind, but before they got within hearing range, they stopped talking. It was strange, but they were boys, so Veirella did not think about it too much.

"Well, it was nice seeing you again Aspen. Wish we could stay longer but curfew," Pax told him, "what curfew?" Veirella asked, "the school has a protective shield, and it becomes solid at midnight, which is quickly approaching" Griffin answered. They went out the door one after the one. When it was just her, Gemma, and Aspen, Veirella stopped him from leaving. “I forgot to ask. Did you receive my letter?” The sword theory was dead after what Luka told her, but Veirella still wanted an answer.

“I did, and the answer is no. Why do you ask?”

“No reason was just curious is all,” she considered telling him the truth, but if he was going to keep secrets from her, she would do the same. “It was lovely seeing you.” Veirella hugged him. “Same here.”

“I will miss you, but we will see each other again once the air has grown warmer,” Aspen told her, following her friends. Veirella stopped and turn to him “Aspen,” he turned to look at her “would you like to say the night, you need a wielder to get home and I think most of them are out for the night, and we could talk some more?” Aspen smiled at her, then nodded. “I would like that.” He answered, then walked over to Veirella and her waiting f riends.

The night was over for them, but not for everyone else. The street was still filled with people. There were far fewer now than there were before, but the place was still crowded. But it was a lot easier to say together.

When they got to the edge of the city, Griffin opened a portal. “Why did we need to come this far out to open a portal?” Veirella asked, “because there is the chance of them leaving residual energy behind and it can do some serious damage to mortals.” Luka answered.

“It does not happen often, but to be safe, we need to go it at a distance,” Pax continued. Veirella wondered what it would do to them and if there was a book, she could read about it. All her friends went through the portal Luka took her hand and they went in together. The last one through was Griffin. He closed it behind him. They went through the gates towards the carriage, but he did not follow. Veirella looked back, and he was not moving.

“Are you okay?” she said, walking towards him. “Veirella stay back” Luka told her she looked up at him confused. He was not looking at her he was only focused on Griffin.

“It hu...hurts,”

Griffin managed to say, Veirella looked back at him, and there was smoke coming off him. His skin went red and started bubbling "hel...help me" Veirella stepped towards him. But within seconds, she was pressed against Luka's chest. "What are you doing? Something is wrong with him. He needs help," she tried fighting her way out of the hold, but it was no use. "You cannot help him" she looked up at Luka again, but he did not meet her eyes. "Then you help him," she told him.

Griffin's eyes coated with blood. She did not know what was happening to him, but it looked horrible. "There is nothing I can do. There is nothing anyone can do," Luka told her. "No...no...no there has to be something we can do, something is wrong with him, he needs our he—" Griffin's screaming cut her off.

Veirella was horrified at what she saw Griffin burst into flames. It started with his hands, then up his arms and down his legs. He reached for her, but Luka pulled her back before Griffin could get to her. His screams got louder and louder as the flames reached his head. Veirella could not tell how long it took for the screams to stop. He fell to the ground, but the screaming continued, but he was dead, and the screams sounded closer.

Eight Years Before

Veirella finished her lessons earlier than expected. She was had a test for history and test days were always short. Veirella did not have anything to do after so she sat in her room by her window watching the birds fly. It was hard to be alone, not having her Aspen and Iris around to entertain her with their games. Made life seem or mundane.

Veirella was never allowed to play with them. The one time she asked, they had both practically yelled the word no at her. She was allowed to watch but never part take, Veirella spent time with both her siblings sometimes together other times separately.

With Iris, she listened to her read stories and sometimes make up ones of their own and other times they did experiment. With Aspen she painted, unlike with Iris, there was less talking. They found peace in each other's company when every other part of their lives was filled with chaos.

Veirella missed seeing them regularly and wished they were there. They left before her seventh reight and had missed her eighth; but they forgot neither for her seventh they sent letters apologizing for not been there and for her eighth they sent gifts, they were exactly what she expected from both.

'The book of Myth's' from her sister, Veirella only knew two stories from it and one of them scared her so bad she slept with her mother for two months' after hearing it, and the one with the cursed princess.

She loved that story and read it to herself several times and had Iris read it to her several more. Veirella asked her for the book every time she read it, but she always said no, and now she finally had it. There were hundreds of other stories in it, and Iris had marked her favorites. And from Aspen she got hand mixed paints, many with colors she had never seen before, none of which she had used yet.

"Darling" Veirella turned to see her mother entire her room. She hesitated before entering fully, then closed the door behind her. She slowly made her way over to Veirella and sat next to her. "Remember what we talked about last week?" her mother asked. Veirella nodded. How could she forget her mother told her; her father intended to send her away for her Ryin training to begin.

Veirella cried to her mother, asking her not to do it, not to let him. She told Veirella she would talk to her father about it. "Yes, did father change his mind?" she asked, her eyes widened, waiting for what her mother had to say. But she did not speak. She looked at Veirella then out the window for a moment, then her eyes found her again. She reached for her hands, taking them into her own and took a deep intake of her air, then released it.

"No." She choked out. Veirella pulled her hands from hers and moved away from her. She promised she would not let him send her away, but she was breaking her promise. "Veirella, I know this is hard for you to understand, but this is what is best for you." Veirella turned to her teared threatening to fall from her eyes.

"Why?" her little voice broke as she asked. "Because you are different." She answered. "How so? How am I different?" she asked, but her mother did not answer her. She stood moving towards Veirella then knelt before her, laying her hands on her shoulders.

"Look, this will not be forever, just a few months, maybe a year or two, then you come home. Okay," she informed her, Veirella pulled away from

her and ran into the bathing room and closed the door. She heard her mother knocking at the door, telling her to open it. But she climbed into the bath, laid no and cried, then she fell asleep hearing her mother's voice called for her.

Clarity

Lorenzo

Twenty-Two, that was the number of people from the school that were dead. Lorenzo did not pay much attention to Pax when he was talking about the about of Centinal's that he heard were died. It was not uncommon. Some could not handle the power they were given, and it killed them.

But Griffin was not one of them. He was a great fire wielder, and Lorenzo had never seen him push himself beyond his limit or anywhere near it. After watching him burn to death, Lorenzo thought about that number. As he watched the boy, he was starting to consider a friend be added to that number.

Now he knew there was some truth to Pax's worry. The flames on his body died off, once there was nothing leave on his body to burn and the crying girl in his arms finally went quieted. All that remained of Griffin was his chard body and the smell of his burnt flesh in the air.

"Get the girls back to the school and alert the Headmistress I will stay here with the body" Aspen ordered them like he was the one in charge, but nevertheless they did as he told them. "The body he is a person. He has a name." Anastasia yelled at him. She was doing a better job at holding herself together than Veirella was, but her reaction was understandable considering what she just watch happen and Lorenzo could see the tears in her eyes, and hear the hoarseness of her voice.

"He was a person, but now he is died, and we have to deal with it. Pax, Lorenzo, get them out of here, and you." He looked to Cyrus who was still looking at his died friends blackened body. "Inform the headmistress, I assume you already know about all of this."

All of what Lorenzo wanted to ask, but he did not get a chance to. His attention was pulled to the sound of horses coming down the road. With all the commotion, he did not notice the other horses ran off. There were two of them, one black, the other gray. They were pulling a black carriage along with them.

Lorenzo looked down at Veirella who was still looking at Griffin's body. He turned away from him so she could no long see it and she made no effort to look back at it. The carriage stopped next to them, Pax opened the door and the fae light came to life.

Pax helped a fighting Anastasia into the carriage, "there is nothing you can do for him out here" she looked at him, for a moment not saying anything then step up and sat down in the far corner and Pax took the spot next to her. Lorenzo helped Veirella in. She did not put up a fight at all, she just let him guide her in. They sat across from Anastasia and Pax, then Lorenzo pulled her back into him, keeping her close. Her eyes were open, but she was not looking at anything.

They all stayed silence will Cyrus went up to the front then they were moving, Lorenzo did not take his eyes off Veirella, and neither did Pax. She had not spoken since she stopped screaming. When they stopped at the entrance of the school, Pax opened the door, got out, turned to help Anastasia, but she pushed his hand away and jumped down. Lorenzo got down, then helped Veirella down. Pax moved towards them.

"I'll take them up, you go find out what the hell is going on." Lorenzo nodded and gave her over to him. Cyrus jumped out of the box and ran up the steps with Lorenzo following behind him.

He opened a port key, which lead straight to the teachers' floor. And wasted no time, ran, and barging into the Headmistress office, "boys, you better have a good reason for barging in here or—" she stopped when she saw the look on Cyrus's face, one filled with pain and anger.

"Sorry for my intrusion, Headmistress, but Griffin is dead," he forced out the name of his friend. It could not be easy saying those two things in the same sentence. Headmistress Conley stood from her desk and walked to the windows behind it. She stood there for a moment, taking in what she was told. She sighed, then turned her head to the side, still not looking at them.

"How did it happen?" She asked, the question was directed at Cyrus because Lorenzo was still in the dark about what was happening. But now was not the time to ask questions. He needed to watch and listen. Questions would come after he had something to go off of.

"The same as the others?" She continued, then she finally turned around to face them. He turned to Cyrus, who nodded in response. Then he told her the details of the events that took place less than an hour ago, not missing a detail. "How are the girls? It must have been traumatic for them to see something like that" it was Lorenzo's turn to speak "Anastasia is angry, and Veirella has not said a word." He could still hear her pained screams and feel how her paralyzed body became.

"We much retrieve his body, this is the first time there has been remains we must learn as much as possible" headmistress Conley wrote something on a piece of parchment them gave it her owl, she opened the window and it was off, then she walked passed them, out the door, both following behind. *What the fuck is going on?* Lorenzo thought to himself as he followed them.

They made their way back to Aspen and Griffin's body. Aspen was leaning against the now closed gates. The shield was up; it was mostly inviable but there was a bit of a blue shimmer present. Cyrus went and stood over the body, saying his final goodbye, no doubt. He and Griffin had been friends since their first year, and now one would keep going, and the other would not.

Scarlet arrived in a second carriage a few minutes later and went right for Cyrus and hugged him. She was also a third year; there were likely friends. Lorenzo gave them a moment alone before walking over. "Do you think you can get anything from him?" Scarlet wiped her fallen tears. She tried to hide it but Lorenzo saw, then she knelt next to Griffin's body and pulled on her magic; blue sparks moved around her fingers, then she moved her hand over his body, checking for something.

"Well, he still has blood in his body so I can work with that," she informed them. Scarlet did not appear surprised by any of it, so she also knew what was going on. Lorenzo wished he paid more interest to what Pax was saying when he was talking about the suspicious deaths. Maybe he would be more informed.

"Good, we may finally get an answer to whatever the hell is doing this" Cyrus responded. His voice was harder that it usually was even harder than when he was giving them orders.

Aspen retrieved the body board from the roof of the carriage and set it next to the Griffin's body. Scarlet gave each of them a set of gloves. "Be careful; we have no idea if this thing can travel from one person to the next, so try not to touch him with your skin" all they nodded in unison, then each took a paired of gloves from her.

Aspen, Cyrus, and Lorenzo moved his body to the board. Where he was on the ground, there were pieces of him stuck to the stones. It was sickening to see and feel he had been alive two hours ago, and now he was dead and his body felt like firewood after it burnt out.

They strapped him to the board, then moved him to the roof of the carriage. Once they were sure he would not move, they got in the carriage and went back to the school. Cyrus, Lorenzo and Aspen brought Griffin's body to the medical wing of the school, saying nothing to each other as they made their way there, following behind Scarlet and the headmistress.

They put him in one of the test rooms so no one would see the body. The first-year students frequented the medical wing almost daily with injuries from classes both wielding and combat. "We can start testing in the morning," Scarlet told them, her eyes still had sleep in them, and her dark red hair was a mess from bed which she had tried to fix by wrapping into up and there were dark circles beneath her eyes.

"I know someone who has experience with something similar to this. I will request his help" Aspen informed them. "I will have the number of guards around the school increased. Just to be safe, you three got to bed, and we will continue this once we have gotten some sleep. Prince Aspen come with me," Conley told them, then she walked out Aspen following behind her, he stopped by the door where Cyrus was standing, he moved as far away as he could get without leaving the room.

Aspen patted his hand on his shoulder a few times, then walked away. Even though the Headmistress told them to get some sleep, it was unlikely any of them would.

They all went their separate ways third year dorms were on the fourth floor of the school, and the royal court was at the top, Lorenzo found the closet port key he could and went through it, he needed a moment to think but had no interest in walking up six hundred steps to do so, he would rather burn alive than do that.

It was a horrible thing to think, all things considered, but no one could see inside his head, so did it really matter. It was quiet in the court. He expected to find Pax waiting up to see what he found out. If he managed to get himself to bed, then it could wait until morning and Lorenzo did not have much to share, anyway. He went to his room, stripped and got into the bath.

It was just that he liked it cold, his skin was hot, so ice cold baths had been his go to for a while now. He could still feel the slash he had taken to the abdomen; it was especially noticeable when he was wet. It did not hurt, but it was a small reminder of watching someone he knew die.

When he got in bed; he could not stop hearing Griffin's screams as he died, and somehow the loudest scream was from the only person not dead, Veirella.

Myths and Truths

Veirella

Veirella laid in bed a wake for most of the night. She could not sleep, she could still feel the heat of the fire on her skin and could still hear Griffin's screams. Burning to death was one of the worse ways to die. She laid there, looking up at the ceiling. She had been looking up into the dark for so long that she could now make out the wood patterns.

There was movement next to her where Gemma was sleeping. Veirella looked over to see if she was awake too, but all she did was turn. She pushed her covers off, watching Gemma as she slowly removed herself from the bed. Veirella made her way out of the room, opening and closing the door as light as she could manage. She heard cracking behind her. She turned and saw the fire going in the hearth, and Pax was sitting next to it. She made her way around the sofa before saying anything.

"Do you think being that close to fire right now is a good idea?" Pax whipped his head in her direction. "I am a water wielder. I can put myself out if I need to." he answered. Veirella got closer and sat across from him and watched the flames eat into the firewood.

"This does not affect you?" he asked. As they were both watching the flames. "No. I thought it would, but other than not being able to sleep, I feel mostly fine. Just it does not give me nightmares when I do finally fall a sleep."

Veirella looked over at Pax. He did not seem to be affected at all. "How about you? He was your friend." She had only met him a few times and only spoke to him once. Veirella may have had the more severe reaction to what she saw happen. But that was natural for her. She wanted to help him and listen to him stand there and burn was terrifying.

"Fine mostly, I spent a few months with the guy, but I cannot say we were friends." Pax answered. Maybe he was good at hiding how he felt or he truly felt nothing for the boy. "It is horrible that any of them are dead." His voice lowered, almost a whisper. Pax did not intend for her to hear him, but she did.

"The others?"

Veirella turned to him. Pax closed his eyes and cursed. "Ignore that, its nothing." He brushed her off. "No, what others?" Veirella asked. She was not going to give up. There was something going on and he knew something. Pax made no attempt to answer her. Veirella watched him, waiting for him to say something. Anything would be better than nothing to her at this point. Pax avoided looking at her, looking down at his hands or into the fire, but never at her.

"You know, at one point I thought we were friends. I know were did not spend much time together as children, but I thought in the times we did see each other we became friends. But in the time I have been here, you have avoided me and lied to me twice."

Veirella stood, brushing away the cinders that had fallen on her dress. Pax watched her stand, then looked away before she could see him. "Your actions have shown me enough to know that we are not friends, and I do not speak to people who are not my friends. It was nice knowing you, prince Sebastian." she continued, then she went back to her room.

"Veirella." He called after her, but she did not stop to hear what he had to say. She had given him enough of her time. She was careful going back in to the room so not to wake Gemma then made her way to her vanity and wrapped her hair, she opened one of the drawers and pulled out a vile filled with amber liquid. She opened it and drank half. She would get some answers in the morning from who she did not know, but in order to do that, she needed to get some sleep.

Veirella felt her head shaking. She felt herself being pulled from the darkness she had come to find peace in. Someone was holding on to her, not remembering where she was, Veirella jumped up. *They found me* she thought. Her heart was raising, and her ears filling with pressure.

"Veirella"

Hearing her name, she looked around, finding Gemma sitting wide-eyed on her bed. She was wearing different clothes than she went to bed in, her dress was replaced by black keives or leather it was hard to tell sometimes. It was once the standard material used to make guards uniforms and what soldiers wore beneath their armer, but it had not been used for that purpose in over two hundred years. It was now just another form of fashion.

Veirella closed her eyes and released the air that had built up in her chest, and her heart began to slow. "Sorry. But I honestly thought you were dead. Your breathing was so slow it was hard to tell," Gemma explained.

"Are you okay? You seem a bit rattled" Gemma laid a hand on her shoulder, pulling Veirella's attention to her. Veirella smiled at her. "I'm fine, I just did not expect that" her friend gave her a sympathetic smile, then apologized again. Veirella removed herself from the bed and Gemma followed. She looked over Gemma fully, now that she was standing.

"Why are you dressed like that?" she asked tilting her head to the side and looking her over again. Gemma looked down at her clothes. Veirella got a closer look at the fabric and it was leather, the shine it had gave it away. Gemma was wearing leather—everything, pants, jacket, and shoes. "You had your shoes on in my bed?" Veirella asked.

"They are new."

"And as for your first question, I went and got dressed when I saw Luka, Pax, Cyrus, and your brother leaving. They said something about going to the medical wing of the school, *sooo* I thought we should go. Lets stop asking for answers and take them." She continued. Veirella intended to remind her that they already did that. But Gemma came to that conclusion on her own.

"Well, we already did that, but my point still stands." Gemma walked around her and went into her closet. Already knowing where this was going, Veirella removed her dress and waited for Gemma to return with what she would be wearing to this confrontation.

"Your lady has great taste" Veirella turned to Gemma who was holding up, knee length green dress made from keif fabric. It was not all the same and some colors were rarer than others, blue, black, and red were common but white, green, and yellow came once every so often. Gemma had a pair of boots that met where the dress ended above her knee. "Lets get you in this, and you are going to need a lot more pants. Versatility is important."

When Veirella finished getting dressed, she looked at herself in the mirror. The dress and had long sleeves, with a small slit in the neckline where a part of her Lovia could be seen, and it was covered in gold patterns to look like roots. Veirella pulled her hair pull and secured it with a band, then she pulled down two pieces at the front.

"If we were not trying to be intimidating, I would say you look good enough to eat, and a certain fire wielder just might take a bite," Gemma said then turned away from her, Veirella turned to look at her so fast her vision blurred. "Let's go. We could be missing vital information as we speak." Gemma ran for the door, hoping to escape the question she saw in Veirella's eyes, and Veirella followed. When they got up the stairs, Veirella finally said something "Do not know how Dragians do things, but I do not want to be bitten" her voice shook will she spoke. Gemma looked at her and smiled as she pulled open the first door, then the next.

Gemma opened the port key in the painting closest to them. She then turned to Veirella and raised a hand to her shoulder. "My beautiful, innocent friend you have so much to learn." she moved her other hand to her chest, "and I will be happy to teach you" Gemma moved away from her then stepped through the port key. Veirella did not like how she said that it sounded more like a threat than a promise.

When she stepped through the painting, there were a set of massive double doors before her. The halls on both sides were empty and there were no other doors nearby. The walls on either side were filled with paintings of faces Veirella did not know. The wall behind them was lined with windows separated by low hanging paintings. Gemma closed the port key, then push the doors open.

The room was a blush shade of white. The only source of light was coming from the glass roof above. Both side of the room were lined with beds, but they were all empty and so was the room. "If they are still in here, they will be in one of the labs." Gemma told her, pointing to the doors that lined the back wall. She opened the one in the center that revealed more doors.

Each separated by four feet, Gemma turned her head to the side and closed her eyes. She stayed like that for a moment. When Gemma opened them, she went straight for the fourth door on the left. Then Veirella heard the voice's, one of which belonged to her brother. She almost forgot she asked him to comeback with her.

They walked into the room; it was bigger than she thought it would be. Everything from the walls to the windows were high up where no one could reach, to the grey storage on the walls, everything else was black or silver. Luka, Pax, Aspen, and Cyrus all had their backs to the door, so they did not see them come in. There were other's in the room but the four massive boys were preventing them from seeing.

"He as some traces of blood left in his body so we could start by seeing if there is something in it."

"That could work. I have not had much in that area but consider he is a Xiakary maybe we could get something more from him."

The woman's voice belonged to Scarlet, but Veirella did not recognize the man's. Gemma walked towards them. Veirella tried to stop her, but she pulled away. "I want to see what they are doing." Them not knowing they were there gave them a better chance to actually learn something, but Gemma announcing them would probably get them sent away.

She moved to stand next to Sebastian, then he turned to look at her. "What are you doing here?" All eyes landed on Gemma who smiled up at Sebastian, then looked over at something, then quickly looked away her skin lightening in color from what she saw.

Veirella assumed it was Griffin's body, which she did not what to see again. Watching him die was enough of a sight for her. "I did watch him die, so I want to know what happened to him." Gemma answered, pushing her shoulders back to make it seem like she was taller than she was. Sebastian looked her over, taking note of what she was doing, and smiled.

He opened his mouth to say something, but Cyrus stepped forward before he could. "You are a first year, princess or not. First years are not allowed to get involved in issues outside of the classroom." His voice was louder than it needed to be, but it did not echo.

"Well, this happened on school grounds, and we—" she looked back at Veirella and so did everyone else. Her skin heated up with the unwanted attention that was now on her. "—watched him die, so we have a right to know why we were just given nightmares for life" Veirella really wished she would stop saying we. Last thing Veirella wanted was more attention on her.

"It still does not concern you, so get out. Both of you." Cyrus looked from Gemma to Veirella. Gemma stepped up to him and he looked back at him. He was much taller than her. Cyrus had about six inches or so on her. "I am not going anywhere. Kids with the same blood as me are dying

I have a right to know what is going on. Not only from my sack, but my people." She was pulling rank on him.

"When you become queen, you can make that choice, but considering you are not and I outrank you, will you attend this school. You do what I say." He pushed back, his voice hardening with each word. "Well, do our parents know what is going on? What are they doing about it?" Veirella skin burned with all the tension between Cyrus and Gemma and would do anything to break it, even get involved in something she wanted no part i n.

"That is not your concern, so get out both." Cyrus did not look at Veirella as he spoke to her, then he took hold of Gemma's arm and moved her towards Veirella.

When Cyrus got close, he raised his hand up to take a hold of Veirella but Aspen stopped him. "Cyrus, myself and everyone else here, are being mindful of the pain you are in at the moment. But you so much as touch a hair on my sister's head, I will cut your fucking arms off."

Aspen did not move from where he was across the room. He was not even looking at them. Veirella could not see her brother because of how Cyrus was towering over her, but she could hear the quiet rage in Aspen's voice.

Cyrus release Gemma, who turned and gave him death glares. Veirella did not think she would be friends with this massive boy. He respected what Aspen said, but not Gemma. Her brother threatened him, but still. Gemma held the same title he did, but Cyrus felt so comfortable dismissing her.

She would be within her right to have his head, for the way he disrespected her. Cyrus was still looking down at them, and Veirella did not like the way he was looking at her. He wanted to say something, but he knew he could not. "Cyrus." Luka walked up to him. He turned and looked at him. They stood at a similar place in stature. Luka looked him down as if he intended to fulfill Aspen's threat. "Move."

He was not asking. It was a command. In that moment Cyrus's illusion of power was stripped away from him, by someone who was to be considered his subordinate. He now understood that Luka doing what he told him was not because he needed to, but because he chose to.

For a moment it did not look like he would move. He just stood there, thinking about his options. "I would not recommend doing anything stupid. Enough people are dead. Let us not add you to that list" Sebastian told him. Cyrus looked over at him, then to Aspen would whose attention was still on the burned body on the table, then back at Luka. Then finally walked away, moving to the other side of the room where Scarlet and the man Veirella did not know but whose face looked familiar.

Scarlet looked at him but did not say anything. Then she returned her attention back to what she was doing. "Now that we have established who has more power here, can we get back to the task at hand?" She looked around at all of them, but the name next to her is the only one to nod, acknowledging her.

He had a white coat on. He was either a physician or doctor. Were those the same thing, Veirella did not always know, the only difference she knew was a Riechea, they did most of the problem solving and discoveries in modern technology, infrastructure, and medicine.

That was what she wanted to be, that or a battle strategist, but considering the war ended thirty years ago, there was no point in her doing it. So, her first choice was going to be her only option. In theory that is, she was still a princess. Veirella would receive titles once she ascended, so her options were truly unlimited.

Once Cyrus settled himself on the wall, Luka walked back to where he was next to Sebastian and Gemma stood next to him. Veirella stayed where she was. She saw a glimpse of the body and did not what to see anymore. "In Fianorea we mostly only had Nievarian bodies to work with, and the other's blood were too corrupted to work with," white coat informed them.

"That is the only thing we have not tested. So far there does not appear to be anything abnormal with the rest of their bodies. Will other than the forest bursting from out of them, that is." He continued. He cut Griffin's arm open to get to what remained of the blood in his body, then took a needle and drew what he could, which was not much. The vial he was using was small and less than half of it was filled.

"Not a lot but we can make it work" he took the vial over to the microscope, then stuck a metal rod inside to collect a few drops then, rubbed it onto a tray, sealed it, then placed it in the silver machine. He looked into the tool, changing the zoom multiple times, looking for the one that worked best. He was there looking at it for a while, not saying anything while everyone there looked at him, waiting to see if he found something.

A few moments later, he moved his face away from the lens and looked down at the ground. "So did you see anything?" Aspen asked. "Maybe. Scarlet, look at this." She moved over to him, white coat moved so she could look at what he saw. She did not take as much time as he did. When she looked away, she looked at him. Then at everyone, but still said nothing. "Luka, can I have some of your blood? You were both fire wielder's you're the best to compare this to."

Luka nodded, then took his dagger from the sheath on his lower right thigh and cut his finger. Scarlet got another one of those silver metal rods and took his blood, then repeated the same steps as white coat.

"The Celicai in his blood is faded" she told them. "Is that not common with when a Centinal is on the verge of burnout?" Aspen asked, "yes and no, when a Wielder is close to the end of their power, the regeneration slows but does not stop, works a lot like Hematopoiesis which Luka's blood is doing at its normal rate, but even slowed down it should still be happening. What is happening to Griffin's blood is closer to Apoptosis."

"So the cells die, but nothing is there to replace them? So something or someone has the ability to just steal it or kill it?" Gemma asked. "Well, unless you know of a creature with the ability to steal magic, in a way that kills its victims in such an agonizing way, this is a virus or an infection that can only affect Centinal's," White coat told her.

"Serabi" Veirella said low so that no one heard her. There was a creature that could do that. It was not real. And it also gave her nightmares as a child.

"So, what do we do now?" Aspen asked, he looked between white coat and Scarlet, waiting for one of them to answer. "Now we use his blood to see if we can find a way to cure it, and as horrible as it is, we need to wait for someone else to die or find someone close to death. We need to work with what we have to try and stop this."

Tragedy and Changes

Veirella

That was the last thing they were told. From what Aspen said, this had been happening for some time now. How was it possible that so many people died and everyone did not know. And why were their parents not trying to work together to stop it? "What are we going to do?" Sebastian asked. His question was not directed and even if it was, none of them had an answer to give him.

Cyrus went to Genevieve's office to update her on what they found and the others went back to the court. They sat around the fireplace. Veirella and Gemma sat together on the sofa on the right. Aspen stood by the fire, and Sebastian sat across from them in the other seat and Luka was on the arm.

"I do not know, and honestly, there doesn't seem to be much we can do." Luka answered him. "What is a Serabi?" Gemma asked. Veirella's eyes widen for a moment, then return to normal. How did she even hear her say that? "What?" Sebastian asked.

"Nothing, just a story." Veirella answered. Just thinking about it made her skin move. "Okay, but what is it?" Gemma asked again. All her friends looked at her, waiting for an answer that Veirella would not be giving. They all turned to Aspen when he spoke. "It is a monster in this book our sister read to her when we were children.

It stole children from their beds at night to feed on their magic. While doing so, it killed them. Then felt their bodies where their parents could find them." Aspen explained. "That sounds close to what we are dealing with. Is there a chance that—"

"—Not even a little. It was a story that Iris never should have told her. It was a stupid fable meant to scare children into doing what their parents told them." Aspen cut Gemma off. She stood and went over to him, "but what if it was real? Most fables are based on reality." That was the last thing Veirella wanted to hear, that there was a chance the thing was real. "Anastasia, if the Serabi were real, there would be more than one mention of it. There would be death recorders of the kids that were killed.

History is to be taught not erased, so we can learn not to repeat it. As heir I have been taught just about every form of threat we have ever faced and I can tell you with certainty that the creature you are talking about does not exist." Gemma's face fell at his words, Veirella knew she would regret saying the words that came out of her mouth but she did it, anyway. "What about the Book of Nazira? It keeps track of all magical creatures, living and dead. If the Serabi is real, it would be in there."

"No one knows where it is. It was lost over six hundred years ago." Aspen told her. Veirella smiled at her brother. There was something she knew that he did not. Veirella knew he looked for it once, but had no luck in finding it. "It is not lost, it is being protected. And Iris knows where it is." She told him.

"Did she tell you, or have you actually seen it?" Competitive as ever, they always threw it in each other's faces when they did something to best the other. But this was one thing their sister kept to herself. "I have. I got to read a few pages before it disappeared, but she knows where it is."

Gemma smiled at her, "then we need your sister. This may lead us to nothing, but it is still worth looking into." The smile on Veirella's face faded at the thought of her sister coming to Astro. She spent so long ignoring her that Veirella did not know if asking for her help would do anything.

"It is worth looking into. There is very little chance we find anything. Considering what Henry said, it is likely a virus or infection." Aspen sighed, dropped his head, then looked around at them. "I guess where are going to get my sister. This is going to be interesting." He continued.

After speaking to Genevieve, Aspen and Sebastian portaled to Estonia the next morning. To ask Iris for her help, they should be back by nightfall if she agreed to come. It was making Veirella's head spin.

Do you think she still hates you? If you were my sister, I would still hate you.

Why did you even come home? You should have stayed in that cocoon. You should be dead.

But no worries, you can still fix that.

Veirella was trying to make them stop, but she could not. The breathing was not working and telling them to shut up only made them louder. Veirella was sitting on her bed, her arms wrapped around her legs as she cried she pushed herself back and forth. It had been a while since she last heard them, and even longer since it had gotten this bad.

Veirella thought they were gone, that she would never need to hear them again. It was so much that she did not hear her door being opened, did not hear her name being called, or feel when the bed moved from someone sitting next to her, but she felt the touch. A hand rubbed her arm, soothing her. Veirella opened her eyes and saw Luka next to her, worry written on his face.

The voice got quieter and quieter until they faded into silence. "Are you okay Dove?" his voice was soft and sweet. Veirella did not know what to say. She knew she was not okay, but how did she explain what she was feeling?

Instead of fumbling over what to say, she wrapped her arms around his neck and hugged her back. Luka rubbed his hands over her back as Veirella's hold on him tightened. She stayed that way for some time, not saying anything, just silencing crying.

Luka said nothing. He did not ask why she was crying or made a joke about how she was drenching him in her tears. He just sat there holding her. Once the tears stopped, Veirella let go of him and returned to where she was sitting on the bed. "Do you want to talk about it?" Veirella wanted to. She just did not know how to get the words out.

"My world is covered in darkness, everyone knows reason for it but not the mark it made, seeing the light is a rarity for me so when I do I grab onto it as tight as I can because I know it will eventually fade away and leave me in the darkness again." Veirella was not sure her words made sense, but that was the best she could do.

"I started hearing voices in my head, saying all these horrible things. I don't know how long it has been and I can not remember when I did not hear them." Veirella choked back tears before she continued, "it happened so much, and there was nothing I could do. I thought I would be stuck like that forever. But," Veirella stopped, looked over at her table, then at Luka, who was watching her, she did not see any judgment or pity in his eyes.

He was not looking at her like she was crazy for the things she was saying. "Onne morning a bird flew into my window, it died. I cried for it, then I heard it, telling me I should go out the window. Over and over and over again." She took a breath, then kept going. "I just wanted them to stop. I have no idea how I got it, but one moment I could belay, think or breathe and the next I was bleeding. I was holding a dagger, I stuck it in my hand.

The pain made it go away. Like me, hurting myself was satisfying for it. The pressure in my chest faded, and I felt better. Doing that made me feel better." She stopped and looked at Luka whose face was still the same "for a while I liked that feeling, and the voices were gone and I thought I found a way to deal with it, I sleep with that dagger, I made small cuts to my fingers every time that pressure would come back. I can't tell you how long I did, days, weeks, maybe even months. All I know is I did hear it."

Veirella stopped thinking of what to say next. When she felt Luka's hand on hers, when she looked at him. "I realized something was wrong with me, because I was willing to hurt myself to be able to function. When the voice came back, I guess small cuts weren't enough anymore. I went to cut my arm open, but I managed to stop myself long enough to throw it out the window. I have no idea how long I sat there listening to it, but eventually I made them stop. I don't know how, maybe I just wanted it bad enough." No one else knew. Veirella kept it all to herself, and somehow she felt comfortable enough to tell this boy she barely knew.

"Is that why you stay away from sharp objects?" he remembered what she told him in the forest, and she nodded in response, "is there something that triggers it?"

"There usually is."

"What triggered this one?" he asked. That was a whole other thing, but it was not worse that telling someone you heard voices in your head. "My sister she has been avoiding me and I honesty do not know what to expect when I see her tonight."

"I am sure if you talk to her, you can learn why she did that." It was a good idea, but what would she say? How would she do it? But instead of asking, Veirella changed the topic, "Why did you come looking for me?" Luka smiled, "wanted to see if you wanted to do some training, but that can wait—"

"—No I would love to, doing that thing with Gemma just make me what more. I will go change and met you in the training room."

Veirella dressed in light blue trainers, putting them on felt familiar like she had done it a hundred times before. Which was likely, she did not remember everything that happening in the time she spent at Nightwell

Castle, but trained skills became a part of you once you went enough time doing them.

Veirella stood before the mirror looking at herself. She was still getting use to what she looked like. Everything about her was different her body, her size, face, and voice; and she got to see none of it happen.

From the reflection in the mirror, she saw Willow appear behind her. She had not shown up for a few days now. Veirella thought about calling for, but thought better of it, Willow may have had a responsibility to her but Veirella knew her way around the place, and the bath that was set for her nightly was a sign that Willow was still around.

"Where are you going?" Veirella turned to her and looked down at her clothes again. "To train with Luka. I asked him to help me." Willow smiled at her. She was probably surprised to hear that Veirella was training again. "You spend a lot of time with the fire wielder. "

"I spend a lot of time with Gemma as well. I do not see your point." She answered. "What about the water wielder? No interest in seeing him?"

Veirella turned away from her and went to her vanity to tie up her hair. She did not want to talk about Sebastian. He lied to her, and she did not want anything to do with him. "Sebastian is never here, and when he is, he spends most of his time outside of the court." She answered.

It was the truth. The few times Veirella had seen him around or attempted to approach him, he walked away, so stopped trying. "Friendships are important. I am sure whatever that he did, to pull this reaction from you can be fixed. People make mistakes, it is a part of life." Willow told her, but Veirella was not interested in forgiving him, not anytime soon anyway. And considering Sebastian, showed her more than once that he wanted nothing to do with her, she would not force a relationship.

"I need to meet Luka, we can talk about your absents in the last few days when I get back." Veirella looked at Willow who turned her head away, whatever it was that kept her away she did not want to talk about it.

"Something you do not want to talk about. How fun is it?" Then she walked out of the room.

When Veirella entered the training room, Luka was doing warmups. She was never taught to stretch or doing anything specific before training. Elizabeth told her she would not get to warmup before someone tried to kill her so cold starts was her norm. Doing so left her in more pain that if she had done something to get her body ready, but over time she got use to it and so did her body.

When Luka finished, he turned to her brows raised, "it is always better to warmup before training it hurts less." She shock her head, "I was taught cold starts, pain is important for growth, and it keeps you alert." Luka nodded, then went to the door and took two bow staffs from the wall, he tossed one to her then got back on the mat and Veirella caught it with ease.

"You do intend to actually fight me, right? The last time we were here, you did not take me seriously." She asked. Luka dropped his head, smiled then looked back up at her, "that does not really count Dove. And I do not like throwing hits at people I like when I am angry." Veirella did not say anything she needed him to say the words.

"But yes, this will be an actual fight. No messing around. I promise" Luka raised his right hand to his chest, over his heart then tilting his head forward. "Lets do this," Veirella told him, then moved to the center of the mat with him following. She turned to him. Luka was going for offense, so she did, too. Disgusted as defense.

"Ready?"

"Ready."

Luka wanted to attack first. The way his body moved showed it was his primary, so she pushed him into protecting, by attacking before he could. Veirella was fast. She went for his head with no intention of landing a hit. When he raised his staff to stop hers, she went for his right, hitting him in the side.

He jumped back and smiled at her, which she returned. "That one was for not using my name." She told him, "why would I do that when I see the effect it has on you," Luka smiling at her. Veirella did not give him time to regain control. She went at him repeatedly. He was good at blocking her moves. Veirella only got three more hits in before he got her. Veirella was fast, so it was more a graze that a full hit.

He was catching on to what she was going, so he started putting more distance between them. When she went after him, he let her get close then spun out of her attack, then swap her feet from under her, knocking her on the mat. Luka offered her a hand up; she took it then backed away. Unlike her, Luka waited for Veirella to pull herself together before attacking.

She nodded at Luka for him to keeping going, then they both attacked, she hit he blocked; he returned an attack she blocked. They when on like that for a while, neither getting the other. Veirella noticed Luka was following a pattern when he attacked her. He did the same three moves in different sequences, but they were the same.

Bo spin into a cross strike, downward smash, Bo spin into an up strike, and a poke strike. The spin was a major move in most of his attacks. Veirella watched him do it a few times, timing how long it took him to get into it and then out. Eight and half second, Veirella let him get close but left enough space to force him to use it and when he swiped from strike to spin, she went for his left leg.

Knocking him on the mat, then holding the head of her staff over his face. Luka's face went from confused to shocked, then he smiled up at. "Okay, you win," he said, trying to catch his breath. Veirella was still breathing normally. Her heart was beating four beats faster. And she had small beads of sweat on her neck, but she was mostly fine. Veirella pulled her staff back and gave Luka her hand to help him up.

It was mostly point less he took it but used his other hand to push himself up. "For someone who has done no trained in years, you seem to be in perfect form." *It really had been years.* She thought. "Guess I am more prepared than I originally thought" she tried to make her words not sound so dry and pitiful but it did not work.

She saw Luka's face fall, and she thought of something to say she had spilled enough to him for one day. "And that was for calling be Dove and not my name" she pointed a finger in his face, a smile broke across his lips "but I like it so much, and know you hate it" he told her then stepped closer, "okay what if I started calling you Enzo, how would you like people calling you a name you do not care for?" Veirella asked.

Her change in name did not have the same effect on him as he did her. "Go right ahead," he told her, then got a little closer, if that was even possible with how closer he already was. "You swell divine" with that Veirella snapped out of the trace and moved away from him. His brows drew together.

"I should go, get ready. The others should be back soon." Veirella turned the bow staff and stretched it out to him. There were a good distance between them far more than there was a moment ago. He took it from her, putting it to stand before him. "Are you okay? Is it something I said?" His voice was soft and filled with concern.

"No, no, not at all. I would just like to be cleaned up." She quickly answered. Luka nodded then dropped his head, clearly not believing her, but he was not going to push for the truth. Veirella nodded, then practically ran from the room.

Eight Years Before

Four weeks, that is how long Veirella had been training with Elizabeth Nightwell. She was one of the first women to ever become a high racking member of the military and she was one of the most difficult teachers to have, or at least that was what Iris said about her.

And Veirella was starting to agree. She was hit from every direction to the point she could not tell which direction she got knocked off her feet from. "You are not paying attention to your surroundings. What if you are have no visibility? You will have no idea what direction you will be getting attacked from.

Now on your feet and try again." There was no warmth in her voice. She was cold and commanding. Veirella would never need any of what she was learning. She lived in a palace where she was protected at all times. When would she need to fight someone? But she did not say that. She just stood and took her place back in the center where she was surrounded on all sides by girls almost twice her size.

Veirella retrieved the bow staff from the ground and took up one of the defensive positions Elizabeth spent the first week showing her, the girl's all took attack positions which she was starting to learn.

"Begin." Elizabeth ordered, and the girl to her left came at her. Veirella managed to move out of the way, then hit her with the staff. She raised hers blocking the attack. Veirella saw her look behind her and she tucked and rolled before the girl behind could hit her.

Then the girl's on her left and right went in for hits, but she raised her staff, blocking them both and kicking the one to her right. She dropped to the ground, and Veirella went for the other, but she moved before she could hit her. That was the last time hit she managed to get in. For the next hour, she was either protecting herself from hits or getting hit.

Veirella was in so much pain after training, she could barely walk. Everyone of her training session's ended with her covered in bruises, then her limping back to her room, where there was a warm bath awaiting her. But that day was different. One of the girls told her that she did good. That was a first for Veirella most days that would just hit her, then leave her on the training mat. That was the first time any of them said anything to her.

"You did good out there."

"Thank you, but considering my butt still hurts from hitting the ground so many times, I think the opposite." She responded. The girl laughed. "well look on the bright side. You got some hits in and you managed to get one of us off the mat and, considering you have never done that before, I think that can be considered good." She told her.

Veirella nodded in response. "My name is Lily by the way," she told her. She had long reddish-brown hair, light brown skin with light brown eyes and wore the same blue Keives Veirella was.

"Nice to officially meet you. After you sent weeks hitting me, it feels nice to know one of your names." They were the only ones left in the room. The other girls left when Elizabeth did. That was the routine. Once they were finished hitting her, Elizabeth would tell her all the ways she failed and everything she needed to work on.

And if she did not mention something, then she had not messed it up, which was currently only her stance. Everything else seemed to be a problem. "Hey, want to see something amazing?" Lily asked, smiling down at her. Veirella nodded and Lily jumped off the mat and went out the door that led to the balcony. Veirella took some time getting herself off the mat and out the door after her.

"What is it?" She looked around, not seeing anything but rocks and plants. She could see most of the forest from where she was and some of the mountains. "I have seen you outside playing with the birds and thought you were the perfect person to share this with." Lily picked up one of the rocks, closed both her hands around it, and green sparks moved around her fingers. Veirella watched in awe as she opened her hands and to rock between them began spinning and then it changed. The rock was no longer a rock, it was now a flower, a lily to be specific. Veirella looked up at her and smiled.

"How did you do that?" she asked. Veirella had seen the gardeners grow plants with the magic but never change one thing into another. Lily changed the flower back into a rock and gave it to Veirella. "I can show you how, if you want?" Lily asked her. Veirella nodded so fast if her head was not attached to her body, it would have fallen off.

"First thing you should know, magic comes from your emotions and if you can control those emotions, you can do amazing things, and negative emotions work best." Lily explained. Veirella's face scrunched together. "What do you mean?" she asked.

"The bad things you feel, like being mad or angry. Sometimes even hate, those are all negative emotions and you can take them and do what I just did. So is there anyone you are angry at or hate?" Lily asked. Veirella thought about it for a moment and thought of her parents. She was angry at them for sending her away.

Veirella nodded at Lily in response, "Okay, think about the person or people. The more negative the emotion, the better. Then close your hands around the rock." She did as Lily instructed. "Then close your eyes and think about how anger they make you," and Veirella did just that. She thought about her mother, who she had not spoken to since she told her she was going away, and her father how made the decision to it in the first place.

And green sparks started moving around her arms and fingers. "Good. Good, now think about what you want it to become. Think of your favorite flower and make it appear." Veirella did as Lily instructed. Lilacs were her favorite flowers, so she thought of them. A moment later she felt the rock pushing against her hands and she opened them to let it move, then she opened her eyes to see what was happening.

The rock began spinning the form the purple flower; she loved so much. "I did it." She smiled up at Lily, who mirrored her. "Yes, you did," she responded. "I need to tell Iris about this," Veirella told her, putting down the flower she created and turned to go back inside.

"No!" Lily yelled, stopping her. Veirella turned back to her, confused on why she said that, "I mean why not wait until you are much better at it. And surprise her with your new skill," she explained. Veirella liked that suggestion. She could make her flowers from stones as a gift.

"Okay."

Spoken Truth

Veirella

Veirella laid in the bath for over an hour after washing herself clean. She contemplated washing her hair but considered she had done it already earlier in the week; she reframed for doing so.

"Do you intend to stay in there until you look like a crone?" Willow asked. She lending against the frame of the door, waiting for her. "Maybe." There were some gifts of magic, like the bath she was in. No matter how long she stayed in the water, it would never get cold.

"This is nice. It will be worth looking aged." She responded. Then sank deeper into the water, letting it get to the tip of her ear; she felt bits of her hair getting wet, but it was worth it. "I think your skin is too smooth for such damage of it, so it is time to get out." Willow grabbed her robe off the hook next to the door, went over to the bath and opened it waiting for Veirella to step in. "Just a little longer." she closed her eyes and lend head back against the golden tub.

"Well then, I will tell your friends to begin without you. Considering you need more time." Veirella opened her eyes and looked up at Willow. She was still holding the robe open, and she smiling down at her. "Why are they waiting for me?" she asked, her brows pulling together. "Your siblings have returned." At that Veirella stood, stepped out of the bath and into the waiting robe.

"When did they return?" Veirella asked as she made her way back into her room, where Willow had already picked out a dress for her to wear. It was blue, darker than she usually wore, with gold flowers intricately sown into it. "Not long. They needed to go see the headmistress before coming here."

Veirella went to her armoire, picked out black undergarments that would go unnoticed in the dress. Then she turned back to Willow, who was holding it out for her. Veirella stepped into it and Willow laced it up in the back.

Most of her dresses did not require help to put on. Meaning no one at home knew about Willow and had packed Veirella's things for her to be self-sufficient. Once Willow was finished tying the dress, she went to the closet. Veirella went back to the armoire for a pair of dark blue socks.

When Willow came back holding matching flats, Veirella shook her head no to them. She was not going further than the commons, which were right outside her door. Shoes felt unnecessary. Willow put the shoes down and when to take Veirella's hair down. They took three braids from each side and used a band to tie it back from her face.

Veirella thanked her, then went to leave the room, but stopped when her hand touched the handle, and looked at the door like she could see what was on the other side of it. "Do you think she will speak to me?" Veirella did not know why she was asking her; she did not ever mention Iris to Willow. But she knew other things about her. Maybe she would know this too.

"I do not have an answer for you. I do not know your sister. But I do hope whatever it is, you two can find a way to work through it." Willow's words helped release some of the pressure built up on Veirella's chest, but not much of it. But she turned and smiled at her all the same. Then turned back to look at where her hand was holding the handle. She closed her eyes, breathing in and out twice, counted to ten, then opened her eyes and finally opened the door.

When she walked into the commons, Gemma was the only one there. She was seated on one of the sofa's her legs crossed beneath her; she was still in her uniform. She must not have been there long. Veirella made her way around to where she was sitting and sat next to her. Gemma watched her as she did so. When Veirella looked at her, she smiled and Veirella did the same.

She looked around the room, seeing if she just missed something. The place was so quiet a feather could fall and it would be heard. The only sound was the crackling sound of the fire burning. Veirella did not know who kept lighting it or if it just happened on its own.

"Where is everyone?" Willow said her siblings were here, but there was no one but her and Gemma in the commons. "Luka is in his room, and Pax took Iris and Aspen to see the headmistress." Gemma answered. "How are you doing, with everything that happened?" Veirella did not know how to answer that question, at the moment watching it happen it was terrifying, but she did not know where her mind was or how to handle any of what she saw. "I don't know" she shrugged, then looked at her friend. "You?"

"About the same" Gemma answered, then looked down at her hands, "are you okay? I mean in general" Veirella asked. Gemma was not one to be quiet, so something was wrong. She sighed, "well my powers are still shit, and Julia has not answered any of my letters in the past three weeks. I think I said something I probably shouldn't have, and she is angry with me. I have a habit of not keeping my opinion to myself."

Veirella did not know Julia. Gemma had written about her in some of their letters, but she had never actually ever met her, but she knew the girl was important to Gemma. "I am sure whatever it is, you will get an answer eventually. And as far as your wielding goes, once you find yourself, I have no doubt it will come back to you," Veirella assured her.

She did not know how Gemma felt; she wanted her powers to work and Veirella wished she could get hers to stop. She wished she could go back to being normal; it was fun watching other people wield. Doing it, on the other hand, did not pull the same feeling from her. Veirella had not tried to wield in a while. It was not important and at the moment. With everything going on, if white coat was right about the virus, then there was a chance she could set it off my using magic if she was already infected.

But a part of her felt she would require magic and that was the last thing she wanted to do.

Moments later, Sebastian, Iris, and Aspen came through the doors. And at the same time Luka came out of his room. "This place is beautiful," Iris stated, looking around, eyes wide. "Thank You" Gemma answered. Sebastian looked over at her, brow raised. "You had nothing to do with the way it looks in here."

She shrugged. "This is our home. The proper thing to do is to accept a compliment when given one." She told. Gemma went to greet Iris, but Veirella did not move from where she was sitting, but she watched them. Veirella could feel someone watching her. But she did not turn to look, she knew it was Luka. He was the only one outside her line of sight.

And he was the only one other than Aspen, who knew why she was not going to greet her sister. She would not acknowledge him, doing so would give away how tense she was, and the boy already knew too many private and personal things about her.

"Iris, it is a pleasure to have you with us, and thank you for giving us your time and help." Gemma switched from relaxed and friendly to polite and diplomatic within seconds. She was still being friendly, but it was different from the way she spoke with the others. Her tone, pasture, were more formal, her head was higher and her back was straighter.

"No need for formalities, our parents are not around to see," Iris told her then smiled, "and it is my pleasure to help, especially knowing that you need my help with something that infringes on my brother's love." She looked over at Aspen he rolled his eyes at her, and Iris's smile grew a little wider.

The relationship they shared was one Veirella always yearned for. Someone who knew you better than you did yourself, and no matter the circumstances, they would have your back. Friendship was similar in a lot of ways, but a friend was more likely to leave you for dead than a sibling was.

Aspen and Iris were twins. They came into the world together, and experienced most things together. Veirella thought they could read each other's minds, the way they could go from two individuals to one mind. She always wanted that. Veirella was close to her brother, but it was not the same he treated her like a child. Their relationship was more mentor/mentee than anything else.

She did not think that type of connections was someone was something she would ever experience, and she did not truly know Aspen or Iris anymore. They grew up, became different people. They had years; five, to be exact. Aspen felt less like her brother and more like a father. He spent more time worrying and taking care of her than making jokes and having fun.

But that was not new. Even when they were younger, she was never allowed to partake in their games just watch. Veirella could understand them treating her differently. After all, she was not a real Greystone. She wore the name but did not share the blood.

"You were always more interested in priestesses than I was so it makes perfect sense why you know and I do not." Aspen's words came from a place of logic but also jealousy. Veirella could hear it in his voice and by the way, Iris's lips found a way to grow wider. She did, too.

"That is not the real reason you do not know the location of Nazira's book. She did not trust men, so even though the book was given to us to protect, no king has ever been privy to that information." She informed him. Aspen turned to her, "if it has to do with who is on the throne then, why do you know? You are second in line." He asked.

"It has nothing to do with who rules and the book was given to us over four thousand years ago. In a time where in was inconceivable for a woman to rule, why do you think our kingdom is the only to require both a male and female heirs?" Aspen shrugged, "Progress." both Gemma and Iris turn their heads to the side, looking at him.

Aspen looked between them, then nodded his head. "Okay, I guess not."

"Okay, let's get back to the topic at hand and not get into how shit the world we live in is." Gemma said, loud enough for them all to hear. "Right."

"As I was saying, Nazira did not trust men, considering they did destroy the tree of life, and are the reason why some of the creatures she wrote about went extinct." Iris stopped and looked at teh three of them.

"She intrusted the book with princess Azalea the day she died. And for generations, the location has been passed from princess to princess." She continued.

"Why not mother to child?" Gemma asked. "She only had sons, so she told her niece, her older brother's child. May mistakenly thought she did it to keep it within the direct royal line, so everyone there after continued the tradition." Iris answered. "That is...a lot."

"And completely understandable." Aspen added, "You said this has to do with all the deaths over that past year. How will the book help?" Iris asked. Aspen signed and looked at Veirella then back at their sister. "Gemma, as it in her head that the creature from that book you gave Veirella might be real. The one doing all of this, and the only way to get her to move past this, is looking through that book."

"No." that was all she said, "Iris, a lot of kids have died and so many more could." Sebastian looked in Veirella's direction and so did Iris, "if we do not find a way to stop this. I know we are asking for a lot, but please think about it." Sebastian continued.

"I will think about it, give me sometime. Because you are asking for a lot." She answered. "Thank You." Gemma sighed, happy that she was thinking about it. The sky grew black some time later, and Iris disappeared with Gemma down the hall. Sebastian tried speaking to Veirella but when he sat next to her, she stood and went to her room.

Sometime later, Gemma came in and gave her a note with two words *written on it: BLACK MOUNTAIN.*

Blood Bond

Sebastian

She hated me, Sebastian thought as he watched Veirella walk away from him. She moved like she could not get away from him fast enough. “What happened there? Luka asked as he watched Veirella close practically run from him. “I helped lie to her about something, unknowingly.” He answered.

“If you did not mean to, then why not tell her that?” Sebastian did not know how to answer him, because there was something else he was lying about and he did not know how well she would take it. Sebastian did his best to stay away from her. Every time he saw Veirella he just wanted to shout the words at her.

The secret pulled at his lips every time he was with her. He wanted her to know the truth, but would she hate him for it? “You have not told her yet, have you?” Aspen asked. Sebastian shook his head. “No.” Aspen sighed, “why not? She has been here for months.” Sebastian stood and went to the window.

“Why didn’t you?” Sebastian asked. Aspen also knew the truth. Why was it only Sebastian’s responsibility to tell her? He was her brother. “Because it is not my secret to tell.” He answered. Sebastian dropped his head and sighed.

"I will do it eventually, when the time is right or if she ever decides to speak to me again." Which he did not think was likely ever going to happen. "What are you two going on about?" Luka asked, his brows drew together watching them. "Ask him. Not likely he'll tell you, though."

Sebastian went to say something to Aspen, but stopped himself when Ana and Iris came in. They looked at all the three of them, then at each other. They could tell something was going on. The tension in the room was so thick it could be seen. "Is everything okay?" Ana asked.

"Asked those two." Luka told her. Aspen turned to them, but Sebastian spoke before he could. "So, are we going to get the book?" Aspen looked at him for a second, then returning his attention to Iris. "Yeah, Iris gave me the location." Ana answered, "When do we leave?" Aspen asked. Iris smiled at him then walked over,and grabbed his arm, "you are not going. You, my dear brother, are not allowed to know where it is, sorry" the look on her face said she was anything but.

"Sure you are. That look on your face is very apologetic."

"So, just you three?" Luka asked. Iris released Aspen and turned to him. "No, Anastasia will stay here; it may take a few days, and first years are not allowed to leave. But Veirella is your loophole. She does not have regular classes, and she does not need to check in with anyone. So, no one will notice she is missing, and you also need an earth wielder to get there," Iris explained.

"How can those two go but I can not?" Aspen asked his sister, "neither of them are Forian. Once they leave, they will forget where it is. All they'll remember is being there." Iris answered.

"When do we leave?" Sebastian asked, "In the morning." Iris answered, *no prep time. This should be fun,* he thought. "The sooner the better, considering the circumstances."

"Then I guess we should get some sleep. Our first blind mission. This should be fun," Luka said, moving from the sofa, then made his way to his room. Sebastian ignored the excitement he heard in his voice. There were some things that would never change.

"One of us should tell Veirella" Sebastian told them. He looked from Aspen to Iris. They looked at each other, then Anastasia stepped forward. "I will" she looked at Iris. "I'll see you in the library tomorrow." She nodded, then Ana walked past him and making her way to Veirella's door.

Sebastian watched the door closed. He stood there watching like he was waiting for her to come back and tell them what she said. "You need to tell her." He sighed, then moved past the twins, headed for his own room. "I will" *eventually.*

Sebastian was up before the sun. He got very little sleep, which was the worst way to start a mission, especially one he had so little information about. He did not know what to expect, and because Iris said so little, Sebastian had a feeling she did not know what they were in for. He sat on his desk cleaning his arrows for the third time or fourth time. He lost count at some point; he would finish and they start over again.

Sebastian was not paying much attention to the act. He was going off memory from doing it so many times over the years. He wiped both sides of an arrow, carefully avoiding the sharp head, put it down, then took another. All Sebastian could focus on was how he was going to get Veirella to talk to him, every time he thought if something to say it would be wrong.

He knew he would need to tell her the truth eventually, but he did not know how to start or where to star from, but he knew it needed to happen sooner rather than later. When he started his next round of cleaning, someone came to his door, knocked, then opened it. Luka stepped in and closed it behind him.

"Are you okay?" He asked, brows pulled together. Sebastian knew Luka well enough to know he was not the type to worry about anyone, included himself. And if he was asking, Sebastian was not doing as good of a job at hiding it as he thought. Luka looked down at the cloth and arrow Sebastian was holding, and his eyes followed. He was not doing as good of a job avoiding cutting himself as he thought. The white fabric was turning red with his blood.

He put down the cloth and the arrow, stood from the table and rain his hand through his hair. "Yes, everything is fine. Just a little on edge about today," he answered. Luka went to the desk and picked up the arrow that Sebastian was holding and examined it.

"Just a little?"

Sebastian took the arrow from him and placed in back in the quiver, and did the same with the others, two of which had blood on them. "Does this have something to do with the big secret you're keeping from Veirella?" Sebastian stopped to and looked at his friend. "Why are you so suddenly interested in Veirella?" Luka shrugged. "She lives with us, and she's quiet. I find it intriguing." He answered, "is that so?" Luka rolled his eyes.

"Are you going to tell me what you're hiding or not?" he ignored Sebastian's words and continued his search so an answer. "You can know when she does." Luka rolled his eyes. That was not the answer he wanted, but it was all he was going to get.

"You ready? We have been waiting for over an hour." Sebastian released the last arrow, watched it fall into place, then turned to Luka. "Why didn't you not come get me sooner?" Luka leaned back against the wall.

"Because I not your mother, or your second. Mange your own time." He answered. Sebastian strapped his quiver across left shoulder and placed his pack on the other. Then he retrieved his bow from its place on the wall above the table.

"Two things, one you should work on your time management skills and, two you should find a better system for travelling. Because this" Luka waved his hand over Sebastian, "is a disaster waiting to happen." Sebastian looked himself over, then back up at Luka. "It has not failed me yet. And in most situations, we have a base set up, so I will not always have the bag with me."

Luka pushed off the wall and went for the door. "Yet, being the focus of everything you just said," Sebastian followed him out. "Scenario; what if we are on our way to an assignment and we get ambushed? With the time it takes you to get rid of you pack and place your arrow, you could get shot."

"So, what do you suggest? No supplies? Or no bow?" part of the Luka's question made sense, but he needed a solution that Sebastian was sure he did not have. "I did not think of that part yet," Luka answered. Sebastian went to say something, but Luka raised his hand, stopping him. "But I will...eventually." He continued.

"You do that, and then I will do something about it. But for now, this works." Sebastian looked around the empty room, then turned to Luka, his brow raised. "Where is Veirella?" Luka shrugged. "She was just here." And as if summoned by her named being called, Anastasia's door opened. She came out, Veirella following behind.

"Ready to go?" She was asking Luka. Veirella did not even look in Sebastian's direction. "When you are?" he answered. "How does this work? The portal?" Veirella asked Luka *again*. "I think it's best if Pax explains that" Luka looked at Sebastian, and he stepped forward. Veirella reluctantly looked at him. "All the continents have wards or shields created by their elemental wielders.

So it limits where on the continents a wielder of another element can go. I could get us on Fianorea, but that is about it. If we needed to go somewhere specific, we would need an earth wielder like yourself to get there." Veirella nodded, taking into what he was saying.

"So do they work like port keys, where you think about where you want to go and it takes you there?" she asked. Sebastian shook his head. "Yes and no, with a port key, the destination you opened it thinking of is the only place you can go and anyone else that goes through will end up in the same place, until the port as being closed and reopened again. But with a portal where you want to go is where it will send you and only you. But if others are going through with you, they think of you instead of a place." Sebastian explained.

"Okay, so I can open a portal and you can follow be through without knowing where we are going?" Sebastian guessed, based on her question, she would not tell him where they were going. "Yes, or if you hold someone." He answered. "Like Luka did for me when we went to Corviac?" she asked. Luka smiled down at her and nodded.

"How do I open a portal?" she raised her hands, and they all stopped her. Veirella looked around at them, her eyes grew wide like theirs' did. "What?" she asked, looking between Luka and Sebastian. "You will not be opening a portal. I will use your energy to do it for you." Sebastian answered, panic taking his voice.

"Why can I not do it myself?" she asked, her brows pulling together. "Because it takes time to learn how to do it. You opening a portal without training could end with you cutting yourself in half. Or worse, send you to another dimension."

If she tried to open one just then, with the amount of power she had, she was likely to kill them all. "Also, long distance is not the best why to start. I will get us to Fianorea, I will pull from you to get where we need to go." He continued.

Sebastian pulled on his magic, then pushed it out. Once he had enough of it in open space, he thought about where he wanted to go, then all the blue sparks on his arm began forming in the air, moving to form a circle; the center looked like water was forming at the beginning of a storm, or waves in the ocean.

"I thought we could not open portal's in places frequented by people, will this not affect us?" Veirella asked, eyes wide looking at Luka. "That only applies to mortals, and considering we all wield, and none of us have had side effects from it I think we will be fine" he answered.

Things like that did not happen often, but when it did. It was not something anyone who liked the ability to sleep wanted to ever hear or see. Neither he nor Luka had ever seen it happen, and he was guessed the same for Anastasia, but she liked to torture people, so Sebastian would not put it past her doing it to someone.

"We should get going" Veirella walked up to the portal, "Where is your pack?" Sebastian asked her, but she did not turn to look at him or answer his question.

“You are going to Fianorea. If she needs something, I am sure nature will provide it.” Ana answered for her. “and she has Willow. Who is literacy just a call away if she needs something.” she continued.

It much be fun being Veirella having a Nyx that actually liked you, his told him to piss off the day they met. “Okay, let's do this.

VEIRELLA

Veirella held Luka’s hand as she went through the portal. It took longer to get to the other side than it had before. Her vision clouded with blue light as it moved around her, which made her head spin. When they made it to the other side, Veirella felt her body moving forward she was going to fall.

“I got. Long distance jumps for someone new is always hard. Also, if you are going to fall, it is best you doing it in the other direction.” Veirella was already having a hard time focusing, and Luka’s words did not make any sense. “What?” she asked, her voice low and hoarse.

“Look in front of you” Veirella managed to open her eyes a fraction to see what he was referring to. She threw herself back against Luka. Her heart sped up. As she saw where there were. They were standing on the edge of a cliff. Down below water was hitting against the rocks hard and fast. If she had fallen over, either the fall would kill her or the waves would.

“I thought he was one of the best at this?” Veirella asked. Her voice was filled with both panic. “He is, but traveling to a continent that is not your own tends to bring you closest to your element.” She looked up at him. From where she was in his arms, Veirella could not see his eyes. “Is that why you did not do it? You could portal us into a magma reservoir?" Luka shook his head, and his body tensed beneath her.

A moment later, Sebastian came through, landing behind them. "Next time you sent someone through a portal warn then about what might be waiting for them on the other side." Veirella's words were meant to come off harsher than they did, but with how light her voice was it did not have the intended impact.

"Sorry about that, but at least you did not fall in." Sebastian attempted a smile at her. It did not turn into a full one. There was caution in his eyes. Like he was preparing for how she would respond or react.

But she did not instead to. Veirella rolled her eyes at him and pulled away from Luka, then stepped around him. "We need to figure out where we are so we know where we are going." Veirella started looking around, trying to find any identifiers. They were in one of three places, Irredia, Cracia, or Atryae. They were the only places on the continent that had such direct access to the water. Irredia had a lot of tall trees no matter where in the region you were, they could be seen, so that was not it.

It could be Atryae because of all the flat land around, most of its citizens lived closer in land and the mountain's that would be seen there were west, however the one's Veirella saw in the distance where south; so they were in Cracia.

There was a small island southwest of Cracia in the direction of the Black Mountains. Veirella turned around and both Luka and Sebastian were looking at her; she was the only one who knew where they were going. There was so much fog around because it was still early in the morning. "We could really use Gemma right now," she said, mostly to herself. "What is it?" Luka asked, moving towards her, "what do you need?"

"Trying to figure out where we are, I think we are in Cracia but I do not know for sure. There should be an island in that direction" she raised her hand to show him and he turned to look where she was pointing, "but there is so much fog in the air it's hard to see anything" she answered.

Luka smiled at her then sent balls of fire into the air, burning away the fog. It took some time, but after a while she could see the tip of a rock formation. "There it is." She pointed it out, "we are in Cracia, that means we are going this way. We should get there by nightfall if we start now and take no stops between." She told them Luka and Sebastian nodded, and a smile broke across her lips.

They walked for four hours, then made the choice to stop. It was not realistic for them to take no breaks, especially on that side of the continent where it was always warmer and, with the sun in the sky, it was worse. If they were up north, they would not have had that problem.

"It is way too hot to be walking around at this time of day." Veirella stated, then found a tree with the most shadows to sit under, then closed her eyes and took in the cool air that hit her. "You grew up here." Veirella open her eyes. Luka was standing before her, holding out a canteen. Shook her head, refusing him. As hot as it was, she did not need it.

"I grew up in the north. It gets warm up there, but not this warm." Veirella looked around for Sebastian, but he was not with them. "Where is Sebastian?" Veirella looked up at Luka when he did not answer. His brow raised, he was looking down at her with his canteen halfway to his lips. "What? Where is he?" she asked again.

"So we are using given names now?" Veirella shrugged at his question. "That is his name, is it not?" she remembered what he told her the day they met or when they were reintroduced. That was the name his friends called him and they were not friends, so Veirella saw no reason for her to call him that. "Whatever happened between the two of you, I am sure he feels shitty about it. As smart as he is, Pax can be oblivious sometimes." Luka told her.

"He lied. I gave him a chance to be honesty, and he was not" Luka went to say something, but she raised her hand to stop him. "And even if he did not have the answer, anything else was better than lying." She continued.

Veirella could tell he wanted to continue defending his friend's honor, but she did not want to hear it. The topic of conversation needed to change, "what are those marks on your arm?" she pointed up at his right arm where the black lines were going up, there was no pattern to speak of they were all curved lines moving over each other.

Luka looked do at his arm, he stayed that way for a while not saying anything. Veirella did not want their conversation to end. If she knew they were a sore subject for him she would not have brought it up, but she knew nothing about him so she was unaware of what was okay to ask about and what was not.

But he made no to attempt to hide them, like she did her Lovia; Veirella was embarrassed and ashamed to have them. The day she passed her final test, she proceeded to almost die. She did not feel deserving of them, and they were not given to her by a priestess. One day they there was nothing, the next they were there.

They were not as bright as the three vined roses Aspen had on his side or the vines that wrapped around Iris's forearm; they were light noticeable but dull all the same. She thought it was her punishment for not fighting her attackers. "It is a curse." Luka finally spoke, Veirella eyes doubled in size as she pushed herself up from the tree, then reached for his arm before stopping herself.

But he raised it so she could see them. Luka pushed up the sleeve halfway up his wrist. There were six lines overlapping, some darker than others. "How are you cursed?" her voice was low and soft as she asked.

"I was born with it, a produce of being my father's progeny." He answered. Veirella looked up at him to find he was already looking down at her, "every child born of his line is destined to die at twenty-one" Veirella looked away doing that simple math in her head, trying to understand; but finding it hard to, she finally thought of the number, but before she could say it, he did. "I will be die in four years, just like all my siblings before me."

"Why? Is there a way to stop it? Veirella asked, her heart dropping lower with every word he spoke. "No, no, why to stop it or slow it down. This mark appeared on me when I was eight; and it has grown a few inches every year since then. Once it reaches my heart, I will die." Veirella laid her hand on his arm and ran her fingers across them.

"Do you know why you are cursed? Why it happened to any of you?" Luka shrugged. It did not seem to bother him the fact that he was going to die. With the way he was acting, he did not even seem to care. "Not really, but it may have something to do with the mother. And the deal they made, he give them something and return she gave him a child," he answered.

"How often?" There was something there, something was missing; maybe if she could figure it out, Luka would not need to be the next victim of what had to be a very long list. "Every twenty-one years, the moment one dies, another is born. To start the cycle again." Luka answered. She wanted to ask more questions, but Sebastian came back.

"Anything?" Luka asked. Veirella looked behind her. Sebastian was making his way through the trees that got closer the further in they went. "All clear." He answered, *did he just check their surroundings?* Veirella wanted to tell him there was no reason to do that. There may not have seen any other sign of life, but every region on Fianorea had soldiers.

But she reframed from doing so consider she did spend five years locked in a cocoon in a forest similar to that one. She was not the best person to defend Fianorea's safety at the moment. "We should get going. As bad as the heat is, sunlight is our friend," Veirella told them, then they continued walking. Veirella stayed as closed to the trees as she could, just because they needed the sun did not mean she wanted to be in it.

Another few hours passed, and they stopped again; it was starting to get dark. But they were close. They passed the start of the mountain a while back. They just needed to keep going until they reached the higher peaks.

"How much further do we need to go?" Luka asked, it would have being a better idea to tell them where they were going after all they would not remember the exact location but she was trying to be safe. She did not think they would try coming back for the book, but it was her family's responsibility to protect it. "Not far." Veirella looked up at the ridges, then answered.

"We are going up the mountain, right?" Sebastian asked, "Yes, we need to get to the higher peaks, closer to the center." She answered. Veirella was aware of how cold she was acting towards him, but she did not care. "Then we can portal. We will land a little under halfway up. We can walk half the distance today, the rest in the morning." Sebastian told them.

"Why can we not just portal all they why there?" Veirella was still learning, but Sebastian took them from Astro to Cracia in one go. Why could she not just open a portal that took them to the top? "One, we have no idea where exactly we are, two was have no idea what is up there, and finally three you do not have enough of a buildup of Cai in you to do distance like that." He explained, "that takes years, and even then it could still kill you." Sebastian continued.

There was that word again. Veirella wondered if anything magic related did not potentially end with death. "You brought us here without knowing where we were going." Sebastian shook his head at her. "I did not bring us here. I just followed you. I knew we needed to come to Fianorea. That is all. Why do you think you went first?"

"Oh" was all she said. "And I also pulled from the Tethers to help us along. So, it was not as much of a strange on me." *Finally, something I know,* Veirella was happy she learned when she was learning about them. Tethers were connected through the continents as they broke off over a thousand years ago. The tethers kept them connected them. They were invisible to the eye, but someone with a connection to the elements could feel them.

It was nice being told something she did not need explained to her. She wanted to bask in the joy she felt, but it was getting darker, and the forest was not a place she wanted to be at night. "Okay, how do we do this?

"Just give me your hands." Sebastian dropped his pack and gave his bow to Luka. Then Veirella laid both her hands into his. "Just relax and breathe. You may feel some pressure, but that is normal." She nodded, and he did the same. "Ready?"

"Yes"

Sebastian tightened his hold on her, then she felt it. Energy moving through her body, but she was not calling for it Sebastian was. Veirella felt something else similar to her own power, but it was not hers, it was his. Sebastian was not just pulling on her magic, he was pushing his own into h er.

The combination of both their powers was too much. Her breathing became erratic, her body was on fire. Veirella felt the pressure of it all building inside her. It wanted out; not just want it needed out. She closed her eyes, doing her best to keep it in. "You're okay. Breathe through it. This ends badly for both of us if you start panicking." Sebastian's words were comforting. "Okay" she asked.

Veirella focused on her breathing to get it on under control, then the pressure in her chest faded and her power along with it. Then she was falling. Veirella opened her eyes, but she was still standing. She looked down at her hands. Green sparks were moving around them. They moved down her wrists and onto Sebastian's, changing from green to blue.

He let go of her one of her hands and raised it. The sparks jumped off his arm and into the air. Forming a small ball that grew the more magic, he pushed into it. The portal was a mix of them both, green and blue sparks weaving around. Creating a hole in the world. She felt Sebastian's energy pull away. "We got it, this should get us a good way up" he was stopping; for him this was enough, but Veirella felt she could do more.

The more magic, the higher they would go, the shorter the climb. So Veirella pushed more power into him. She did not know where that bust of energy came from, but she gave it all to him. Her eyes glowed, and the portal doubled in size, gold sparks overpowering the blue and green.

"That's new." Luka said, moving away from it, not knowing if it would keep growing. Veirella's head began pounding like something was trying to push out of her. Sebastian released her hand and the connection between them broke.

Veirella felt something run down the side of her face, raised her hand to touch it and saw blood on her fingers. She quickly wiped away because Luka or Sebastian saw. "We should get going." Sebastian grabbed his pack off the ground, then Luka handed him his bow. Then he went to Veirella took her hand, and they went through together, Sebastian only a few steps behind.

The second Veirella stepped through to the other side, she fell onto Luka. "Hey, hey, hey, you okay?" her body was so weak it was hard to stand. Everything around her was dark and hazy. "Everything looks strange." She told him, her words jumbled and faint. "Is she okay?" Sebastian's panic ridden voice was the last thing she heard. It went dark.

When Veirella woke, she was lying on Luka. A fire was going next to them and Sebastian was on the other side of it, sleeping. Veirella slowly pushed off Luka, trying not to wake him. But her effort were futile, his arm tighten around her. "You, okay?" he let her go a moment later and she sat up.

"What happened?" Veirella looked around. She did not remember them moving after they came through the portal. "You fainted. You seem to be a bit of an overachiever; we got a lot further up than original estimated," he answered. Everything was covered in darkness, so she could see where they were. “How far up did we get?” she asked, looking up at the mountain, trying to see how much further they had to go.

Luka let out a low laugh, almost silent, but she felt it. Veirella looked down at him, brows pulled together, not understanding why her question was funny to him. “What is?”

“We are at the top, highest point of the mountain you can get.” He sat up, his face coming close to hers. “You are one powerful wielder,” he told her, voice low and thick, “and you are quite the swordsman.” She responded, her eyes never leaving his. “How would you know? You have never seen me wield a sword.” He asked. Veirella did not truly understand how she knew things about people’s abilities. It was something she was just always able to do.

It was hard to explain to others the things she saw when she looked at someone. “Well, I have seen you train. You do not have a favored side, perfect balance. That is a trait mostly found in those who wield swords.” She answered.

“Secori.”

“What?” she asked, tilting her head. It was not her first time hearing the word, but Veirella did not know the meaning of it. “Nothing. what do you know about the Celestials?” Veirella wanted him to tell her what *Secori* meant; but that was a question that could wait for another day.

She sighed, then turned away from him, looking into the fire. “Not much. They are our gods. There are twelve of them and each continent has three that they worship.” Veirella knew what she was taught, everyone chose a god to worship. Many called them different things, but their true names were unknown to most. “I have no idea what my blood mother’s name is. I know only the priestesses are given the blessing to hear it. But I thought by now I would be told.” Veirella continued.

“We do not get to know what their names are. If you were taking normal classes, they would have told you that to them we are not important enough to have such the privilege.” Luka answered. There was resentment in his voice. Considering he was cursed because of his blood, he had every right to be. "They say that to you? That sounds a little harsh," Luka shrugged. "Not those words specifically, but close enough."

"Earth created the world, Water gave it life, Air gave it breath, and Fire gave it light. Then they each broke pieces of their souls and created two more." Veirella looked at Luka, who was still looking at her. "That is how they teach us about gods here." She continued.

"You really had no idea what you were?" Luka asked. "I guess my parents were waiting for me to manifest powers to break the news. But I never did, so no point in telling me the truth." Veirella told him, her voice dropping lower with every world she spoke. "Maybe they have a good reason for keeping it from you. And when you see them again, you can ask, considering you can now speak."

Veirella smiled at him, "maybe" she heard something move and they both turned to look at Sebastian who was turning, then a faint sound came from his lips. When he stopped moving, they looked back at each other, trying their best not to laugh. "The sun, while not be up for another few hours, you should get some more sleep." Veirella nodded at him, "so should you." She went to stand, intending to find somewhere to lie down next to the fire, but Luka stopped her.

He held her arm, keeping her next to him. "You can stay right her, I am a lot softer than the ground." Veirella did not intend to argue. Sleeping on the ground was not ideal, but she was willing to do it. But he offered, and she would not refuse. Veirella moved herself around, then laid her head on his chest. She closed her eyes and just before she was gone, something warm hung over her body.

When she opened her eyes again, the sky was lighter. The sun was not out yet. But from what she could see, it would be above them soon. Veirella sat up and something fell down her body. She looked down and Luka's jacket was on her. She looked over at him. He was leaning against one of the many massive rocks around them, with his eyes closed.

She looked to where Sebastian was sleeping, to find the spot empty, and the fire was still going as strong as it was when she first saw it. Veirella stood, took Luka's jacket and laid it next to him. She did not know where Sebastian had gone off to; he could not have been far, there were not many places for him to go to. But she did not want to sit around and wait for him to return or for Luka to wake up.

Veirella went looking around for an opening, someway for them to get into the mountains. She did not find much. The more she walked, the more rocks she saw. They all looked the same. It felt like she was walking through the same place repeatedly. Veirella finally gave up and went back after seeing nothing but more rocks.

When she made her way back to their camp, Luka was awake, and Sebastian had returned. "Where did you go?" Sebastian asked her. He was sitting against one of the smaller rocks his pack before him. "Looking for an opening." Veirella answered.

"Well, I found one, about a mile and a half that way," he pointed behind him. "We can check it out to see if we find anything. Also, that showed up for you." Sebastian nodded toward a green pack similar to his own, next to him. "There should be boosters in there for you to take. The elixir will help with hunger and thirst, it's a green liquid." Veirella nodded at him, then retrieved the bag. It was mostly filled with medical supplies.

And small vials, with two different colored liquids. Green the boosters, and another a light amber liquid similar to the one mother gave her. There were three greens and one amber. She took the booster, which had no taste. "There is no taste. What exactly is it?" Veirella asked. "A combination of everything our bodies need, mixed with stardust. It makes it so we do not need to eat as often as mortals. It also helps speed up our body's ability to produce Cai." Luka explained.

Veirella did not feel any different, "I feel the same, is that normal?" she was already strange she did not need to add more things to the list. "Yes, anything else would mean that your body is rejecting it."

Veirella did not need Luka to say what would happen if she did reject it. Most things in the world of magic seemed to have the same ending death. “But you have nothing to worry about in that regard to that only ever happens with the other two Asphies.” Luka continued.

“We should get going. The sun will be up soon, and we are so much closer to it than we were yesterday. I think it’s best we do not get caught in it.” Sebastian told them. It did not take much time for them to be ready to go. They did not have much laid out. Luka absorbed the flames and filled the hole in with the dirty they dug out, then they left.

By the time they made it to the cave, Sebastian found the sun was halfway over the mountains. "How far in did you get?” Luka asked. “Not very. I just checked to make sure it went somewhere. At the end, there are three large openings.” It was not much to go on, but they already knew so little what was adding one more to the list. *As long as it got us closer to where we need to go, it was be fine.* Veirella was trying to assure herself of the possible death they were about to walk into.

They got halfway in when Veirella heard something. “Do you guys hear that?” Sebastian was ahead of them, leading the way, and Luka was next to her. “What?” they both asked. They looked at each other, then back at her. “The tapping.” She answered. Veirella looked up at them. She could see the concern written on their faces. “Do you seriously not hear that?” She asked again.

The tapping not was getting louder, but she it was getting closer. Veirella looked around, trying to find where it was coming from. “What do you hear?” Lukas asked. “It sounds like something is hitting the wall.” The hits became faster, more rapid, more aggressive, and then they stopped.

She located the sound. “I think it's coming from beneath us.” Veirella felt the ground shift. It was going to break. “We need to get out of here now!” Her words were rushed and panicked. Something was beneath them and she did not want to find out what. They started running in the direction they came; they did not get very far before the ground disappeared from beneath them, then they were falling.

Veirella came to, and her entire body was in pain. Whatever she landed on broke her fall because nothing was broken, just badly bruised. She slowly pushed herself up, wincing with every move she made. There were rocks beneath her from the broken ground, but there was also something else, something that crumbled under her hands when she pressed into it.

It took her some time, but Veirella finally made it to her feet. It was dark all around her, and the floor she fell through did not offer much light. "Luka, Sebastian." She called out to them, but did not get an answer back, they were probably still unconscious. Veirella would need to fill around until she found them. Preferably, Veirella would like to find Luka first. He had the ability to bring light, and she hated being in the dark.

"Luka, Sebastian," she called again, still no answer, Veirella did her best to move around considering the ground was covered in with rocks and something that fell oddly close to bone. Her foot got stuck on something and she fell over, it was not a long fall but she was already in pain so hurt like hell. "This is getting boring, and I am hungry." Veirella stopped moving at the sound of that skin crawling female voice. Fire appeared next to her in a torch. Veirella closed her eyes from the sudden change.

When her eyes adjusted to the light Veirella saw what she was laying on and quickly jumped to her feet ignoring her pain. They were bones everywhere, not just animal, human as well. "What the hell." She whispered." Remembering the voice she heard. Veirella watched as torch after torch lit up the room, revealing more bones. She looked behind her, trying to find the owner of that voice, but there was nothing but more rock and the wall.

When Veirella looked back around, her eyes widened at the sight before her. Eight very long legs stood before her. She was terrified to see what they were attached to, but she look up anyway. Black fur covered body, six onyx eyes that reflected the fire around them, and two very long fangs. *Spider, very, very, very big spider.*

Looking at her, Veirella did not think the creature would need to bite her. It could swallow her whole. "I have been dying to play with someone and lucky me you came up here. I heard you last night. I just had to wait for you to find my little cave." The creature's voice was both sweet and disturbing.

"Now that you are awake, we can finally play. You get to choose which one I eat and which one you keep," she continued. The creature moved back, revealing Luka and Sebastian webbed to the wall behind her. On her left, Luka was unconscious. His body was so warm he was burning through the webs, but they grew back almost instantly. Sebastian was on the right and he, on the other hand was awake and struggling to get himself free. "Let them go." Veirella demanded, her voice echoing off the walls.

"No. I give you one and I keep the other." The massive creature's voice echoed through her mind. Veirella would not choose. She went there with two and she would be leaving with both of them alive. "I will not do that." She answered.

"But why? It is such an easy choice, the pretty one you do not know, or your own blood. Now, who would let their own brother die?" Veirella head whipped from Luka to Sebastian, and everything stopped all she could hear was that one word over and over again.

Brother, brother, brother

Sebastian was her brother, but that was not possible. She had met his mother. She had a mother, two in fact, one was mortal and the other was a Celestial. The only way Sebastian could be her brother was if they shared a father, but his father was also a Celestial.

It was a lie. She was letting this monster get inside her head; Veirella pulled her eyes away from Sebastian to look at the spider. "You are a liar" her voice was not as high as it was moments before. Her words came out in a whisper, a part of her believed it.

"Really, you think so? I suggest you ask him." Veirella looked at Sebastian, who had stopped struggling when she removed the webs covering his mouth, then his eyes found hers.

It was hard to see him fully from how far up he was, but Veirella could have sworn she saw his face fall and his body got limp, avoiding her gaze.

"Sebastian, tell her she is wrong." There was no chance of it being possible. They may not have spent much time together as children, but they did see each other occasionally, someone would have told her.

A moment passed then he finally looked at her, "she is not, I am your brother." Her heart fell at hearing his confirmation. "I can explain everything if we get out of here." He continued. Veirella did not want to hear anything he had to say.

"*Stop.*"

"I will tell you everything." He continued.

"Stop!" Veirella yelled. She was louder than what was normal for her, but Veirella needed him to hear her. "Just stop, *please.*" She could not take it anymore.

"Does this mean I get to keep him? You take the other one. I am sure you will enjoy his presence a lot more, considering the circumstances." Veirella wanted to rip the things, voice from its throat; unfortunately she could not reach it to do so. And there was a chance it was the guardian; the book would need to return once they were finished with it so it, so it was not the best idea to kill the thing protecting it, no matter how much she wanted to

.

And if it was the guardian, there was a question to be answered. If Veirella got the answer correct, the beast would vanish, not permanently the moment they left the mountain it would return. Veirella took her chance. She would not choose who to save, she would rather be the one eaten. "What is your question?" She asked. It was a risk Veirella did not know what the guardians looked like. The reading she did on them did not provide drawings for her to look at.

"What?" the creature asked. Veirella could hear the surprise in her voice, as creepy as it was. "What is your question? You are up here near not one but two of the most populated regions on the entire continent, but you stay here. Why is that?" If she was killing the people that lived in the area, there would be more bones, and a lot more fresh ones at that.

"Because you cannot leave. You are bound to this mountain." She continued. Veirella stopped when she saw one of its legs move towards her, and she stepped back.

"So, I ask again. What.Is.Your.Question?" The creature did not say anything and, for a moment, the cave was silent. If she was the guardian, it would be something complex designed to make her work for it. It would test her skills, mind, and knowledge. "Very well. I am everything and nothing at all. I can be made but not unmade you need me but you rarely see me, what am I? You get one chance, you answer wrong I eat all three of y ou."

Veirella could have laughed in her face from how simple that was. If the bodies at her feet belonged to those who had answered wrong, maybe they deserve to be devoured. But then again, when ego was at play, no one would give the obvious answer. For many, their pride was more important, and that was always the downfall of me. Ego was a funny thing, and in order to win something, you needed to lay down your pride.

"Air"

"What?" the creature was obviously expecting Veirella to get it wrong because she started moving closer before she even answered, "not possible. I have asked that question to many before you, older and wiser and none have answered correctly." Veirella could also most feel her anger.

Guess they were not as wise as they believed themselves to be then, she thought. A moment later, the spider started to fade, one leg after the other, then her body, then her head, and finally her webs. Once the webs were gone, Luka and Sebastian fell to the ground with a loud *thud* that echoed through the cave.

The fall woke Luka up; Veirella ran to help him up. "Are you okay? Anything bent or broken?" She asked, helping him off the ground then looking him over. "I'm fine, just a little bruised, both my body and my pride." He answered. Veirella took a hold of his side and he wincing in pain, she looked up at him, eyes wide. "Okay, maybe a broken rib ... or two," he admitted.

"We need to find the book. This seems to be where all the bodies are, so this must be where it is." Sebastian told them. Luka pushed off her to stand on his own when Sebastian came to stand with them. He was looking at Veirella but she would not look at him.

Veirella would deal with him later. She wanted out of that cave and into a bath, then bed. Her headache had returned, and it was worse than before. Veirella hoped she could hold up long enough for them to get the book and back to Astro. "Feel around the walls for any openings or something that moves." Both boys nodded at her, then they split up, each taking a different corner.

They were all also finished with their sections, but they found nothing. Sebastian got to the end of his and he called for them. "Over here," he pushed the rock in and the wall and the cave moved around them. Then a space in the wall opened up next to him. Red light poured out, lighting the cave, which was both good and bad. Veirella could see better, but that also meant she could see the bones more clearly and saw just how high they went. Sebastian moved his hand, and the wall started closing. He pushed back down, and it opened up full once again. "I guess this is a two-person jo b."

Veirella stepped forward, but Luka stopped her. "What?" she asked, her brows pulled together as she looked up at him. "The air is warm. There is a ward around it. If you touch that, it will burn your skin off." He answered.

Veirella looked back into the space, but she did not see anything past the red light. And unlike Luka, she did not feel the warmth. *Why did a book given to earth wielders to protect have fire wielder wards?* From what Veirella remembered of her early years, Dragia did not have a good relationship with Fianorea.

Luka moved around her and went into the light. When he walked through it, smoke went up in the air. It was burning him. But he did not stop, as if he could not feel it. He disappeared for a moment, then he appeared again. He was holding a massive light grey book with more pages than one book should physically have. Veirella wondered if it could even open all the way.

On the spine, there was a tree carved into the leather with Nazira's name above it. Luka got closer, and she saw the top had the same thing. "We should get out of here. If that thing is still alive, I would like not to be here if it comes back." Veirella knew it would not be back until after they were gone, but she did not intend to tell Sebatian that she wanted out just as much as he did.

"You two need to go find your things," Veirella told them. She looked over at Sebastian as he pushed off the wall, letting it close. On some level, she wanted him to put his hand back up there. The torches were still burning, but it was much darker, and a lot more disturbing.

Luka gave her the book, which was so heavy Veirella almost fell back from the weight of it, Luka waited until she caught her balance before letting got. "You got it?" she nodded. "Go find your stuff. I really want to get out of here." Luka nodded, then went to the other side of the room to look through the rocks and bones where they fell through. Sebastian lingered for a moment, then followed him.

It took them a while to find everything. Their packs were under a pill of bones on one side of the room and their weapons were webbed to the wall, Veirella was still wearing her own, Veirella was happy she was not taken up by the spider, so she did not need to rummage through dead people to find it.

Her arms grew weaker as she watched them try to get their weapons off the wall. Veirella had to lean against the wall to get some of the weight off her back or she was going to fall.

She watched them argue about how to get to them. For two of the most powerful wielders of their asphies, they were not acting like it. "If we move this over there, we can climb up and get them" Luka pointed to the massive bolder next to them. There was no chance they could move on their own.

"Guys, how about you use powers? You're both Celerians. One of you can control fire" she looked at Luka. "and the other water blase them down" Veirella looked at Sebastian, "wood burns" Sebastian answered, "and swords break." Luka followed up. *Did he have so little control over his abilities that he could not direct it? And Sebastian could stand there and catch them.* Veirella thought the words but did not speak them aloud.

It took some time, but they finally reach them; Veirella was wrong about one thing, their ability to move the bolder. With their strengths combined, Luka and Sebastian were able to push it to the wall, then climb up and retrieved their weapons.

Finally

"How are we getting out of here? There does not seem to be a way out other than the hole up there. and unless either of you know how to fly we are stuck done here." Veirella asked.

"Luka's going to portal us off the mountain and I will get us to Astro. That way we can go all the way to the Academy." Sebastian answered. "There is some risk," *death. It was always death.* "But if you two are okay with the chance of burning to death, we can do that." Luka continued, their options were limited if they went with Sebastian's plan, Luka could kill them; it could work, just one thing needed to change.

"I get that of the two of you, Sebastian is better at portals. But what if we switch who does what? Sebastian gets us down, and based on how the first time went. We are likely going to end up near an open body of water, and from where we are now, the closest water source is in Irredina. Which, if I remember correctly, is closer to Astro island, so less work for Luka." Veirella explained.

"That could work, do you think you could do it? I know long distance jumps are not your thing, but considering the school has open wards, there is less risk." Sebastian asked Luka.

They looked at each other exchanging silent words Veirella did not understand. "I can." Veirella admired Luka's confidence in what he could do, he on said two words but the finality in them did not leave room for questions.

So, that is what they did. Sebastian got them to Irredina and Luka got them to the school. They appeared in the court. The second they were through, Veirella handed the book over to Luka. She had been holding the thing for so long she could hardly fell her arms.

Every part of her hurt, but the worse was her head. The pain had gotten worse, and she could no longer pretend it was not there. Veirella needed to get in the bath, then into bed. She looked around, looking for which way she needed to go to get to her room; in her search, she spotted Gemma and Iris sitting in the sofa.

Iris was holding Gemma. She was crying. Veirella wanted to walk over to her to ask what was wrong, but her feet would not move, and no sound left her open mouth when she tried to ask. The pressure that was building in her head finally exploded, and it suck the life from her body.

Mixed Reasons

Anastasia

Julia was died she was gone. I would never see her again, hear her voice, or apologize for the fight we had before I left. And now Veirella was going to die. The thoughts ran through Anastasia's head as she watched her friend's lifeless body.

She was trying to wrap her head around the fact that one of her oldest friends, someone she considered a sister, had been dead for three weeks and she did not know. And here she was, watching it happen to anyone. Veirella was on the floor shaking, blood coming out of her nose, eyes, ears, and mouth.

"Veirella!" Aspen yelled, as he ran to her side. But she did not respond. Pax pulled her up off the floor and brought it to the table. That Iris and Luka quickly cleared, "what is happening to her? What happened when you went to get the book?" Iris asked. Anastasia could hear the panic in her voice and the sound of her racing heart. "I-I don't know. She was fine an hour ago." Pax answered, still holding onto her.

Anastasia was still standing in the same place, still holding the letter she received from home, looking from it to the table that her friend's blood was spilling on to. Anastasia stepped closer to the table, getting closer she saw something and the letter in her hand, "that's not blood."

Everyone looked from Veirella to her, all sharing the same look of confusion. "What are you talking about?" Aspen asked, his tone filled with both anger and fear. To someone who did not spend time with prisoners, it did look a lot like blood but, there was one small difference, blood was smooth and much thicker. Greviger dust, on the other had had a shimmer to it and ran more like water.

"It is Greviger dust. They use it to torture prisoners Iriea, her body much be fighting it off." Anastasia told them. "How would something like this happen?" Pax asked. He turned to look at Anastasia, but she did not have an answer for him. She walked over to him. Luka and Iris moved so she could get to Veirella's head. "There is a way to stop it. We need to find the voice. And pull it out before it kills her mind."

"*Voice*?"

Luka said it was low, so no one but Anastasia heard him. She did not say anything to him because she did not think it was a question for her. "How do we do that?" Aspen asked, his eyes never leaving his still shaking sister. "Not we, me." Everyone looked at her, Iris and Aspen with relief, Pax and Luka with worry. They were the only ones who knew she was having trouble with her magic. She was getting better, maybe not good enough to help Veirella, but she had to try.

Anastasia did not know how long this had been happening to her or how much time she had left. Veirella could be dead by the time it would take them to find another air wielder who knew how to do an extraction. Anastasia raised her hands to Veirella's heads. "Hold her still." Aspen took a hold of her helping Pax holder done on the table.

With a hand on either sides of her head, Anastasia closed her eyes and pulled on her magic, and listened.

"*She is not good enough to be queen.*"

"*It should be Andrew.*"

Anastasia shock her head. She needed to get out of her own and into Veirella's. *Come on, focus. You have done this a hundred times. If you don't, she dies.* She told herself, Anastasia pushed through the voices, all the judgment and pain.

From people who did not in her, so she could help the one who did, and she was going to die if Anastasia could not push them away. She pushed everything away until it silence was in her mind. She could no longer hear her friends. It was all empty. Anastasia could see the threads of her mind and Veirella's. They were faint, but they were there.

She moved for them, pushing as hard as she could. Anastasia heard her name. The voice was faint and distant; she ignored it and kept pushing, then she moved for Veirella's mind thread again. When she grabbed it, she was pulling from memory to memory of Veirella at different ages.

Something was wrong, Anastasia could feel it. Veirella's mind was a mess. Nothing was solid it was all in pieces. She could not tell if Veirella was doing it to herself or if it was the Greviger. Usually there was a door she needed to open, but everything was moving too fast for her to see anything.

Anastasia knew what type of memory it would take to, something painful and significant. Grevigers fed on pain thrived on it. If she could not find it with her eyes, then she would find it with her ears. Anastasia closed her eyes and listened. She heard her laughter and how much joy Veirella was filled with.

Then she felt it, terror. *"Iris"* Anastasia opened her eyes to see what direction it was coming from. Veirella was running through the forest. She was running from something. She was so small, and she looked so scared.

The night of the attack she thought, Anastasia reached for the memory and pulled herself into it. Veirella ran right through her, Anastasia watched her run off then turned to what was chasing her but the only thing coming towards her was a red dust storm.

She got catch in it and was thrown against a tree. ***"She's mine."***

"Go find another soul to save."

"No"

"What are you going to do? She is far too gone. Leave!"

Anastasia tried to stand, but it pushed her back down. *No, Veirella was still breathing, which met she could still be saved* Anastasia pushed herself up, something hit her across her face and she was thrown back again the tree. Anastasia felt the blood run down her face and the pain that came with it but she pushed thought it.

"You will not have her. I will die first."

"If your death is required for us to eat in peace, then so be it."

The wind pushed her back, and she grabbed on to a tree to help keep her feet on the ground. Anastasia raised her free hand and drew on her magic, pulling the storm to her. The winds got stronger, but she would not give. A ball of red air began forming in her hand. It did not get bigger but condensed in on itself, forming a cone of wind in her hand.

"No! You can not do this"

"She is promised to be us. She is ours. You can not have her."

"She is not yours to take," Anastasia told them, then absorbed the storm. Once all the wind was in her palm, Anastasia condensed it more, then crushed it. Anastasia wanted to stay and see what was after Veirella, what tried to kill her than night. She heard footsteps approaching, but she was pulled out before she could see a face.

Anastasia opened her eyes. The same time Veirella did, she jumped up gasping for air, trying to catch your breath. "What—what happened?" She looked around he her brother, "You're okay, everything is going to be okay." He assured her, pulling her into his arms. Iris grabbed a hold of Anastasia's hand, squeezing it in thanks. She wanted to nod at her, but she was not the floor before she could say the words.

Seven Years Before

Veirella was a fast learner. It had taken her a matter of weeks to learn defensive maneuvers. For people older than her, it would have taken months. For a nine-year-old to be progressing that quickly, it was mind blowing magnificent. Every bruise was a lesson to be learned, how to better prevent it from happening again.

Veirella had only trained with a bow staff. She had little to no interest in swords; it gave her multiple points of attack if she was surrounded, she did not have to compromise on any direction. Her main weapon of choice were daggers. On choosing day for her fifth reight she choose the weapon.

Veirella did not spend much time using them when she was younger, but she did not want to train then, so her parents let her be. But now she was learning to use them, the twin blades were plain, and silver. No one was teaching her how to wield them. She just gravitated to them on her own. A few months after she began her training, after she was left alone in the training room, she took them off the wall and tried throwing them at the target board.

Because of the sharpness go the daggers they stuck to it but they did not stay in. They touched the board, stayed for a few seconds, then fell. She did not use enough focus to throw them. Veirella went over and retrieved them and went back halfway across the room. She was just getting started, so she shortened the range.

She threw them again, and again, and again. But they never stuck. And of the six rings on the board, the closest one she could get to was the edge of the third. She was throwing them from over shoulder like one would an axe, but that was starting to hurt her arm.

So Veirella tried doing it from under instead of over. Aspen liked to throw stones across the river that way and they would run on the water before stopping and sinking to the bottom. Veirella tried doing it that way, retrieved the daggers from the ground for the fifth time to begin her next attempt. She turned her body slightly to the right and pulled her arm to the side, took a deep breath, then threw it.

She watched as it spun around until it landed on its intended target. She watched it not moving, a smile began to form on her lips, then it moved. "No stay, stay" she begged. It shifted a little more down, then it finally fell out. Veirella dropped her head and sighed, walking over to the blade, not bothering to throw the others, knowing the result would be the same.

And she did that for weeks. Same result, Veirella knew there was something was off with how she was standing or the angle she was throwing it.

Veirella was walking back to where she was standing for all her attempts before, but stopped halfway and turned around. 'Maybe I am standing too far', she thought to herself. She was already close, but maybe she needed to be closer.

But she did not have the chance to test that theory because Lily walked back into the room, ready for their private training session, from what Veirella could tell no one else was aware that Lily could do magic, even though she had only seen her use her magic once, the first time she showed her who to shift things.

"What are you doing?" she asked. Veirella looked at her friend, who was leaning against the wall next to the door, with her brows raised. "Trying to throw dagger." Veirella was annoyed with herself for not getting i, after so long. "And how is that going for you?" Veirella turned back to look at the

target board and threw the dagger she was holding in her right hand and watched it fall moments later.

"How does it look like I'm doing?"

Lily did not answer. "We should begin." She walked out to the balcony they had been using for their lessons. Lily did not want others seeing them together, so she made the rule that they would only meet once per week.

Most times they worked on her wielding and others they walked the grounds, looking for different types of stones and gems she could change. "Did you practice what we started last week?" Veirella should have been trying to turn rubies into diamonds, but she made no progress in doing so. Rubies were by far prettier than diamonds, but they were not as durable, and Veirella's attempts to change them had only left her with cuts on her hands and fingers.

"Yes, but still the same," she answered. Lily turned, removed the green flowerpot to the far right and pulled the four small red gemstones. And handed them to Veirella. She knew what she needed to do, but it was not working.

Veirella closed her hands around them and pulled on her anger which had depleted over the time she had been at Nightwell, between her Ryin training and Lily's lesson she had little anger left to give, but she pushed all her energy into them trying to get the stones to change.

The green sparks formed around her arms and moved down to her fingers; Veirella felt them move around her fingers. She pushed and pushed until she felt the pain of her fingers been sliced open, Veirella opened her hands, and the blood covered stones fell.

Lily received the stones from the ground and put them back in her hands. They were starting to heal but Lily never waited for her to finish healing or give her a moment to catch her breath before wanting her to go again; she said if she went easy on her she would never learn.

"Can you show me how you do it, so I can see ho—"

"No!" she cut her off. That was her answer every time Veirella asked her for help. Lily said her magic was a one time only show. Veirella closed her still bleeding hand around the stones and pressed them into her palm, and pulled

on everything she had left, the pain she was feeling, her annoyance with Lily and the disappointment in herself for how she was to her mother.

Veirella focused on her hands and drew the energy to them. She felt the magic move through her body, but green sparks did not appear around her hands. Instead, her eyes began glowing bright gold. Veirella felt movement between her hands and opened them. The four small red gems began floating and glowing, the red of the rubies grew brighter than changed into pink and finally became clear.

A smile broke across Lily's lips as she watched Veirella do it. The light faded and Veirella felt the gems return to her hands. When she could see them, there were four uncut blood-stained diamonds before her. "I did it." Veirella smiled at what she had done.

"Yes, you did. "Lily's voice was so low Veirella almost missed what she said. Veirella looked up at her friend, then her eyes filled with darkness.

Mended Wounds

Veirella

Veirella laid in bed, looking up at the ceiling. She had done nothing but that for the past two days. Coming to terms with everything that was happening in her head. Sebastian was her brother, and she has known how to wield for most of her life.

It was hard coming to terms with it all. Every few minutes, or hours, she got a new flash of images going through her head. That was the best part. She could tell how long apart the flashes were. From things she did not remember to ones she did, but only in small detail. Veirella remembered meeting Gemma and Sebastian, but she did not remember how or where she saw them first.

She remembered Lily but just the parts where she helped train her and when they would take walks through the forest, but she still could not recall why they did it, it had something to do with wielding she put that much together, but they why was unclear.

She sat up when she heard something fall on the floor. The sound came from Gemma's room. Veirella did not get to check on her after she received the news of Julia's death. After Gemma fainted, so did Veirella. Gemma saved her life, and she needed to thank her for it, and also see if she needed someone to talk to. Veirella felt like a horrible friend. Part of her knew it was not a rational thing for her to think, considering she did not intentionally try to die. It was just bad timing.

She went to her closet, removed her nightdress, and put on a white dress with ruffled sleeves. Veirella counted the buttons as she did them up.

Then she went to her vanity and unwrapped her hair and let her freshly done braids down. Veirella wished Willow could magic the style to her head instead of her having to sit for hours the day before while she did it. Once she fixed it, Veirella made her way over to Gemma's. She raised her hand to knock. "Come in Ella"

It slipped Veirella's mind that she could do that. She opened the door and saw Gemma putting a pack together. She was getting ready to leave. "Came to see if you were okay, or needed someone to talk to" Gemma stopped and looked at Veirella.

Her eyes were swollen, and she was red all over. Veirella made her way across the room and stood before her. She did not know where to go from there, so she waited for Gemma to take the next step. She threw her arms around her and cried.

"No. She was family. We shared no blood, but she was still my sister, and now she is dead. And I did not even get to say goodbye" her voice broke a little more with every word she said. "I am so sorry" Veirella did not know if that was the right thing to say or if it helped at all, but it was what she had to offer. "Where are going?" She asked. Gemma pulled away and wiped her tears. "Julia does not have any family. She was an only child and both her parents are gone. So I will complete her Ecuovear."

That was not possible. Ecuovear was not a one person task. It required three days of watching over the dead until the body became ash. "*Alone*?" Veirella's voice shook as she asked. "I know how dangerous it is, but she has no one else, and if I do not, they will just throw her in the fire pit with all the other unclaimed." She explained. Veirella could not argue with her. If she was in that position, she would do the same thing.

So she nodded, then helped her finish packing. Veirella walked her to the stairs, "thank you for saving my life." Gemma smiled at her. "No need to thank me. You would do the same for me." She would. They hugged, then Veirella watched her leave. Gemma could not make a portal herself, so she needed to find an air wielder who could.

Veirella prayed the gods would protect her. Traditionally, three people were required to complete an Ecuovear burning, and that was still dangerous. What would it do to one person?

A new room appeared in the court in the time she had been out. It was across from the training room. And just as big, if not bigger, there was a massive circular table in the center of the room, along with chairs for each of them. Veirella made her way done the hall. It was her and Luka's turn to read through the book; heavy, so it was nice having a designated space for it to live where everyone had assess. As Veirella made her way to the door, she saw Iris coming out.

"Hey." Iris slammed the door behind her, then reluctantly turned to look at Veirella. "Hey." She responded. They stood there in silence, while Iris tried looking everywhere but at her. *She really does hate me.* Veirella thought. She moved towards her. "Can we talk—"

"I need to get to the library. There is something I need to check out," Iris cut her off. Veirella dropped her head, her chest tightened. She thought she was imagining her sister's rejection, but it was not in her head. Veirella looked at her and nodded, then moved so she could pass.

The hallway was big enough for both of them to pass with room. Iris moved past her as fast as her legs could carry her, Veirella watched her until she disappeared around the corner.

Then she went to the door, but she still watched the empty hallway. Until Luka appeared; he smiled at her, but Veirella did not look at him.

Her eyes remained in the spot her sister her sister just walked away from. His smile faded, replaced with concern. “Are you okay?”

“I think my sister hates me.”

“What? Why would Iris hate you?” The way Luka said the words made her feel ridiculous for even thinking them. “She has avoided me since I came home. She has been here for over a week and has kept as far away from me as possible.” She sighed, then looked at Luka. “I am sure there is a reason, you should talk to her.”

Veirella opened the door, and Luka followed her. The book was open on the table, a page marker was on the last page they was read. Luka pulled out a chair for her, Veirella thanked him and he pulled one out next to her, then he pulled the book closer. “How did you guys come up with is system? Are we just going page by page or are we going by species?” She was still unconscious when they started going through it.

Veirella wanted to be there when it was opened. Many may have found that strange but, for her it was a piece of history she wanted to be a part of. “Chapter by chapter. We have no idea what is it that was are looking for.” He answered. They were going based off a storybook for children. Gemma thought it could real. Luka, Sebastian, and Aspen were just covering their bases, and Veirella was hoping Gemma was wrong and this was all a waste of time.

But they were not taking it serious. If they were, they would have been searching by species and not just reading through, hoping to find something that would take too long. “We need to go by species, it while take less time if we do it that way.” Veirella turned back to the contents pages which was fifteen pages long. She did not know there were that many different species to classify.

The Serabi stole children, so demons were the best place to start. “Do you know anything about demons?” Luka pushed forward to look at the book. “I little, we deal with a few different types on our assignments.” Veirella pushed the book to him and grabbed one of the notebooks to write the possible options if they found any. “Then you should read first.” She told hm.

Luka did not look at the book before him. His eyes were on her. “Do you want to talk about it?” Veirella did not know if he was asking about Sebastian being her brother or the thing that had been eating away at her mind for months. “No.” Veirella was still dealing with all of it. She was still trying to understand how she was supposed to feel. It was all too much, and the last thing she wanted to do was talk.

Three Night's

Anastasia

Family was a precious thing. It was to be cared for, protected, and cherished. One many only consider someone family when blood is shared, but not all families were forged through kinship. A bond made through shared experiences, such as pain, could create an unbreakable bond between two from different paths off live.

Anastasia and Julia were from different houses, age groups and their status in society were miles apart, but they shared an element. And created a friendship from it. Julia became the older sister Anastasia wished she had. Julia taught her how to wield air like no other. And she helped Anastasia learn one of the most dangerous skills to control in their element 'the cut' Julia knew it and taught it to Anastasia.

With her power as heir, she got Julia a place in her house, which gave her the chance to attempt for Astro Academy. Julia thanked her for it, but Anastasia did not think it was necessary.

Now here she was sitting on a stone, washing over her body as her soul passed on to the other side. It was an important ceremony and a show of respect for Centinal's. Protecting them from the chance of being possessed by a wondering soul that was never put to rest or a demon.

Her sliced up body was surrounded by flames prepared to engulf her. Ecuovear was three days long, death was common among their kind. Anastasia was only allowed those three days to grieve. That was how long it took for the cai to burn away, and for the body to become ash. The three closest to the dead were usually the ones on how watched over until the ceremony was done, but it was just Anastasia. Julia's parents died when she was a girl, so she was all she had.

There were three rings on the Ecu leading to her body. As the flames moved up to Julia's body, she began to burn from the heat alone. The smell of her burning flesh made Anastasia sick, but she would hold it in, she needed. The first day was the easiest and the hardest. She was the most awake, but she was in the most pain. Anastasia made herself comfortable because she would be sitting in the same place for the next three days.

She cried silent tears, trying her hardest not to make a sound, spirits like the quiet. If her pain was heard the soul would not leave, the mind and body may be no more, but the soul knew no such thing. If it realized what had become of itself, it would stay and eventually become vengeful and dangerous.

On the second day Anastasia's eyes were dry from all the crying and her skin was so hot it hurt to breathe, not that it was easy with the burning and rotting flesh before her, the last of the cai had burnt out of her body she was of a lower rank so it only took a two days. Anastasia saw the last spark leave her body, along with what remained of her soul. Both were pulled from her up into the sky. One would go to Cala, the other would be taken by the wind.

On the third day, she lost track of time. The world was moving around her, but Anastasia did not notice. Her eyes never left Julia's body to see if it was night or day, and it hurt too much to do anything but watch. She watched aa the last of her friend's body blackened. and her body crumbled, once the last of her was dust the ashes moved through the flames and into the awaiting urn, once she was all inside the fire went out and the room went dark for a moment then brightened again with the sunlight shining from above.

Anastasia took the last remaining of her strength and move to retrieve the urn. She walked out of the cave, using everything she had, once she say the trees. Anastasia pulled on the little strength she had left and sent her ashes into the air. "You were a great friend and I hope to see you again someday in Cala."

Discovery

Veirella

A week passed of them doing them reading through Nazira's book. Veirella did not think it was possible for one book to have so much knowledge, in the detail it did. The others thought it was a waste because of how much time they were spending on it.

But Veirella did not share the same opinion. For her, even if the creature from her story was not real, she was still learning about others. She did not see a situation where she would need to know anything about fairies, considering they all died out after the breaking.

Veirella was the only one not training. Luka was with Sebastian when he was not doing research with her. Sebastian attempted to speak to her more than once but she was avoided him. She would need to talk to him at some point, but it was not a conversation she was ready to have. On some level, it felt wrong doing to him what Iris was doing to her, but she needed time and Sebastian needed to give that to her.

Gemma was still in Iriea, so she did not have anyone else to talk to, and the way Luka watched her, Veirella knew he wanted to talk. Her life was a mess, and she was tired of people pitying her for it. Sebastian was pushed to work with Aspen and Iris until she got back. If she was coming back, that is. Veirella did not see much of her siblings. Iris was off in the library, doing research for their father when they were not going through the book. At least that's what Aspen told her, Veirella was done caring, if her sister wanted nothing to do with her, she was have the same.

But that was also all he was willing to say, and he spent most of his time in Genevieve's office. But Aspen did not share the details of their meetings. It was either something for their father, like Iris or it was about Veirella. Night fell and morning came, and Luka was at her door. As he was every morning.

"Do you have an internal clock?" Veirella groaned, still half asleep. He came there at the same time every morning, ten past seven. He was never late or early, always on time.

"Maybe," he smiled down at her. Veirella closed the door and got dressed. She took her time like she did every morning. He could wait. Which he always did, or he could go on without her. Once Veirella was presentable, she went back to the door. And he was in the same place. She was in their uniform and so was he. This was the first time she saw him in it. His was not much different to hers. He had on a tie but no vest.

Luka moved so Veirella could get out of her room, then he closed the door behind her. "What sections do we have left to go through?" Veirella's change in how they were working made everything go may faster, the others mostly stuck to the abilities and descriptions then moved on when they did not find a match, some species did not have as many sub-species as others and many were in the same family they did not need to go through them all.

Veirella was the only one reading every word. She read fast, so it was only taking them a few minutes more to do through, but Luka did not seem to mind. "Water dwellers, and Demonology, the others are working their way through the rest of the earth species." Veirella answered. Those three were the longest sections of the book. It would take them another week or two to finish.

They started on demons, but the things made Veirella so uncomfortable to look at and read about that they left it. "Ready to say the monsters?"

Luka asked. She could not tell if he was making fun of her, for the way she reacted to the creatures, or if he was just asking.

"I do not think I will ever be ready for this, but it must be done." She could have asked to switch with the others and gone through the water section. But it was shorter by about a hundred or so pages. It did not seem right to ask that of them. They would give it to her if they asked. Aspen took even the most irrational of her fears as if they were actual threats. Probably the true reason he was going alone with this idea in the first place and the last thing Veirella wanted was to be babied by her brother.

They entered the newly forged room, where the book laid open. As it was every morning, with all their notes scattered around it. Veirella took the seat closest to the window. She wanted to look out at the birds as a reminder that the creatures in the book were just one of many. She would read first, then Luka. It was usually the other way around, but if she got it over quickly, she could not run herself mad waiting.

An hour of reading and Veirella now knew, there were several different types of demons, listed by levels instead of species, and some levels had more than others, the more of them there were the lower the rank and power, and the levels with less were more powerful. The lower level demons served higher ranking demons, higher-level demons were called Celveri and lower-level demons Demei.

Demei's could leave their dimensions, but Celveri could not. Some demons had different names for male and females, like the succubus and the incubus, both were sex demons. Veirella stopped reading and looked at Luka. "What exactly does a sex demon do?" Luka looked at her, then at the book to see what she was reading. "Ah, Succubus and Incubus. They tend to procreate with not so willing men and women. The succubus goes after men to get themselves pregnant while the Incubus impregnates woman. Mostly very young, not much older than us."

Veirella was already not very fond of demons, but that just made her hate them all together. "That is so wrong."

"It is, and we do as much as we can to stop them. Some would say men get the better end of the deal, they do not remember and can go on with their lives never knowing the truth, but for women it is different they are the ones' whose bodies are used as incubators to create more of those things." Luka's words were heavy, but his tone remained unchanged.

"Just because the men do not remember the violation does not mean it did not happen. Two people suffer the same wrong. Just because the aftermath affects one more, does not mean the pain is not still there. For them, it may be like it is for me. I know something happened to me. I don't remember it but I can feel it." Veirella told him, Luka did not say anything he just nodded. Veirella took one last look at the winged beast. She was beautiful, but looking at her Veirella could see nothing but ugliness.

She turned the page to the next creature and went back to reading. Before her eyes made it to the words, Veirella noticed it was different from the others. There was no drawing. There was a place for one, but it was empty. She paid little attention to it before, there should have been a drawing, the book wrote itself. Veirella found the name and focused on it. The creature was called a Sirabus.

The name was not the same, but it was close. "I think I found something." Veirella pushing the book to Luka, "There is not drawing." Veirella knew it had to be something a part of her just knew.

He looked at it. Then she pulled the book back so she could read. "The creature was thought to be a crossbreed, half siren and half succubus. The Sirabus could not claim one or the other, it was both but also neither. The creature is classified as an abomination, something of unnatural origins, both in magic and nature.

She has an ability to steal Celicai from anyone she comes into contact with. She can then use their power as her own. Because she does not have the ability to create her own Celicai, so she must stealing it, but she can only use the powers short term, but she can pass the stolen magic to another, as long as they have Celicai or stardust withing them and this transfer is permanent, unless she take it back which would kill them."

Veirella stopped and looked at Luka, who was looking at her. Veirella wished she was having one of her nightmares. If this was in her head, she could wake up, but is it was real. But she needed to be sure, so she kept reading, "side effect of her stealing Cai the wielder she takes it from will lose their ability to generate it, and when they do wield their power, reflect back in on them, killing them in the process."

And there it was. She could not deny the words before her. The creature was real and somehow it was back out in the world. The pages were older by a few centuries at least. That meant someone had stopped her. It was done once maybe they could be done again.

Veirella kept reading but the more she read the worse it got the Sirabus could shapeshift to look like anyone she wanted to, she had a song like sirens did, but she could use it on both men and women, and she was extremely fast and strong. The Sirabus had no known weaknesses, and no way listed on how to kill her. The last time the creature was seen was at The Azaldir Temple.

"On some level, I was hoping it was not real, but this is undeniable proof that it is." Veirella still wished it was not real, but Luka was right there was no way to deny it. "If it is the one doing this, how did it get out of the temple?" *And why were they not told about it, to begin with*?

"They are obviously trying to cover it up." Luka answered. "But why would they do that? All four royal houses have a child with celestial blood. Why would they risk their own children?"

"We need to go to the temple. We need to see for ourselves that she is no longer imprisoned. And how she got out in the first place." Luka was right, but the last thing Veirella wanted to do was leave the school. "That sounds like a bad idea. We should speak with others." Luka shook his head. "No, just Pax and Ana when we see her." Veirella was confused, "Why not Aspen and Iris? If it was not for them, we wound not even know any of this." She asked.

"Because one they are not one of us, and two if your parents are unaware of this learning that a creature under Iriea's control that could kill their daughter is free, and they were not informed of it could send us into another war." It did not sit right with her to lie to her siblings. Aspen was always there when she needed him, and Iris, as broken as their relationship was, she put herself on the line so they could get the book.

But if Veirella was being honest with herself, neither of them would keep it to themselves if they knew she would be in danger, not after what happened. "We can just tell them that your parents need to meet with the other families. That is as much as we can give away until we know what we are dealing with." Luka continued. Veirella looked away from him. She did not like lying, especially not to her parents.

"Dove, this affects me, it as much as it affects you, as well as Pax and Anastasia; but this has nothing to do with them. This is Celestial business. No concern for mortals until we say otherwise. Everyone will learn the truth, just after the fact." Luka assured her. Veirella thought about it for a moment, but she could not find a way or reason to tell him he was wrong. "Okay.

The next morning, Sebastian took Aspen and Iris back to Fianorea. They needed to speak with their father, so Veirella did not need to lie to them about where they were going. "Why are we traveling so little?" Luka and Veirella were waiting in the commons for Sebastian to return. "This is more of a day trip. It will take most of the day to get to the temple and back, but we need to be back here by morning."

"Why? We did not have a time limit when we went to retrieve the book?" she asked. Veirella should have asked more questions before going and doing something. Maybe she would have the answers if she were there when the plans were made.

"Because you are not allowed to leave, I am technically still in recovery, and we should not be going anywhere without Cyrus. What we did a week ago was only possible because you brother and sister were here, so the headmistress felt no need to come check. Because Ana went to all her classes."

Genevieve had not checked in on her in a few weeks. Veirella did not mind her absence, but it was strange not having someone older watch everything she did. There was a part of her that liked the freedom it gave her, but another side of her felt like she was being abandoned. "What will you do once you leave school?" Veirella knew he would be king someday, but she was interested in what he would do until then.

Luka stood by the windows. He was quiet for so long Veirella thought he would not answer. "I will not live long enough to have plans after graduation." Veirella understood he would die, but he would still have two years left after he finished school. "You will be nineteen when you graduate. That gives you some time." Again, Luka said nothing.

"If you were not cursed, what would you be doing?" She asked.

"I do not spend my time daydreaming about a future I will not have. That is a cruel form of torture, and I have no interest in pretending." His words were cold and empty. Like he had already given up.

"Considering you care so much about the future, what will you be doing when you leave this place?" he was deflecting. They were more alike than she thought. But she would follow his lead in this. Veirella did not need to think about the answer to that question. "My future has being planned out since the day I was born. After my Ascension, I will be given a title the same as my brother and sister.

And I will study I trade. It will be my job to keep the relationship between our kingdoms. If we were still at war, things would be different." Luka turned to look at her. "How so?" no one outside of her family knew that her father was teaching her. "I would be a battle strategist. So instead of making peace, I would be plotting her downfall." The way Luka looked at her, for saying that, forced her to look away.

"I can see that."

"You know soon or later you are going to need to talk to him, you can not pretend he is not there forever. And even if you tried to, he wouldn't let you." Luka continued. Veirella did not know what to say to that. Luka did not want to talk about his problems, but he wanted to push her to talk about hers. But she was saved from answering by the person she did not want to talk to or about. A portal opened in the middle of the room, and Sebastian walked through it. He did not close it because they were about to leave.

They were all wearing black keives it was the hardest of the six colors to cut, through so it was what soldiers wore. The fabric was, by far, easier to move in that leather was and it was more comfortable, Veirella would still choose a dress if it was an option, but that was not great for travel or fighting. The skills she was taught were so she could protect herself if she ever needed to not so she could willingly put herself in danger. "We should get going." Sebastian told them it was still early morning, and the sun was barely out.

Sebastian went through the portal, then Luka took Veirella's hand and they followed him. On the other side it was still dark out, "Where are we?" Veirella had been to the palace two when she was young, and even in the dark she knew they were nowhere near it. They were on the ground and most of Iriea was built in the sky. "The Under City" Luka answered.

"I sent a letter to Ana, letting her know we were coming. Our ride will be here soon." Sebastian told them. They were on a hillside. From what Veirella could see of the city below, everything was close together. She wondered how they had enough space to move about. There were lights in some places, some had more than others, likely people getting ready to start the workday.

Veirella knew enough to remember they traveled through the air on birds the times she visited. Hosheau, was a beautiful city. When the sun was out, the white marble was the most mesmerizing thing to look at, and she could not wait to see it again after so long.

They were there for half past when Veirella felt a gust of wind pass over her. When she looked up, there was nothing there. Then she felt the ground beneath her move, Veirella turned around and saw a gryphon behind her. It was a massive creature. One of its four legs could crush without thinking about it after.

Its body was filled with dark feathers, but its head was far lighter, Veirella had to force her body to stay, she wanted to run before it had the chance to eat her. *"There is no need for you to fear me child, I will not harm you"*

Veirella's eyes widened at hearing the creature speak. Luka and Sebastian were walking towards the gryphon like they could not hear her. "There is no need to be scared. She will not hurt you," Luka told her. "Come, it is a lot like riding in a carriage." The gryphon looked down at Luka. *"Did he just compare me to a horse, him I might eat."*

"Can they hear you as well?" Veirella asked, pulling her attention away from Luka, and focusing on the massive bird-like creature looking down at her. "*No, they cannot. You smell familiar, like the creator. We gryphons could speak to her. Are you of her blood child?"* Veirella did not know what to say. She knew the creator in question was her blood mother. *"No."*

She bent all four of her legs and tucked her wings, revealing a gold and white structure atop her back. "What is that?" Veirella asked, pointing up at it, "that is called a gryphocart, that is how travel here works," Sebastian told her. They climbed up on her back leg. There was a lot more space to move than Veirella thought there would be. The gryphocart looked identical to a carriage, just wings instead of wheels. The doors did not open out, they slid into the frame.

From the outside the windows were dark, but when the door slid open, the inside was bigger somehow. Luka pulled Veirella around him and helped her inside. "Thank you," he nodded, then sat next to her. The walls were red and white with gold lines that took some similarities to lightning bolts.

Sebastian came in and sat across from them, then the doors slid back into place, fading in so smoothly the opening disappeared. Veirella felt something moving over her. She looked down to see what it was, and there was a black belt covering her waist.

"W-What is that?" Veirella pushed closer to Luka, getting ready to jump away from the thing trying to trap her. Luka laid a hand on her shoulder, attempting to calm her down. "It's strapping you in, so you cannot move or get thrown out if the door open." That did not help her much, *"this is the way everyone travels here, accidents such as that rarely, if ever, happen"* the gryphon told her. Veirella had yet to be given a name for the creature and was not sure if she should ask.

Once they were all securely locked in place, the gryphon took off into the sky. The launch was the hardest park for Veirella; it felt the same as being on a frightened horse. There was no rocking in a carriage, there was just nothing. If Veirella could forget that they were in the air, she would like this form of transport.

There was only one type of transport Veirella has never used, and that was a ship. The ocean was great in size bigger than all the continents together. Her father told her once that the ocean was so great in depth that it was as dark as the night sky, even during the day at the bottom. *"You will not fall. This is secured to me"* the gryphon told to her.

"Can you read my thoughts?" Veirella hoped the answer to that question was no. She was an animal and could not tell anyone, but it was still an intrusion. *"No, but you are thinking very loud so it is not to hear"* she was not aware that such a thing that was possible. How were thoughts loud? They were thoughts they were in your head. *" What is your name?"* The creature cared that she felt safe so Veirella took a chance and asked. *"My name is Do'ala."*

"That was a beautiful name, if I remember correctly it means peace."

"Thank you, and it does." She answered. *"And yours means daughter of light. There is a legend about her. Have you heard it?"* Veirella did not know there was another meaning to her name, let alone that a story went with it. It was nothing special *provei'ta* translated, it meant guarded or protected. Her mother told her she was nature's delight and no matter where she was,

if she called out for help, everything from the plants to the animals would come to her aid.

"No."

"Would you like to hear it?"

"Maybe another time. But thank you for offering."

The sun was rising over the mountains when they finally made it to Hosheau. They flew over the marble city up to the palace. Every building beneath them was made of white and grey marble. Everything was flat, some building small other larger, but it all went together perfectly.

They landed on top of one of the tallest buildings around them, there were other gryphons at least twelve from what she counted and those were just the adults. There were young boys and girls attending to them. Some were being bathed, others fed, and a few were being prepared for flight.

Sebastian was the first out was Do'ala landed, then Luka and Veirella last. She tucked her wings and lowered herself so they could get off her back. They climbed down her leg, where there was a boy waiting with a ladder they did not need. He walked away without saying a word once they were all on the ground. "Is Gemma coming to meet us?" Veirella asked.

The place went silent. Everyone stopped what they were doing to look at them, like she said something strange. They were all looked different ages, some younger than them, others older. They were all dressed in red and white tunics with black pants and shoes that matched. There was not a crease or speck of dirt anywhere on them. It was an impressive task to look perfect and undisturbed while working with animals.

"No, she sent Gia." Sebastian answered. The name was not familiar to her. Veirella could not recall any mention of her in any of the letters she exchanged with Gemma. "Who is Gia?" Gemma was her oldest friend, but in reality Veirella knew very little about her. She grew and changed over the years. But Veirella was still the same. "You are about to find out." Luka told her Veirella looked up at him.

Luka was looking past her. When Veirella turned she saw a girl coming towards them. She was dressed in a dark red coat that curved to her body, and loose fitted matching pants. "Luka, Pax, it has been a while since I have seen your faces around." She smiled at them, Gia gave them each a hand and they both kissed her, "always a pleaser Gia." Luka smiled up at her, then released her hand.

"It has not been that long; I was here not so long ago." Sebastian told her, then he released her hand. Gia crossed her arms, then looked over at Veirella. "Mind my manners, but I do not know your name?" the girl's smile seemed genuine and welcoming. So Veirella stepped forward, "I am Veirella Greystone of House Greystone daughter of King Dorian Greystone, a pleaser to meet you." Her introduction was practiced, learned from the moment she could speak.

Aspen sometimes laughed at her for telling people more than her name. It was not needed for her to tell people who her father was. They knew who he was just by her name. But Veirella was proud of who he was. "It is an honor to meet you, princess; I am Lady Gianna Riv'kiana." Gia bowed.

It was a show of respect, not because she was a princess, but something else. It was not required for people not of your kingdom to bow to you if you were not the king, queen, or the heir. "How do you know Gemma?" Gia's brows raised. "Who?" It was not one of Gemma's given names, it was something only Veirella called her. "Anastasia"

"I am her High lady" it was not a new turn, it was just never used. It was the title given to a woman chosen to be a queen's hand. "Will Gem—Anastasia be meeting us here, so we can go to the temple?" Veirella asked. Gia's smile fell. "Unfortunately, no she quiet busy at the moment, you will be going without her. But no more two outsiders are allowed at the temple at a time, so one of you must stay." She told them. Veirella would pull herself out. Luka and Sebastian were a team, so it was best they went together.

Gia pulled a small satchel from her pocket and handed it to Veirella. she opened it and two small crystal balls were inside, one blue the other yellow. "The treats are for the gryphon. Give her the blue and it will give her a guide to the temple, give her the yellow, and she will bring you back. Do not lose these. The yellow crystal is the only way she will be able to find her way out of the temple. The clouds around it are like a maze, and you can get lost within them." She explained.

Veirella retrieved the small blue crystal and went to Do'ala opened her hand and waited for her to take it. She lowered her head slowly and snatched it up in her beak. "You two go. I will stay behind. I wanted to check on her, anyway." Sebastian told them.

Veirella was going to pull herself out, but he did it before she could, she was not going to give him a chance to change his mind. She wanted to see the temple, and this may be her only chance to do so. "You best be leaving now. It takes quite some time to get there," Gia told them. "Make sure she's okay," Veirella told Sebastian. "I will." Luka and Veirella then returned to the gryphon. Everyone standing close to Do'ala moved as she launched.

A few hours into their journey, it began raining. It brought Veirella some comfort and helped take her mind off the fact that they were nowhere near solid ground. She always thought it was normal how at peace she was when it rained or when she was near a river or pond, but it was not normal, it was because of who her father was. Every aspect of her world was changing, moving before she, Veirella wanted it to stop so she could have a moment to adjust. She wanted a moment to breathe without every breath she took being something new to discover about herself.

"You okay over there?"

"Fine" Veirella did not want to talk, her thought were all jumbled together, which was making it hard to think, much less speak. "This is a lot to get used to, but eventually it will feel like second nature. Some spend their whole lives wielding others only a few years, but they all get there in the end and you will too."

If that was her only problem, it would probably be the same for her. "Five months ago I could not speak, and what I could stay could barely be heard in an empty room, and a few waving of my hands and suddenly something I struggled to do for months, bleeding every time I tried is like it never happened.

I should be died, a normal person does not survive having their throat slit open." Veirella raised her hand to the scar on her neck. It was automatic every time she thought about it. Her hand went there. "But you lived."

"Why did it happen in the first place? Was it because of who my mother is, the Celestial Goddess, the creator of all that is, or my father the king or a nation most people fear just thinking about? The nightmares are gone, but the fear of not knowing why this happened to me is still there and the pain will never go away." Veirella did not know why she felt so comfortable sharing such personal thoughts with him. She barely knew him, but she continued.

"I want a normal life, but I am the furthest thing from it. I do not even have a normal family. I know my mother and father love me."

"But do they love you the same as your siblings?" Luka said the words Veirella could not bring herself to. "Listen, love does not come from blood. My mother's blood courses through my veins and she is a bit of a..."

"Word you should not call your mother," Veirella cut him off. She did not think it was his first time referring to her that way, but she did not want him saying anything bad about the woman to make her feel better. "Yes" he answered.

"You have a history of where you came from, what the ones who came before you could do. I am my mother's first. As far as anyone knows, I may also be the first ever crossbreed between two Celestials, so what does that make me? I am still a Celerian or am a Celestial or something else?" Veirella was not really asking. It was not like Luka had the answers she needed.

"I don't know Dove, from the little I know about know about you Celestial or Celerian you are one amazing person." They were still looking at each other and Veirella saw his eyes change. She wanted to say something, but she was interrupted.

"We are here." Do'ala told her, Luka looked out the window and came to the same conclusion. Veirella had no intention of looking out of that

window. She could see the dark fog they were flying into just fine from where she sat. "No, turning back now," Luka told her. As they went through the clouds, that got thicker and darker to the point they could barely see anything. Fire appeared before her from the palm of Luka's hand.

Veirella did not know what to expect. Each temple was different. Some priestesses had the power to make you never want to sleep again, and others were just mean, but none of them were nice. If they were, it was because they wanted something.

Veirella did not know how different the priestess there were to their sisters on Fianorea. "I intended to give this to you before we left, but there is no time better than the present." Luka retrieved something from his pocket. He had two small daggers in his hand. Veirella pushed them back at him and shook her head. "I know how you feel about them, but we have no idea what we are about to walking into. I hope you will not need to use them, but just as a precaution."

Veirella looked at his hand for a moment before picking them up. Veirella did not want him to worry about her being unarmed, if they do get into any trouble. The daggers were thin and flat, perfect for throwing, but they were also incredibly detailed with vines carved into the hilt. These were not his own daggers. He had had them made specifically for her. Before she could ask him why they landed.

The door opened and Luka split the flame in two, and sent them into the darkest. He got down, then helped Veirella down. *"Look behind you"* Do'ala warned. Veirella spun around. What she saw made her want to climb back onto the gryphon and go home. There were guards in every direction she looked and their faces were covered with white masks and black hoods and they holding spares pointed at them. "Luka, turn around" when he saw what was before them he went for his sword. Veirella stopped him before he could draw it.

"Let us not start a fight. We do not have any chance of surviving; they are guardians of the Temple. They are probably more skilled than you and

I combined." Luka's hold on his weapon loosened, but he did not let it go. "Then what do you suggest? They do not look like the talking type." Veirella pulled out the satchel Gia gave her. She felt something else in the bag. She just did not look to see what it was.

She opened it and threw the contents into her hand. Along with the yellow crystal, there were two golden coins with a castle like structure, with long pointed tops on one side and sound waves on the other.

Veirella held them up to the guards. She waited a moment for something to happen, then looked at Luka, who was watching them, ready to attack if they did. Then they stood straight and started hitting their spares on the ground. Then they disappeared. Veirella looked around, waiting for something else to happen, but she could not see anything pass what Luka's fire balls lit. There were walls on either side of them at a distance. They were not on solid ground. There were crystals above them. Crystals that are not common to Iriea *"Did an earth wielder help build this place?"*

"Yes." Do'ala answered. Veirella did not intend it as a question. But she got an answer. She would need to work on quieting her thoughts, if that was even possible, having her mind be open to others was unnerving. "We should go see if we can find someone." Luka moved his flames forward, Veirella grabbed his arm stopping him, "what about her?" Veirella did not what to leave the gryphon alone and risk the guards coming back for her. *"I will be fine, die've"*

"She will be fine here. Gryphons have their own way of protecting themselves." Veirella looked at her once more, then turned and followed Luka.

An eternity or walking later, they finally found something that was not flat ground. Stairs, they went walked up and about a hundred steps later they were met with a line of women. Standing before two massive doors, dressed in red cloaks, *the priestesses*.

Veirella showed them the coins, and they moved aside, revealing a single woman wearing a white cloak. The High Priestess. She moved towards them and the others lowered their heads as she passed. When she stopped before them, Luka and Veirella did the same. In the outside world, they outranked her, but inside the temple there was no one with more power than the high priestess. They served as messengers of the Celestial's and could speak for them.

"My Lady—"

She raised her hand, stopping Veirella. "I know why you are here, child. Come." She turned and walked back into the temple. And they followed her. At no point did she look back to ensure they were there. If they were not, it was unlikely she would stop and come back for them. "How do you know we were coming?" Luka asked her.

"I figured someone would come, eventually. I just did not know who. And I heard you the second you step on the continent we hear all the goes on here." She answered. That was the creepiest thing anyone had ever said to her. If it were any other person telling her something like that, she would have been worried. Having such abilities could give one power no one should ever have. However, the priestesses did not have allegiance to anyone. They could not. It would break their oaths to do so.

After turning down hall after hall and more halls, they started going down. And the stairs felt just as never ending. Seven hundred steps later, they finally stopped going down. They went down some more hallways, then stopped. "This is way you are here." She moved, then turned to them. Veirella and Luka shared the same confused expression. There was a hole in the wall, like something broke through it. Luka sent his flames in and followed after them. And Veirella went to the priestess. "What is this?" Veirella did her best to focus on the woman while keeping an eye on Luka. Neutral or not, you could not count on them to not stabbing you in the back. "This is the tomb that held the creature you are hunting." She answered.

"If you knew, she broke free. Why were our parents not informed?" It did not matter how much leadership hated sharing information with outsiders. The Sirabus being free affected everyone, not just Iriea, "it is a recent discovery. There was an incident some years ago that damaged half of the temple. We were vulnerable at the time." Passover it was the only time a temple was unprotected. When the last High Priestess dies, another is chosen. All they are all needed for the ceremony so no one would be guarding. "We lost a few books, mainly knowledge on Celicai, nothing too harmful, but still a tragedy non the less. And that is just what we know so far. My daughters are still going through the archives to see what else is missing."

Temples protected the history and knowledge of everything, so it would take them a few more years to get through it all. "They finally made it down here a few weeks ago. When they realized what happened, I sent word to the queen." She continued. If Gemma's mother knew the truth, why had she not told the other families, or she did and was choosing to keep it quiet.

Veirella went into the tomb. Luka was looking at the walls. There were drawings everywhere. And the ground was covered in pieces of it. Veirella went to see what he was looking at, but stopped when her eye caught something. The fire Luka was using to light up the tomb was reflecting off something. Veirella got down to see what was there, but it was trapped under a large chuck of rock. She tried pushing, but it was pointless. "Luka, there is something under here."

He went over to her and helped her move it. "What is that?"

He retrieving the white crystal sphere and gave it to her. "I think this is a Lin'greaia in common tongue it translates to sonic orb. They use them to ward off sirens. Look for any others. They go in a set of four." Luka made more fire to brighten the room. He looked on one side, she the other. Veirella found another, and Luka found the other two. Veirella had nowhere to put them and wished she had brought a pack with her. She gave them to Luka. His hands were bigger and he could carry far more than she could.

Veirella looked around the tomb. There were ancient symbols carved into the ground and the walls. She could only make out a few of them. The only ones she knew were the elements. All in different language, and almost all of them were dead.

"Have you ever seen anything like this before?" she asked Luka. "No, never dead languages are not really my thing." He answered. They stayed and looked around to see if they could find anything else, like a name carved into the wall, but no such luck. Even if there was, they could understand any of it. "Unless you can suddenly read any of this, we should go before we run out of time." Luka told her. Veirella looked over at him, and her brows pulled together. "What do mean by that?"

"The coins Gia gave you, they are our key in here, but once they fade we die." This was information that should have been given before they went in. "Why are you just telling me this now?" her tone was laced with panic. "I thought you knew. You showed them the coins." Veirella wanted to throw something at him but restrained herself. "Why act all weird with the guards if you knew what would happen?" Luka shock his head, "I did not know about them. I just assumed all temples worked the same."

Veirella had been to one of the two earth temples of Fianorea and did not recall anything about a coin or time limits. They were there for hours, and they had only been in Azaldir for two, maybe three hours. Veirella pulled the satchel from her pocket and looked at the gold coins that were fading into black. She showed them to Luka, and his body stiffened. "We should go. It will take longer to go up than it did to come down." Veirella nodded, then made her way back into the hall, where the High Priestess was still waiting.

When Luka came out behind her she took one of the orbs from him and held it up to her. "May I take theses? They could be of some use to us." She nodded. "Yes, I hope they serve you well." She looked down at the coins in Veirella's other hand, then turned and walked away them following behind her.

They were cutting it close, but they made it outside just in time for the coins to fully turn black, then turned to dust in the palm of her hand. "Thank you for granting us entry into your home," Luka told her, then they bowed. "The pleasure was all mine." The softness of her voice made Veirella almost believe she meant that.

They made their back to Do'ala. *"That took you long enough"* Veirella could hear the annoyance in her tone. *"Sorry to keep you waiting"* She was probably not in favor of being left out in the dark. *"Can we go now?"* Do'ala asked. Veirella pulled the yellow crystal from the satchel and gave it to her. *"Yes, we can."* Luka helped her up, then pulled himself up; the second they were strapped in Do'ala shot into the sky.

Veirella fell asleep on their way back. When she woke, it was dark out. "Are we almost there?" She asked, her voice still riddled with sleep. "We should be there soon." Veirella raised one of the Lin'greaia's observing it. A Lin'greaia was meant to hold power for eternity, "what happened to them? For something that should always be glowing that looks pretty dull," Luka asked.

"I have no idea, but traditionally Lin'greaia's are used to protect sailors from sirens. The Sirabus is part siren, so they work on her. But the difference is sirens do not have constant contact with them, like the Sirabus. I think over time she learned how to take the magic from them, which gave her enough to break herself out." Veirella explained. She could not be sure that was what truly happened. But it was all she had at the moment. They would need power. Lin'greaia was powered by song. Something more beautiful than that of the seas witch, and that meant Veirella would be going home to a place she always thought about.

Most of their journey back was smooth. Then Veirella felt the Do'ala turning. They should not have been turning to go anywhere. They went in one direction all they why to the temple and it should have been the same coming back. "What is happening?" she asked Luka, her chest grew heavier with every second her question went unanswered. "I'm sure it's nothing.

We could just be going a different way." Luka was trying to comfort her, but Veirella saw him reach for his sword.

"*What is happening?*" The gryphon did not answer. "*Do'ala what is going on out there?*" Still nothing. Veirella did not know if she was ignoring her, or she somehow turned the connection off. They did not make anymore turn be they still had no clue as to where she was taking them.

A while later they landed. Luka unbuckled himself, and Veirella did the same. He raised a finger to his lips, telling her to be quiet, "You stay here, and I will see where she took us." Veirella nodded. Luka reached behind him and pushed on something, then the door slid open. She watched him climb down Do'ala's leg, pull his sword and disappeared behind her. When Veirella could no long see him, she sat back in the seat where it was dark, and she would not be seen if someone was out there.

A few minutes passed, then Luka reappeared. Veirella pushed herself to the far side of the gryphocart. "We are above the Under City. Pax and Ana are here." He told her. Veirella ability to breathe returned and the weight on her chest lessened. Luka went back down the Do'ala's leg and Veirella grabbed the satchel with the Lin'greaia's inside and followed. She had no idea the bag could expand until she put the first two inside and she saw that there was still more room. Magic was a strange thing.

Luka helped her door, and once they were clear of the Do'ala's wings, she took off into the sky. Sebastian and Gemma were standing on the other side of the creature. Sebastian looked anger and Gemma was both sad and *hurt*. Veirella started going towards her friend. She left the Academy a week before; she wanted to comfort her. Veirella knew the rules of Ecuovear. She heard of how it worked.

When the physical body faded, the grief went with it. To respect and remember them for the life they lived, and not the way they died. Veirella understood some of it, but not all. The pain one felt after losing someone they care about should not be dictated. Everyone heals in their own way and time.

Before Veirella could say anything, Gemma spoke, "Pax filled me in on everything. Seems like we have our work cut out for us." She put a smile on, but Veirella could tell it was fake. Her eyes didn't light up like they normally would. But she would not push her. Veirella did not want others forcing her to talk about how she felt so she would not do it to someone else. Sebastian opened a portal, and they went back to Astro. They landed back in the court in the commons. The fire was going, which was strange because none of them were there.

"So, you all finally decided to return." they all turned not to see Genevieve sitting behind them. Her voice was calm, but her face was far from it. She stood and moved closer to them. "Do you three have any idea how reckless and irresponsible what you did was? Those with Celestial Blood are dying, and I do not know if you have forgotten, or you were just not thinking, but you are at the top of the food chain. Luka, Pax, you are second years, not third. You may only leave school grounds under the supervision of upperclassmen, which you are not, and Veirella." She looked down at her, it was the same look her mother gave her siblings when they did something they were told not to, and she did not like being on the receiving end. "You are not allowed to leave at all, you have zero experience in the field you could have gotten yourself killed."

Genevieve stopped, looked them over, then took a deep breath to calm herself. "You are all my responsibility while you are a student at this school. I am the one who is responsible for what happens to you. You all of power greater than anything I have ever seen before, but raw power will not save you when you are up against someone one with skill and knowledge." Genevieve's concern made Veirella feel bad for making her worry.

"Do any of you have anything to say for yourselves?" she asked. Veirella was the one to speak. "We are sorry for not telling you we were leaving or where we were going, and unfortunately, nothing came of it. We were following up on something, but it turned out to be nothing." She told her. Veirella could feel all her friend's eyes on her. She hated lying, because she knew what would happen if she told Genevieve about the Lin'greaia's. And they did not have time to follow the proper ways to get this done.

The Sirabus was still out there killing, and could save some lives, but cutting down the time it took to get everything ready. "Not all roads will lead you to an answer, but at least you tried." Genevieve told her, Veirella hated lying but in that moment, it was necessary, she broke into her office and stole information she should not have, so what was one more offence.

"Do not let this happen again, or I will inform your parents of this." That was mostly intended for Pax. Veirella's parents would be happy she was doing something and with other people, no less. They all lowered their heads to make Genevieve think she did something with that speech she gave them.

"Headmistress, I would like to go see my family for a day or two if that allows?" Genevieve turned and looked at Veirella, "yes I am sure your mother and father would love to see the progress you have made in the time have been here." Unfortunately, they would not be seeing her or see that progress anytime soon. "And may Luka accompany me? I know he is not a third year but, I feel safest with him, than I do a stranger. "Veirella told h er.

Genevieve looked at Luka and smiled. "Yes, he may." Then she turned and felt the room. "Where are we really going?" Luka did not need to ask why she lied. He knew as much as she did. Veirella turned to him and a smile broke across her face. "Soul Mountain."

Truth of the Past

Veirella

"I still cannot believe you lied to her," Gemma exclaimed again, out of everything Veirella told her that was what she was stuck on. "If I told her the truth, then she would have given to someone else. And that would require asking for permission to enter. That is time do not have." Veirella told her.

They were leaving in a few hours, and Gemma was helping her pack; Soul Mountain was one of the coldest places to be any time of year, but in winter most never tried to go there. "What do you think will happen to us?" Gemma asked, and her voice was barely there. "I wish I knew; we don't know how powerful she is. We could die. On second thought, maybe we should at least tell the Genevieve about the Sirabus, just to be safe." Veirella had a feeling she was still on the island. She killed Griffin.

Why would she just leave when there was an entire school of Centinal's with power she could steal? She was sure Genevieve knew enough to think that whatever was happening finally reached the school. "You go get those Lin'greaia's charged up and I will bring the book to her so she can see what we found. And I while keep the whole climbing a deadly mountain to get to some singing flowers part to myself." Gemma's attempt at making it all seem normal was not working, but Veirella loved her for trying.

They finished packing her things. It was not much, a heat pack, a few veils of the booster, but none of the other elixir. Gemma told Veirella she only needed to take it twice a month, she would not mind taking it twice a day if it met, she would never feel like that again. They also packed a few herbs, just to be save Veirella was taught how to use nature to heal; it was a requirement for all Forian girls to know how to save a life.

They made their way to the commons; then Gemma went to her room. She needed to get ready for class. She would be playing catch up for the weeks' worth of work she missed, Veirella would love for that to be her main problem. But unfortunately, they had bigger problems to deal with. Veirella went to the training room where Luka and Sebastian were putting their weapons away. Sebastian looked at her, but she pretended not to see him. "I am going to go clean up, then we can go." Luka walked up to her on his way out.

Veirella looked up at him, "you two should talk, I mean it. We cannot function as a team if all four sides do not click. Hear him out before you decide to hate him." Luka did not wait for Veirella to say anything. He just left. Luka was right she needed to talk to Sebastian. She could not avoid the fact that he was her brother forever. She was not truly angry, Veirella was just tired of having everything change, and having everything that she was be a lie.

Veirella also did not know why he kept it from her. She watched him put the swords back on the wall, then he turned and looked at her. "Can we talk?" Sebastian both relaxed and tensed up from her question. "Yes."

For a while, that was the only thing shared between them. He waited for her to make the first move for her to start the conversation; but Veirella did not know what to say. "How long have you known?" it took Sebastian a while to answer. He did the same thing with his hands that she did when she was nervous.

"My whole life, I was told about you right after you were born. It was the first time we met." Veirella had to force feet to stay where they were, it was already too much. Sebastian knew who she was the day they met. Well, the first time she remembered meeting him at is. "Why didn't you tell me who you were the day we met in the garden? You had the chance." She asked.

"I was told not to say anything about, you are a first in our world. No Celestial's have ever had a child together. It should not have been possible. Yet here you are. No one was to learn of our shared parentage, but I was to keep you safe if the day came were someone tried to hurt you for what you were. *Which I did such a great job at that.*"

"What do you mean by that? How did you fail to protect me?" Sebastian dropped his head and cursed. "Nothing, forget about it," Veirella walked further into the room and closer to him. "No, you do not get to do that. You do not get to keep things about me from me. You want us to have a semblance of a relationship. You tell me the truth." She told him there was more to her voice than she thought herself capable of.

Sebastian sighed then looked at her; "Okay," then he nodded to himself. "I remember the day you got hurt; I got hurt in training earlier that day. I always had visions of you. Sometimes you were really happy others you were in distress. I never worried because someone was always with you, protecting you. But that night I felt how terrified you were. I saw you running. I felt when the arrows hit you, then when the cut. And all I could do was watch because I barely had enough cai felt to heal, let alone move.

But I still tried. I was still shit at making portals. I tried three times, but then I had nothing left and all I would do was watch you there dying. I thought you were dead because I didn't feel you anymore." Sebastian's eyes filled with tears, but he wiped them away before they could fall.

Veirella didn't know what to say, or what to think. She shared one of the worse moments in her life with someone she hardly knew, and she could still didn't remember what happened that night. "I had one job, and I failed. I failed you, and I will forever be sorry for not being there for you that day." he continued. She felt the tears running down her face. Veirella did not even realize she was crying. "Sebastian, you are a little over a year older than I am. I was ten. That would have made you eleven. I was not your responsibility; I am still not your responsibility. And the person who put you in that position is horrible for doing so." Sebastian heard her words, but he was not listening to them.

For a while, neither of them said anything. "Where do we go from here?" he asked. Veirella did not have an answer for him, and she told him just as much. "I don't know." His face fell, "but we can figure it out. Together." He looked up at her and the first tear fell. He wiped it away, and she did the same.

"We can talk more. Once there is not an ancient monster trying to kill us." Sebastian laughed, "that sounds like a good idea."

With Sebastian's help, Veirella opened a portal just outside Soul Forest. They were on the other side of it, so she would not see the castle and the way they came meant they were far closer to the mountain. And a good distance away from where she was cocooned.

They made their way into the forest. It would take them a few hours to get to Soul mountain, but it was a walk she did not mind, nature was peace for her and Veirella hoped some day she could find safety in it again. Soul forest was smaller than most of the forests on the continent, but it was a maze to get through. "Are you okay being out here?" Luka asked. She was trying not to think about where they were. This was her first time going in after coming out of the cocoon.

"Navigating is keeping my mind busy." She stopped and turned to look at him, "since Gemma went into my mind, I have been having these flashes of memories, I do not know if they are real or just something my mind came up with, because in some of them I am wielding. And my parents did nothing about it. For weeks I have been trying not to think about it but at the moment, it is the only thing keeping me from noticing where my feet are." She felt the pressure building in her chest, which usually meant she was losing control of herself.

But this was not the time she could not lose control. She had something she needed to do. So Veirella closed her eyes and began counting her breaths in and out until the pressure lessened. She looked back at Luka; he saw what happened but did not question her about it. Which she appreciated. "Let's keep going. We should be there in two or so hours." Veirella did not wait for him to answer she just turned around and kept going.

They walked in silence for a while. The only sounds being made came from the ground they walked on and the birds in the sky. "So, how did things go with Pax?"

"It was okay. We have a lot we need to talk about. This is all still a lot to wrap my head around. Every time I turn around, there is something else to rip it from under me." She answered. Veirella wanted the world to stop spinning long enough for her to get some footing.

Her shoe got stuck and in pulling it free, she lost her balance; Veirella grabbed a hold of the tree next to her. *"If you can touch it before I do. Then You get to choose where we go for training Irredina or Atryae." Aspen told Iris, they were children, this was years before they were even old enough for their Ryin. "Okay" Iris responded. They competed for everything. Their father encouraged it, their mother not so much. She thought they should work together, not against each other.*

"Oh, and Iris. You should pack for the cold because when I win we are so going Atryae." She rolled her eyes at him. They were currently the same in height, but that would change soon. Growth would come for them soon, and Aspen would become much larger. Iris looked around them, searching for something. "Where did Elle go?" Aspen turned around to find Veirella was gone they knew they shouldn't have brought her out with them but both their parents were busy entertaining guests and they did not want to leave her alone with her wet nurse while they went and played. "Come on, she has small legs. She could not have gotten far." Aspen told her, "Elle" they called out for their sister.

They went in different directions, looking for her and calling out for Veirella hoping she would answer. Iris was the one to find her. Her eyes grew wide as she watched Veirella walk towards the wiping willow tree. None of the branches had gone after her yet, but they were preparing to. Iris ran for her sister. She got her as a large branch from the right came at them. Iris pushed Veirella out of the way and out of the tree's reach.

Veirella hit the ground and started crying, but before Iris could help her up, another branch came at her. She did not react fast enough, and it threw her into the trees. She hit her head and fainted when she hit the ground.

Veirella heard her name. She could not tell where it was coming from, then she felt someone pulling her up. The vision faded, and she saw Luka. His hand was on her waist, keeping her from falling. "Are you okay? You disappeared there for a second." Veirella straightened herself. Then he let her go. "Yeah, everything is fine. A little distracted is all. We should be at the foot of the mountain soon."

Veirella had memory flashes before but nothing that clear, and it didn't feel like it was coming from her. It felt as if she was watching from someone else's eyes.

The rest of their walk was silent. She was thinking about what she saw, and how much of a danger she was, and Luka did not seem like much of a talker so he did not push for conversation. When they made it to the base of Soul Mountain, it was dark. "Why didn't we do this in the day? It would be easier to see." Soul Mountain had some was differences that made it more unique to other mountains. It had its own magic. "It would be easier to see, but a lot harder to climb. In the day the mountain pushed things down, with spark waves, and it the night it pulls them up. So instead of it taking us an entire day's journey to get to the top, we should be there in two and a half hours, if that," Veirella explained.

She looked back at Luka, and he was smiling at her. "What?" she asked her skin heating under his stare. "You know a lot more about magic than you let on." Veirella knew magic was real. She saw others do it. She was just unaware that she could or she did now and forgot. Because the memories in her head told a different story. "Magic is not new to me, having it is. And I also know everything there is to know about Fianorea." She told him.

"We should get going." Luka told her then looked up at the mountain. Veirella did the same, then she looked down at herself. "Are you sure we have enough on? It will not take that long to get up there, but it will still be cold." *And it will still get colder,* she thought. Veirella was wearing keives with winter boots, and gloves to match, along with a fur coat to keep her body warm. Keif was designed for the cold. But Veirella was not sure she wanted to test that with her life. Luka was dressed the same way she was, but he could wield fire. He would be fine. "Yes, you will feel a little chilled, but nothing too much. And you also have me as your personal heat source." He answered.

Then they started going up. The further up they went, the colder it got, and they still add a good distance to go before they saw any snow, but there was still ice on the ground. Luka switched places with her after the third time she almost fell over. He was using his magic to melt the ground, which helped them go faster. Veirella could not see his sparks, but she could feel them. It warmed her and made the cold air easier to bear.

The moon was almost above them when they made it to the slope, where Veirella saw small patches of snow. "We need to get up there before the moon fully rises. The Nives will bloom when it reaches its peak." Veirella informed Luka they would stay bloomed for a few hours, but Veirella had waited for so long to hear them, she wanted to catch every second of it.

"How do we get up there?" Luka asked. She spent so much time reading about the mountain she knew every detail about it. "Look for black rode sticking out, in pairs and about five feet in distance from the next pair." Luka nodded, then summoned fire. He split it in two and left one with her. Soul Mountain came with its own magic and it wanted to be seem, so the mountain made ways from mortals to see her in all her glory, different rods lead to different places, and the distance of the rods indicated what direction one needed to go to experience what she had to offer.

Veirella found singular rods four feet in distance, which led to a cave with glowing crystals, then she found rods that were several feet apart, which lead to cave with water that was somehow always cold but never froze. Nioloes were the only ones who ever went to it. With all the training and work they did, they were always in pain.

Veirella thought she found a third, but she did not see any rods above it to show that it went somewhere. There were other places to see on the mountain, but many never survived going to them. Lost souls that will never go home, so many lives were lost on the mountain that people started calling it Soul mountain. Veirella did not know if anyone remembered its true name. That made two things she did not know about the place, its name if it had one and if the Se'vi was real.

The fireball started moving, and she followed it. At the end, Veirella saw Luka. Then both balls became one. "I found it." Luka moved so she could see the rods. They were obsidian, they were at least four inches wide, and had dips like pieces were broken off over time. Veirella looked up and there was an identical pair above them at the right distance.

Luka helped her go up the first two, then she used the snow to push herself up to the others, then she felt the pressure of her body fade and she could move freely. She was grateful for the light the moon offered, but she also hated seeing it go up. It was halfway up and the more it moved into place, the colder it got, and the slower she moved.

Twenty rods up Veirella could not feel her hands. It was either from how many times she pulled herself up or the cold air biting at her bones. The mountain's magic made the climb easier, but she still had to do soon work. She could feel her grip weaken, but the gods must be smiling down at her because the next time she pulled herself up, she saw flat ground.

Veirella pushed her body up into the snow; she got to her feet and pushed through the snow. It was so high it covered half her legs. Veirella got a good distance away from the edge and sat down, then pulled her feet out. She removed her pack and pulled out her canteen. She went to drink from it, but nothing came out. The water was frozen and she would need Luka to rectify that problem. Veirella watched the cliff side, waiting for him to appear.

By the time he got to her, the temperature had dropped again. Every piece of snow that he touched melted away, inch after inch disappeared beneath every step he took. Veirella returned her canteen to her pack, then pushed to her feet. When Luka got close to her, she felt the heat coming off hi m.

The numbness in her faded slightly, just enough that she could move again. She turned around and saw the massive opening in the mountainside she somehow missed while sitting in front of it. Luka melted them a path towards in and as they got closer, the snow melted away. The further in they went, the less white was around them. Luka sent flames into the air when it got darker. They also helped her warmup.

"Do you know how far in they are?" Veirella shook her head. She was still too cold to speak. The book said the song would be their guide, but the moon was not up yet. They han a few more minutes of waiting to do so she stopped and removed her pack, and picked up her canteen. "Do you mind?" her voice was low and raspy.

It was nothing compared to the pain she felt when she tried speaking before she got her voice back; it was more uncomfortable than anything else. "Sure." Luke answered, then took her canteen. Small red sparks appeared around his hand, then around the silver bottle. Then he gave it back to her. Veirella drank half of it. She would have finished it if she did not remember. She would need it for the climb down.

She returned the canteen to her pack and sat down. She looked up at Luka, who did not look like he just climbed up a mountainside. "How are you not tried?" Veirella asked once she could speak again. "I have done things like this so many times that it no longer affects me." He got closer to her and his heat covered her more than it was before. "You climb snow moved mountains on the regular?" Veirella met his eyes. She never noticed the beautiful shade of green they were until that moment. It was not forest green, something much brighter.

"Something like that. All fire wielders with the ability to become riders hear a dragon once they tap into their power, and upon their Ascension, they made the climb to Calos to claim that dragon if they are proven themselves worthy." He explained.

"So you have trained for this?" she asked. He nodded his answer. "So do all fire wielders have a bonded dragon?" Veirella wondered how many differences there were between the different elements and if she would share earth and water gifts or be something different. "No, just some. A few centuries ago many more were chosen, but as few eggs hatch now, they are more reluctant to bond."

"But there were dragons at Corviac. If they are so reluctant to bonding why let the young leave?" Veirella thought they would be more inclined to keep them on the hatching grounds. "They use them to test babies, see if some day they will become wielders. So they can start training them. It just so happens that hatchlings love to dance." Luka smiled, more to himself than her.

But it made her smile. He was always so stone faced; it was nice to see him relaxed for once. Veirella intended to say something, but the cave started singing. Luka stood to his full height, then helped her up. They followed the sound, which was harder because it echoed off the walls. They made it to an end with four separate openings; the song coming from all of them. "Its hard to tell which way it's coming from." They could go through all of them until they found the right one, but that would take hours depending on how far in they went.

"We should split up and search." Luka stayed quiet. Looking down at her, Veirella turned to look at him because of his lack of input. "You go left and I will go right. If I find them, I will come and find you and you can do the same." Veirella turned to walk off, but he grabbed her hand, stopping her.

"We both know there is a faster and much easier way of doing this." Veirella's brows grew together. "What are you talking about?" If she could find them, Veirella would have already done so. "Greviger dust makes a person's thoughts turn against them. That's how it tortures, but you heard the voices when it was in your head, not your own them. If you want to find the Nives, you need to listen to them in only a way you can," Luka told her. Veirella looked away from him. "*I can't*," her response was low and her words broken. Luka pulled at her hand, trying to get her to look at him, and when that didn't work, he moved to stand before her.

"This all sucks, I get that. Your entire life is being torn apart one piece at a time, and it is terrifying. I have no idea what happened to you, and I may never be able to understand it, but one thing I can say about you is that you are not one to give up, I can't say I know anyone else that could have survive what you did, that shows strength. So find that girl and tell me where we need to go." Veirella nodded at him. A tear rolled down her face, but he wiped it away before she noticed.

"Okay, I can ... I can try" Luka stepped back releasing his hold on her. Veirella closed her eyes and called on her magic. She felt the sparks moving through her, warming her as they went. She listened to the beautiful sound touching her ears and pushed past it. The sing washed over her, pulling something from her but also giving her something back.

Then she heard the voices "*come come to us, we want you to see us. Be with us, come to us.*" Veirella's feet moved, her eyes were still closed, but she trusted them not to tell her wrong. She went to the second cave, the song was the same, and the word changed, "*there you are, look at us are we what you expected? Are we what you wanted?*"

Veirella opened her eyes, and they changed from brown to gold. She was standing in a field of white flowers. They opened into a curve with the tips curved under then out; the center was gold and the spurs were being pushed into the room and the petals were glowing. They moved side-to-side dancing to their own song; it was the most beautiful thing Veirella had ever heard, and she did not think anything would ever come close to it. "*Yes, you are exactly as I expected.*" She answered.

Veirella pulled her pack off and retrieved the satchel with the Lin'greaia's they were already glowing, as she laid them down before her. The white light was as bright as the Nives petals. Veirella sat down and watched them move. She did not care that it was cold anymore. She felt nothing but them, and they made her safe and warm. Veirella stayed in the flower bed until they all faded and closed back up, into an unnatural circular shape.

Veirella returned the Lin'greaia's to the satchel, then put it in her pack. She stood, then turned to find Luka standing off to the side. Veirella had sat there for hours watching them as he watched her.

They slept for a few hours, waiting for daybreak. They needed the magical pressure of the mountain to change. The sun was not up yet, but they needed to leave before it was. "You said the energy that helped us get up here would help get us get down. Why the rush?" Veirella turned and looked at him, "I do not think those were my exact words. The mountain pushes everything up at night and down during the day. The wind moves down when the moon sets. If we wait for the sun to be full, then we will be thrown off." She told him.

Veirella took her booster, then fixed her pack. Luka woke before her so she assumed he took his already. Then made their way through the caves taking turn after turn. Veirella did not realize how far in the Nives led her. They made it out and started climbing down. It was not as cold and there was less snow, but that had more to do with Luka than the weather.

The wind picked up the closer they got to the bottom. It pushed at them, but they made it down before it could get any worse. It would take them half the day to get from Nightwell to Cracia, which was the last thing Veirella wanted to do after going up and then down a mountainside. "Why are we going that far out?" Veirella asked. They portaled into Nightwell from the school. Why could they not go back the same way? "I am not as good at portals as Pax is. He has done it for far longer and is much better at it, so the more distance we can cut, the better." He explained.

"You could just do what he did and pull energy from me, combining our powers." Veirella was begin understanding how it all worked, power was important, but so was control and skill. She had the power she knew that for a fact, but her lack of control over it made doing things more complicated.

"That will not work. We do not share blood."

"Converging only works if two wielders are related?" seemed like a flaw. "No, a wielder taking energy from another can only happen if you share blood, converging requires combining energy. There is a difference." He explained. Veirella stopped walking, and so did Luka. "What?" Luka asked. His hand went to his sword as he looked over her for a threat he would not find. Veirella turned to look at him.

"You knew that he was my brother?" She asked. Veirella was getting tired of everyone keeping secrets from her. "I guessed when he suggested the idea, but I did not know for sure until the cave," he answered. Veirella sighed, then turned and continued on.

The sun began to set, and they still had twenty miles to go. Veirella held her tongue about how much her feet hurt and how tired she was. Luka likely felt the same. He took her pack an hour before, which she did not ask him to do or protest. It took some weight off her and she was able to move more freely and faster.

They heard something running behind them and by the sound it made it was big and there was also more than one. Luka pulled Veirella behind a tree because it was coming their way.

The branches being snapped got louder the closer they got, Luka pulled his sword preparing to attack. The panic in Veirella's chest turn to something warm and comforting. They made it to the tree and Luka went for the attack, Veirella turn to see what was following them. Then her eyes landed on the tracker. "Stop!" she yelled. Veirella moved from her hiding place and jumped between Luka and her dogs.

"Veirella what are you doing?" There was panic and fear in his voice shocked her two things she never thought she would ever hear from him. He tried pulling her towards him and ways from the large black creatures. But when he reached for her, the bigger one growled at him. "Put your sword down, you cannot hurt them. And they will not hurt you." She told him. For a second, Luka's grip on his sword tightened. Veirella looked at him.

Pleading with him, hoping that he would trust her. Luka looked from her to the two creatures behind her, still growling at him, then lowered his weapon, then sighed and sheathed it. "Thank You." He nodded, then Veirella turned her back to him, facing the dogs. "If he has to stop, so do y ou."

The bigger one pulled back and put his teeth away, but the smaller one growled at Luka again when he got closer. Veirella looked at her, then she stopped. "Luka, this Artemis and Kal'eri. My pups." She told him, Luka looked from them to her, "Dove, they are bigger than you are. How are they still considered pups?" He asked.

"They are not big enough to be considered adults yet." Veirella went to stand between them and lowering their heads to her. Then she rubbed them both. "I missed you. You have both gotten so big since I last saw you." The last time Veirella was with them, she was eight. They were a gift for her reight that year. She only got so spend a few months with them before she was sent away and they could both fit on her bed then.

Veirella looked at Luka, who was watching her. Veirella held a handout to him. "Come, they like to be scratched." Luka looked at them, then back at her. Veirella could not tell if it was fear or surprise in his eyes, but something was there. "If we want to get to Cracia faster, we are going to need to ride them. And neither will let you near unless they know you can be trusted." Veirella explained.

Luka stood there watched the three of them for a moment before slowly making his was to her. Then she took his hand and moved it along Artemis's head. Once she felt him relax, Veirella moved her hand, continuing to scratch Kal'eri. She watched them, hoping Artemis would not reject him.

He got closer to Luka, and Veirella held her breath, waiting to see what Artemis would do next. But she relaxed when he rubbed his nose against him. Luka turned to face Kal'eri "I do not recommend doing that, she is not as nice as Arty." Luka nodded and drew back his hand.

Veirella moved away from Kal'eri towards Artemis and he laid down, "Ready?" Luka raised his hand to the back of his neck. He was nervous. "No, but let's do it." He answered. "We will ride on Arty, as much Kal'eri loves me and I her. I have no interest in getting on her ever again."

They climbed onto his back, and Luka wrapped his arms around her waist. Then Artemis stood. "Here we go." Veirella gently pulled on his fur and his took off. "Wow." Was all the words Luka could form, riding Artemis was a lot similar to horse riding. Only he was bigger, faster, and he jumped further. "Who gave them to you?"

"I no idea, they just showed up. My parents were terrified they would eat people. Artemis had a letter attached to him. No name for them or the sender. It just said they were for me." She answered. Veirella hoped to find out who sent them, so she could thank them in person for one of the best gifts she had ever received. "Some gift." *That they are,* she thought.

It didn't seem like they were moving for that long, but Veirella saw the Black Mountains and Cracia's ridges ahead of them. Artemis took them all the way to the cliff side, then stopped. He laid do, Luka jumped off, and Veirella slid off him. "That was faster than expected and exhilarating," Luka told her. He rubbed Artemis again, his hand disappearing beneath his thick fur.

Luka stepped back when he stood to his full height. Both pups went to Veirella lowering their heads to her. She laid a hand on both of them. "I wish we had more time together, but I need to go. When I get home, I promise to give you all my attention." She kissed Kal'eri then Artemis, then she released them and watched them run off.

Red sparks of flame appeared around Luka's arms, then a portal matching his power formed before them. He took her hand, and they walked through it. On the other side, they were surrounded by green; they were in a forest and it did not look like the one at the academy, Veirella looked behind her and saw a cliff she let go of Luka's hand and went to see what was on the other side.

There was a city in the distance, "We're in Asiza. We can get horses there to get back to the school." Luka informed her. Veirella looked over at him and saw his skin was red and grey. It was not a significant difference from his earlier color, but they had been together long enough for Veirella to notice. "Are you okay?" She reached up to touch his face. He was also a lot warmer than a moment again when she held his hand. "Fine, just being wielding too much power for too long." Veirella took her pack from him and took her last booster and have it to him. "No, you take. You need you strength." Luka pushed it back at her. "Luka, you need it more than I do. We can get some real food when we get into the city before we leave, but for now take this. I do not need you dying on me."

They stood there looking at each other with the veil between their hands, then he let her go, holding out his hand waiting for Veirella to give it to him. She opened it, then gave it to him. Luka drank the green liquid, and the color returned to his skin seconds later.

It was dark when they finally made it into the city. There were people all over the place, some dancing to music, other stumbling about, and a few trying to sell the trinkets. Luka led her to the building with the less amount of people near it. The sign above the door read 'The Cruel Raven'. All the tables were full, so Luka brought them to the bar. They found two seats at the far end away from everyone, where they could see the entire room.

The large man behind the counter, with red hair on his face, came to them. "What can I get you?" He is accent was thick, which made his words hard to understand. "Two cider's and whatever taste the less shit." Luka answered. The man nodded and walked off. Then returned with two glasses filled with amber liquid. Luka gave him silver coins with dragon heads on them. That was her first time seeing coins like that.

When Luka was halfway through his drink, the red-haired man returned with two bowls. She barely touched her drink she was too worried about him. "Lucky for you two, this catch is fresh." The wooden bowl was filled with a creamy liquid. "Thank you," Veirella said to him. He nodded then went back to survive the other patrons.

Luka finished before her, then left to get them horses. When he return half an hour later Luka somehow managed to look worse the before. "Are you okay?" she asked, her voice laced with concern. Veirella raised her hand to his head. His skin was cold. "Fine, we should get going, even on horseback. It will take all night to get back to the school."

Veirella nodded and followed him outside, where two brown horses were tied to the poles. Luka helped Veirella into her saddle, undo the halter he went to give them to her, then stopped. "You do know how to ride? Right?"

"Yes" Luka nodded, she took them and tended to his own horse "Luka a word of advice find out if someone can do something before you put them on an animal that has a tendency of kicking people to death when frightened." Veirella smiled at him.

Then she tightened her hold on the reins, moved from him, not waiting for an answer. Veirella did not go far. Luka did not look well, and she wanted to keep an eye on him, but he was not too far behind and was managing to keep a similar pace to her.

As they moved, Veirella made sure to look back at him every few minutes, making sure he was still with her. When Veirella looked around to check on him again, she saw him fall forward, then off the horse. "Luka!" she yelled. Veirella pulled her horse to stop her. Then turned him to stop the other. She jumped off her horse and ran to her friend.

Luka rolled onto the side of the road into the grass. His was face down, and he was not moving. "Luka?" Veirella called out, her voice breaking. *Not dead anything but dead,* she thought. Veirella got down and turned him over. She raised her hand to his face and signed with relief when she felt him breathing.

"Luka, wake up." Veirella shook him, hoping it would wake him, but nothing. She heard movement back to the road. She needed to find help. Veirella looked in the direction of the school, they were not close enough for her to see the gates, she heard something behind her, Veirella turned around there was someone walking down the road towards them from the town, she could not see their face it was cover with a black hood.

But she was thankful that someone else was on the road. Veirella ran up to them. "Hey, I do not mean to be a bother but my friend is very sick. Could you help me get him back on his horse? Please." They stopped but did not say anything, "If you require payment, I have money. I just need to get him some help." Veirella was willing to give as much as they asked for as long as they helped her get Luka back on his horse and she got him to the school.

"I would accept payment, just not money." The voice belonged to a woman. And the way she drew out the words made Veirella step back. It was strange, but familiar, but hard to place why that was. "Wha—what do you want?" Veirella felt she would regret asking, but she did it anyway.

The woman did not answer. She slowly raised her hands to her hood and pulled it back. Veirella's heart stopped, and she forgot how to break when she saw her face. "You." Lily answered.

Six Years Before

This would be her final test after two years of training. This moment could determine if Veirella would get to go home. She was surrounded by six girls as usual, but instead of wooded weapons they held double sided blades, Veirella did not have a weapon. The point of the test was to see how well she could handle herself.

If she could get one of their blades and take them all down, she would pass, and her Ryin would be complete, then she would be given her Ceremonial Marks, which all Forians were marked with after passing. Traditionally, Ryin took three to four years to complete, for a variety of reasons. Either they fail one of their final tests or the Lavia rejects them and they need to work harder to prove they are worthy of wearing the Goddess's marks.

Aspen should have already finished his train. Three years seemed like enough time for him to complete Ryin. Iris, on the other hand, did it in a year. It was not required for one to learn how to wield all weapons to finish training and, but most choose to because it was not needed she opted to only learn the one she chose on choosing day. The lasso, it was not a common choice but her sister was not a common person.

Veirella cleared her mind. Her thoughts were wondering, and she needed to focus to remember where she was. She took a deep breath, then looked at Elizabeth, signaling to her at she was ready.

"Begin"

The second the word left her mouth, three girls came at her, two from the side and one from behind. Veirella got around the one to her right and pushed her into her place. The one coming at her from behind stuck the blade in her neck. Then she pulled forward, cutting her throat open. She fell to the ground and bleed out. Veirella looked at her for a second, but she could not lose focus. None of her other test had ended with anyone dying, but maybe that was the true test.

To see if she was capable of taking a life. The girl next to her went for her head, Veirella dodge the attack and went at her, she was the closest and her weapon would be the easiest to take, Veirella considered going for the dead girl's but her body was covering it and that would leave her open, if she tried.

She kicked the girl's knee back, and she lost her balance. Veirella went for her arm, twisting it until she released her hold on the blade. She got a hold of one side when one of the other girls came at her. Veirella used the girl she was trying to get the blades from to push herself up and kick the other in the face.

She fell back, Veirella was still in the air. She used that to her advantage and flipped the girl over her, and finally she released it. She attempted to stand, but Veirella stuck the blade in her throat before she could. The other three came at her together. Veirella noticed that the blades could split in two, and she pulled them a part then threw one at the girl in the middle. It went through her head and she fell back.

Veirella let the other's to get close, then slip between them and stabbed the one on the left in her thigh. She pulled the blade out and the girl fell to her knee, Veirella quickly retrieved the other half of the blade and stuck them back together, she spun for the other girl and aimed for the center of her blades separating them, then she spun to her feet and cut her head off and did the same for the other.

But she wasn't finished. There was still one alive. She stood then pulled her blades a part, so she had one in each hand, then ran at Veirella. Before she could get closer, Veirella threw her blades at her. It went right through her chest and landed in the wall behind her. She fell to her knees, dropped the blades, and fell over.

Veirella looked around at them. There was blood everywhere, but there was not a drop on her, from them or herself. "Well done, princess. You have completed your training. The Goddess will be pleased with our gift." Elizabeth told her.

"Gift? What gift?" Veirella turned and looked at the girls she just killed. They were a sacrifice. Lovia Marks were not a gift, they were a reward for doing something for her, "many fail this part of the test it takes them years to be able to take a life, and for other's it takes them time to realize what they need to do" Elizabeth explained, she got closer to Veirella and laid a hand on her shoulder "You child realized what was happening the moment it happened and you did not hesitate to act." She continued.

"It was a kill or be killed situation and I have no interest in dying." She responded. Elizabeth smiled at her, then turned and got off the platform. Veirella followed after her. "For someone so young to understand that will get you far, most never get that morality and survival do not go hand in hand."

"Morality is a concept for those who can afford to have it. And in a world were being bigger and stronger keeps you alive, I cannot afford to sympathetic."

Veirella told her. She hadn't grown much in the last two years or three for that matter. "Thank you, for teaching me how to be strong" Elizabeth opened the door then turned and looked down at her. "I did not teach you strength. All I did was pull it to the surface. All that you are, came from you," she assured her. Veirella nodded, then Elizabeth moved so she could go through the door.

"Remember to stay close to a fire tonight. The winds are moving down. It will be the coldest night of the year," Elizabeth informed her. Veirella nodded. "I will." The second Elizabeth closed the door, Veirella took off. She

knew what night it was. It was the only night in the year the Nives bloomed, and Iris promised to take her to see them.

After telling her the story of how they came to be, Veirella had wanted to see and hear them and now she could. They started planning to go months before, and the day had finally come. When she got to her room, Veirella knocked four times, then waited for Iris to open the door. When she did, Veirella was too excited to greet her before asking.

"What time are we leaving?" By the look on her sister's face, she had forgotten, "What do you mean? Leaving for what?" she asked; and her words confirmed Veirella's suspicions. "To see the Nives bloom, remember you said we could go see them this year" her excitement faltered for a moment, but she was reminding Iris of it now so they could still go.

"I am so sorry; with all the studying I have to do I completely forgot" she had forgotten how could she have forgotten. Veirella never stopped talking about it, but somehow it had slipped her mind.

"So, we are not going?" the disappointment in her voice was not what she wanted her sister to hear. Veirella did not want her to feel guilty for focusing on her studies. It was not her intention, but it was how she felt, and it was hard to hide that. "I know how much you wanted to go before we left, but we can always come back up here and do it next year." Iris responded.

Veirella had waited so long for this, and now she had to wait another year. She was not too sure she ever wanted to return to Nightwell Castle. As grateful as she was for the lessons she learned, the place would still give her nightmares for years to come. "I know how much you wanted to go, but it is not safe to do the climb without the proper preparations especially for someone as small as you are" Iris explained, but Veirella did not like that answer her size had benefited her many times in the past two years.

"How is my size a problem? I do great in training because of how small I am," she pushed back. Veirella was truly curious to know why her sister thought that. Iris knelt before her and took her hands into her own. "You know how after a baby bird is born, it still needs its mother to feed it because it cannot leave the nest?" Veirella nodded, "A Nestling" Iris smiled at her

correction. If she was going to use bird analogies, she should know the correct terms.

"Well, you are like that bird—Nestling, you need someone to help you go up Soul Mountain because you are young and small. If I were to take you there without someone to regulate your body temperature, you could get sick and then something bad could happen to you," she explained.

Veirella shook her head, taking in everything Iris said. "So, what you are saying is that without proper warmth. I could get hypothermia and then I would die" Iris nodded at her in responded, then she stood up and released a pain breath.

"Yes."

Veirella could not argue with that. Dying was not on her list of things to do in the near future. "Okay, well, I guess it is better we be safe; I want to do a lot of things before I die." Veirella was disappointed, but she understood. "And you are also too pretty to die so young," Iris told her, then pinched her nose. Veirella slapped her hand away and stepped back, and Iris laughed. She hated when she did that. Veirella figured it was why she did it so constantly.

"Why do you always do that?" she asked, her tone filled with annoyance, which her sister could hear. "Because I know you hate it, and that makes it all the more fun." Iris reached for her again, but Veirella was quick and moved before she caught her. She got closer to the open door, putting some distance between them.

"Well, I am going to take a bath and do some reading. I am all sticky from training." She pointed at herself, emphasizing her words. Veirella did not know why she was still considering it training. She had finished two weeks prior, and had been doing testing since, but that was what she called it for two years. So it was automatic at this point.

"I will let you get back to your studies," she looked towards the open books on her desk behind her then she turned to leave the room, but Iris stopped her "Come here" she asked her, Veirella stepped back now going through the door. She did not trust that Iris did not have some ulterior your motive.

"Why?" she said. Her tone was one filled with caution and suspicion of the request. "I just want a hug from my baby sister. Is that such a crime" Iris moved her hands apart waiting for Veirella to come to her. "You are not going to do that thing again, are you?" Iris shook her head.

"No, just a hug"

Veirella took a moment to think about it, then went to her sister and wrapped her arms around her waist. Then Iris closed her arms around her, and Iris did exactly what Veirella had hoped she would not. She pinched her nose again and tickled her before she got away from her. Veirella was annoyed, but she was also trying to keep herself from laughing.

"You lied" she said as harsh as she could manage. "What can I say" Iris raised her shoulders then dropped them. Veirella made her way out the door, not saying another word. "I will see you at dinner," Iris called after her, as she closed the door. Iris had insisted they have dinner in the dining hall that night. Veirella did not know why, but she also did not care. Spending more time with her sister did not need to be questioned.

Halfway to her room, Veirella saw a face she hadn't in months. Lily; someone she once considered a friend, up until she left her unconscious on a balcony, several months passed. Her dark hair was braided up, and she was wearing black Keives, a color mostly only worn by fighters, for its strength and durability.

"Lily, what are you doing here?" Veirella's tone towards the girl was cold and uncaring. The night she changed the gems was the last night she saw her. Veirella never asked about her, she did not care to know where she was. And even if she did, who would she have asked? She did not speak to the other girls that trained her, and Elizabeth did not seem like the type to freely give that information.

And Iris was also the only one that knew that Veirella was spending time with her. Lily had told her not to say anything about their lessons, but she still spoke with her sister about it. She wanted to learn, but she was not willing to hide and keep secrets from Iris.

Then had never met for obvious reasons. The night Iris found her passed out on the balcony she did lied, Veirella told her, she fainted. Iris was not all for their friendship, but she never pushed Veirella to not spend time with her. She might have if she was just someone random Veirella had met outside the castle, but Lily was one of the girls helping her train, so she did not see the harm in it.

"I had some things at home that needed my attention. I asked to be pulled from your training teaming." She answered. "And it was so urgent you left me outside on cold ground?" Lily went to say something, but Veirella raised her hand, stopping her. "In all honest I do not care. I know saying that makes me sound spoiled and lacking understanding of the privileges I have. But it does not matter, you cannot call yourself someone's friend, then do that to them." Veirella told her, then stepped around her, then made her way towards the stairs.

"Look, I am sorry; I just panicked. I did not want to be blamed for what happened to you." She explained. Veirella stopped and turned to her. "One I was not dead. I fainted, and Two when I woke, I could have told them you had nothing to do with it, but instead you took off. So goodbye Lily thank you for helping me but this friendship" she pointed between them.

"Is over and down." Then she turned and continued up the stairs. A moment later, she left. Something hit the back of her head. There was an echo of pain, then darkness.

"Are we killing her here? It will send a message if they find the youngest daughter of the King. The man who rules over the most powerful realm in a Millennium, how easy it is to get to him." The person speaking was male, Veirella could tell by the deepness of his voice.

That was the first thing Veirella heard when she woke. She did not remember what happened. One moment she was going to her room, the next she was waking with her hands bound behind her back.

Then she heard a voice she knew, "We're not killing her, if she is dead then I will not get what I want and I did not spend two fucking years teaching that little shit how to shift for her magic to be wasted like that. Maybe after I am finished with her, you can finish her off." Lily told the man. Her voice was different, more cold and detached.

Veirella opened her eyes, slighting just enough so she could see around her, but not enough for them to see that she was awake. Veirella could feel the tree behind her, so she knew they were in the forest, but were they close enough to the castle for her screams to alert the guards? The chance of that was unlikely, so she stayed quiet, from what she could see around her.

There were four bodies, one belonging to Lily. The others were all man, Veirella considered her chances of fighting them off, but based on her size, theirs and how much more of them were there. The better plan was to run and hoped she ran towards the castle where she could call for help.

But she would need help to get out of the predicament she was in first; Veirella was in her element. Her chances of getting away were high. ***"Help me. Please"***

She called out to everything around her, both plant and animal, ***"what do you need daughter of daughter's?"***

They all asked together.

"Help me get away, help me get home," *she asked. For a while, no response came. Veirella thought she had asked for the impossible and began thinking of other ways to free herself, but then it came. Veirella felt something moving behind her, and then her hands came free, but still she did not move.*

"When you see the birds run."

"Okay"

A few minutes passed, then she heard something moving in the trees. "What the hell is that?" one of the men asked, then he looking up at the trees to try and see where the noise was coming from. "We are in the forest; animals live in here idiot," another told him. Then, seconds later, all the birds in the forest came down on them.

"Run"

"Run"

"Run"

Veirella did not hesitate. She got up and ran as fast as she could; she heard a few screams and pained grunts. "The girls gone," one of them pointed out to the others, and Veirella tried to move faster. She heard movement behind her, but she did not turn to look.

She did not know how long she moved for before she reached a clearing in the forest; it was bright with moonlight and she ran into it, then she felt something stab her in the back, and she fell to the ground screaming from the pain, Veirella attempted to stand but another hit her in the leg.

She laid there trying to move, but it was no use. She heard footsteps coming towards her, then felt the arrows leave her body, which was somehow more painful than them going in. "Neat trick using your little pest to help you get away," the man said to her, then pulled her to her feet, pulled her against him and put a knife to her throat.

"Do anything like that again and I will carve you it little piec—" he either did not finish what he was saying or Veirella did not hear him, because all she could think about was the fact she could not breathe. One moment she was standing, the next she was on the ground, the cold hard ground. Veirella felt something moving down her chest and she raised her hand to feel it. Something wet and sticky was on her fingers.

She held them up so she could see, and they were red, so, so very red. Why was it red? Something was on her legs, but she could not move to see it or stop it. Veirella tried calling for her sister. ***"Iris,"*** *she thought. She was trying to say her name but the word would not leave her lips, but she kept trying.* ***"Iris. Iris. Iris."***

She tried and tried but still nothing. The thing on her legs was moving higher, it was trapping her. Veirella was getting tired; it was getting harder to keep her eyes open. She closed them for a moment to rest, then she heard a scream, then Lily flashed before her eyes. She was bent and broken. She was only red, like Veirella's fingers.

'What did I do? She's dead. I killed her. She's dead.' That was the last thing Veirella thought before her world was covered in darkness.

Plan Of Attack

Veirella

Lily, her friend she thought to be, dead. The woman that plagued her dreams at night. Was standing before her well and breathing. No broken bones or odd shaped body parts. How that was possible? Veirella did not think she wanted an answer to that question.

"Lily, you should be dead." Her words came out lower than she intended them to, but she heard her. "I should be a lot of things but yet hear I am," she answered, as the smile on her face grew wider. She stepped forward and Veirella stepped back. She did not intend to do it, but a part of her did not trust the girl standing before her.

Light brown wavy hair, warm light skin, and hazel eyes. It was Lily. Everything about her was the same. Well, almost everything. She had a scar running down one side of her face, going down her neck and disappearing beneath her coat. "How have you being Ella, its been a while. Well, not for you." She laughed. The sound struck a shiver up Veirella's back.

Lily stood there staring her down. The way she was smiling at her made her skin run cold. Veirella did not know or understood what was happening but, something told her not to let her get any closer to her or Luka. "How are you even alive? I have memories of you dead." Veirella did not know what she expected her to say, but her laughing was the last thing she wanted to hear.

"You cannot kill that which is not whole." Lily answered, her being alive was unnatural, all living things died, there were curtain parts of nature that one could not avoid or run from, Lily was dead, Veirella saw that she should not be talking to her. But Veirella should be dead, so did she have a right to question how Lily survived.

"Enough with the questions. Like I was saying, you want to help the fire wielder. You give me you." Veirella heard her the first time, but what did that mean? "What do you want?" She tried to keep her voice steady, but there was still a slight shake when she spoke, and by the way Lily was looking at her, she heard it too. "I want what has been taken from me, and the only why to do that it with your type of power." Lily moved closer to the side of the room where Luka was and Veirella reached for her power.

She did not know how to use it to attack, but she would do anything to keep her away. "I have been killing, wielder's for months and it's still not enough to break through. But then I got my hands on that one and, what a surprise it was to see you together." Lily laughed again, then slowly turned her attention back on Veirella.

"You seem to care about him, so I am willing to make a deal. You give me your magic and I will release my hold on him. The little prince over there gets to live and you die in his place. Do you want to make a trade?" Lily asked, drawing out the words.

Veirella released the power she summoned. She was clueless to how Lily's power worked and attacking her could just end with her getting what she wanted. Veirella looked over at Luka, then back at the girl she once considered a friend, "it's you? You're the Sirabus?" Veirella's pack was on Luka's horse, with the orbs.

She could not get to them without Lily attacking her or going after Luka. "He looks pretty dead to me," Veirella told her, "not even close that is just the first step. I may have sped it up a little, but he will wake soon." She answered. They both looked over at him. Veirella did not want to die, but she would not let Luka die either, so she had to buy some time.

"If I agree, I need to get him back to the school and out of the way. Because he would try to stop you," she told her. Lily thought about it for a moment before she answered. "Fine, meet me in the forest outside the school tomorrow at nightfall, or he dies." Lily waved her hand at Luka. "I returned some of his power." Then she vanished.

Veirella heard Luka grown. She ran to his side and helped him sit up. "What happened?" Veirella was going to need to tell everyone what she knew, and she did not want to do it twice. "A lot, I will tell you once we get back to the school. But right now, we need to move." She told him Veirella helped Luka up. He managed to put himself back on his horse, then they moved.

Veirella helped Luka inside, but he did most of the work. The boy was bigger than her and was a lot heavier, too. "Are any of these port keys?" Veirella did not remember much of the tour that Genevieve gave her and Aspen the day she arrived, so she could not recall if it was mentioned.

"The one at the end." Luka pointed at the gold framed portrait on the wall by the stairs. It was of an older woman. Her skin was a light brown and her hair was perfectly braided back, and she dressing in silver armor. It was a rare sight from what Veirella knew. Women had only been allowed to serve for the last five decades.

And even then there was still restriction. Unlike men, it was not mandatory but optional; and unlike highborn men who were not exempt from military service, highborn women could not serve at all. Only women from families without titles or money could partake.

Veirella helped Luka down the hall, then he pushed himself up on the wall next to the painting. He raised his hand to open it, but Veirella stopped him. “NO! I can do it.” She remembered what happened to Griffin when he used his magic.

Veirella thought Lily’s power could kill on contact or slow like she was doing with Luka, but if her victim used their magic, it would kill instantly because she was draining the thing that made it possible to wield.

She was not sure how accurate her theory was, and she was not willing to test in with Luka. “Okay.” He said, then pushed himself back so she could get to it. Veirella raised her hand and called up on her energy, once she felt it moving through her, down to her finger’s Veirella thought of where she wanted to go, she needed to speak with the other’s but Luka needed help and that was more important. Green and blue sparks appeared around her hand, then the port opened into a vortex, matching her magic.

“Go, I will be right behind you.” Luka told her Veirella looked at him, her brows rising as she watched him barely hold himself up. “No. You go first, and if you try to argue with me, I will push you through myself.” Luka attempted to smile at her, but the action seemed to pain him. Veirella moved so he could go through. He watched her for a moment, then pushed himself off the wall and toward the vortex.

Veirella pulled his pack from his shoulder, he looked back at Veirella watching her pushing it up her shoulder. Before she noticed, he looked away, then stepped through the empty space. Veirella counted to ten, then followed him.

When she appeared on the other side, Luka was against the wall next to the painting. And the massive doors to the med center were before them. “Why did we come here instead of the court?” Luka’s words were stranded, “because you need help.” He went to say something, but Veirella raised her hand, stopping him. “Real help, let’s go in.” Veirella was never one to give orders, but Luka was being difficult.

Veirella pushed open one of the doors and waited for him to walk through it. To their luck, Scarlet was in the main room, and all the beds were empty. “Scarlet, we need your help.” She looked up from what she was doing. Her eyes locked with Veirella’s. Then she looked at Luka.

“Absolutely not.” Aspen told her. After Scarlet got Luka into a bed in the back away from where students frequented, she sent for Sebastian, Gemma, and the headmistress. Once Veirella informed them of everything Lily told her, Sebastian portaled away, then came back with her brother and sister. “We need to do something.” She pushed back. Sebastian and Aspen were standing before her. “He will die if we sit here and do nothing.” She told them Veirella had no intention of giving herself over to Lily, but she did not need to know that. She hoped Lily, though Veirella was too naive to try anything. “Veirella.”

She looked over at Iris, who had barely said anything to her. “You cannot do this. Getting yourself killed in his place will solve nothing. Whatever she wants, she does not have it for a reason, and you helping her get it by making yourself a martyr will help no one.”

“Wow, Iris, first full sentence you’ve said to me in years, and it is to call me a martyr.” Suddenly Veirella could not remember why she hated her ignoring and avoiding her. “Maybe you should stop trying to make decisions for her and let her choose.” Gemma said, stopping Iris from saying anything else.

“Maybe we should figure out what she wants. If she is willing to kill all those people to get it, it must be important. And where is she trying to go?” Gemma asked. *Once you leave, you cannot return.* Veirella remembered those word’s she did not know where she heard them but she knew what they meant. “The Black Forest. If something is born there once it leaves, it can never return." The Words were leaving her mouth, but she did not know where they were coming from.

"How do you know that?" Sebastian asked her. "I have no idea, I may have read it in a book somewhere." Her memories were still all over the place, so she could not put together the details clearly, "not likely, the magic of the forest is a protected secret. You, knowing anything about it, should not be possible," he continued.

"Okay, but am I right?" Veirella asked, and Sebatian reluctantly nodded. "Then we start there, see what we find. Maybe it could help us stop her." Gemma suggested. "We don't know what she wants, and the forest is not a small place." Sebastian told them, "isn't it close to a shoreline?"

"Yes." Veirella understood what Gemma was asking, "Siren caves." Both her and Sebastain said in unison. "Exactly, she is half siren she was probably born in one. Start there and work your way out." Gemma continued.

"Okay, so Sebastian and Aspen can go to Ataria, and we will stay here and make sure Luka doesn't die." Veirella told them it was a great idea tracking down what she wanted, and use it against her to help Luka, and if they did not return before sundown the next day, she wound meet Lily. "Even so, what are we looking for? Sirens hoard everything. It could be just about anything." Aspen brought up a great point. What did Lily want that was worth killing for?

"You cannot kill that which is not whole."

"What?" Gemma asked. "It was something she said. It could be nothing, or it is. We are going into all of this blind, and our friend is dying in there. We need to do whatever we can." Veirella never had more than one friend before, and she was not willing to lose one so soon after getting him.

Retrieval

Sebastian

Cyrus was the last person Sebastian wanted to be stuck with at the moment. They hadn't been in the same room since what happened with Veirella and Ana. Sebastian understood the anger he felt after watching his friend be killed. He felt the same for years after watching Veirella get attacked, but that did not excuse what he did. They did nothing to have him direct it at them.

But his presence was not their choice, even with Aspen going with him. Headmistress Conley would only let Sebastian leave if Cyrus came. He asked for someone else, but he was the only one without a charge to attend to. They left early, before day broke. If they wanted to get to the caves at all, they needed to go before the tides came in. Atarian's did not enter the black forest, it was not a safe place to be. The creatures within it could not leave, and going in was serving yourself up for dinner.

"Are you two just going to ignore me for the entire time we are here?" Sebastian and Aspen did not want Cyrus there. They came through the portal and walked off. Sebastian just closed it when he felt him come through, and he has been behind them since. "I have nothing to say to you, and I am certain he would say the same." Sebastian answered.

Cyrus signed, “look I get that I was a bit of an ass. But my best friend just died, so could you cut me some slack? I am sorry of how I reacted.” Sebastian stopped and turn to look at him. Cyrus did the same, “if you think I am the one you should apologize to, then you’re not sorry enough.” There was one thing Ataria had over the other continents; well, other than their superior skill in the water. It was their respect for their women.

Yes, men were considered the head of house, but a woman made sure it did not all fall apart. Gender had never played a part in their society. Ataria had lords, but it also had ladies. A man did not have power or ownership of his wife, and women held the right to all their children. A man could not create life. Why should he be given control over it?

But Forian men did not seem to understand that Sebastian knew their laws had changed, but it had not been enough for the ideation to die out and Cyrus still thought women were beneath him. “And who would that be?” Sebastian turned and continued on.

He would not dignify that question with an answer. Aspen was leaning against a tree not too far ahead. And he was still close enough to hear their conversation. Sebastian wanted to hurt Cyrus, but he was sure Aspen wanted to kill him. He looked at Sebastian, then behind him at Cyrus. “In normal circumstances, I would cut your tongue for the way you spoke to my sister.

Then I would shove it down your throat and watch you choke on it.” Aspen pushed off the tree and went on, “one thing you should know about Veirella, she is the sweetest person you will ever meet. But she does not give second chances and you already crossed her once. Do it again and she just might kill you herself,” Aspen continued. He did not look back at Cyrus and neither did Sebastian and, by the way his blood moved through his veins, the threat reached him.

They made it to the edge of the forest without running into a demon. There were some that still walked the plain. When the barriers were created they were protected by the magic of the forest. And unfortunately they were not the easy to kill kind, it was the same for siren's the magic of the sea protected them from being sent back to the dimension they came from.

The shoreline was white with sand. The water moved in and out, and with every retreat it went further out. "The tides are going down. It should be safe enough for us to go into the caves by the time we get across shore." Sebastian informed them. With the resistance of the wet sand and the rockslides, it was take them a while.

"Watch where you go. This place is not fond of people. It will try to kill you." Sebastian pointed out the line of rocks that surrounded the shore. "We need to say close to rocks because of the sandworms. Do not touch anything we need to keep our presence as minimal as possible." Sebastian continued. Aspen nodded, then they made their way down the path. Why there was a carved out path to walk in the first place was more terrifying that Sebastian than anything they would face down below. The demons could not leave the forest and sirens did not have legs for land, and no one wanted to see that side of Ataria enough to risk walking through the forest.

Not when there were so many places just like this one all over the continent. "You know, for future rulers of two kingdoms that were at odds for so long, you two seem quite close." Sebastian could not tell if Cyrus was asking a question or making a statement. Whichever it was, he would still not get an answer. No one outside of his friends, which only included Anastasia and Luka, and his family and Aspen's, knew that he and Veirella were related, and it would stay that way. Cyrus stayed quiet when neither of them fed his curiosity.

Sebastian led the way. He got as close to the hill as he could be. Making sure to change how he walked with every step he too, so he did not leave a pattern to be followed by the creatures beneath the sand. Sa'nchiens ate just about anything. The bigger the meal, the more they wanted it. They created holes in the ground big enough to pull their meal through and once you were in, there was no getting out.

Sebastian heard screams from behind him. The last thing he wanted to see was a grey, faceless worm with itself wrapped around Cyrus's leg, sucking on him. The Sa'nchien pulled at him and he grabbed onto the rocks behind him. Sebastian and Aspen ran to help him. Sebastian grabbed his arms as the worm pulled him free of the rock, which caused a few to fall. Aspen pulled his sworn and began cutting at it.

But it did not work. His hits did not affect the creature. To it, they were not even there, just Cyrus's leg for it to feed on. "This is not working." Cyrus was still screaming and Sebastian could hardly hear what Aspen was saying. The worm pulled Cyrus, and the force made Sebastian slip. If they could not get him free, they would need to leave him behind or die with him. Because the boulders above them were getting ready to fall. He looked back at Aspen, who stopped hitting the worm and began cutting through with a dark silver dagger; he was halfway through when the first few rocks fell around them.

When he finally got through it, white liquid spilled from the Sa'nchien separated body and it disappeared beneath the sand. Its head released Cyrus's led and screamed, it was lower but his ears still felt it. Aspen pulled its body from Cyrus's leg and threw it further down the sand. Sebastian looked up and saw a massive boulder shaking. It would fall in seconds.

"We need to move now." Aspen grabbed Cyrus's arm and threw it over his shoulder. Then Sebastian did the same. "You need to stay awake. You pass out on me, you. I will leave you behind, got it?" Aspen told him, "y-yes" he answered, voice low and pained. "Good, now move." He ordered. They moved as fast as they could with Cyrus between them. He helped by jumping on his uninjured leg, but Aspen and Sebastian did most of the work.

The rocks above them were falling faster, but they were moving at a decent pace. They were almost at the cliffs, when a Sa'nchien shot up from the sand and lunged at Aspen, Sebastian looked at it and it stopped right before it grabbed his arm. A thin layer of glass covered its body.

They made it to the cliffs with seconds to spare. Sebastian made it on just in time to hear something fall behind him. He turned to look and saw a boulder twice his size merely inches from his leg. Another second and he would be died.

They set Cyrus down, pushing him up against the cliff side. "You can leave me here until you get back. I need some time to deal with this. You need to search those caves before the tides rises." Cyrus told them, Sebastian nodded at him. He got a closer look at his leg and there were black lines going up his led spreading from the small circular bite. He was right. The more time they wasted helping him, the more time they lost. Cyrus pulled off his pack, drank one of his elixirs, a bright blue liquid. They moved towards the water, Sebastian looked around for the water lines. Knowing the level it rose to would tell how much danger they were truly in, waist level wound be easy for him to navigate, shoulder would cause him some problems but he could do it.

Unfortunately for him it was much height then that, as least six inches above their heads, Sebastian hoped they would not be down there long enough for tides to rise that much because even with the danger of drowning they would have bigger problems to deal with. "What are his chances of surviving?" Aspen asked.

"Low." He answered. If they went back to the school now, his odds would go up, but that would take a lot of energy, energy Sebastian needed for the search. It was a choice between Cyrus's life and Luka's. And it was not up for question who he would choose to save.

Aspen had no problem swimming into the cave. The water was calm, and the opening was not so far down that he would struggle. Sebastian could breathe underwater as well as he could above it. The currents were not a problem because he could control them. Sebastian's skills were limited to himself. He knew it was possible to share his ability with others he had seen it done for children who could not wield.

But that was not a skill he ever cared to master or tried to. Perfecting his other abilities was more important to him. Sebastian knew he would need to learn how to use all of his powers eventually, but on the list of things he wanted to master, creating air pockets was not very high up.

When they broke the surface, it took Aspen a moment to calm himself. He was breathing hard and his coughing was erratic. Sebastian didn't think the distance was that much, but he based that off an Atarian metric and Aspen was not Atarian. "You okay?" Aspen's breathing was heavy and starved for air. He closed his eyes and took a long intact of air, then release. He repeated the action until his chest slowed. "You said it was a short distance. That was at least nine minutes." Aspen snapped, "for an Atarian child that is a short distance. How long can someone of your land stay under?" Sebastian did not know must about Forian's or how their bodies functioned, but they could not be that much different. "Two to five minutes, several if one dives regularly." Aspen answered.

"Two minutes' babies stay under longer than that." Sebastian's voice rose echoing off the walls. Of all the numbers, he expected to hear that was so low it was almost impossible. "Well, your babies are born in the water, and they spend most of their lives in it. That is not surprising." Aspen swam towards the flat rock in the center of the cave, which was perfectly placed between the other caves.

All siren caves were circular in shape and had at least seven smaller caves within. Some had more, others less. It all depended on the size of the rock formation they built them in. Sebastian followed Aspen, then used his magic to push them up. "Thanks" Sebastian nodded. "For an heir, your knowledge on us does not seem great, and considering we share a sister, I thought you would be more inclined to understand us."

He always knew he had a sister. He was there the day Veirella was born. He did not remember much of it. He was only a year when it happened. But the memories of that day were printed into his mind so he would never forget. "Can you tell me about her? She does not share much, and this is still new for her. It is unlikely she is willing to share anything with me," Sebastian asked. Veirella was still cautious with him, but she wasn't ignoring him anymore and he was grateful for that.

Aspen laughed. "Veirella is the one person you should not wait for to open up about anything. She is headstrong and hates having people put attention on her. If she is willing to tell you something she will simplify so it does not seem as bad as it is. Getting my sister to tell you anything means things are really bad. I think she spends more time trying to live up to our family name than anything else. She watched how our father did things and how others preserved us and she feels like she needs to live up to that." Aspen sighed and continued.

"She will not handle any of this well. Finding out who she thought she was is a lie will be hard for her to deal with. Right now, she has this Lily thing to keep her from thinking about it. After that, I don't know what to expect. A few years ago I could read her better than anyone, but now." Aspen did not finish. He went to Sebastian, then laid a hand on his shoulder. "For the next few years you will see her much more than I so look after her for me?" Aspen asked, "of course." There was no need for him to ask, but by the way Aspen relaxed at his agreement, he needed to hear it.

Then they began their search, not truly knowing what they were looking for, but hoped they would know when they found it. Aspen went to one cave and Sebastian another. The first cave Sebastian swam into was covered in jewels. And none of it was made by the sea.

All trinkets stolen from ships they sunk over the years. Sebastian had never seen a siren up close; they had warning bells if they came too close to the surface, but they mostly stayed deep down. The only time they attacked was if people entered their territory. Sebastian knew they killed hundreds but, seeing what was left of their destruction, made it different.

Each cave he entered was worse than the last. There were even bones still attached to some of the things that they stole. He was relieved to see pearls and shells in the fifth cave he entered. *At least they made some effort to keep their own,* he thought. Once again, he looked through it all, but he found nothing worth killing for, most of it could be caught on a dive.

The water was rose around him. Sebastian was not keeping track of the time and the sun was still bright above, so he did not expect it yet. He made it back to the main cave, and the water was running onto the rock, that was a few inches above the water when they came in. Then Aspen shot up to the surface, just as tired as Sebastian. "Anything?"

"No." They either missed something or got it wrong, and Luka did not have time for them to be wrong. They made their way to the rock. Sebastian didn't need to use his magic the water was high enough for them to climb on.

"There is nothing in here but jewelry and bones. Nothing here is worth killing for." He snapped. Sebastian needed to calm down. It was hard to think when he let his emotions rule him. "Maybe it's not a thing she wants. Maybe she just wants to come home." Aspen could be right, but he had to be wrong. If there was nothing, someone he cared about was going to die, and he couldn't live with that. "There has to be something we missed. We need to look again," he continued.

But Sebastian stopped hearing him. Something was pounding in his ears, it was in his head, and it was all he could focus on. Sebastian looked around, trying to find, but saw nothing. Then he felt something drop on his face. He touched it; he pulled his fingers away, and they were covered in blood. Sebastian looked up and saw something that shouldn't have been impossible. "I think I found what we were looking for, or better yet, it found us."

Aspen looked at him, his brows pulled together. Then he looked up and saw it too. "That isn't something you see every day." There was a heart floating above them, in a silver cage, and it was still beating.

"How is that even possible?" hearts needed a person and blood to stay alive. Magic was weird, but that was something different. "That is not a question I think anyone has an answer to." Aspen answered. Sebastian pulled on his magic, calling the water to him. He formed a whip, then wrapped it around the cage and pulled; but it did not move. He pulled harder, but still nothing. "Are you broken?" Aspen asked. "It's not moving." His words were stranded as he pushed move water and energy into it. "Freeze it" Sebastian looked at Aspen. "What?"

"Is that not one of your gifts? Water Manipulation is a common form of wielding for water wielder, is it not?" Changing the shape of water was not as easy as it looked. Sebastian had done it once, and it was not intentional. He released most of the water and it fell around them, splashed up to the walls, then he formed a ball around the cage, and spun it.

Controlling water required creating a flow between it and yourself, freezing it, required stopping that flow. Sebastian understood what he needed to do, but that did not mean he could do it. The one time he froze, something was the night he saw Veirella in the forest that night. He hated thinking about that night but it was the only why he could get it to work, Sebastian closed his eyes and focused on everything he saw, her run from something, he could not see but he felt how scared she was, then the pain she was in.

Veirella went down, but that did not last long someone pulled her up, but then she was falling again and it became harder to breathe. Sebastian opened his eyes, and the water spin faster. That night he felt pain and disappear at seeing what happened to his sister. But now the memories made him angry. Sebastian wanted to hurt whoever made her suffer, and Lily was on that list.

His body ran cold, blue sparks shot up his arm, and the water solidified and stopped moving. A moment passed, and it fell, shattering between them. Aspen grabbed the cage. The heart looked unaffected; He tried to open it but there was no lock or opening of any kind. "We need something to cut through this. It seems to have been built around it," Aspen told him

.

"We should get out of here before the little see demons come back." Aspen jumped in the water, then Sebastain followed. They made it down to the opening. Aspen went through, Sebastain used some of his power to push him to the surface. As he began making his way through, he was hit with visions of Veirella. She was hurt, and a girl was standing over her. *Lily*, he thought, finally putting a face to the name. A face he now hated. They were in the forest, at the school.

He felt like he was watching history repeat itself. Lily raised the sword to Veirella, but before he could see what happened next, Sebastian felt something pulling at his leg, and his vison cleared.

He looked down, and there was a scaly grey hand with sharp nails wrapped around his leg. *Siren*. Sebastian tried swimming up, but it was no use. She was stronger. He got a better view of her. A part of him was relieved by what he saw. She was young, about his size. There was a chance he could survive. The younger ones were faster in the water, but much weaker in strength.

Their skin was also much softer and easier to cut through. Sebastian kept fighting her. As she hissed at him, she came up intending to grab his other leg and he kicked her in the face. She loosened her grip, and he pulled away. Sebastian moved for the opening as fast as his legs could carry him, but she was still with him. He stopped and used the water to pull him down, and she hit the wall. He pulled his dagger and waited for her to come for him. It took her a moment to find him. When she did, she charged at him without hesitation.

She grabbed at him; he pushed around her, then stabbed her in the neck and pulled the dagger through, splitting her throat open. The life left her body, then she fell through the water. Her want for him had to have overtaken her other senses, because killing her was far easier than it should have been. Sebastian used his power to move through the water and up to the surface. Aspen was standing on the edge watching for him.

He reached a handout and helped him up. "What took you so long?" Sebastian's breathing was shallow, and weak "Siren" was all he could manage to say, "well congratulations, you did the impossible."

"We need to go. Let's get Cyrus's body." As much as Sebastian didn't care for him. He deserved to be put to rest the right way. "He is still alive.

Just sleeping. Guess he beats the odds." Aspen told him, "Okay, but we need to go now. Veirella's in Trouble."

Vengeance

Veirella

Veirella sat by the window, watching Luka sleep. Aspen and Sebastian left before they woke. She stayed with Luka until they put him to sleep the night before, according to Henry or Link, as Aspen called him. Luka's body was constantly channeling energy. By putting him to sleep, it lowered his body's need to create that energy, which should keep him alive.

Veirella wanted to listen to her brothers, do what they wanted, and stay. She would give them the chance to fix it another way. But if they were not back by half a day, she would be meeting Lily. "You care for him?" Veirella looked over and saw Iris. She was not wearing a dress like the last few times Veirella saw her. She wore silk blue pants with a matching shirt that covered her hands. Veirella could not recall ever seeing her without sleeves. Her hands were always covered. Even the few times she saw Iris at home, she had her arms covered, and that was in the warmer months.

It seemed like a form of self-inflicted torture that Veirella did not understand. "Yes, I do." She answered, then returned her attention to the boy sleeping in the bed. He looked at peace without understanding the situation. A person would look at him and thought he was fine, but if they looked closer, they would see how pale his skin was.

"Will he be worth dying for? Because if you go and meet with her, that is exactly what will happen." Veirella was not in the mood to be lectured, she never thought she was ever feel annoyed again. It was nice knowing she could feel more than sadness and pain; Iris was the last person she wanted to explore her newfound emotional range with.

"I don't want to hear it, Iris. I already had this conversation with Aspen and Sebastian. I do not need another." The things Veirella felt were new. She did not remember feeling them as a girl. She could not decide them, only that it made her want to scream at everyone trying to dictate her choices.

"And my opinion, as your sister does not count for anything?" Veirella stood and turned to her, "you do not get to play the older sister now just because it benefits you to do so. You spent months avoiding me every time I tried to talk to you. You made an excuse to leave the room, so no, at the moment, your opinion does not count for much."

Veirella told her. Iris looked away from her and focused on her hands. She brushed them down her shirt, pushing away lines that were not there. "I informed Genevieve of what you intend to do. She wants to see you in her office. If I cannot get you to see how much of a bad idea this is, maybe someone else can."

Iris did not wait for a response. She just turned and left the room. Veirella wondered how Aspen put up with her for so long, without getting the urge to throw her off a roof. But then again, they shared a womb. He was probably born with a tolerance for her.

It had been a few weeks since Veirella met with Genevieve. She saw her a few times, but they never made time for a proper conversation. And the first time they do have one, she was getting a lecture. Veirella stood outside the door for a moment. It did not matter what she said if Aspen and Sebastian were not back in time, or found something she was going to meet Lily. She finally found it in her to knock on the door. When she opened it Genevieve was sitting in one of the sofa's pouring tea.

"Welcome, come sit." Veirella did as she asked and sat on the sofa across from her. Genevieve offered her a cup, but she refused. She did not think she was above giving her nightshade if she did not comply with what she wanted. "You asked to see me?" Genevieve returned the cup she offered Veirella and took the other. "Yes. Your sister has informed me of what you intend to do.

I am all about letting the students here make their own choices, but there are some things that I will not allow." Veirella could block her out and still know where the conversation would end. But to her surprise, Genevieve did not say anything she was expecting.

"Your mother did not want you to come here, your blood mother, that is. She never gave your parents a reason as to why she did not want you learning how to wield; but they sent you here anyway because it was what you needed. And they were right to do so." Veirella understood that when she was younger, but the goddess did not want her to learn at all.

"Makes no difference me being here or at home, I am no better at it now then I was months ago." Veirella did not care to talk about her other mother, and she did not understand why Genevieve was pushing away from the reason she was there to begin with.

"Are you sure about that? Because when you came here you could not speak. And now here we are having a conversation that does not include paper. Celerian's are very different to mortal's and the other two Centinals, Cai is a part of you, it must be used or you will suffer for it.

You did not use much when you were a child, so you never grew, what you did kept you alive. You learning to grow flowers was more to wake your magic up, which then triggered your healing. For someone so smart, I expected you to question that more." Genevieve explained.

Veirella did not question it because it did not feel new to her. Time passed around her and through her in ways she did not understand. She recalled things she did not remember happening and did things without knowing she did them. Her voice returning felt the same. Veirella knew she could not speak well one day and the next she could without causing herself pain.

"You have a long road ahead of you, not just in your journey to discover yourself and the things you can do, but in your healing as well. The first step in moving forward is closure, so I think you should meet with this Lily and get what you need from her. But do not promise her anything. We will find another way to help Lorenzo. The power you hold is too great to give up." Genevieve told her. Veirella was sure she intended to try and talk her out of it or order her to stay in the school. Neither of which she would have listened to.

"I remember some of what happened that day. I just want to understand why." Genevieve stood and Veirella did the same. She moved closer to her, then raised her hands to her face. "People sometimes do things for reasons we may never understand." Genevieve dropped her hands and moved so Veirella could pass. Veirella did not need Lily to explain why she tried to have her killed. That question answered itself. She wanted her power, she did not get it, and now she was going after someone she cared about and that was worth her head.

Veirella went back to the court. She still had a few more hours for Aspen and Sebastian to return or for her to leave. She had the time and thought spending it with the only person who would not try talking her out of going would be best. Luka was unconscious, so he could not try to dictate her choice. She went to his room, and to her surprise, he was awake. He was sitting on the side of his desk, looking out the window.

"You should still be sleeping." Luka looked over his shoulder at her, "well I have never been one to follow the rules or do as I am told. And neither are you from what Ana says." Veirella had to resist the urge to roll her eyes at him. "How are you even up right now? That doctor gave you enough nightshade to knock two war horses out." Luka smiled at her shift in conversation but did not comment on it.

"Those things are not very effective on someone whose blood is as hot as the sun. I burn through it three times as fast," he answered.

"How much does it hurt?" Luka's body stiffened. "Why do you think it hurts?" he said, his voice still calm and sweet. "One, it sounds like it hurts. Celerian or not, you are still part mortal. Some things affect you, and two of your reaction at the question." Veirella answered. He dropped his shoulders and sighed. "A lot. And I can guarantee that whatever you're thinking about right now it is still worse." Veirella moved closer to him. "How long?"

"A year and a half. Over time, it has gotten more tolerable. And it didn't just start its not like I was fine one day and in pain the next. It was gradual from the moment I got my powers. I ignored it at first, but then it became too much to ignore anymore." For a moment Veirella heard the anguish in his voice, but then it disappeared and the calm sweet tone returned that she noticed he only ever used with her.

"Other than Sebastian, who knows?" Veirella assumed they told each other everything. Well, almost everything he did not know Veirella was his sister until recently. "Only you. I never felt the need to share."

"At least Sebastian does not need to feel as bad for keeping a sibling from you, considering you are keeping the fact that you live in pain from him." She was trying to make him smile anything but sadness would do. "I think his secret is still bigger." Luka argued, "a secret is still a secret no matter how big or small it is." She told him.

"Fair. So what is the plan for this meeting with the crazy killer?" And they were back to what she did not want to talk about. "Well, I intend to trick her into freeing you from whatever control she has. Lily remembers me as a little girl who had no one to turn to for help. She may still see me that way, so I intend to use it to my advantage." Veirella explained, and by the look on Luka's face, he did not seem impressed or even a little convinced that it might work.

"That is an idea, but I have a better one. We went through all that trouble getting those orbs charged up, we should use them. Trap her and force her to release me. Sirens hate those things because of how much pain they cause. We bargain for my powers in order for us to set her free or buy enough time for Aspen and Sebastian to get back with whatever it is that she wants so bad." Luka's plan was arguably better, but Veirella was not sure if the orbs would have that effect on her.

She spent centuries caged by them. What's to say she was not used to the pain they caused? "Two things, one yes that could work, but considering how far she is willing to go for whatever is in that forest I do not think giving it to her is the best idea, and two what do you mean by we, you are staying here away from her." Veirella told him, Luka stood up and Veirella steps back but stayed close enough to help him if he lost his balance. Luka's skin was not as pale, but he still looked ill.

"If I am not there, how can you be sure she did it if you do not see it happen?" He waved his hands over his body. "Luka, I may not know you well, but you do not seem like the type to stay out of a fight, especially if death is involved. You can come running or whatever it is that you do after I save your life."

"And how do you intend to trap her on your own?"

"Gemma will come with me." Luka moved around her. "Now I am definitely coming. I love Ana to pieces, but she barely has control over her wielding, and you do not know how to. I think it is better if I am there with you." Luka's reasoning made no sense considering the state he was in.

"And you are just as useless. If you wield you die." Luka did not stop or look back at her, he just walked into his bathing chambers. Veirella contemplated going in after him, but she did not know what she would see if she did, so she waited for him to return.

Sometime passed before Luka came out. He changed into keives and had a sword in his hand. "Then we can all be useless together. The more of us, the better our chances of not dying." Luka said to her, never looking away from the sword. Veirella watched it as he got closer. There was a red dragon on the black hilt, and a red stone at the head. Veirella felt strange just being close to it. "Where did you get that?" Veirella pulled her eyes away from the weapon to look up at the boy holding it.

"My mother gave it to me as a gift after my first hunt. She has been used to take many lives and has won more battles than most men will ever live to see. Death Singer." Veirella wanted to laugh. The same sword she thought caused his injuries was the very one he was holding.

Luka raised it to her, but Veirella made no effort to take it. "In this situation you are the best person to wield it. I know that you are not a fan of anything with a sharp edge. But like the with the dagger's it is better to be safe than dead." Luka explained, but even so, she still did not touch it. "Then you keep it. If I have need for it, then you can give it to me. Can we agree on that?" Luka nodded, then place the beauty of a weapon in the sheath on his back.

"Very well then. We should get going so we can set the trap." Luka looked down at her. "You might want to change into something more practical for the setting." Veirella looked down at her uniform. There was nothing impractical about what she was wearing a fight was based on skill, not clothing, but Luka was right. If the option was there to be in something more battle friendly the only logical choice was to take it.

Gemma helped Veirella get dressed. She was only going to wear pants, but Gemma insisted she put her keives on. According to her, they may never get another chance to wear them for their intended purpose. "This is very restricting" Veirella told her as she pulled on her jacket, "can you walk?" Veirella turned to Gemma. Who was sitting on her bed watching her. "Yes."

"Then your perfectly fine. We should go if you do not want your sister to interfere." Gemma jumped to her feet and made her why to the door. Veirella grabbed her pack with the Lin'greaia's, then followed her.

Luka was leaning against the wall next to the door. He stood up straight when he saw them. "Does it really take that much time for girls to put clothes on?"

"Appearance is everything, no matter the occasion." Gemma answered. They made their way up the stairs, and Luka opened the door. "Spoken like someone who has never been in a fight. I am sure the pretty clothes you wear will prevent someone from trying to cut your head off." Veirella went first, and Luka looked her over.

Gemma followed, then turned to him, "well you seem to appreciate the effort." She smiled at him. Luka pulled his eyes away from Veirella and ran a hand over his face. "Are we doing this or not?" Veirella when to one of the paintings and opened the port. She looked over at her friends. Luka's face was a darker shade of red, and Gemma watched him smiling. Luka looked down at her for a moment then walked over to Veirella. "We should go."

"Are you okay? You look a little red." She wished he stayed in bed. He was in no shape to fight if it came to that. "Great." He told her. Veirella watched him for a moment, then moved so he could go through. Once he disappeared Gemma went to her, she was still smiling, "you could ask him for anything right about now and he would say yes." Gemma told her.

Veirella's brows pulled together, "what?" she asked. She looked down at her chest, then turned and walked through the vortex. Veirella looked down at herself. The shirt Gemma gave her was low cut and showed part of her marks. It was not much, but it was more skin than she was used to showing.

It did not take long for them to make it to the forest; it was not that far from the school. "We need to find somewhere where we have the upper hand, and Ana can hide." Luka told them Veirella had only been in the forest once and she was not there long enough to know anything about the place.

"What about the clearing where they have the bonfire? A lot of surrounding coverage and a big empty spot in the center for us to trap her." Veirella's chest tightened and her heart moved a little faster than it should. The last time Lily got her into a clearing in the forest, it did not end well. But she had a chance to return the favor. "Okay, lead the wa—"

"No," They all turned around to see Iris coming towards them. "You are going against what Genevieve said by doing this, and against what you told Aspen and Sebastian." Iris was yelling at her. Veirella thought about turning and walking away, but she did not know where she was going. If she walked long enough, she would eventually find the place, but that would take time they did not have.

"Genevieve said I could go, and even if she said I could not, I would have done it, anyway. Because Luka's life is on the line, how do you not get that?" Veirella did not raise her voice, but she spoke with more force than she normally would. "She almost killed you once. How do you not get that?" Iris pushed back, "how do you even know that?" Veirella did not tell anyone that she remembered some of the attack; it was the clearest memory she could recall.

"It was not that hard to put together. I met her once and I could tell something was off with her. So when I saw what happened to you she was the first one I suspected, she has a lot more power than you do, we are going back inside, I sent a letter to our parents they will be here in a few days, and they can figure this out." Iris lowered her voice the closer she got, then took hold of Veirella's arm.

"No!" She pulled away so hard Iris stumbled back. "Luka does not have a few days. You can either come with us or stay here. Either way, you are in my way." The heat Veirella felt in her chest was new and primal. There was a part of her that wanted Iris to try and stop her. "We should get going if we want enough time to set up an ambush." Veirella turned to Gemma. She smiled at her and Veirella felt the heat fade away.

The clearing was similar to the one she was in for all those years, but it was bigger and the grass was lower. Veirella, Iris, and Gemma hid the

Lin'greaia's on different sides of the forest, forming a circle around the center. Luka tried to help, but they refused it. Veirella had the fourth orb, and the plan was for her to throw it into position and the others would roll into place. They tested it to make sure it would work.

Their first attempt failed, so they marked the ground were then were moved them and tried again. It worked, but they did not have enough time to try again. Put them back in the second marked spot, Veirella marked where she needed to throw hers, and Iris and Gemma hid themselves in the forest.

Far enough that they would not be seen by anyone coming for any direction but still close enough that they could still hear everything. A little while later, the sun began to set. She would be there soon. Lily was never late to any of her training sessions. She was usually the first or second one to show up, and Veirella hoped her timing was still that impeccable.

"You okay?" Veirella was watching the forest for any sign of movement. She was twisting at her finger's something she always did when she was nervous about something. "I should be the one asking you that." She looked back at Luka. He was sitting on one of the many lodges around them.

"Well, I asked first." Veirella smiled at him for a moment. It was faint and faded away like it was never there. "Well, we are about to face a killer that I once called friend, but she was not really my friend because most of the things I remember about her she was horrible to me. She basically left me for dead on a roof top, then came back and tried to kill me, and she has killed a lot of people since then, now she trying to kill you." Veirella's heart sped up but she did not feel the pressure that usually followed.

She looked around again checking for movement, then she heard him laugh. She looked back at him brows knitted together. "You find someone trying to kill you funny?" She asked, Luka shook his head "no I just think that is the most I have heard you say."

"Well, I am happy my ability to speak is so amusing to you."

"Come here." Veirella looked around again checking for what felt like the hundredth time. "Dove" Luka called, she looked back at him. She wanted to tell him to stop but the name was growing on her.

Veirella hesitated for a moment then she went to him. Luka's eyes followed every move she made until Veirella was sitting next to him. "Take a minute and just relax." He took her hand into his, she looked away from him giving her attention to creatures on the ground most never noticed or cared to.

Sometimes she wanted to be just like them, be able to move around the world without everyone watching. "I do not have the time to relax, your life is on the line. All our lives in fact, until she has being delt with there is no room to relax." Veirella hoped her words did not come across as defensive, it just felt like everything was falling apart again.

"Or maybe focusing on everything else makes it easier to ignore the fact that your hurting." Veirella tried to pull away but he would not let her. "No one knows how any of this is affecting you and you don't seem that big on sharing, but everyone can understand it being a lot. In the last four and a half months you found out your parents are not who you thought. You have a brother you did not know existed, and powers you barely understand, that is a lot for one person to deal with." He continued.

He made her want to run and hide. She did not like to talk about her feelings. No one in her family did, they all delt with it themselves. *Just another thing to make me different from them,* she thought. "And what about you?"

"What about me?" Luka gave her a half smile, Veirella looked up at him watching to see if what she intended to ask would get him to give something away. "You might die. I told you what she did to you and barely reacted to it. Like you had already come to terms with the idea of death." Veirella searched his face and his eyes for anything.

But there was no change. "I am going to die, that is a given. So when faced with death I welcome it." He answered. "We are all going to die, that is how nature works. You just have a little less time and a clock over your head, but that does not mean you should give up. Find something you want to live for and fight for it. Because I am going to fight for you curse or no curse I will make sure you live life." Luka's half smile grew fuller.

"Is that so?"

"It is." She answered back. "Well Dove let's see you do the impossible." His voice lowered and deepened as he spoke. "Luka, that is still not my name." Luka went to say something but he was interrupted.

"Well aren't you two adorable." Veirella and Luka jumped, Luka pulled his sword pointing it at Lily, ready to strike if she did anything. "Relax lover boy, we had a deal and as long as Veirella holds up her end of it you'll be just fine." Lily's voice made Veirella's skin run cold, she did not remember her sounding so disturbed when she was a girl.

Around them the forest came alive torches going up in flames. "Pity I have to give all this power back. The fire wielders before you did not have this much of a kick." she looked at Luka. And Veirella used that her diverted attention to slowly reached up behind her and pulled the orb from the satchel. Luckily for her Lily was standing far enough in the center that she could trap her.

"Are you going to say there and talk or are we going to do this?" Veirella tried removing the emotion from her voice but it was not something she did well. Lily looked at her and smiled, she started moving towards her but Luka stopped her with his sword. "I am going to need to get close to her, to take her magic."

"She will come to you." Luka told her, his voice colder than it was when he spoke to her just mere moments ago. "Very well." Lily raised her hands and stepped back. Veirella slowly inched forward tightening her grip on the orb as she went. Lily's showing off played in her favor, the light around them made seeing her mark that much easier.

"You release Luka then you can have me." Veirella told her, Lily raised a finger and waved it at her. "Not how this works sweetheart." Veirella tilted her head, "I think you misunderstand you do not have much of a choice."

She looked down the X before her, Veirella pulled out the orb and dropped it
.

Lily looked down at it and laughed. "Was that you're big plan? You need a set for them to work, and for that little stunt I might just kill the both of you." Lily began walking towards them, Veirella raised her hand stopping her, "wait for it." A second later all four orbs rolled into place glowing around her, the next Lily was on the ground screaming in pain and covering her ears.

Veirella could not hear anything, "If you want it to stop you will let Luka go--" Veirella was cut off by her laughing it was pained but cold. "What exactly are you going to do? I cannot be kill. Many have tried, but when you don't have a heart to stop it makes that a little hard." Veirella heard movement behind her, she looked back and saw Gemma and Iris running up to her.

"Oh, more of you." Lily scoffed, Veirella did not pay mind to anything else she said she was still trying to understand how she did not have a heart. "What does that mean? You don't have a heart, how is that even possible?" Veirella asked. "Well I am very special." Lily answered.

"How did you lose it to begin with? Not like you can just take it out." Lily laughed again, "well that is exactly what he did." She answered. "Who?" She looked up at Veirella and smiled, the look in Lily's eyes sent a shiver up her spine. "That you will find out soon, you'll meet him eventually." She answered, *why was in so hard for people to just answer a question?* Veirella was getting tired of getting half answers to simple questions.

"Or you won't. You know I spent years with these things, they are not as effective as they once were." Lily dropped her hands from her ears then stood. Veirella stepped back, not knowing what to expect. Then Veirella felt a wave of energy throwing her back. Veirella hit the ground, and pain shot through her body. She opened her eyes and everything was blurred and wrong, when her vision finally cleared Lily was above her holding Luka's sword. "I think it's time I finished what I started. Men are so useless." Veirella looked around but could not see any of her friends, but she had Luka's sword.

Veirella hoped he dropped it when he fell, and Lily did not kill him to get it. Lily inched closer moving the blade up her body. Veirella searched around for something, anything to hit her with and grabbed onto a tree branch. She would hit Lily in the leg when she was close enough, but she did something even better. Lily got down close to her face, close enough that Veirella could hit her. "Let's play." Lily voices conniving and cold. And Veirella wanted nothing more than to stop it.

"Yes. Lets." Then she swung the branch hitting her over the head, Lily fell back losing her hold on the sword in the process. Veirella stood and grabbed it, branch in one hand sword in the other. Lily turned over, blood running from the gash on her head, Veirella did not think she hit her that hard. She looked at the branch, it was different covered in silver. "I see you remember some of the things I taught you? You, and I are the same." Lily laughed again it was a sound Veirella was getting tired of hearing. She dropped the branch and it reverted back to bark. "I am nothing like you."

"If you say so, abominations are still abomination's even when the mix is different." Lily got to her knees, but before she could stand Veirella raised her hand trying to stop her, the pained look on her face said she did something more.

Veirella had no idea what she was doing or how she was doing it but she kept going. "Let. Luka. Go. I can do this as long as it takes, I may not be able to kill you but I will back you wish that I could." Veirella told her, her voice hard and cold.

Lily did not do anything but watch her, Veirella pushed harder, and Lily screamed. But Veirella did not care, she would keep going until she released him, "let him go." Her voice was calm but distant. "I will. I will, just end this please." Lily cried, her voice shaking from the pain of screaming so much. "*You* first."

Lily raised her shaking arm as far as if could go, and red sparks pulled towards it. Then she sent them into the forest behind Veirella until the faded from her. But still Veirella did not stop. She did not know how to and she did not want to.

Lily's screams grew louder and louder until they finally stopped. Veirella's mind cleared and she saw her head bent back, she dropped her hand releasing Lily from the hold she had on her and her body hit the ground with a loud thud. Veirella stood there watching the dead body, she killed someone it was not her first time Veirella remembered that much.

"Veirella!" she turned around and Gemma was walking towards her. She moved with a limp, maybe a twist but nothing broken at least. Behind her Luka was holding her unconscious sister. "Is she okay?" Veirella asked, she hated that she was the reason Iris got hurt again. "She hit her head really hard, we need to get her back to the school." Gemma answered, "well at least she's live" Gemma limped over and wrapped her arms around Veirella and she did the same. "We all landed so far from you, then the screams I thought—" Gemma shook her head, "not my screams, I'm just happy that the three of you are okay." Veirella told them.

"What about me?" Veirella knew Lily would come back, she just thought they would have a little more time before it happened. Gemma released her, and she turned to face Lily. "You are not as innocent as remember. That hurt. So I going to take my ti—" Lily didn't get to finish what she was saying.

Because she was pushed away from them, Veirella looked at Gemma, she had light blue sparks woven around her fingers, and she threw Lily into a tree. Veirella looked back at her when she heard her scream, Gemma was using her magic to hold her up against a torch. "All she does is talk, how did you listen to her for so long?"

Luka laid Iris down against a lodge and went to them. "What are we doing? We can't exactly killer her." Luka asked, Veirella hoped her brothers found the heart and were on their way back. "Then we buy time, enough for Aspen and Sebastian to get back. If we give her heart back maybe then we'll be able to kill her, we just need to stay alive long enough to do that."

Veirella told him, "how are you so certain they found it? Our whole plan depends on that one detail." Gemma asked.

"They are my brothers, I have faith in them. I how much longer can you keep this up?" Gemma did not seem to be struggling, but she did not have full control so it was not guaranteed to hold. "I don't know."

"Okay, Gem's when it becomes too hard to hold her back, let go don't fight it, then run back to the school, alert the headmistress and get some guards out here." Veirella instructed, "what? I am not leaving to guys out here alone,"

"If the boys are back they don't know where to find us, you do. And out of the three of us you are a lot lighter on your feet. If all else fails we need to at least get her off school grounds so we can raise the barrier." Luka told her.

"She starting to push back" Gemma told them, then the sparks on her arms faded. "Go" Gemma nodded at Veirella then turned and ran. "We need to keep her bad as long as we can. She has time on her side. I know offensive is where your skills lie but this calls for defense, give Gemma as much time as possible." Luka nodded, but Veirella didn't see it, they were both focused on Lily. She was on the ground not moving. Red sparks began moving down Luka's arms he was preparing himself.

"I may not prefer to use defense, but I am good at it." Luka answered. Lily pushed herself up of the ground. It was slow and it looked painful, she had burn scars all over her back, and she was still steaming. When she made it to her feet she locked her eyes on Veirella, Luka stepped forward an action that took more effort than it should have. Once she was back in the clearing, he pulled the flames from the torches and formed a ring around her

.

Stopping her from getting any closer, Veirella looked up at him. Making sure he was okay, he had his power back but she wanted to make she there were no lingering effects of what Lily did. His skin was not as pale and the darkness around his eyes was fading. Veirella returned her attention to

Lily, the Lin'greaia's did not hold her but she hoped the possibility of Luka burning her to a crisp was motivation enough for her to stay put.

Veirella needed answer's. Nothing Lily could say would change how Veirella felt or what happened, she was already suffering with the pain and there was no undo it. Veirella went towards her stopping when she felt the heat on her skin. "Why did you it, any of it?" Lily smiled at her. "The world stole from me, I just wanted it to feel the lost I did." She answered. "And all those innocent people had to die for your revenge?"

"Well, you know blood of blood an all."

"And me? If you killed all those people for something their ancestors did, why did you try to kill me? You were imprisoned centuries ago, and until recently my family had nothing to do with Iriea. What could I have done that was so bad?" Veirella asked her voice softened as she spoke making her feel more valuable to Lily.

"You. You exist, all that power in someone so undeserving of it." She screamed. "You know the first thing I tried to do was go home. But then I got the edge of that forest, and it through me out. A group of water wielders found me, I did not mean to kill them, but I did and if felt so good." Lily's voice shook for a moment making her almost sound human.

"I tried going in again and I got further, but again it push me out. Then I realized I needed more power, and so I just kept killing. People started noticing, so I started taking less. It killed them slower, but I still kept moving. Then I moved to Fianorea where I met the most beautiful girl. Lily that was her name, she was an earth wielder. She was chosen to train their princess."

Veirella's skin ran cold. She was not Lily. Veirella should have guessed the name was fake but not that it belonged to someone else. "I killed her the day before she was to leave, then I became her, her name, her face, her life everything and they were none the wiser. Then I met you and the raw power I felt coming off you was so pure, it was just what I needed but you had no idea what you were and I could sense it growing every time you wielded.

It didn't matter how much you used it still grew. So, I pushed you. I made it grow. Fatten you up so I had more to feed on. But when I came back you were so different, and I didn't feel like waiting anymore. All that power in someone who knew nothing of it. Power. Money, Privilege and *Love.*" The way Lily looked at her, she hated Veirella for what she had, but she was also envious.

"I wanted you to know pain, what the world was really like; it would be the last thing you felt before I killed you. But then you got away and that stupid beast of yours got to me. When I was strong enough I came looking for you and saw the cocoon. So, I poisoned you if you ever came out you would die, slower than I wanted but same outcome." Lily continued.

"It was you; you sent me the flower?" Veirella's grip on the sword grew tight, she forgot she was still holding it, and now she wanted to use it. The stone in the hilt grew red, and the heat from before return more intense and hungrier. "Drop the flames." She told Luka.

"Veirella."

"Do it." She was done asking, either he let Lily out or she was going in. Seconds passed then the fire fading only leaving the burnt ground behind. "Let's play game."

"And what would that be?" Lily asked edging her way to Veirella. "How many limbs does it take before you scream blood." Veirella's eyes glowed and the ground grew around Lily's legs trapping her in place. The roots in the ground broke through moving for her wrapping her legs then her arms.

The roots pulled her from all sides and Lily was raised into the air. "You tortured me all because you were jealous, I had something you wanted. You killed people, for the mere fact that they were born" Veirella got closer, and the roots pulled tighter. She screamed, the sound was music to her ears. "It took me a minute to put it together, but I know who you are. Not your name there was no name in the story but all the same it is still you." Veirella told her. "*What*?" Lily asked the words strained with pain. "The story about how you fell in love with a man, and when you did not do what he wanted he forced you to." Veirella watched her waiting for it to click.

For a moment Lily's face fell, and a second later it was gone, but Veirella saw it. "When I heard that story as a girl, I felt sorry for her. It was wrong that someone had to live through that, but now I feel nothing for you. You suffering does not give you the right to do it to everyone else." Veirella told her holding the sword up to her neck.

"This is where your story ends." Lily began laughing, put it was different almost sad, but the roots pulled tighter. "You think you can kill me? Many have tried but none have succeeded, what makes you think you can do what they could not?" She asked. "I hate you enough to never stop trying. They wanted a problem gone so they locked it away, I just want you dead."

Veirella sensed someone coming towards her from behind. "Pax and Aspen are back they have it." She turned around and Gemma was running towards them. She stopped when she saw Veirella's eyes. "Wow, Ella your eyes."

"What?" Veirella asked, she lost focus and they faded. A moment later she heard snapping then a loud thud. Veirella spun around, the roots were in pieces and Lily was coming at her fast. Luka through her back with his flames. Lily hit the ground then got back up like it was nothing, then ran at her again. "Here" Veirella raised the sword to Luka, "seems like you're the one that needs it." He took it from her, then put himself between Lily and the girl's. He did not let her get too close he keep pushing her back with flames. "How far back are they?" Veirella asked, she did not know how long Luka could hold Lily back, Veirella had never seen him fight and on any other day he could hold her on his own. But he was still recovering from what she did to him. "Not too far, but how exactly are we going to kill her?" Gemma asked.

"That part is still in the works." she answered, "well do you think you can work faster?" Lily needed her heart in order for them to be able to kill her. The part Veirella worried about was how much stronger she would become when they gave it to her.

If she had the time she could test what type of connection it was, if it was symbiotic then the heart needed to be in her body when she died in order for it to die too, but if it was nolmiotic then they would need to strike them at that same time. Lily seemed stronger than before, Veirella thought killing her again would only make her stronger.

The next time she died it needed to be permanent. "Finally" Veirella was pulled from her thoughts by Gemma's voice. Aspen and Sebastian was running towards them, Sebastian's hands were covered in blood, and he was holding a silver box that was dripping with it. "Good news, and bad news." Veirella sighed. "What is it?" she asked. "Well we got the heart, but we can't get it out of that." Aspen pointed to the cage in Sebastian's hand.

He raised it so Veirella could get a better look at it, the heart was beating. It was by far the most unnatural thing she had ever seen. "That is going to give me nightmares for life." Gemma admitted. "You and me both." Aspen agreed.

Veirella recalled some of what Lily taught her, she wanted her to change the structure of objects, maybe she could do it. No. She needed to do it. Everyone's lives depended on her being able to do it. "Okay. This is what we're going to do. Seb you and Gemma go help Luka hold her off, Aspen get Iris back to the school, and I'll deal with the heart." She ordered.

Aspen's eyes searched the forest looking for their sister, "where is she?" Veirella pulled Gemma closer to her so he could see her. Iris was still unconscious lying by a tree away from the commotion behind them. Aspen ran to her, picked her up and laid her head on his shoulder.

"How exactly do you intent to open that thing?" Gemma asked. Veirella watched the heart floating in the center of the cage. "A little trick she taught me." Sebastian gave her the cage, removed his bow, leaned it against the tree next to him then pulled out his daggers. They were closer to short swords than dagger based on the length of the blades. "We'll buy you as much time as we can. Do what you need to." He told Veirella then took off towards Luka.

He stopped through fire balls at her and began cutting at her. But the cuts did not seem to faze her. "You should go help them" she told Gemma. She looked over at them then shook her head. "I would just make things harder." Veirella heard the pain in her voice, they had a lot to talk about once they delt with Lily.

Aspen made his way back to them. "The last thing I want to do is leave you out here." Veirella felt how worried he was, but there was nothing she could do about that. At point he needed to let go. "We all have things we need to do, if we do not work together this all ends badly. Iris needs you more than I do right now, go get her some help. I'll be fine, I promise."

Aspen nodded, looked at her for a moment, then turned and went back the way they came. Veirella wrapped her hands around the cage doing her best to touch all four sides. It should be possible for her to turn it into whatever she wanted it to be. So she chose to make it water, it would fall away and do the least amount of damage to the heart.

Veirella closer her eyes and pulled on her power, calling it from every corner of her body that it existed. She felt it all move towards her hands, then green and blue sparks manifested forming rings rotating over her arms down to her fingers. She reached for the cage, connecting herself with the metal. The coldness of it ran through her bones, the blood became her own. She felt the vibrations of the beats in every inch of her body. Once she was one with the cage and everything it was she pushed her magic into it, willing it to become what she wanted it to be.

But nothing happened, she wanted it to turn but it would not listen to her command, Veirella pulled harder and harder, but still nothing; Veirella did not stop she remembered doing it. And she needed it to work now, she pulled so hard, her nose bled. Then the vibrations became too much for her body to handle.

Veirella screamed dropped the cage and fell to her knees. "It's not working. *why didn't it work?* Why can't I every do anything right." she cried, Veirella dropped her head into her hands. Her friends would die all because she was useless, and there was nothing she could do about it. She gave it everything she had, but it still did not work. "Try again." Veirella raised her head and Gemma was kneeling next to her holding the cage out for her to take it. "I have nothing left in me, that was all my Cai." She told her.

"I don't think it works the same way for you. I saw your eyes glow, they were gold. You held her up and it seemed like nothing for you. So reach for that, there is something different about you Ella. She taught you how to do whatever this is didn't she?" Gemma asked.

Veirella nodded she could not find the words to speak, "but she is nothing like you and you are so far from her that you don't belong to the same world. So do it your own way, make it listen, make it hear." Gemma told her, Veirella sat up, and took the cage from her. When she wanted to give Sebastian more power she did it without his help or effort, she wanted to make Lily suffer and the forest did as she wanted.

Now, she wanted the cage to disappear. Veirella closed her eyes and pulled but this time it was not power she reached for it was something more. Her feelings, the things she thought would be lost to her forever. The emptiness in her chess that that had filled without her ever noticing. She needed to believe in what she was, what she could do. She did not bend to nature it bent to her. Veirella's grip tightened, she opened her eyes and they glowed. She focused on the metal cage in her hands willing it to change.

The bars softened piece by piece, then it became a liquid, and then it became water. Slipping through her fingers into the ground. Then the heart fell into her hands, and it started beating faster. Veirella felt something wrong, she looked over at the clearing just in time to see Lily through Sebastian across the forest. Lily's eyes found hers then they went to the heart in her hands. She smiled at her, then through Luka back like he was weight less. He dropped his sword in the process.

"I think she knows we freed it." Veirella told Gemma. "Good, now we give it back to her and end this." Veirella was contemplating if it was a good idea, but before she could say anything Gemma took the heart from her and ran into the clearing. "This is what you want right? This is why you killed all those people." Lily slowly made her way to Gemma who positioned herself in front Veirella so Lily would not see her moving. She made her way into the trees, watching where she stepped, and Gemma at the same time.

Veirella got behind her and waited for Lily to take the heart from Gemma. When she did Veirella made her way out of the forest. She wanted Lily to pay for what she did, Veirella wanted her death to take time, she wanted it to hurt. She picked up Luka's sword and the stone in the hilt glowed red. The heat she felt before returned and hotter and raging, Lily absorbed her heart. Then she threw her head back and sighed.

Veirella nodded at Gemma and she stepped back, then she made her way around Lily taking Gemma's place then kicked her to the ground. She opened her eyes and looked up at Veirella. "That's not really fair is it?" Lily's voice did not sound as cold but she did not seem anymore human. "I have no interest in being fair. Stand up." Veirella ordered.

Lily stood, "well now that I feel things. Tell you what I'll let you save one of them. The pretty one or the brother?." Lily stretched her arms out, to where Luka and Sebastian each laid. Veirella raised the sword and cut her arm off before she could say anything else. The scream that came from Lily's mouth as she stumbled back could wake the dead.

"How about you?" Veirella moved closer to her, swords still raised, "you may have been able to heal that in no time without your heart, but not so much now. And to make sure lets just get rid of this." Veirella stepped on her arm and it melted beneath her boot, into a puddle of blood. Lily's eyes shot open at the site.

"That's better. Now fight me, try an earn your right to breathe." Lily did not move, her eyes still on the spot her arm once was. "Plea-"

"No!, you do not get that word. Fight or I will come over there and skin you piece by piece then I will take each finger one for every crime you have ever committed and make your death slow and painful." Lily looked at her, fear crossing her face for a moment then she stood. No longer a threat, not the predator, but the prey. No longer the hunter but the hunted. Lily let go of her shoulder were her arms was the blood still gushing out and running down her body.

Then she ran at her, Veirella let her get in close then spun and cut her other arm off, then melted it the same. "You taught me how to do that remember, all those nights in the cold trying to get me to turn rocks into metal, Rubies into diamonds; looks like it paid off." Veirella turned to look at her on the ground looking more like a sickly bird than someone who took the lives of innocents. "That one was for coming after my family, get up!" She watched as Lily struggled to get to ger feet. She was crying it was a little unsettling to see, someone so evil being vulnerable. "You know what to do."

"Pleas—"

"Shut up and fight me." Lily dropped her head back, looking at the night sky, then she ran at her. She let her get a lot closer than before, then Veirella spun again letting her get past. Then sent the sword through her spine and into the heart, she did some much to get back, just to lose it mere moments later. Veirella got close her ear. "Now you know what it feels like to be stabled in the back."

"I am so-sorry, for the wa-y I lived. But the wor-ld does no-t like diff-er-ent and y-yo-you and I are a lot alike in th-at way." Lily told her as blood ran from her mouth. "I am nothing like you." Veirella pulled the sword out and cut her head off letting want remained of her body fall to the ground.

"Veirella drop the sword!" Veirella turned and all her friends were running towards her. She looked down at the sword in her hands, her brow furrowed as she looked at it. Then little cracks began forming all over it, red light pouring from them.

Then it shattered, hitting her. A blast of energy set her friends flying a piece of shrapnel hit her in the throat, and she went down. Veirella could not see what was happening with the others she, it became harder to breathe then everything went dark.

EPILOGUE

Rebirth

Veirella's ears ringed, as she slowly regained consciousness, her body hurt all over, as if something had fallen on her. She opened her eyes and they burned, all she could see was white.

She closed them then tried opening them again. And the white slowly turned into blue, it was the sky; but it was night. Veirella sat up groaning as she did so. She was atop a cliff; she looked down she was surrounded by flowers vast in color. And there were massive trees in every direction. She slowly got to her feet and looked over the hill that she was on where she saw animals beneath her.

Some of which she had never seen before, most species of animals did not mix well with each other, it was strange to see lions around so many creatures that they considered a food and not try to eat them.

"Fascinating, isn't it?" Veirella turned around to see who was there but she was alone. She turned back and caught her something moving next to her. When she turned there was a woman standing next to her. She is quite tall, and her dark skin glistened in the sunlight, and her hair was braided back, which stopped at her hip and her eyes were as dark as midnight.

Veirella had never seen someone with such beauty before, it was hard to believe that there was someone alive with such ungodly features. She moved away from the woman not knowing who she was or how she ended up in the middle of a field. She would not make the same mistake twice, she almost died the last time she trusted someone. Veirella would not put herself in a position like that again. "Who are you and how did I get here?" Veirella's tone was a bit harsh, but she would not appear naive or too trusting.

"Take a look at yourself and guess, only a child of mine could have a face with such beauty that others would envy" the woman answered. The Goddess, her blood mother. Humility did not seem to be one of her traits, maybe that was something she got from her father, "where am I?" She asked not acknowledging what she said.

"You are in my dominion." She answered. "And how exactly did I get here and why am I here?" The Goddess looked over her as if expecting an entirely different reaction to her presence, but what did she expect? for Veirella to praise your existence and thank her so creating her. She had no interest in doing that, she created her and then abandoned her with powers she did not understand.

Then forbade her from learning how they worked, she had nothing to thank her for maybe she would not have suffered so much if she was allowed to be her true self. "There was an accident, and I pulled your mind here." She answered, Veirella did not remember an accident, all she remembered was being outside, then a pain in her neck. Then she was there. "What kind of accident?" She asked hesitantly.

"Your school collapsed in on itself, the school you should not have been in to begin with." She answered her tone biting, "what do you mean collapsed where are my friends? What happened to everyone else?"

"They're all dead, along with everyone else in that wretched place."

Acknowledgements

Thank you to my family for the encouragement to keep going and finish this story, and to myself for finally being able to write the end. This book was made possible because I have a hyperactive mind to the point that if I do not do the thing that I cannot stop thinking about, I will not be able to function or focus on anything but that thing. My mum says I have an inventive mind, but I mostly think it is annoying, but only a little, because if not for the mind that I have, this book probably would not exist right now. The world this story is built around has existed in my head since I was fourteen, but the main point of the book came from teenage experiences. As someone who pays attention to the world around them and can somehow always find people to relate to, I felt it was important to put those experiences in a story; many people look at kids just like me and say we cannot have real problems because of the environment we are raised in. There are parents out there who hurt their kids with intention, and there are parents who do it not knowing that their actions and choices hurt. Neither group ever talks about it; one is too scared, the other feels guilty for complaining, even though that is not what it is. Starborn is about this second group; even the things done with the best of intentions can have terrible outcomes. Something else this book also focuses on is teenage struggle; youth does not determine your pain level, life does. Being young when something bad happens to you does not make it matter less than if you were older. Terrible things are not going to avoid you because you're a kid, unfortunately. But we survived and made it to the other side, which is what matters. So, every time you look in the mirror, remember to tell yourself, 'I did that,' because you did. This is my acknowledgment, so I felt it was important to acknowledge the main reason this story was written and thank you to all those who have given it a chance.

About the author

Aliyah C. Coulson is a fantasy lover and an avid reader; give her a book with dragons and she will be complete because in her world everything is better when dragons are involved. She took her love of fictional worlds and stories and decided to create one of her own. Her love of writing developed in her junior year of high school because she loved writing essays for her AP English class, so she decided to write a book and Starborn a world she has had in her head since she was fourteen became real.

Instagram: @aliyahccoulson
@archerypress
TikTok: @aliyahccoulson
@archerypress
Website:
https://www.aliyahccoulson.com/

www.ingramcontent.com/pod-product-compliance
Lightning Source LLC
Chambersburg PA
CBHW020916310726
48980CB00011B/916/J

* 9 7 9 8 9 9 2 0 8 8 8 0 9 *